Anthony Price was born
educated at King's School,
at Merton College, Oxford
peace-time soldiering he h
beginning as a reviewer on
Editor and finally Editor of

He won the Crime Writers' Association's Silver Dagger for
his first novel *The Labyrinth Makers* and later their Gold
Dagger for *Other Paths to Glory*. All his novels reflect his
intense interest in history and archaeology, and in
particular in military history.

THE OLD *VENGEFUL*

'He has done it again . . . yet another cunningly put
together spy thriller, with an ingeniously complex plot:
highly readable, extremely engrossing – and even, in
addition, historically enlightening'
Times Literary Supplement

'Hyper-complex mix of skulduggery, donnish sleuthing
and double bluffs'
The Guardian

'Stimulates intellectually and infuriates delightfully'
The Times

'Lovely labyrinth . . . Mr Price unbeatably blends
scholarship with worldliness, flattering us to bits'
Sunday Times

By the same author

ANTHONY PRICE

The Old *Vengeful*

GRAFTON BOOKS
A Division of the Collins Publishing Group

LONDON GLASGOW
TORONTO SYDNEY AUCKLAND

Grafton Books
A Division of the Collins Publishing Group
8 Grafton Street, London W1X 3LA

Published by Grafton Books 1984
Reprinted 1984, 1986, 1987

First published in Great Britain by
Victor Gollancz Ltd 1982

Copyright © Anthony Price 1982

ISBN 0-586-05818-4

Printed and bound in Great Britain by
Collins, Glasgow

Set in Times

For James Price

PROLOGUE:
Loftus of the *Vengeful*

'There's nothing wrong with funerals,' said Audley. 'I met my wife at a funeral.'

Mitchell studied the picture again. In the original newspaper it had been a good sharp reproduction, but the photo-copier hadn't improved it. 'I hope the weather was better than it was for this one.'

'It was bloody cold, as I recall – an east wind and an open churchyard.' Audley peered over his shoulder. 'Yes . . . they do seem a bit bedraggled, I must say. But that's because it's never been considered conducive to good order and military discipline to carry umbrellas into action – though I believe Sir Thomas Picton carried one at Waterloo, didn't he?'

'Or naval discipline, in this case.' Mitchell ran his eye down the line of officers. 'Two captains, three admirals, and a flag-lieutenant – and the two-striper's the only dry one . . . or half-dry, anyway.'

Audley smiled evilly. 'And that's only because he's holding an umbrella over the hero's daughter. Smart fellow! And the C-in-C looks rather unhappy, I do agree. But then he never did like Loftus – they were at Dartmouth together, and Loftus pipped him for the Sword-of-Honour, or something . . . although, to be fair, I don't think that was the whole reason.'

Mitchell went down the line again, and on to the civilians. They too were in the rain, and bare-headed as the bugler called them to attention, two bald as coots and three with their variously grey and white hair plastered to their scalps, but all wearing their medals proudly.

His eye was drawn to the other picture on the page, of the *Vengeful* burning furiously, with a list to port, but still spitting gunfire from her 4-inchers, and with a couple of mortally-wounded E-boats in foreground and background. It was a painting, and it had probably never been as dramatic as that, but the artist's untruth conveyed the truth of the battle, which was that the elderly ship had died well and not alone.

'Those old boys are the surviving Vengefuls, I take it?'

'"Vengefuls"?'

'That's the term for the crew. Like "Hampshires" and "Norfolks" – and your "Wessexes", David.'

'Ah! We called our chaps "Westdragons" actually – because of our cap badge . . . but I take your point. And – yes, they are. Plus two of the admirals, who were midshipmen at the time – or one was a midshipman and the other a sublieutenant, to be exact.'

That exactness cooled Mitchell's ardour somewhat: if there was anything the big man was, he was exact in his details; and if there was anything that he wasn't, he wasn't a fool.

All the same, facts were facts, so he had to gesture to the scatter of papers on the desk. 'But I don't see that there's anything for us here – honestly, David.'

Audley adjusted his spectacles to study the papers.

'THE LAST ROLL-CALL –

'*The Royal Navy remembered one of its war-time heroes yesterday: Loftus of the "Vengeful"* – '

And the bald, prosaic, low-key *Times* obituary cutting: '*Commander Hugh Loftus, RN, VC, who died yesterday* . . .'

There had been a gap between those two: the obituary was out of departmental records, filed and dated from three weeks ago; the pictures of the funeral and of the last fight of the *Vengeful* were from some other source – at a guess from the *Daily Mirror*, or some such. There was no clue on the photo-copy, so it must be something of Audley's own notoriously catholic culling, which ranged from *The Sun* to *Pravda*, or the *Buffalo Courier-Express* to the *Bicester Advertiser* – the only clue here was that there was no clue, which was in itself a tell-tale indication.

'Why do you say that?' Audley challenged him.

'Well . . .' He had to get this right, even if it was wrong. 'Well, someone's done the routine search on Loftus – and he was living way above his pension . . . But there's nothing unusual about that, in this day and age – he was prematurely retired a long time ago, that's why he never got beyond commander . . . War wounds and ill-health – quite straightforward, no black marks, although he was never a well-loved man among his equals . . . His wife left him a bit of money: she came of a well-to-do naval family. But that was also a long time ago – she's been dead nearly thirty years. They weren't married very long.'

'He wrote books though. "Naval historian" is how *The Times* described him.'

'That's right. Naval histories. He probably made a bit from them. Not a lot, but some.'

'What are they like?'

Mitchell shrugged. 'Carefully researched . . . he took his time over them. He liked travelling around staying at good hotels – he knew his food and drink. Drove a Daimler.' He thought for a moment. 'The books . . . they weren't bad. Maybe they weren't quite one thing or the other – detailed, but not quite scholarly, and not quite popular either.'

'You don't like them?'

'There's something about them . . . a certain irritability . . . a preference for blame above praise. I can't quite put my finger on it.'

'Perhaps he was embittered by that premature retirement.' Audley tapped the picture. 'Those two admirals were his junior officers, after all . . . But you don't know?'

'I don't think I'd like to have served under him, hero or not, that's all.'

Audley pointed again. 'But they turned up to see him buried. "The last roll-call".'

'Yes. I may be doing him an injustice – I probably am.' Mitchell looked at Audley. 'The point is, for whatever it's worth, he's – he *was* – absolutely clean. No contacts. No hint of anything.'

'But he's dead.'

Mitchell shook his head. 'Nothing there, either. I had Bannen check that out. He'd had a dickey heart condition for years – his doctor had told him to go easy, but he took not the slightest bit of notice. When his Daimler was boxed in on that car park he tried to manhandle a Ford Escort out of the way. It was a hot day, and he was angry . . . There are plenty of witnesses, and Bannen talked to the owners of both the cars that had boxed him.' He shook his head again. 'Pure as driven snow, both of them.'

'No one is as pure as that.'

'Then . . . pure enough for Bannen and me. David . . . the man was seventy-one years old – he had a heart attack. Short of digging him up again you're going to have to accept that. He certainly spent a bit more money than we can readily account for – and he had a big car and a biggish house . . . But that doesn't make him a traitor, or a security risk – and for Christ's sake, the old boy's dead now, anyway! And if he was up to anything he'd have been much more careful about the money angle – '

'I didn't say he was a traitor – or anything else,' said Audley mildly, bending over the picture again.

'Then what the hell have I been doing this past week?' Mitchell let his cool slip. 'Damn it – you had me pulled off the Czech link with Dublin just when it was beginning to look good!'

'Waste of time!' murmured Audley, without looking up. 'They'll never let you go back to Dublin now your cover's blown . . . Besides which, you were taking too many risks there latterly.'

'I'm only doing research now. I like doing research.'

'More waste of time . . . Is this the daughter?'

'Yes.' It was never worth arguing with Audley.

'Not a good likeness . . . at least, I hope not for her sake!'

Mitchell fished among the documents on his left, and then slid the enlarged photograph in front of Audley.

Audley studied it for a moment. 'Oh dear! A good likeness.' He frowned at the daughter. 'It looks like a prison picture . . . or maybe a "Wanted" poster?'

'It's from a hockey group. We enlarged it.'

'A hockey group . . . mmm . . . the nose is a problem, and so are the teeth – an orthodontic problem, left too late . . . I hope she plays hockey well, poor girl.'

'She got a Blue at Oxford. And a First in History, at LMH.' For no reason, except perhaps his exasperation with Audley, Mitchell felt defensive on the woman's behalf.

'That's good to know.' Audley nodded. 'It's always comforting when nature indemnifies in other ways – even though Miss Loftus herself may not look at the mirror so philosophically.'

'I think she's got an interesting face. Not beautiful, certainly, but . . .' Mitchell searched for a word ' . . . but interesting.'

'Plain? "Homely", the Americans would say . . . *Equine* is a word that springs to my mind. But no matter!' Audley turned to Mitchell. 'A good hockey player – "Take your girl", they used to shout at Cambridge, as I remember, when I once watched our Blues thrash theirs . . . and ours did seem to take the game much more seriously than they did – when they came off at the end . . . I shall never forget it . . . one of them slapped her winger on the back and cried out "Well played, Anthea, well played – good man, good man!" And I must confess that I did wonder for a moment, when I looked at Anthea, whether we might not have put an unfair one over on the Dark Blues.' He grinned at Mitchell. 'But . . . a good hockey player and a good historian . . . So what does she do now?'

13

'She teaches history part-time at the local high school.'

'Only part-time? What does she do with the rest of her time?'

'Nothing at the moment. She waited on her father hand and foot while he was alive, so they say – so Bannen says, anyway.'

'She didn't share in the good life, then? The wine and the food and the good hotels?'

'Apparently not. But we didn't inquire too deeply into her.' Mitchell studied Audley's face. 'That wasn't in the brief. Should it have been?'

'Mmm . . . Maybe it should at that.' Audley pursed his lips and held the picture up again. 'Maybe it should . . .'

'For God's sake – why? She's a plain, thirtyish spinster schoolmistress who's never said "boo" to a goose since she scored the winning goal in the Parks at Oxford ten years ago!' This time Mitchell's cool snapped unplanned. 'What the hell are you up to, David?'

Audley set the picture down carefully. 'I'm not up to anything, Paul. But Colonel Butler is . . . and Oliver St John Latimer is too, I shouldn't wonder . . . and the Prime Minister and the President of the United States and the Central Office of Intelligence certainly are.' He looked up. 'Will they do for a start?'

The cool came back together instantly, with the join hardly showing even though Mitchell was angry with himself for underrating both Audley and Audley's summoning him from the safe and rather boring job he'd been doing while he put the finishing touches to his own new book, which had been the cover for his tour of duty in Dublin, and its by-product.

'Yes, I'm sure they'll do very well, for someone. But not for me.'

'Why not for you?'

'Because Jack Butler said this was a one-off, David.'

'And so it is. But you haven't finished yet.'

'But I have.' Mitchell selected the green folder from

14

among the papers on the table and pushed it towards Audley. 'You wanted Loftus of the *Vengeful,* and there he is – investigated, signed, sealed and delivered. And cleared. And *dead.*'

'But you still haven't finished, Paul.'

'And I still think I have,' said Mitchell obstinately. 'You wanted a good quick job, and you've got it. I had Bannen doing the leg-work over here, and he's a first-rate man. Smith in Paris covered his research trips there, and Frobisher handled his American jaunt – and they're good men too . . . And *I* put the whole thing together.'

'And you're smart too, of course.' Audley smiled to take the offence out of the statement.

'I'm smart enough not to want to waste any more of my time and the country's money.' Mitchell decided not to take offence. 'Look, David . . . if we were Inland Revenue, or maybe Fraud Squad, I'd maybe recommend our digging into his apparent excess of spending over income . . . though until his affairs have been sorted out even that's a long shot. But for the rest, if there was the slightest smell I think we'd have picked up a whiff of it between us.' He pushed at the folder again. 'And my assessment of the man is that he was probably embittered – he was undoubtedly bad-tempered and quarrelsome and dogmatic . . . he always made more enemies than friends . . . and he treated his daughter like a servant. But he was also brave as a lion and utterly devoted to Queen and Country and the Royal Navy. In fact, he was the archetypal old-style naval officer, pickled in aspic . . . or brandy, more like – like someone out of his own history books. And I'd stake my job on that.'

Audley nodded approvingly. 'That's good, Paul – I accept that – all of it. But now we need more field work.'

'More *field work* – ?' That approval and acceptance, and then *more field work* could mean only one thing. 'So you know something that I don't know – that I couldn't know –?'

'Of course! I've no wish to waste time and money either, Paul.'

For a second Mitchell was tempted, but only for that one second. 'Well . . . I'm not a field man now – you know that, David. The Dublin tour was my swan-song – you know that, too.'

'Yes.' They both knew that, and Mitchell was pretty sure that Audley had always known why, after Frances Fitzgibbon's death, he had taken the job. And, when he thought about that, it was a strike to Audley, and an unpaid debt too, that the big man hadn't vetoed his private war with the KGB in Dublin. Vendettas were usually grounds for disqualification, not promotion.

'Yes.' The fleeting look of remembrance, of that shared sadness, confirmed Mitchell's suspicion. 'But this time you're the square peg for the square hole, Paul. I wouldn't have asked for you otherwise.'

'Bannen would do as well – I like him, David.' It was odd how liking a man could be a reason for endangering him. 'James Cable would be even better – he's Navy . . . and I can't even swim very well!' Mitchell grinned. 'And I'd guess you need a naval man for this one.'

'Cable's busy . . .' Audley cocked his head ' . . . and aren't you into naval matters, in your next book?'

As always, Audley was disconcertingly well informed. 'First World War naval matters. I hardly think – '

'That will do very well! There was a *Vengeful* at Jutland – sunk, of course . . . but then *Vengeful*s tended to have a submarine tradition – the last of them was actually a submarine, I believe. But fortunately it was transferred to the Greek navy before anyone could submerge it permanently . . . But the First World War will do well enough, for a start.'

Mitchell sensed the job closing in on him, like the infantry subaltern who had volunteered for the safety of the RASC in 1915, because he knew how the internal

16

combustion engine worked, and found himself commanding one of the first tanks on the Somme.

'What is it that you know, that I don't know, David?' That was the crucial question – the tank question!

'Some of it you do know: the PM went to Washington a fortnight ago.'

Mitchell knew that: the Marine band had played on the lawn outside the White House, and the BBC had transmitted the sound of the music and the platitudes.

'They got on rather well – they exchanged gifts – the special relationship was renewed.' Audley closed his eyes for a moment. 'The PM gave him cruise missile promise, and the okay on Poland . . . And the President gave *us* a top secret – an ultra-secret – from the CIA's inside man in the Kremlin, whom they've just pulled out one jump ahead of the chop – a *Politburo*-KGB liaison officer, no less.'

That was more like it: now they were into the real business of the Research and Development Section, which had nothing to do with routine security checks on long-retired and palpably innocent naval heroes and everything to do with hot potatoes which no one else wanted to touch.

'It seems that some time back their man got a sight of a list of KGB projects to which the Kremlin was giving operation approval.'

'Projects?'

Audley nodded. 'Just the names – no details. But of course project names are the real thing. And we know these are the real McCoy because there were six of them, and the Americans have confirmed their five as being in progress.'

'And the sixth was British?'

'The sixth was British.'

Mitchell thought for a moment. 'How long ago is "some time back"?'

'You can assume that ours is in progress too.'

He thought again. 'But if the Americans have identified theirs . . . and pulled their man out since . . . everything he ever handled will be compromised by now, I'll bet. In which case won't they abort?'

Audley shook his head slowly. 'The received wisdom is that they won't. They always accept higher risks than we do . . . besides which they may not have twigged yet – the man hasn't been out long, and the Americans did try to cover his departure in confusion. So we may have a little time in hand.'

More thought. It was certainly true that the Russians took greater risks, partly because their resources were so much greater and they could afford to squander them, and partly because of the dominance of military men among the planners, who subscribed to the Red Army's belief that no defensive position could be held against attackers who were ready to pay the price for taking it.

'What was our project name?' The jackpot question was overdue.

'I'll come to that in a jiffy.' Audley smiled at him, and the smile hinted at an odd mixture of satisfaction and apology. 'There are some complications to this one, Paul.'

First the bad news, thought Mitchell. And then the worse news. 'I can see that. If the President gave this to the Prime Minister as a gift, then she'll want results – she won't want egg on her face. No wonder no one else wanted it!' That last was a guess – but no guess really: this was what R & D was for, and Audley himself was notoriously attracted to eccentric and dirty jobs – they were what he got his kicks from.

'Oh – of course *that* . . .' Audley waved a hand vaguely '. . . that goes without saying. But there's an internal political angle to this one. Which I ought to explain to you since it will affect you, Paul.'

'Oh, yes?' The reason for that apologetic cast was on its way.

'Master Oliver St John Latimer wanted this job, you

18

see – ' Audley's unlovely features became unlovelier '
. . . he's consumed by this strange compulsion to *shine*
for our masters . . . or our mistress, in this instance . . .
to *shine* – and he has a strong competitive instinct.'

What Oliver St John Latimer had was ambition: with
the noble, honest and decent Colonel Butler as acting-
Director of Research and Development the Director's
job was up for grabs, and Oliver St John Latimer wanted
it.

'And you don't want to shine, of course?' said Mitchell
nastily. 'You don't want to be the next Director?'

'I don't give a stuff, either way – no.' Audley was
impervious to nastiness. 'I don't want to be the next
Director, or the Duke of Plaza-Toro, or the Kabaka of
Buganda, or the Akond of Swat – Jack Butler is a
perfectly good Director – his overwhelming qualification
for the title is that he doesn't want it, if you ask me.'

The irony about that, thought Mitchell, was that it was
probably true. And the other and greater irony was that
Jack Butler favoured Audley for the very same reason,
so rumour had it.

'But, as it happens, Latimer would have made a dog's
breakfast of this one – Butler's quite right, as usual –
Latimer's a high IQ plodder: he can set up an operation
much better than I can, but he's no good at this sort of
thing – this is something else, I suspect.'

So Audley had won . . . if this particular prize could
be called *winning*! 'So where are the complications, for
God's sake, David?'

'Season your impatience for a moment – the *complication* is that you can't take this one single-handed, and
Master Latimer is as artful as a cartload of monkeys – '

'I've not got a partner?' Mitchell's chest expanded:
Frances had been his partner, and Frances slept in a little
country churchyard now – now and forever. 'I don't *want*
a bloody partner – '

'Not a partner. More . . . a bodyguard – a driver . . .

19

someone to watch your back and do the chores, Paul. And he'll be good at all those things, I assure you.'

He – ?

'No!'

'Yes. Do you know a man named Aske? Humphrey Aske?'

'Aske?' Mitchell ran the tapes. There was a new Special Branch man taking over from Cox – Andrews – *Andrew* . . . and an Agnew, who was half-French and a Hull University Law graduate . . . Aske – Christ! – *Aske!*

'He's a – he's a – oh, *shit* – ' Mitchell ran out of words, into outrage.

'Odd? Queer? Gay?' Audley raised an eyebrow. 'A cupcake? I heard that word recently, from one of our new recruits – you know of Humphrey Aske, then?'

'David – no, for God's sake – '

'I might have known you'd know him. You always know too much, Paul.'

'I've only seen him a couple of times – I've talked to him once – '

'But once was enough? Tchk, tchk!' Audley tutted at him. 'Prejudice is a terrible thing! And since it takes all sorts to make a world – and particularly *our* world – has it never occurred to you how useful the Askes of this world can be, once we've stopped trying to sweep them under the carpet?' He gazed at Mitchell. 'What was he doing when you encountered him?'

'He was poncing around in records.' Mitchell recalled his incredulity from the encounter.

'In the Balkan Section? He has been covering one of their embassies – probably the Bulgarian . . . the old Bulgarian heresy?' Audley was at his most maddening. 'That's one of Master Latimer's areas of activity, and he's one of Latimer's creatures. That's why we've got him now – or you have.'

More incredulity. 'Latimer isn't – ?'

'No. Latimer *isn't*. Latimer is neither homo nor hetero,

so far as I can observe. He is merely and unfortunately very smart, in this instance. So I'm afraid you have Aske as your back-up.'

'Why not Bannen? I like him.'

'Because Bannen doesn't have the right qualifications. Aske does – and Latimer has kindly made him available, because he wants to know what I'm up to . . . and Jack Butler is being obstinately fair-minded, because Aske needs more field experience at the sharp end, to qualify for promotion.' Audley gave Mitchell a wicked look. 'But you don't need to be nice to him, or to let him into your confidence. He's just there to hew wood and draw water for you, and to die for you if he has to.'

That was altogether too close to the bone: there was no answer to that, only another pang of remembrance.

'Now . . . the project.' Audley dismissed the complication of Aske as though the truth had exorcized it. 'It was *Project Vengeful* – and the *Vengeful* was in English, not Cyrillic, so there are no semantic or etymological arguments about "avenger", or "vengeance", or "vindictive", even though they were all Royal Navy ships in their time too.'

Loftus of the 'Vengeful', thought Mitchell automatically. *But that was two-thirds of a lifetime ago –*

'There were twelve *Vengeful*s – the twelfth was a submarine in '44, but that's being attended to elsewhere, and you don't need to worry about it. You've drawn the other eleven, and I want you to eliminate them . . . or not, as the case may be.'

Ridiculous, thought Mitchell.

'And Loftus was the expert on all of them. So you will start with him,' said Audley. 'Or, seeing that he's dead, you must start with his daughter – even if it means playing mixed hockey!'

The hero's daughter

1

Elizabeth only became fully aware of the handsome young man after an intermediate sequence of more casual emotions.

There was a Victorian mirror on the bric-à-brac stall, opposite her own bookstall on the other side of the gangway – a big, ugly old thing, mahogany-framed, solid as an old battleship and as unsaleable – it had been on the same stall in the previous sale, and hadn't sold that time either, and wasn't going to sell this time at half the price. But now he was looking into it, and he was looking at her.

The first time, she had put it down to accident – to the accidental adjustment of the mirror; then, when she noticed that he was still looking at her, she put it down to brief curiosity – to the discovery that he could stare into it without being noticed, without knowing that she had observed his curiosity. But the third time, after she had moved down her stall and had then come back to her original position beside the cash-box . . . then he was still there, and she began to wonder what it was that held his attention.

It couldn't be the cash-box, because his suit fitted too well for that – a nice summer suit that was never straight off the peg – that suit was too good for what there was in her cash-box, and so was his haircut; even the three young tearaways from Leigh Park, whom she had observed casing the stalls earlier, had dismissed the box at a glance as containing too much silver and too few notes.

But then it couldn't be *her*, either – that was equally unlikely, to the point of being ridiculous, even though she now represented a very great number of bank notes – because he couldn't know *that* . . .

Or could he?

She began to day-dream pleasurably along the lines which dear old Mr Lovell at the solicitors' had sketched obliquely, even though he was unaware of the half of her good fortune. It still amused her, the new deference – not plain Elizabeth any more, now that she was an esteemed client and not Father's messenger; she was still plain Elizabeth herself, but in Lovell, Cole & Lovell she had become Miss Loftus; and dear old Mr Lovell, who had never been unkind to her, had tied himself into a Gordian Knot trying to warn her of the temptations and pitfalls waiting to ambuscade her, now that she was a woman of modest wealth and property, and all alone.

There were people, he said –

(He was still watching her: she was sure of that now!)

There were *people* – old Mr Lovell couldn't bring himself to say *men*, just as he would not have dreamed of telling her that she was no oil painting even if she now had a golden frame – there were *people* who might come to her with . . . ideas . . . She must be careful of the company she kept, careful of new friends who might not be friends at all, careful . . .

Some hope! thought Elizabeth: it was she herself who had all the ideas – even silly ideas about impossibly good-looking young men who watched her surreptitiously in mirrors at church fêtes – mysterious young men like the hero in that Mills and Boon romance she'd confiscated from Angela McManners last term, when Angela should have been deep in Lockyer's *Habsburg and Bourbon Europe* for her A-level.

And there, as a reminder of that episode, was huge Mrs McManners herself, just a few yards down the stall, browsing on the cheapest and tattiest paperbacks – it would never do to let her catch Miss Loftus ogling young men!

'I'll take these two,' said Mrs McManners. 'Both from the 10p box, dear.'

'Thank you, Mrs McManners,' said Elizabeth sweetly. '*Purity's Passion* and *The Sultan's Concubine* – shall I wrap them for you?'

'They're for my daughter – she's very fond of history.' Mrs McManners hastily stuffed her purchases into her basket. 'I must fly, dear.'

The idea of fifteen stone flying diverted Elizabeth momentarily as she dropped the coins in the box. Then a hand came into the corner of her vision, its index finger running up the titles towards her.

'And I'm very fond of history too.' The finger came to rest on one of Elizabeth's own contributions to her stall. '*From Trafalgar to Navarino: The Lost Legacy* – by Commander Hugh Loftus, VC, RN.'

But it didn't say all that on the dark blue spine, thought Elizabeth. There was only *From Trafalgar to Navarino* and *Hugh Loftus* picked out in gold there.

They looked at each other directly for the first time, eye to eye, but whatever she let slip in her expression she could see no sign of any acknowledgement in his that they had already scrutinized each other in the mirror.

'How much would that be, then?' he inquired.

In second thoughts, now that he was right here in front of her, he not only looked ten years older, but Elizabeth had the strangest feeling that she had seen him before somewhere; not before during this same afternoon, in some unregistered fleeting glance in the crowd, but before somewhere else . . .On a television screen? In a newspaper?

He leaned forward slightly towards her. 'How much?'

With an effort Elizabeth shook herself free of second thoughts. 'I'm sorry – it's £1.50,' she said, fumbling the book out of the line.

'£1.50?' He smiled at her.

'It's a mint copy.' It was one of Father's author's copies in fact. 'And it's in aid of the church tower restoration fund, so I don't think it's too expensive.'

'I wasn't questioning the price, Miss Loftus.' He took the book from her and opened it at the fly-leaf. 'I was just hoping that it would be signed – I see that it isn't . . . but it's cheap at the price, anyway. Only – it would have been even cheaper with a signature – at the price – wouldn't it?' He smiled again.

Elizabeth swallowed. 'I'm sorry. I haven't got a signed copy.'

'No matter. Perhaps you could sign it instead?' He produced a pen, and held the book open for her.

'I don't see . . .' Elizabeth trailed off.

'The next best thing, Miss Loftus. If not the hero himself, then the hero's daughter. I would have preferred *The Dover Patrol* – more my period. But this will do very well.'

He was an academic, she ought to have guessed that even though she hadn't started to try to guess what he was: the mixture of confidence and that slightly dégagé air, plus the Oxbridge voice, were clues enough. Yet, if he was an academic TV or newspaper personality, she still couldn't place him. But there was an easy way of getting round that now.

She accepted the pen and the book. 'To whom shall I inscribe it?'

'Paul Mitchell – "Mitchell" with the usual "t".'

That didn't help matters, even though something still nagged at the back of her mind.

'"To Paul Mitchell from Elizabeth Loftus" – there, for what it's worth.' She smiled back at him. 'That's the first time I've ever signed a book. But I don't think I've added to its value.'

'On the contrary.' He studied the inscription for a moment then looked at her appraisingly. 'For such a unique collector's item . . . shall we say £5?'

Elizabeth's worst suspicions were pleasurably encouraged. Fortune hunters were out of date, and in any case the details of her official inheritance – let alone the rest of

28

it all – couldn't possibly be common knowledge. But he was up to something, that was certain.

'The price is £1.50, Mr Mitchell. I couldn't possibly accept more.' She took his £5 note.

'Mint condition?' He raised the book between them. 'The going price in Blackwell's at Oxford for this is £9.95, you know.'

So he had done his homework, but if he was trying to pick her up that was to be expected.

'It's still £1.50.' That 'Blackwell's at Oxford' was a nice touch, well-calculated to arouse her happiest memories, if that was what was intended. Yet, once identified for what it was, it armoured her against him. 'Do you mind taking your change mostly in silver?'

'I don't want any change.' Her intransigence was beginning to unsettle him. 'Keep it for the church tower.'

She began to count out the 10p pieces from her cash-box. 'You can give them all to the Vicar's wife, then – she's sitting just down the end there, and she'll give you raffle tickets in exchange. You might win a bottle of whisky or an LP. And even if you don't win anything, she'll give you a pamphlet on the history of the church for free . . . seeing as you're interested in history, Mr Mitchell.'

That, and £3.50 in 10p pieces, ought to damp down his ambitions, whatever they were. And besides, there was a customer waiting further up the table.

She pushed the piles of coins towards him. 'Excuse me . . .'

But when she had completed the sale of *One Hundred Great Lives* and *Civilization on Trial*, at 40p the pair, he was still there with his coins untouched, looking just a little forlorn.

'Yes, Mr Mitchell?' Elizabeth's conscience tweaked her slightly. It was after all a church sale, and she had not given him the benefit of any doubt whatsoever, in all Christian charity.

He spread his hands. 'Miss Loftus, I confess . . . I was also hoping to buy a little of your time.'

So at least they had come to the crunch on her terms, thought Elizabeth smugly. 'My time?'

'Just that. At least, to start with . . . I want to put a proposition to you.'

Elizabeth's hackles rose. She looked up the table for more customers, but there were none, so she could hardly set any price on her time, which patently had no value here and now.

'A proposition?' She could hear the harshness in her voice which was normally reserved for scholarship girls who allowed their precocious sex lives to intrude into the work which had to be done, and who then attempted to fob her off with transparent excuses. 'What proposition?'

At least he had picked up the danger signal: she could see that by the set of the jaw. 'It's about your father, Miss Loftus. It relates to him.'

As it invariably did, the direct mention of her father froze Elizabeth, activating her public face to assume its sorrowing-daughter expression.

'I was very sorry to learn of his death.'

There was no earthly reason why he should be very sorry, if he was a stranger. And if he wasn't a stranger – it occurred to Elizabeth that it was quite possible, if this young man was an academic of some sort, that he might have met Father somewhere, sometime. But then, if he had, it seemed to be unlikely that Father would have endeared himself sufficiently to make him 'very sorry'. So, either way, it was merely a conventional insincerity preparing the way for the proposition.

'I read the obituary in *The Times*.'

Everyone had done that –

. . . *after a long illness bravely borne . . . although badly wounded, refused medical attention . . . continued to direct the engagement . . . successful conclusion of a brilliantly-handled operation . . .*

Well, *The Times* always did its duty by VCs, and, with the original citation to go on, the panegyrist's work had been largely done for him in advance, for all that it mattered now, which was no more than any other sea-wrack from those sunken E-boats of his.

But everyone had read it anyway, even Mr Paul Mitchell.

'That's why I'm here, really . . . Perhaps . . . perhaps I'm rather rushing in – so soon after . . . But I'm hoping that you won't think so.'

What Elizabeth was thinking was that her silence was getting to him. And that, if it had merely been a matter of small talk about her irreplaceable loss, would have been fine with her. But with his proposition as yet unproposed it called for a bit of encouragement.

She indicated the stacks of 10p pieces. 'You've purchased some of my time, Mr Mitchell – remember?'

He gave her a curious look, almost as though she had given him an inkling of the true face behind the mask.

'Yes, of course . . . Well, the obituary stated that at the time of his death he was engaged in writing a history of HMS *Vengeful*, the destroyer he commanded in the Channel fight in '42. Is that what he was doing?'

The question was delivered with a slight frown, indicating doubt if not actual disbelief. And that was interesting because of all the facts recorded in the obituary, other than the long illness *bravely borne*, this was the one *The Times* had got wrong. And – not doubt, but certainty – Mr Paul Mitchell knew as much. But how?

'Why d'you want to know, Mr Mitchell? Does it matter what he was writing?'

He shook his head vaguely. 'I seem to remember . . . about two or three years ago . . . he wrote a letter to *The Times* trying to get in touch with anyone who served on the previous HMS *Vengeful* – the one which fought at Jutland in 1916, or any next-of-kin with letters and suchlike . . . And he also explained then that he was writing a book about all the ships of that name which had ever served with the Navy – am I right?'

'Yes, Mr Mitchell.' She had typed the letter herself, as always, from that scrawl which only she could read. And there was no point in denying it because there was nothing vague about his memory, it was exactly right.

'So *The Times* was wrong?'

Elizabeth nodded. But she had asked *why* and he had answered *how,* she realized.

'All the *Vengeful*s.' He nodded back. 'And there were twelve of them, I believe? Or nearly thirteen, but the Admiralty changed its mind about the last one, and finally called it something else – *Shannon,* it is now . . . so that doesn't qualify. And your father commanded the penultimate *Vengeful*, then.'

Elizabeth nodded again. 'You're very well informed, Mr Mitchell.'

'Not really. I just read the newspapers, that's all.'

'Then you have a good memory.'

He grinned at her. 'Especially for letters in *The Times*. Because that wasn't the only one your father wrote, was it!' The grin started to broaden, then disappeared instantly as he remembered also that such levity was inappropriate to the occasion. 'I'm sorry . . .'

'There's no need to be.' It didn't suit Elizabeth for him to become inhibited by her bereavement, not now that she understood exactly how he had become so knowledgeable. 'You mean the *Vengeful–Shannon* correspondence, I take it?'

He nodded cautiously, still doubtful about her reaction to the memory of that long, acrimonious and ultimately hilarious battle of the letter-writers in the columns of *The Times*.

'You found it amusing?' Elizabeth fabricated the ghost of a smile to take the sting out of her question. She could well believe that outsiders might have considered it so, that passionate and useless controversy about the naming of a warship which the letters editor had headlined variously, tongue-in-cheek, as 'The last fight of the *Vengeful*' and 'A hard-fought engagement'.

He took encouragement from the ghost-smile. 'To be honest . . . I thought it was the jolliest *Times* correspondence since those dons got to arguing about how fast and how far the ancient Greeks could row their triremes.'

Of course, he couldn't know how she had suffered through it all, with Father tearing into each morning's newspaper and his alternate bouts of rage and triumph as the argument swung this way and that.

They had shamed her, those letters, for the contempt the recipients must have felt for him; and doubly shamed her, as he made it so very clear that in some twisted way he had come to regard his immortality as descending somehow through the renewed name of his beloved ship, rather than through his unloved daughter, who was plainly useless – very plainly – for such a purpose, and fit only to type his letters and his books, and cook his meals, and wash and fetch and carry and clean for him.

Well – so much for that! It was all flotsam now that time and events had revenged her on the last captain of the penultimate *Vengeful* – time and events and the Admiralty!

'My father didn't find it so funny.' This time she didn't pretend to smile.

'No, I rather gathered that.' He took his cue from her. 'But to a landlubber like me ships' names really don't have much significance. In fact, they often seem to me to be rather idiotic – like the names people give to racehorses.'

'Oh, I wouldn't say that.' Elizabeth found the mention of racehorses slightly unsettling, however accidental it might be, as a reminder of Father's weakness. Except that, judging by the contents of the safe deposit boxes and the cash-box under her bed, it could hardly be called a weakness.

'But didn't they call one of the Flower class corvettes in

33

the last war "Pansy"?' countered Paul Mitchell. 'I can't imagine what the sailors made of that!' He lifted *From Trafalgar to Navarino*. 'And what was it Nelson's sailors turned the *Bellerophon* into . . . because they couldn't pronounce it, let alone spell it – "Billy Ruffian", eh?' The grin came back. 'God knows what they made of the *Euryalus*!'

So the landlubber knew something about ships, Elizabeth noted. But if ships' names drew him out towards his proposition, then so be it.

'Ah, yet that merely illustrates the primacy of the classical education in those days, Mr Mitchell. It was just the same in the French navy – the French had an *Hercule* at the battle of the Saints in 1782, and a *Hector*, and a *César*, and a *Scipion* . . . and then after the Revolution you have new names like *Fraternité* and *Franklin*, after Benjamin Franklin, creeping in – and the *Droits de l'Homme*, even.'

Paul Mitchell nodded. 'I see what you mean. Like the Reds renaming the Tsar's dreadnoughts *October Revolution* and *Marat* in 1919 – Marat to them being like Franklin to the French revolutionaries, of course.'

He nodded again. 'Education, politics . . . and history too – naming your ships after the battles you've won, and the men who won them . . . yes – *Midway* and *Coral Sea*, and *Rodney* and *Nelson*, and that weird dreadnought we had at Jutland, the *Agincourt* – '

Good heavens! thought Elizabeth. He even knew about *Agincourt*, which had started life as *Rio de Janeiro*, then had turned into *Sultan Osman I*, only to be taken over in the nick of time on Tyneside in 1914 by Churchill, to fire its ten salvoes of 12-inch shells – at Jutland. The very mention of HMS *Agincourt* had always made Father quite dreamy, with a mixture of envy and pride oiling the waves of his bitterness.

But she had never heard anyone else speak of it – she had never met anyone who had ever heard of it – until now, with this strange young man –

34

' – and religion too . . . *Santissima Trinidad,* and all the other Spanish saints we blew apart at Trafalgar.' Paul Mitchell waved his bargain again. 'Yes, I can see that there's a lot more in ships' names than has met my ill-informed eye until now! So I'd better be careful, with an expert like you around, in case I say something stupid.'

'I'm not an expert.' Elizabeth was resolved not to be caught again.

'Not an expert?' He tried to make his disbelief sound polite. 'But a history degree at Lady Margaret Hall . . .'

The contrast between the qualification and the unpaid secretarial work flicked her on the raw. 'I mean, I'm not an expert on naval history,' she said stiffly. 'Just what was it that you wanted to talk to me about, Mr Mitchell?'

'Ah . . . well, about your father's book, Miss Loftus – ' he gave her a direct look ' – am I right in thinking that he hadn't finished it?'

He knew the answer. But, although there were plenty of ways he might know it, he knew more than that, and it was still the *why* which plagued her.

'No, Mr Mitchell. As a matter of fact he hadn't.' To get more she still had to give more, she sensed that. 'My father was a sick man – he'd been unwell for a long time . . . he behaved as though he wasn't, but he was. And he had his good days, and his good weeks, and his bad ones, therefore. May I ask you why you want to know this?'

'How far had he got?'

It was on the tip of her tongue to repeat her question, but she sensed that it might be easier to let him reach the answer in his own way. 'He was revising a chapter on one of the earlier *Vengeful*s. He hadn't really got down to collating the material he had on the last three *Vengeful*s, if you must know.'

He brightened. 'The twentieth-century ones, those would be?'

'The ninth *Vengeful*. That's how far he'd got, Mr Mitchell.'

He thought for a moment, and then nodded as though she had confirmed information he already possessed. 'The Jutland *Vengeful*. Improved Admiralty M Class – 975 tons, three 4-inch, four 21-inch torpedo tubes, 34.5 knots. Built by Hawthorne, Leslie & Company Limited on the Tyne at Hebburn, commissioned at Chatham – 1913–14 Estimates. Right?'

'If you say so. There was one that fought at Jutland certainly.' If she had not already been inclined towards caution his finger-tip facts would have made her so. 'But you obviously know all about it already. You wouldn't be a naval historian by any chance, would you?'

He shook his head. 'No, Miss Loftus, not a naval historian – a military one. Actually the 1914–18 War is my field – the war of the tenth *Vengeful*. Only it's the Western Front that's my speciality. The trenches . . . if you can call them a field.' The corner of his mouth twitched. 'I don't suppose you can discern any connection?'

'Is there one?'

'It was the same war, Miss Loftus.' He paused for a moment. 'You see . . . a few years ago I was re-reading one of my favourite books, Charles Carrington's *Soldier from the Wars Returning* . . . Charles Carrington being the "Charles Edmonds" who wrote the best and truest eye-witness memoir to come out of the trenches, *Subaltern's War* – do you know it?'

'No.' But what she did know was that he was what he said he was, she could recognize the glint in his eye, and the dogmatic assertion of the obsessed specialist, from her own experience.

'A pity. But no matter . . . At one point, just before he comes up to Third Ypres . . . Passchendaele . . . he lets slip that the British soldiers in the line didn't know a thing about the French Army mutinies. But they did know about the troubles in Russia and the U-boat crisis. Now . . . I'd never really thought of the other two crises going on at the same time as Third Ypres – do you see what I mean?'

Elizabeth blinked. 'I can't say that I do, Mr Mitchell.'

Her obtuseness didn't seem to worry him. 'Contemporaneity, Miss Loftus, contemporaneity. That's the point.'

'Indeed?' What she could still see was that glint. And that was the way it took some men – the pursuit of an idea and the thirst for knowledge. It was related to avarice, but it wasn't the same thing; it was more about finding than keeping, like gold fever.

'The same applies in 1916 – Verdun, Jutland, the Somme – to me they'd become isolated events because of my over-specialization: I knew all about the first and the last, but virtually nothing about the middle one. Whereas in reality the good scholar *must* look at the whole spread of contemporaneous events to find out how they interlock, if he's ever to understand the truth about his smaller detail.' He paused for breath. 'Did you know that the first convoy system – which was the answer to the U-boat – was developed to get coal from South Wales to France . . . because the German army was sitting on most of the French coal supply?'

She had to humour him. 'No, Mr Mitchell, I didn't know that.'

'Yes – ' He caught himself suddenly, as though he realized that he was about to lose his broad spread in detail ' – well, the fact is . . . I've been busy for some time familiarizing myself with naval history. And when I read the obituary on your father, and I recalled his earlier letter . . . I'm used to handling research material and pulling it together – I did as much for Professor Emerson's book on the Somme a few years back, when he died before he'd finished it . . . it occurred to me that I might be able to finish your father's book for you, Miss Loftus.'

Good Lord! thought Elizabeth, frowning at him with a mixture of astonishment and irritation. He had indeed been after something – but it wasn't her money, let alone she herself – it was Father's research he wanted!

She opened her mouth, but he spoke again quickly before she could do so.

'Miss Loftus – let me make myself plain, I beg you!' He had clearly read the expression on her face. 'I'm absolutely not interested in either making money or a name for myself – I don't need to do either. The book would have your father's name, and you can have the royalties – you can have your own solicitor draw up any agreement you like. You can even veto the whole thing at any time if you don't like it – or me . . . providing I can do the same, of course. Because I'd have to see the work that's already been done, naturally . . . My own contribution, apart from any necessary editing, would be to put together the twentieth-century chapters only, because I'm not an expert on the earlier periods . . . But otherwise, you can call the tune absolutely. So don't say "no" out of hand, without thinking.'

That was exactly what Elizabeth was doing – she was thinking very hard indeed, trying to adjust her first reaction and her instinct and her prejudices with the apparent generosity of his offer. Because there must be a catch in it somewhere.

'I don't quite see why you want to do this . . . under those conditions, Mr Mitchell,' she said tentatively, shying away from the direct rudeness of 'What's in it for you?'

He shrugged. 'Let's say . . . I'm not a naval historian – I'm not ready to write a whole book of my own on naval matters. But . . . I admire your father's work – I think *The Dover Patrol* was a fine book . . . and I *could* do this.' He paused. 'Also . . . I'm between books myself at the moment, so I have several spare months.'

Well, there was an opening, even at the risk of emphasizing her ignorance. 'Forgive me for asking . . . but you must understand that I don't read books about the World Wars . . .' It was harder than she'd expected, and she felt the blood rising in her cheeks.

'What books have I written?' The laughter lines crinkled on his face as he came to her rescue, making it older again, where his recent embarrassment had made him seem younger. 'Or were you going to ask whether I write under my own name?'

'Oh no – that's the coward's question!' She felt herself melting under such candour. 'But honestly, I haven't seen any of your books – and I'm sure that's my fault for being unobservant – '

'I doubt it. But I did have a modest success with my book on the Hindenburg Line a few years back. And then there was the one on the battle of the Ancre . . . after which I completed Professor Emerson's definitive work on the Somme, though I can take no credit for that, of course . . . And finally, I have a new one coming out in the spring, about the Irish Guards in the war – *Watch by the Liffey*, that is . . . When the last survivors of the 1st Battalion were hanging on to the edge of Zillebeke Wood on the outskirts of Ypres in '14 they heard a German band playing "Die Watch am Rhein", and one of them said "Well, we'll give the bastards 'Watch by the Liffey' in reply".'

On the back of a book in Margaret's shop – was that where she had seen him, his face? thought Elizabeth.

'Plus the obligatory thesis, and the articles on this and that.' He fumbled in his top pocket. 'Perhaps I should have given you my card to start with.'

She read the card: *Paul Mitchell* . . . and on one side beneath, *The King's College, Oxford*, with a telephone number; and, on the other, 21B Namier Street, London WC2E 8QJ, with another number.

'And, if you'd like to check up further . . . I'm really a sort of civil servant, but I have this prolonged sabbatical, and the Hobson Research Fellowship at the King's College to make it economic – for me and the Civil Service both . . . In a year's time Whitehall and Oxford and I must decide where my proper home should be.' He smiled disarmingly at her. 'But in the meantime you can call either the Master's secretary at the King's or Sir Terence O'Shea at the Home Office, and they'll each give you the same dull answer. I'm perfectly respectable.'

In spite of her previous second thoughts about him Elizabeth was perversely disappointed. The respectability was all there, but the romance was lost in the safety of such references.

'The only thing is that I'd like to – ' Paul Mitchell stopped abruptly, staring past her.

'Ah, Dr Mitchell!' The Vicar materialized at Elizabeth's shoulder. 'I see that you have found our Miss Loftus . . . Elizabeth, I confide that you have had a profitable afternoon?'

For the first time the 'proposition' became real to her. Since Father's death she hadn't seriously thought about his unfinished book – indeed, she hadn't really thought about it at all. Yet now she realized that in its relatively advanced state and with this man's expertise – alleged expertise, anyway – it could become a real book, making real money for her . . . Except that money was now something she didn't need.

But then, she didn't need to keep it: she could easily solve that problem, and even assuage her conscience a little, by assigning the royalties to St Barnabas' tower.

That thought, and the discovery that having so much had not made her eager for more, raised her spirits. 'Yes, Mr Bickersteth, I do believe that I have.' She swept the piles of 10p pieces into her cash-box with a flourish so that each of them could take that how he liked.

'I'm glad to hear it.' Dr Mitchell's cheerfulness clearly indicated his interpretation. 'And I liked that "confide" too, Vicar. Would that be ecclesiastical usage or something from your naval background? Didn't Nelson try for "Nelson confides" first before Trafalgar, only his signal lieutenant edited to "England expects" to save the extra flags?'

The Vicar chuckled, but Elizabeth found herself specu-

lating about Dr Mitchell again. It was reasonable enough
that he should have asked the Vicar to point her out, and
Crockford's Directory would have supplied details of the
Vicar's naval career. But why had he gone to such
trouble?

'You've met before, then?' She spread the inquiry between them.

'Only this morning, Elizabeth, only this morning,' said
the Vicar. 'But we have an admiral in common – eh, Dr
Mitchell?'

'Hah – mmm . . .' Dr Mitchell appeared not to have
heard. 'I was just going to ask Miss Loftus, Vicar – but I
can ask you just as well, or even better – how long her
duties are going to detain her here? I'd very much like at
least a sight of the manuscript before I go back to London,
Miss Loftus . . . Perhaps I might call on you early this
evening – and then dinner afterwards?'

He was certainly taking her at her word in the way that
word suited him. But, what was more, he was carefully
doing it in public in such a way that she could neither
doubt his intentions nor refuse him without insult.

'Well . . .' she looked to the Vicar for help.

'Of course, Dr Mitchell!' The Vicar's help came in the
form of disastrous approval. 'It would do you good to get
out, Elizabeth. Beatrice can easily clear up the stall – she
can store the books in the Vicarage, and the Scouts will
attend to the trestles . . . As soon as I can find my
daughter, Dr Mitchell, Miss Loftus shall have an honourable discharge from her duties.'

It was all happening too quickly – and it was also so well
organized to be inescapable that all Elizabeth's suspicions
started to swirl again deep within her, not quite surfacing,
but disturbing her calm.

'Well . . .' She cast around for an excuse, but her wits
seemed to have deserted her.

'I'll call at your home, then.' Dr Mitchell looked at his
watch. 'Shall we say 6.45?'

She could feel the trap closing on her. She could still be too tired, or have a headache, or plead her mourning state, or simply be rude.

Or was it that she didn't want to plead an excuse – didn't *want* to, even though everything right and respectable and explicable about Dr Paul Mitchell still added up to a sum total in which she instinctively disbelieved?

'Very well – 6.45,' she said, snapping the trap herself.

2

It wasn't true that there was one law for the rich and another for the poor, thought Elizabeth as she parked on the yellow line outside Margaret's bookshop: the law was the same, it was simply that the punishment no longer mattered. Besides which, anyway, the restriction time had only another ten minutes to run, and the street was empty of cars not for fear of a questing traffic warden, but because all the shops had closed.

Margaret's was no exception, but Elizabeth hammered on the glass door, confident in the knowledge that if friendship wasn't enough to summon her, the thought of next term's sixth form reading list would do the trick.

Sure enough, one look over the 'Closed' sign transformed the bookseller's grimace into a welcoming expression.

'Elizabeth dear – I shalln't say "we're shut" to you, even though you have spent your afternoon ruining my business with unfair cut-price competition at that sale of yours.' Margaret re-bolted the door. 'Have you come to apologize, or is this a social call?'

Elizabeth smiled at her warily. The social call Margaret was half expecting might well be for her answer to that tentative offer of partnership 'if ever you found yourself free to consider it', which Margaret had made over coffee last year. But that 'free' had also meant 'and with sufficient capital to buy in', and now that she had both freedom and capital selling books didn't seem so enticing after all.

'My dear, you've no call to worry – ' the thought of books recalled her to her intention ' – you wouldn't have given house-room to the books I sold, and I didn't sell

43

many of them either . . . Besides which I'm here as a potential customer, if you're open for business – and if you've got what I want . . . which you probably haven't.'

'I never turn a customer away.' Margaret swept a hand towards the shelves and the piled tables. 'Take your pick – the usual discount for the school, two-thirds to you, dear. What's the title?'

'I don't know the title, but the author's name is Mitchell with a "t".'

'Mitchell . . .' Margaret thought for a moment. 'Lots of Mitchells – but *Gone with the Wind* I haven't got, so cross off Margaret Mitchell . . . But there's Julian for novels, and Adrian for poetry, and Gladys for whodunnits, and Paul for battles – '

'Paul?'

'Not your cup of tea, my dear – History, Military, twentieth century . . . I'm sure there's another Mitchell somewhere – ' she frowned at her shelves.

'Paul Mitchell,' said Elizabeth. 'Have you got his book?'

'I've got two of his titles. But don't tell me you're changing your A-level syllabus next term, for heaven's sake! I've just stocked up for the Tudors and the Stuarts.'

Elizabeth shook her head. 'This is personal. Can I see them?'

'Of course.' Margaret scanned her shelves again. '*The Breaking of the Hindenburg Line* is just out in paperback – that'll save you a few pounds. But I'll show you the hardback first . . . Let's see now – Marder, Mattingly . . . Middlebrook – Mitchell, *Paul* – here you are – *The Breaking of the Hindenburg Line*.' She regarded Elizabeth curiously.

It was a substantial book, its dust-jacket festooned with barbed-wire, stark black on white, leading her to the blurb inside.

'*On the morning of April 9th, 1917, the men of the British Fourth and Fifth armies had their first sight of a new*

German defensive position which was named by its builders the Siegfried Stellung, but which became known to the British as the Hindenburg Line.

'Sergeant Alfred Hannah, of the 2nd/4th Royal Mendips, saw the morning sunlight shimmering on what seemed like a river separating him from the village of Fontaine-du-Bois in the distance. Yet it was not water which had caught the light, but the sharpened points of a jungle of new barbed-wire 75 yards wide . . .'

Elizabeth's flesh crawled as she remembered how she had torn her second-best skirt on a single strand of barbed-wire on a ramble beyond the Trundles. *Not your cup of tea* was right!

She turned to the back flap, and Dr Paul Mitchell stared at her from it – a younger version, unlined and fuller-faced, and more arrogant too, but unmistakably the same man.

'Paul Mitchell was born in Gloucestershire on September 29th, 1945, twenty-seven years to the day after his grandfather was killed in action while commanding a battalion during the crossing of the St Quentin Canal. Dr Mitchell was educated at – '

So here, encapsulated, was all the research she had hoped to do, easily come by: school – grammar school or very minor public school, she couldn't recognize the name – Cambridge and a British Commonwealth Institute fellowship; then a research post with the Ministry of Defence (where did the Home Office come in?) and 'now researching the battle of the Ancre, the hard-won victory which led to the German withdrawal to the Hindenburg Line' . . . Definitely not her cup of tea, any of it; and yet the obsession with the 1914–18 War was here made explicable, even if she couldn't quite grasp the Theory of Contemporaneity which had drawn him from the Hindenburg Line to Jutland and HMS *Vengeful*.

'And here's the other one,' said Margaret. 'And the paperback of the one you've got there.'

The Battle of the Ancre was slimmer, but although Elizabeth had already had her fill of carnage it offered her critical assessments of the first book.

'Is this the Mitchell you want?' said Margaret doubtfully.

The critics appeared to have approved of Dr Mitchell's work; though of course the publishers would naturally have picked their quotations with care, for effect.

She looked at Margaret. 'Do many people buy this sort of thing?'

Margaret shrugged. 'About the same as for your father's books, allowing for the fact that Portsmouth's just down the road from here, so I expect to sell more naval books. It's surprising how well all the war books go – astonishing, even.'

Margaret was CND – anti-Polaris, anti-Trident, anti-Cruise, anti-practically everything . . . Elizabeth had to make allowance for that, just as Margaret did her best to make allowance for Elizabeth being her father's daughter.

'And he's got another coming out in the autumn – I think I read about it in *The Bookseller*.' Astonished or not, Margaret never let her principles get in the way of her bookselling. 'I can't remember the title, but it has something to do with the Irish.'

'*Watch by the Liffey*,' said Elizabeth.

'That's it. But how – '

'I'll take the two hardcovers. Put them on my account, dear.'

Margaret was still registering at her unsuspected specialist knowledge, and the temptation to increase the score was irresistible.

'It comes from what the Irish soldiers did in France in 1914 – the Germans were singing their "Watch am Rhein" in the trenches, so the Irish gave them back "Watch by the Liffey", Dr Mitchell says.' She smiled sweetly at her friend. 'And I need the books, you see, because he's taking me out to dinner tonight – '

* * *

There was no ticket on the car and no traffic warden in sight, and the street was still empty except for a car parked even more blatantly further down, where the yellow lines were doubled, no doubt encouraged by her example.

She sat for a moment, reading more of the dust-jacket blurb:

'Seventeen months later, when he next laid eyes on that same piece of the Hindenburg Line, Lieutenant Alfred Hannah of the West Hampshires failed to recognize it at first: the village of Fontaine-du-Bois had vanished off the face of the earth, and rust had dulled the barbs of the wire. But the wire was still there, unbroken . . .'

What was it, she wondered, which drew men like Dr Mitchell – he wasn't much older than she was – to the contemplation of such horrors? With Father it had been different – it had all been part of re-living glory for him, as well as pain. But Dr Mitchell . . .

She drove homewards abstractedly, her mind hardly on the road but ranging more on that conundrum, and then on her own recklessness in allowing herself to be propositioned so easily by a stranger. And such a strange stranger . . .

Then, suddenly and out of nowhere, a brace of leather-suited teenage motor-cyclists from Leigh Park roared past her, waking her up to the discovery that she was out of town already and on the edge of Father's woods – *her* woods, now.

Shocked by her own inattention, she checked her driving mirror carefully for further motor-cyclists before she turned into the concealed drive. But there was only a car way behind her, and that was pulling into the verge . . . It looked not unlike the same car she had observed in the street below Margaret's, and she wondered for a moment if it might not be Dr Mitchell at the wheel solving the problem of locating her home simply by following her, since she had clean forgotten to give him any directions. But then she dismissed the thought as pure imagination:

47

the Vicar could supply those directions just as well, and she couldn't see a man like Dr Mitchell worrying about such a small matter anyway.

She sighed as she searched in her bag for her key. It was no good dreaming about Dr Mitchell merely because he was going to take her out to dinner. In another second or two she would step into the hall, and put her bag on the table under the mirror as she always did, and would look into the mirror to check her appearance, as she also always did out of pure habit. And the mirror would then tell her all she needed to know, as it too always did – and this time it would also remind her that it was Father's research in which Dr Mitchell was interested, not her . . . not her . . .

She sighed again, and turned the key. Perhaps it would be better to vary the habit this time, and not bother to look in the mirror.

She put the bag down on the table –

There was a sudden flurry of movement in the mirror – she glimpsed something – and then darkness descended on her and arms crushed her –

'Don't scream, girl – an' don't struggle neither.' The voice was as rough as the hands, but unhurried. 'If yer do then I'll give yer somethin' to scream about – I'll break yer bleedin' arm. Got it?'

Elizabeth wasn't aware that she had made any sound since the bag – or whatever it was – had descended on her head, surrounding her with impenetrable dark. Nor, for that matter, had she attempted to struggle, for the hands and the rock-like bulk of their owner left no scope for resistance: it was like being grabbed by a gorilla.

But perhaps she had cried out in surprise and pain, and the gorilla had misinterpreted both the sound and the weakness in her knees.

'Got it?' The voice grated in her ear and the pressure on her shoulder-blades increased agonizingly.

This time she heard herself cry out – almost as much in

astonishment as in pain as her brain started to sort out the unbelievable signals it was receiving: nobody had ever done anything like this before to her – *no one had ever held her like this, hurt her like this!*

'You're-hurting-me!' she gasped.

The pressure relaxed to its original implacable grip. 'Just so you know this ain't nothin' to what I *can* do, eh?'

She was being robbed – freed from pain she fought against rising panic – she was being robbed, and she must keep her head . . . or he would beat her into a pulp . . . or . . . she felt the fear of what he might also do to her spreading inside her – the fear founded and fed on a hundred newspaper headlines –

She must keep her head – she must remember what to do, even though the fear was choking her!

But she couldn't think straight any more. Was it better to fight, and risk injury – or did submission encourage them to do what they might not have intended to do in the first place?

But trying to fight this sort of strength would be sheer insanity –

'I've got 'er – an' she's got the message I reckon.'

The voice outside the darkness wasn't directed at her: *Oh, God help me!* thought Elizabeth, despairingly – not *him,* but *them!*

'Bring her in here, then.' The new voice wasn't rough, like that of her captor: it was educated, but at the same time unidentifiably classless.

Before she could deduce anything more about it – before even she could decide whether to derive hope or greater fear from it – Elizabeth was manhandled round in a new direction and propelled forwards.

'Sit her down there,' commanded the educated voice.

Again she was manoeuvred, until the back of her legs came up against something hard – the edge of a chair – and then forced down into it . . . on to it – a hard chair, with arms.

49

Inside the hood she hadn't known where she was, but this chair reduced the choice to the dining room or the study, though without sense of smell it was impossible to tell which.

'Well, Miss Loftus, we weren't expecting you back so soon. But, now that you're here, we can turn that to advantage I think.' The voice paused for an instant. 'Indeed, I don't think – I *know* that you will help *uss*.'

Half of Elizabeth was irrationally terrified by the confidence in the voice, and by its smoothness, in which the sibilants hissed and slithered snake-like. But the other half whispered *robbery* to her, discounting rape and unnecessary violence.

Even, it was easy to imagine what had brought them, for it must be common knowledge now that she was alone, and a lone woman in a large secluded house would be an open invitation to men like this. She should have thought of that before, but now it was too late.

So . . . better to get it over with. Because even if she could spin out the agony until Dr Mitchell came knocking on the door, she didn't fancy his chances against the gorilla who had grabbed her.

'There's . . . there's money in a box upstairs – a wooden box under my bed.' There was no point in directing them to the silver in the dining room and the sitting room, they would have seen that at once and would have got it already.

'Under the bed? Tut-tut! How very bourgeois and careless!' The voice hissed the double-s at her contemptuously.

'A lot of money – more than two thousand pounds.' The contempt stung her. 'Just take it and go, can't you? There's nothing else worth taking – except the silver.'

'Nothing else?' No sound penetrated the hood except the voice. 'You're sure of that?'

Fear returned, instantly dissolving the contempt. 'I – I promise you that there isn't – you can see for yourself . . .

I haven't got any jewellery.' It was hot inside the hood, she could feel her cheeks burning.

'Nothing else?' That hateful hiss again.

She shook the hood. 'I swear it. Honestly – *please*!'

For a moment she thought he had accepted the plain truth. Then, without warning, her hands were seized from her lap and held on the arms of the chair. Something sharp bit into each wrist in turn, and then into each ankle.

Nightmare! She couldn't see and she couldn't move! She couldn't even rock the chair – something, or someone, was holding it steady, and the very effort of trying to rock it stung her wrists.

'Don't struggle, Miss Loftus. You'll only hurt yourself.'

Elizabeth sat rigid. 'Please – I've told you – '

'Shut up – and listen! I don't intend to waste a lot of time, Miss Loftus, so just listen . . . We don't want your silver, and we don't want your money – we'll take it, but we don't want it – do you understand? You know what we want. So just tell us what we want to know, and then we'll go.'

Elizabeth heard herself sob.

'Don't be silly, Miss Loftus. Crying won't help you – and saying "please" won't help you either. Because there's only you and me, and I'm not a kind-hearted man – quite the opposite, in fact. Do you understand?'

With an enormous effort Elizabeth brought herself under control. 'W-What do you w-want to know?'

'That's better.' He sounded curiously disappointed. 'But just remember now . . . two things: I *never* give anyone a second chance . . . and I'm *very* good at hurting people. Do you understand?'

Elizabeth nodded dumbly. Whatever it was that he wanted to know, she would tell him.

'Good. Then tell me all about the *Vengeful*, and those trips your father made to France.'

The *Vengeful*? Those trips – ? The questions simultaneously took her by surprise and also horrified her.

'Come on, Miss Loftus. I have his notes, and there's nothing in them. What I want is inside your head.'

It wasn't the safe deposits at all – *it wasn't the safe deposits at all!* And there was nothing inside her head except blind panic now.

'But I don't know what you mean – '

'Ah! Now there – I told you, didn't I?' Suddenly he sounded brisker, almost happier. 'You can't *sss*ay I didn't tell you!'

'But I don't!' wailed Elizabeth. 'He did research – he did research – I didn't go with him – I don't understand – '

'Of course you don't! You don't remember anything – of course you don't!' The snake-voice paused. 'Your memory has *s*suddenly deserted you entirely. *Hold her!*'

Hands clamped down on Elizabeth's shoulders from behind, pressing her back against the chair.

'W-what are you doing?' She began to struggle instinctively, but the pressure on her shoulders merely increased. 'Please!'

'Please!' The snake-voice mocked her. 'Thi*s*s is a little problem I often encounter, you know. But I'm very good at s*s*olving it . . . I'm going to help you get your memory back, Miss Loftu*s*ss. That's all!'

Something hooked into the neckline of Elizabeth's dress, pulling her forward against the pressure from behind. The thin summer dress strained for an instant, then tore apart as the material ripped and the buttons gave way.

Elizabeth tried to struggle again, more wildly but just as uselessly, the wires cutting into her wrists. Then she went rigid as she felt something hook into her brassiere between her breasts: the brassiere stretched for a second, then seemed to fall apart as though it had been cut –

Oh God! Oh God!

But then nothing happened. The hands released her shoulders – and she was sobbing again. But nothing happened.

'Ssso . . . very nice, Miss Loftus! So . . . just listen, then.'

Still nothing – nothing but the pounding of her heart, which hammered the blood in her ears in the darkness, and the sweat on her face.

'Did you hear that? No? Well . . . I was striking a match to light my cigarette . . . which is strange, because I don't smoke, you know.' The voice was animated by pure pleasure. 'Smoking is bad for you – and particularly bad for *you*, Miss Loftus.'

Still nothing.

'Evidently you don't understand – or you're very brave – brave and foolish.' More pleasure. 'Nowadays they have lots of equipment – microchips too, I shouldn't wonder – but I'm old-fashioned. In fact, although they say the Gestapo got it down to a fine art, I believe it was the Okrana and the Cheka who pioneered it . . . Apart from which it's highly cost-effective – even now, with cigarettes the price they are. One packet and a box of matches, and you're in busine*ss*.'

Just as the unbelievable dawned on her, and she opened her mouth to scream, something soft pressed through the material of the hood between her lips – something soft which was then pulled tight as the gag was fastened, so that she could only make incoherent sounds of hysteria, doubly muted.

'Yesss . . . I know you want to tell me *everything* now – of course you do! But you didn't take me at my word the first time, and I don't want you to have second thoughts again, so I propose to demonstrate the technique just a little in order to concentrate your mind absolutely on my requirements.'

A hand gently parted the wreckage of her clothing.

'There now!' The voice and the hand both caressed her. 'And I see that you don't much indulge in sun-bathing . . . which is really just as well, because you won't feel like wearing your bikini for quite a long time to come, if at all, you know.'

Elizabeth wanted to faint, but her senses refused to leave her. If anything they seemed to have become sharper, even to the gossamer touch on her skin.

'Wait a mo' – 'old on.' The rough voice came suddenly from above, just behind her.

'What is it?' Irritation harshened the snake-voice.

'I thought I 'eard somethin'.'

'Heard something? Where?'

'Out back. Just 'old on a mo', like I said.'

They were listening, and Elizabeth listened with them, yearning for any sound, but above all for Dr Mitchell's knock on the front door. It didn't matter to her now what might happen to him if he fell foul of the gorilla-man – nothing mattered but her own deliverance from those other hands, which had crawled over her with such sickening gentleness.

'I can't hear anything,' hissed the snake-voice.

'No, nor I can't neither – not now,' the gorilla-man admitted grudgingly. 'But I could swear I 'eard somethin', an' that's a fact.' The pressure on Elizabeth's shoulders slackened. 'Better 'ave a look-see, I reckon – just to be on the safe side, okay?'

The snake-man sighed. 'Very well – if you must. But make it snappy. We don't have all the time in the world at our disposal.'

Time, thought Elizabeth desperately. Like them, she had heard nothing. But just as the hood disorientated her sense of place, so the dark tide of fear within her had swamped her sense of time, and what had seemed like only a few minutes of nightmare might in reality have taken much longer.

The pressure lifted altogether, and she could move again within the painful constraints of the bonds which held her wrists and ankles.

Time was what she had to hold on to – she had to think of ways to spin it out: she had to hold on to it, and get control of herself.

Then, out of the darkness, he touched her again, and the control she was striving for slipped from her mind in a wave of sick revulsion and instantly-revived panic. The chair rocked and the bonds cut into her flesh agonizingly. Whatever it was that she had been on the point of thinking vanished from her mind, and all she wanted to scream was *Please don't – please don't!*

But she couldn't scream, and even the incoherent sounds she started to make were stilled as it came to her with a flash of bitter clarity that all pleading was useless, and worse than useless: *please don't* had been the ultimate encouragement he wanted from her, adding spice to what he was giong to do, and had always wanted to do . . . and nothing she could say or do – there *was* nothing she could say or do – would change that. She didn't even know any of the answers to his insane questions, but resistance or submission was all the same to him now.

So . . . there was nothing left to her but helplessness and terrible numbing fear in the dark – and the quiet of his silent enjoyment of her terror, which joined him to her.

The crash of noise which broke the bond between them was so unexpected and so shattering that for a fraction of time she thought it was inside her, as though her brain and her heart had exploded simultaneously.

Then the noise was outside her, repeated and so loud that it convulsed her into movement, regardless of the pain which tore at her again and as the chair toppled turning black into screaming red into nothing as her head hit something hard –

3

There were colours, bright as flowers, but crowned with stars –

'Come on, Miss Loftus – Miss Loftus, come on now – wake up, Miss Loftus . . .' The voice surrounded her, hectoring and encouraging her at the same time.

The colours revolved, and then became flowers in reality: the flowers in the curtains of the study, with the evening sun shining through them and starring the gaps in the folds of the pelmet with light. Elizabeth blinked the tears out of her eyes and fought her way upwards into consciousness.

She could see again!

More, she could see and her hands moved – hands, wrists and arms . . . all of them moved, freely though painfully, falling where gravity took them.

'Come on, Miss Loftus – damn it!' The voice became peremptory and irritable. 'Wake up!'

First, she felt aggrieved – then she became aware of hands holding her, lifting and dragging at her, which roused her into a flurry of fresh resistance against them.

The hands became arms, imprisoning her again. 'No! Come on, now – it's me – *stop it!*'

The hands weren't *those* hands – they crushed her, but they didn't *touch* her . . . it was as though, even though ungentle, they were unwilling to hold her, never mind to touch her –

Elizabeth relaxed, suddenly boneless.

'That's better! Now then . . . I'm putting you down – it's all right, but I'm putting you down – do you understand? Don't move – it's all right . . . I'll come back . . . right?'

There was no way she could answer any of that. But she accepted the soft-hard feel of the carpet against her cheek, and the movement of the bright flowers of the curtains and the stars twisting at impossible angles – and the desk and table legs horizontal when they should have been vertical.

She wrinkled her nose against the smell of burning carpet . . .

Burning carpet! The smell registered in her brain, triggering consciousness and a proper focus on her surroundings at the same time.

The desk blocked half her view of the room from ground level, but there at the end of it, a yard from her face and sending up a spiralling blue-grey smoke signal to her, a cigarette smouldered on Father's best-quality Wilton carpet!

Elizabeth hauled herself on to one elbow and reached out towards the cigarette. But it was too far away after all, and she had to go on hands and knees in order to extend her reach. To her annoyance she saw, as she picked it up, that it had already gouged an ugly brown mark into the thick pile of the Wilton, and –

God! *There was someone lying behind the desk!*

She froze on two knees and one hand, the cigarette pinched between thumb and forefinger of the other hand, hypnotized by the dark suede shoes, and the grey trousers rucked up to reveal socks and an inch of hairy white leg.

'Don't look,' said a voice from behind her.

Elizabeth hadn't wanted to look, there was no danger of that: not only the legs themselves, but also their stillness terrified her. But she found it impossible to take her eyes off them.

'Look at me instead,' commanded the voice. 'Come on, Miss Loftus – look at me.'

She didn't want to turn round either, but in the end it was the lesser of two evils.

'There now . . . it's all right, Miss Loftus – Elizabeth –

can I call you "Elizabeth"? And you can call me "Paul" – right?'

Elizabeth stared at Dr Mitchell uncomprehendingly.

'There's nothing to be afraid of. It's all over, and there's nothing to be afraid of – do you understand?'

She didn't understand . . . except that she knew he was trying to reassure her about . . . about things for which there could never be reassurance.

'It's all right, Elizabeth.' He was speaking to her as though to a child, in exactly the same way that she had spoken to little Helen Powell when she'd come off her bike outside the school and broken her wrist.

'Dr Mitchell . . .' she heard her own voice from far away, half-strangled.

'Paul.' He advanced towards her. 'Here – you put this on, Elizabeth.'

She frowned at what he was offering her: it was her old raincoat from the peg by the kitchen door. What could he possibly have in mind – that she should wear her old raincoat?

Then she looked down at herself, and saw with horror how her dress gaped open, and fumbled instantly in a panic of embarrassment with her free hand to draw the torn edges of her dress across her breasts.

'Here – ' He held the raincoat out with one hand and took the cigarette from her with the other ' – put it on . . . and then we'll get out of here.'

Elizabeth rose to her feet and tried to take the coat from him, but her knees were so weak that she found herself holding to his hand through the coat to keep her balance.

'Are you all right?' He asked.

'I'm all right.' Belatedly she realized that one edge of the torn dress had escaped her, and one breast with it; and the sight of it somehow put strength back into her knees and allowed her to get the coat round her, for modesty's sake.

He was trying to propel her out of the study, but she saw the legs protruding from behind the desk and the sight of them immobilized her again.

'He can't hurt you.' Dr Mitchell's voice suddenly became harsher. 'Come on!'

She had known that already in her heart, or at least half-known it, from the stillness of those suede shoes; but although she believed him she could not take in her own belief with understanding, so that she turned to him in horror at his confirmation of what she had known.

And then she stared at the open doorway.

'And the other one won't bother you either.' Dr Mitchell read her mind, but this time he had control of his voice. 'He's got two bullets in his chest, so he's not going anywhere. *Come on!*'

Elizabeth allowed herself to be half-led, half-pushed, and half-supported out of the study, and across the hall, and into the sitting room.

Bullets –

There had been those noises – they still rang in her head, she could still hear them – before her head had hit the desk – noises – *two bullets in the chest* – and the suede shoes protruding from behind the desk –

He pushed her against an armchair – it pressed against the back of her legs, and she collapsed into it, letting it engulf her.

She hugged the old raincoat against her. 'I'm cold.'

He knelt down obediently in the fireplace, to switch on the electric fire which stood in it during the summer. She heard the switches click – one, two, three.

'Where do you keep your drinks?'

'In the cabinet – in the corner,' she answered automatically. There was a thing in the back of her mind, just beyond her reach – like the cigarette on the carpet.

He tried to put a glass in her hand, and she could smell brandy.

'I don't drink – not this.'

'You're drinking it now. And so am I.' He paused to drink. 'Go on.'

She drank, and the fiery stuff burnt her throat, squeezing tears from her eyes.

'Here you are.'

He was offering her something else. Incredulously, she saw the same blue-grey smoke curl from a cigarette.

'Take it – go on.'

'I don't smoke.' The cigarette brought back an obscene memory, making her shiver involuntarily.

'But you were – ' he bit off the end of the sentence. 'Christ! Was that . . . *Christ!*'

She drank again. This time it didn't burn so much – *burn!* She shivered again, her teeth rattling against the cut-glass, and focused on him.

He was staring at the little golden packet in his hand, as though he was seeing it for the first time, and she was seeing him for the first time too – not as he had stared at her from the dust-jacket of *The Breaking of the Hindenburg Line* – not the *Paul Mitchell* born in Gloucestershire and educated at Lord Mansfield's Grammar School and Cambridge University –

'Who are you?' Suddenly she knew what it was that she had been reaching out for, beyond the smouldering cigarette. 'Have you phoned the police?'

He took another drink. 'You know who I am.'

'Have you phoned – ?' The question died inside her as she repeated it, and a terrible fear invaded her across the gap it left in its fall – a fear which took her back to the question he had left unanswered. 'Who are you?'

Who are you? *What are you?* She shrank away from him into the softness of the armchair, graduating from fear again into greater and uncomprehending panic.

'It's all right, Elizabeth – ' he put his hand out towards her, but she tried to shrink farther into the chair, away from him.

He pulled back his hand quickly, and she watched it

turn into a fist and almost thought for a moment that he was going to hit her. But instead he dropped it to his side and looked down at the cigarette he was still holding in the other one.

'All right, Miss Loftus. I can understand how you feel.' He flicked the cigarette into the empty fireplace, behind the electric fire.

He couldn't possibly know how she felt, thought Elizabeth. But there was no point in telling him so. There was only one thing worth saying, though perhaps that was pointless too. But she had to say it.

'I'd like you to call the police, Dr Mitchell – the phone's in the study.' She licked her lips. 'Or . . . if you won't . . . then I intend to call them.'

'No.' His eyes left her, switching first to the French windows behind her, then to those on either side of the fireplace. 'No phoning. It isn't necessary.'

'It isn't – ?' She stopped as he moved past her, watching him draw the curtains on each of the windows in turn. They had drawn the curtains in the study too, she remembered.

But he was already between her and the door. 'But that was necessary – a necessary precaution.' He switched on the light.

She tried to lick her lips again, but her mouth was dry. 'What do you mean? Why can't I phone the police?'

'Because I am the police, Miss Loftus.'

Elizabeth could feel the heat from the electric fire on her face, but under the raincoat she was shaking now. 'I – I don't believe you.'

He shrugged. 'There are different sorts of policemen. I'm one of the different sorts, that's all.'

His lack of concern angered her – it surprised her that she could be so frightened and yet still also be angry. 'The sort that shoots people, you mean?'

'Or gets shot by them – yes.' He watched her. 'But this time the sort that shoots people – yes again. Fortunately for you this time . . . yes?'

Suddenly Elizabeth was half-way to believing him. But she knew that was because she wanted to do so, against all the evidence of what had happened from the moment she had first set eyes on him at the fête. 'But why . . . why . . .' she trailed off.

'Why did I shoot them? It's called "self-defence", Miss Loftus.' He looked at his watch. 'But if you want me to regret it then I will.'

He was waiting for someone, thought Elizabeth. That was why he was merely talking to her, and not doing anything else.

But what was that 'anything else'? The thought queue-jumped all the other questions which were jostling each other in her head.

'Please – '

He held up his hand to silence her while he concentrated on some other sound. In the distance she heard a car on the road outside, but the sound diminished. 'Yes, Miss Loftus?'

He still had only one ear for her. 'What are you listening for?'

He considered her for a second. 'It's possible that your . . . visitors were not alone.' He pointed to the curtains. 'Hence the precaution . . . though fortunately your windows are burglar-locked, and I've wedged the back door . . . so I don't think we'll be disturbed.'

'But . . . they got in.' She heard her voice tremble at the thought of the snake-man having other animals with him.

'But they had all the time in the world – and an unattended house.' He shook his head. 'Don't worry.'

Don't worry? *Don't worry!* Elizabeth hugged herself even more tightly as the awfulness of her situation possessed her: it wasn't a nightmare – he was here, she wasn't dreaming him, and he *was* waiting for someone – it was a daymare, and it was real: *there was a dead man lying behind the desk in the study – and she dared not imagine what he might have been doing if he hadn't been killed . . .*

and there was another man desperately wounded, lying somewhere else . . .

'What about the man you shot – the other man?' She clutched at the only straw she could find. 'Shouldn't you phone for an ambulance?'

'He'll keep for a while,' said Dr Mitchell brutally. 'He's not bleeding to death, and he's a big strong fellow. Have another drink, Miss Loftus – your teeth are chattering.'

Elizabeth watched him pour. 'I'm cold – I'm hot outside, and cold inside . . . I don't know that I should – ' she looked up at him ' – I don't know anything any more, Dr Mitchell . . . I don't even know if you are Dr Mitchell – who are you?'

'Why not have another try at calling me "Paul"?'

She drank, and this time it didn't burn her throat.

'Well?'

She wanted to be reassured – to stop fighting, to stop thinking . . . just to let go. 'Paul.'

'There! That didn't hurt at all – did it! Everything is going to be all right – don't be afraid, and don't worry.'

She knew that none of that could come true just by wanting it to be so. Nothing was all right, and she was still afraid.

But his voice was soothing. 'Paul . . .'

'Yes, Elizabeth? May I call you "Elizabeth"?' He pulled a stool across the floor and sat on it, coming down to her eye-level. 'What do you want to know, Elizabeth?'

Although he was close to her it wasn't easy to focus on him in the feeble yellow light. Yet she felt absurdly grateful to him now, just for coming down to her level – for being human just for a moment.

'P-please . . . can you t-tell me . . .' she had to concentrate hard to hold her glass steady and to keep the coat wrapped round her at the same time '. . . why all this is happening?'

'Well . . . I should have thought you knew the answer

63

to that much better than I do, Elizabeth,' he chided her gently.

'But I don't – I don't!'

'Well . . . somebody thinks you do. In fact, somebody is very sure that you do . . . so perhaps you do.'

'But I don't – honestly.' She shook her head. 'I really don't . . . Paul.'

'I believe you, Elizabeth.' He nodded encouragingly. 'But, you know . . . sometimes we know things without knowing that we know them. That's happened to me – oh, lots of times.'

Elizabeth grappled with the possibility. But it took her back hideously to the study.

'It's all right – they can't touch you now – ' he started to put out his hand, and then drew it back quickly as though he knew not only what she was thinking of, but even sensed how her flesh crawled at the mention of the word 'touch' ' – I'm here now, and you're safe.'

'Yes.' She rocked backwards and forwards, and then steadied herself, and took another warming gulp of brandy.

'Tell me what happened.' He leaned forward and poured her some more brandy. 'Telling helps, while it's fresh in your mind – it gets it off your chest.'

She tightened the old raincoat around her. 'They grabbed me as I came in – they just grabbed me . . .'

'Uh-huh. And tied you up. But what did they want?'

'They said . . . *he* said . . . he asked me questions.'

'About what?'

She frowned. 'It didn't make sense. They wanted to know about the *Vengeful* . . . and Father's trips to France.'

'So what did you tell them?'

'There wasn't anything I could tell them. He said he'd got Father's notes, but that they weren't any use. But I don't know anything that isn't in the typescript – and I didn't even go to France with Father . . . I tried to tell him that. But he wouldn't listen.' She shivered.

'Yes?'

64

'Then he tore . . . my dress.' She drank again.

'Okay – forget that, Elizabeth.' He shook his head sympathetically. 'It didn't make sense because you couldn't tell him his answers – is that it?'

'It wouldn't have made sense even if I could have answered him.' Elizabeth tried to concentrate. 'Father was only researching for a chapter he was re-writing – that was why he went to France. I do know that much.'

'A chapter about the *Vengeful*?'

'Yes. But . . .' Concentration still didn't make for any better sense.

'If the man wanted to know about your father's ship – ' Paul Mitchell stopped suddenly. 'What is the connection between his ship and France? I wouldn't have thought there was much – 1941 and 1942?' He frowned.

'That's the point. It wasn't *his* ship – it was for the chapter on Number Seven.'

'Number Seven?'

'The seventh *Vengeful*.' She nodded. 'We used to call them by their numbers. Father's was Number Eleven.'

'Which was Number Seven?'

'She was a frigate – a 36-gun ship in the Napoleonic War. She was wrecked off the French coast after she'd been damaged in a fight with a French frigate named the *Fortuné*. They both went down, actually – the *Vengeful* captured the *Fortuné*, but the French ship herself was lost off Portsmouth when the prize-crew were bringing her in.' She gestured helplessly. 'But that was all back in 1812.'

'You never went to France with your father?'

'No.' She could never remember going anywhere with Father, let alone France. 'No.'

He thought for a moment. 'Did the *Vengeful* – Number Seven – have anything interesting on board?'

'Interesting?' It was a stupid question. 'She was just an ordinary frigate coming home for a refit. Or maybe to be broken up – she was in a rotten state even before the fight with the *Fortuné* . . . What do you mean "interesting"?'

Elizabeth heard herself slur the word, and shook her head. 'Interesting?' she repeated.

'I mean treasure, or something like that, Elizabeth.'

'Treasure?' Another stupid question. 'Good heavens, no! She'd been on convoy duty for months and months, escorting supply ships for Wellington backwards and forwards, and backwards and forwards . . . Nothing at all interesting happened to her until she was coming home that last time, and met the *Fortuné* – the French ship. She was so dull before that, that Father had to put in pages and pages about frigates, and how they were built, and so on, and so forth . . .' She nodded. 'I typed out his books – and cooked his bloody meals, and cleaned his bloody house, and washed – ' *What was she saying!* – 'I mean . . . I know all that because I did his typing for him.'

He was staring at her, maybe with surprise, maybe with embarrassment, maybe with pity. But it didn't really matter much now, because she was obviously useless to him as a source of information if that was what he wanted.

'So you see, it really doesn't make any sense at all – twice over, it doesn't.' She wanted to go on talking now that she'd started, even though she had nothing to give him. 'A man . . . a man like that, wanting to know about Number Seven – the seventh *Vengeful*, I mean . . . or any of the other ones, come to that . . . It's just naval history, you see, that's all . . . And if it wasn't . . . I mean, if it was something to do with Father in France . . . then I'd be the last person to ask.'

'But your burglar didn't know that,' said Paul.

'No, I suppose not.' Elizabeth conceded the point miserably.

'So you don't know what he was after?' He sounded disappointed too.

'I know he wasn't after my money – the money in the house – because he said so.' The misery deepened; in another moment her eyes would be swimming. 'I've got rather a lot of it, Father left a whole box full of it. It's in Father's *Vengeful* box.'

'His what?'

'His *Vengeful* box. It was the surgeon's box, for his instruments, with his name on the top picked out on a brass plate – he kept his money in it . . . they gave it to him.'

'Gave it to whom?' He frowned at her. 'Whose name?'

'The surgeon's name – the ship's surgeon – Williard – no, *William* Willard Pike – ' Elizabeth corrected herself ' – he kept his scalpels, and his forceps, and saws and things in it – at least, that's what Father thought.' Something seemed to be confusing him. 'They gave it to him.'

'Who gave it to whom?'

Now she was confused too. 'What?'

'The surgeon kept his instruments in it.' He scratched his head. 'But your father also kept his money in it. Did the surgeon give it to your father? Not that it matters – '

'Of course not!' How could he be so obtuse? 'The surgeon's patients gave it to him – it says so on the inside of the lid. Father kept his money in it – my money now.' She caught herself slurring her words again. 'I mean, it's just an old box – an old mahogany box with brass hinges and the inscription plates on it, that's all.'

'I see.' He nodded. 'And the surgeon gave it to *him*.'

'No! I told you – '

He lifted his hand. 'It really doesn't matter – '

'No! Father's *crew* gave it to him – the survivors in 1942. They found it in an antique shop in Portsmouth, some-where . . . not with the instruments in it, of course – it was empty, but it just had room for a few bottles of very old wine – or port, or brandy, or something. It was their present to him – a sort of keepsake, the box was, after they'd drunk the brandy – you see?' she looked at him hopefully.

'Yes . . .' He listened as another car went by. 'And that was why he called it his *Vengeful* box – I see.'

67

'Yes – *no* – no . . . that was because of Dr Pike.'

He frowned again. 'What? Dr Pike?'

'The surgeon – I told you!' Elizabeth was consumed by a desire to get the facts straight, if that was possible. 'Dr Pike was the surgeon on Number Seven – the old *Vengeful* . . . only he must have drowned with the prize-crew when the *Fortuné* went down on the Horse Sands off Portsmouth – ' She hiccupped suddenly. 'Pardon! It's all in the Number Seven chapter in Father's book – he thought the box must have drifted ashore from the wreck . . . It was really the box that gave him the idea of writing the *Vengeful* book, I think. Do you want to hear about it? Because Father thought – '

'That's all right – I can read about it, Elizabeth,' said Paul Mitchell quickly. 'And he kept his money in it – that's very interesting.'

He didn't look as though he was very interested, thought Elizabeth. He looked as if he was listening to something else.

Suddenly she wanted to interest him. 'Father was a gambler, you know – he *gambled* . . . And I never knew it – would you believe that?' It was almost a relief to tell someone at last. 'He left me a letter – and he left me lots of money. Lots and lots and lots of money – would you believe *that*?'

Now he was interested. 'Oh, yes?'

'Oh, yes – ' After a brief moment of gratification, caution set in abruptly ' – it's all . . . quite safe. Apart from what's upstairs in the *Vengeful* box.'

'That's good.' He stared at her. 'What was it – the horses? Or the football pools?'

'He didn't like football.' Come to that, thought Elizabeth, he hadn't liked horses either. 'But . . . I don't really know – ' she was about to add 'Would you believe that?' when she remembered having said it several times before, and decided against a further repetition ' – he didn't say, actually.'

He stood up suddenly. 'You stay here – just stay where you are, and don't move. Okay?'

She blinked at him, unaware that she had shown any sign of wanting to move. She didn't even think that she *could* move, even.

The front-door bell pealed out before he was half-way across the room.

In the doorway he turned back towards her. 'It's all right. Just you stay put, Elizabeth,' he said soothingly.

She watched the door close. For a few seconds his words reassured her, then her brain began to work again, and she was no longer reassured.

He had heard something which she had missed – that was why he had moved before the bell rang: she had been listening to her own voice – she had been talking too much – *God!*

And – *God! She couldn't just sit here like a dummy!*

This was the reinforcement he'd been waiting for – it had to be that, because burglars' friends would surely never ring the bell. But even so, when she heard the safety-chain rattle before the clatter of the latch it was evident that he was still taking his precautions.

There came a faint murmur of voices, and then the chain rattled again as he released it. Elizabeth almost sank back into the chair with relief, but the spark of her curiosity refused to let itself be extinguished: she still couldn't be sure that it was relief she ought to be feeling, and this might be her only chance of confirming it on her own account.

Levering herself out of the chair was more difficult than she had expected, and her knees wanted to fold under her so that she had to support herself from one piece of furniture to the next for the first few steps, until she could stumble the last yard to reach the wall beside the door.

Leaning against it, she put her ear to the crack –

'I wish to God that I did!' That was Paul Mitchell's voice, but it was no longer soothing. 'Only that's the least of our problems at the moment. You'd better send Bannen to the nearest phone – that's the one I phoned you from, about a mile down the road, just where the houses start . . . I don't fancy using the one here. We need an ambulance . . . gunshot wounds, two in the chest, one in the lung by the look of him . . . and one in the leg . . . and Bannen must get on to the local Special Branch to get him put under wraps, wherever they take him – no, wait!'

'What?'

'We need a meat waggon too. And we'd better have that first.'

'Christ!'

'For two. One's in the room there . . . the other's in the garden at the back, in the bushes by the back-gate – '

'*Christ!*' The second voice graduated from surprise to consternation. 'What the hell's happened?'

'Sssh! I've got the woman in there. I don't want her to hear all this.'

'You haven't shot her too, by any chance?'

'Don't be funny, Aske. Just tell Bannen to get moving.'

Two?

Two! Elizabeth's knees weakened, and only the wall supported her. She wanted to get back to the safety of the armchair in case he came to check up on her, but her legs had mutinied.

She heard the car start up, and then the front door closed again. Relief flooded over her as she heard the second voice again.

'What the devil have you been doing, Mitchell? You said this was just routine, damn it!'

Paul Mitchell half-grunted, half-groaned. 'So it was! If I hadn't spotted Novikov . . . my God, man – I'd have walked in here like a lamb to the slaughter!'

There was a moment of silence. Then she heard the study door open with its characteristic squeak.

Again she wanted to move, but couldn't.

In the garden at the back, in the bushes –

Lamb to the slaughter – *meat waggon* –

The door squeaked shut. 'Who the hell's that?'

'Don't ask me – I don't know any of them, they're not in any files I've ever seen.' Paul Mitchell sounded as though he disbelieved himself. 'They're all new to me.'

'What about *her*?'

'You may well ask!' Pause.

'What d'you mean?'

Elizabeth held her breath.

'They were just about to do something very nasty to her when I crashed their party.' Pause. 'I tell you, Aske . . . whatever they want here, they want it badly, and that's the truth.'

'What sort of state is she in?'

'Not bad, considering what she's been through – and considering what I've done to her, filling her up with brandy while she's still in shock. I wanted her to talk and now I can't stop her.'

'Charming! What are you going to do to her next?'

A tear ran down Elizabeth's cheek. He had been so kind and sympathetic, she had thought. And she had confided in him.

'I'm not going to do anything to her – you are.' Pause. 'I'm going to take this house apart.'

'And just what exactly am I going to do to her?'

'Take her to the safe house. David Audley will have to decide what to do with her after that.'

'And if she doesn't want to go?'

Elizabeth's knees weakened, and she slid down the wall to the floor.

'She's in no condition to argue,' said Paul Mitchell harshly. 'Tell her it's for her own good – tell her anything you bloody-well like, Aske. But just get her out of here.'

'Mmm . . . well, if this massacre is anything to go by, it probably *is* for her own good. Because, I must say . . . it *does* rather look as though the Russians mean business this time, old boy.'

The Russians? She must have misheard – the Russians didn't make sense . . . But then nothing made sense.

'For God's sake don't mention the Russians – I didn't mean that. She's frightened enough as it is, I don't want her to have hysterics,' Paul Mitchell whispered angrily.

She hadn't misheard. It still made no sense, but she hadn't misheard.

'She's the hysterical type, is she? Just my luck! And Bannen tells me she's plain as a pikestaff, too,' groaned Aske. 'All right – let's get it over.'

Elizabeth closed her eyes for an instant. Then, because she didn't trust her legs, she began to crawl back towards her chair.

She wasn't going to have hysterics – she wasn't going to give them that satisfaction: that was what anger did for her.

On the other hand, the way she felt, she was about to be unpleasantly sick to her stomach.

4

One thing she had learnt in nearly 24 hours, thought Elizabeth, was that none of them looked like any sort of policeman – not hateful Dr Mitchell, not polite Mr Aske and monosyllabic Mr Bannen, and certainly not the man in the doorway.

'Good afternoon, Miss Loftus.' He closed the door behind him. 'I'm so sorry to have kept you waiting so long.'

The voice was wrong. He was a big ugly broken-nosed boxer running to seed, in an old shirt with a frayed collar and a pair of clean but paint-spotted khaki slacks. But for that tell-tale Oxbridge voice he could have been the gorilla-man of hideous memory from yesterday.

'But we've had a lot to do, and Sunday isn't the best day for doing it – please don't get up – ' he motioned with his hand as she started to move ' – not if you're comfortable where you are.'

Elizabeth rose from the scatter of Sunday papers on the carpet around her. Mr Aske had said his boss was coming, it was almost the only thing he had said. And this gentle-voiced paint-spotted thug was that man, those words and that voice both told her – and therefore more to be feared than any of them.

'I'm afraid you've had a bad time – and I don't suppose we've made it seem any better . . . Do please sit down – ' he indicated the one comfortable chair in the bedroom ' – and then I shall be able to sit down too.'

Elizabeth pulled the stool from under the dressing table and sat on it. It seemed strange to her, with all she wanted to say, that no words came to her at all. But then, when she began to think about it, silence seemed quite sensible.

The big man sank into the armchair and stared at her for a few seconds.

'No questions, Miss Loftus?' He smiled suddenly. 'But then my colleague, Dr Mitchell, did say that you were a brave young lady. And a resourceful one, too.'

That was so far from the truth as to be laughable, if she had felt like laughing. And praise from Dr Mitchell was something she could do without, anyway.

She cleared her throat. 'I asked Dr Mitchell questions yesterday evening, and I protested to Mr Aske last night. But it didn't do me any good on either occasion. Will I do any better now?'

'A fair question.' He nodded. 'But I am neither Dr Mitchell nor Mr Aske. So why not try?'

He was testing her. 'Very well. You could start by telling me who you are, I suppose.'

'That's better!' He rolled slightly sideways in order to fish a small black wallet out of his hip pocket ' – my name is Audley, and I work for the government . . . *your* government, Miss Loftus.' He displayed the contents of the wallet for her. 'This is what you might call my credentials . . . my right to do what I do, as it were – do you see?'

Elizabeth studied the words and the names, but hardly saw them with her attention drawn towards the photograph, in which a pair of fragile metal-rimmed spectacles had been perched incongruously on his nose, just below the break.

'You're a policeman.' She found her voice again. 'A *sort* of policeman?'

The second sentence was better, less like an accusation, more like a question. But as she said it she thought of Paul Mitchell with a twinge of anger.

'You might say that, yes.' He watched her.

Elizabeth's stomach churned. 'A *secret* policeman – might I say that, Mr Audley?'

'You very well might, Miss Loftus.' To her disappointment, he smiled again. 'And you might be right – a few hundred miles east of here you would be exactly right, in fact . . . But, of course, you wouldn't say as much *there*, you'd be too frightened. So there could be a difference, don't you think? Because you don't need to be frightened of me, you see.'

Elizabeth steeled herself against his kindness. Paul Mitchell had been kind yesterday, but with men like this kindness was only one side of a coin which had a very different face on the other.

'You don't believe me?' He spoke gently.

'I wasn't thinking of you, Mr Audley,' she lied. 'I was thinking of your colleague, Dr Mitchell.'

He frowned slightly. 'With disapproval?'

She was committed now. 'Violence frightens me. And he's a violent man.'

For a moment he stared at her without speaking. Then he shook his head. 'No, you're quite wrong there . . . But if he were, you should be grateful for it, rather than disapproving, after what he did for you yesterday. For that was no small thing, Miss Loftus, believe me.'

His mildly chiding tone stung her. 'I'm very grateful for that – of course.' She was conscious that she'd talked herself into an ungraceful position. 'Though he did actually describe it himself as "self-defence" . . . But then it isn't that, exactly . . .'

'What is it, then . . . exactly?'

She didn't want to go any further, ungraceful or not. 'It doesn't matter.'

'It does matter. It matters a great deal, believe me.' He pinned her with a look from which all the mildness had vanished. 'I need to know – exactly.'

The opportunity of revenging herself on Paul Mitchell had presented itself more quickly than she had expected. But now revenge seemed petty, as it always did.

'Come on, Miss Loftus.'

There wasn't time to think of a lie. 'He killed those men – but he didn't seem to care. He said – '

'Those *men*?' He snapped up her mistake, then sank back into the armchair. 'Ah . . . so he was right! You *were* resourceful enough to eavesdrop . . . On your hands and knees?'

Elizabeth stared at him.

'You left scuff-marks on the carpet – he noticed them.' Audley nodded. 'Paul Mitchell's not just a fine scholar, he's got a sharp eye. For which you should be eternally grateful, Miss Loftus.'

'I said I was grateful.'

'So you did. But I don't think you're grateful enough, so I'm going to tell you *exactly* why you should be much more grateful.' He pinned her again with that fierce look of his. 'You see, you're wrong about Paul Mitchell, Miss Loftus . . . perhaps there are extenuating circumstances for that, I agree . . . but you *are* wrong about him, nevertheless – quite wrong.'

Elizabeth squirmed on the sharp point of his concentration. It was like being at school again, but not as one of the teachers.

'He killed those men for you, Miss Loftus – for your sake, not for self-defence – *for you*.'

'Yes – '

'No! You don't understand because you *can't*, not because you don't want to – I'll grant that. But I'm going to rectify that. So just listen.'

Elizabeth licked her lips.

'It was partly my fault. I told Mitchell this was just a routine job – no problems, no danger, just routine. So after he'd talked to you at the fête and arranged to visit you he could very well have gone off to the nearest pub to fortify himself for a boring evening.'

He was trying to wound her now, thought Elizabeth. And he was succeeding.

'But being Paul Mitchell . . . for which you should be

76

thankful, Miss Loftus . . . he didn't leave it at that – he decided to look around just to make sure everything was all right, even if it was just routine.'

She felt the knife turn.

'So then he saw . . . something . . . which made it *not* routine – something which frightened him, because he didn't expect it.'

Something? There was too much that she couldn't remember –

'So then he had a problem. Because the first thing he had to do was to phone for back-up – for help . . . which he did.' Audley nodded. 'But help was at least thirty minutes away, and he got to thinking that maybe you didn't have thirty minutes – maybe you didn't have any minutes at all.' He paused, and as the pause lengthened she realized that he was letting it elongate deliberately, to give her time to remember what she had been trying to forget. 'So what should he have done then, Miss Loftus?' Shorter pause. 'Go and knock at the front door, like a Christian?' Pause. 'If he was wrong – no harm done.' Pause. 'But if he was right . . . then he was in trouble too.' Pause – unendurable pause. 'Because he didn't have a gun, Miss Loftus – he isn't "licensed to kill", because no one is, contrary to popular legend. Not even policemen – they're not supposed to *kill*, except in very special and well-established extremities. And you certainly weren't an extremity – you were just a guess, Miss Loftus.'

He was hammering *Miss Loftus* like a dentist drilling without any pain-killer –

'So he went round the back, and he was very lucky there –'

Don't say 'Miss Loftus' again, prayed Elizabeth –

' – because there was a look-out man at the back, but the man was careless.' Audley shook his head. 'He was very lucky – and the look-out man was very careless . . . So then he had one dead man on his hands – and having a dead man on one's hands makes one sick . . . would you believe that, Miss Loftus? It makes you *sick* – sick to the stomach. Do you know what a dead man looks like? Do you know how his body reacts to being dead? Would you like the details?'

She couldn't even shake her head – she didn't want to, but she couldn't anyway.

'So *now* he had a gun. But he also had another problem, because there are only two rules for that sort of situation: you either run like hell or you go on like hell, SAS-style, before the other side knows what's happening.' This time he neither nodded nor shook his head, he just looked at her. 'And you never really know what you're going to do then until it happens – the question has to be asked each time, and you never know whether you were right until afterwards, which can be too late. So don't ask me what I would have done – I've a sneaking suspicion that I might have run, and justified it by thinking of my wife and child after – but you know what *he* did – '

Yes, she knew – or she knew now, anyway –

'He went on. And he shot the big one in the kitchen – in the kitchen, and in the leg, and then in the lung . . . and finally in the spine, Miss Loftus.' He still just looked at her. 'They think he's going to die too . . . although Mitchell doesn't know – he still thinks he only killed two men, not three . . . But when he asks me – as he surely will – I shall have to be as brutally frank with him as I am being with you, Miss Loftus.'

Brutally frank was what he was determined to be: she hated him for it, but she couldn't stop him, any more than Paul Mitchell could have stopped in the kitchen – she understood that now.

'He had one bullet left then. But he probably wasn't counting by then – he was probably too scared to count his shots by then, and the SAS rule is to *keep moving* – it's like the old house-clearing discipline in the war: *once you're in the house you must go through it like a dose of salts*, that was the rule – if you stop, you're dead. So he didn't stop.'

'Please, Mr Audley – '

'I haven't finished. The last bit is the best: he killed your little man with a single shot, right through the heart – a professional couldn't have done better than that, Miss Loftus – with a snap shot. But that's the shot which may get him into most trouble, unfortunately.'

He let her think about it this time, until she could formulate the obvious question. 'But – why?'

'Because the little man wasn't armed. He had a scalpel in his pocket – an adjustable typographical scalpel. But that was *all* he had.' Audley shook his head sadly. 'And that won't look good on the report . . . apart from the fact that we'd have liked to have talked to him, and now we can't.' His voice became gentler again. 'It was an accident, of course. But it won't look good.'

'But . . . but he couldn't have known . . .'

'That's what we'll be arguing, certainly. And with your supporting statement – and the gun – we ought to be able to manage "Justifiable homicide", with a bit of luck,' agreed Audley. 'There's a button on the wall there – by the bed . . . Would you press it please, Miss Loftus.'

Elizabeth rose shakily, and stepped over the Sunday papers, and pressed the button.

'Thank you,' said Audley politely.

She sat down again, and waited, and tried to think coherently.

He had done it deliberately, of course – all of it, intentionally and with deliberate brutality designed to shock her. But, deliberately or not, he had succeeded: he had shackled her to Paul Mitchell for ever, with unbreakable chains of obligation.

The door opened, and Paul was there in the doorway – and she didn't know where to look, with the way she must look, *sans* the slightest advantage of make-up, and her hair every which-way, and the old dress which Humphrey Aske had offered her yesterday, when it hardly seemed to matter what she looked like.

79

'It is customary to knock, Mitchell,' snapped Audley testily. 'Have you brought the box? And the form?'

Paul Mitchell hefted a suitcase on to the bed, snapping the catches but leaving the lid closed. Then he felt inside his breast-pocket and produced a folded document.

'This is an Official Secrets form, Miss Loftus.' Audley unfolded the document and handed it to Elizabeth. 'Sign it at the bottom there – '

'But read it first, Elizabeth,' said Paul Mitchell.

'Shut up, Mitchell,' said Audley. 'Just give her a pen.'

Elizabeth took the form from Audley and the pen from Paul Mitchell.

'Sign it, Miss Loftus,' said Audley.

'You're signing away your rights,' said Paul. 'Once you've signed, they can shut you up and throw away the key.'

'She's not stupid.' Audley gestured towards the form. 'After what you've done, she knows she hasn't got any rights – except maybe the right to be shot by you, Mitchell. *Sign it*, Miss Loftus.' He paused. 'And the copy underneath – sign that too.'

Elizabeth signed. In the silence of Paul's failure to reply to Audley's last remark she heard the scratch of the pen on the paper.

'Good.' Audley folded the forms and transferred them to his hip pocket, where the identification folder was stowed.

Elizabeth observed that Paul looked decidedly miserable, and not at all the confident young man she had first seen in the mirror. If she'd wanted to go on hating him it would have been difficult, but now it was impossible.

'*Elizabeth Jane Varney Loftus*,' said Audley reflectively. '"Varney" for the naval Varneys, on your mother's side, from way back – from Boscawen and Hawke, and the Seven Years' War, and all the other wars thereafter . . . There was a Varney who was Admiral of the Blue in the West Indies, I remember from my history books – and that must have perked up the family fortunes, with his admiral's share of prize-money – how much was that in those days?'

'One eighth.' The mention of money made Elizabeth uneasy. 'One eighth up to 1808, less after that.'

'This was back in the eighteenth century . . . one eighth? Plus head-money, and gun-money, and sundry other trifles – very nice!' Audley nodded. 'So . . . an old and distinguished naval family, and you the very last of them, after the Dogger Bank in '14, and Sulva Bay in '15, and the Murmansk run in '43.'

He wasn't reading – the suitcase was open on the bed now, but from where she knelt she couldn't see its contents. But he hadn't dipped into it, anyway; so this was what was already in his head, about grandfather and his uncles, and all her other Varney ancestors.

'Beside the Varneys, the Loftuses were pretty small beer – in trade in the West Country, was it? So your mother was a good catch, at least in naval terms, for Lieutenant-Commander Hugh Loftus, even with his VC? Would that be right?'

How much did he know? Did he also know that Mother had been beautiful, judging by those portraits which were all that she had inherited? Or that Grandmother Varney, judged from the same source, had been even more beautiful, in her diamonds and her dresses?

It occurred to Elizabeth that if Paul Mitchell had had the run of the house last night those might be exactly Audley's sources, with much more beside – and that she had the right at least to disapprove of such an intrusion into her privacy.

'I can't say I've really ever thought of it, Mr Audley.'

'No . . . of course, they were all gone before your time – and your mother too, when you were a baby – very sad!' Audley commiserated insincerely. 'Which just left you and the Commander, and in somewhat straitened circumstances when he was invalided out, I take it?'

She had been right to feel uneasy: it was the money he was working towards. But how much could he know about that, beyond what she had blabbed yesterday to Paul. But how much more could old Lovell add to that?

'Father had his writing, Mr Audley.' Her apprehension increased as she thought of Mr Lovell. If she was now a most valued client he was nonetheless a pillar of the Establishment, and if the Establishment leaned on him he might well bend his ear to it. Yet, at the same time, her own backbone stiffened: if they thought she was going to give in easily, they were very much mistaken. 'He made a new career for himself with his books.'

'Yes. Just so!' He flicked a look at Paul Mitchell, who seemed to be busy studying the pattern on the carpet. 'But Dr Mitchell and I have some small experience of the writer's trade, Miss Loftus . . . and the fact is, your father didn't write many books over the years – good ones, I'm sure, but not many . . . and not best-sellers.' Audley's voice harshened. 'Or, to put it another way, I've spoken with his publishers, and I don't think his royalties matched his tastes.'

Now Elizabeth knew where she was, and what she was: she was the USS *President* making a run off the Long Island shore in 1815, straight out of Father's article for the *British Naval Review* . . . heavily laden, and damaged below the water-line while crossing the bar off Staten Island, and with half the British fleet in hot pursuit. But a run for it she was going to make, nevertheless!

'Mr Audley, I really don't see what this is leading to – or what business of yours my father's royalties are – or his tastes.' She had to get the mixture just right, with equal parts of incomprehension, irritation and innocence. 'And I certainly don't see what it's got to do with that document I signed.'

Out of the corner of her eye she saw Paul Mitchell half-smiling at the carpet, as though he had noticed a joke in the pattern.

'Are we going to play games after all, Miss Loftus?' Audley gazed at her. 'You disappoint me.'

'*I'm* not playing games – '

'Mitchell.' Audley ignored her. 'The box!'

It was the *Vengeful* box, of course – and Audley made his point by emptying a cascade of five pound notes on the carpet in front of her.

Audley looked at her. 'And if you're about to tell me that your father was a gambling man . . .' he shook his head '. . . please don't, because I'm not about to believe it.'

It wasn't going to be a 36-hour stern chase after all, thought Elizabeth desolately – she was going to strike her colours long before Decatur had done. But it wasn't really Audley who had beaten her.

'I know you told Mitchell that – and when he might have believed you . . . that was resourceful, Miss Loftus – I grant you that.' They both knew she was going to surrender, she saw that in his face, as he looked down at the money, and then back at her. 'There's more than this, isn't there? You've got safe deposit keys lodged with your solicitor – oh yes, *your* safe deposits, I don't doubt that . . . the Commander was resourceful too – like daughter, like father, I don't doubt that either.'

Mr Lovell had talked. But, what was worse, Mr Lovell had been much more observant than was good for her.

'Your safe deposits – but *his* loot.' He had her in range now. 'And this is just the tip of the iceberg.'

She felt cold enough for it to be just that. And she couldn't fight him any more because she had never in her heart really believed the gambling story, but had simply chosen never to question it.

A token resistance, for form's sake if not for honour's, was all she could make. 'What makes you . . . so sure . . . that he didn't win it?'

'My dear – practically everything.' He gazed at her with a suggestion of sympathy which she found humiliating.

'Like, for instance, retired naval officers of an academic persuasion aren't often given to gambling . . . or, if they are it's usually common knowledge. And the house would have been full of bits of evidence, from bookies' phone numbers in his address book to old race-cards shoved behind the cushions . . . And if it wasn't horses, then he'd be known around the clubs – especially if he was a big winner, believe me.' He paused. 'Which, of course, he wouldn't have been – he'd have been a loser. And that's almost the clincher by itself. He just didn't have the right form.'

Of course, they would be experts on this sort of thing, reflected Elizabeth, because gamblers would always be security hazards. And, anyway, if Father's story had never really convinced her, it would be no match for them, just as she was no match for them.

'Apart from which there's your statement – Mitchell!' Audley passed the stapled sheets to her – not the original, she noted, but a photo-copied copy. 'This is your account of what happened yesterday, between the time you left the village fête and . . . Mitchell's second coming, if I may call it that – as witnessed by Aske and written and signed of your own free will?'

He was closing in on her now. But however disastrous the revelation of the safe deposits might be, that wasn't her real worry, not now.

'Yes.' Being the only daughter of a new-deceased hero and an unworldly schoolmistress ought to count for something; and she might as well start rehearsing that rôle as of this moment. 'Actually, Mr Aske said I couldn't have the Sunday papers until I'd written it.'

If Father hadn't won it, *where on earth had it come from?*

'Very well. Page two, towards the bottom of it.' Audley had his own copy of the statement. 'You offered him what was in the box, and he said "I don't want your money".'

She saw that he had produced the spectacles he had

worn for his photograph, and had perched them in the same ridiculous place. 'Yes. That's what he said.'

'Uh-huh. And that's also what you said to Mitchell – "he didn't want my money". So what was he after, Miss Loftus?'

'I don't know.' Elizabeth blinked at him. 'I said that to Dr Mitchell too.'

'But it had something to do with France, and your father . . . and HMS *Vengeful* – you told him that also.'

'Yes . . .' What had been rather vague and disjointed in her memory came back to her suddenly with disconcerting clarity. In the state in which she'd been, and with both the brandy and Paul Mitchell egging her on, she'd said much more than she needed to have done. 'But it didn't make any sense – I told Dr Mitchell that too.'

'Why not?'

She gestured helplessly. 'How could anyone possibly be interested in the *Vengeful*?'

'Your safe deposits aren't in France, by any chance?'

'No – no, of course not. They're in London.'

'All of them?'

'Yes – there are only four . . .' Elizabeth faltered as she realized that this was the line of questioning the snake-man should have pursued yesterday, instead of fruitlessly pursuing Father's *Vengeful* research trips.

Audley nodded. 'So we come to the big question, Miss Loftus: what have you got in those precious boxes of yours?'

'I'm sorry?' She looked at him in surprise, then at Paul Mitchell.

'Come on, Elizabeth,' said Paul Mitchell. 'Get it over with. We're bound to find out, one way or another.'

She frowned at him. 'Well – money, of course. I told you!'

'Money?' Audley returned the frown.

'What did you expect?' Now they were frowning at each other, as though she'd given an unexpected answer.

'Just money?' Audley persisted. 'In all four deposits?'

'Yes.' She shared her own bewilderment with them.

'Look, Elizabeth . . .' Paul Mitchell abandoned his position by the suitcase, coming round the bed to squat on his heels in front of her, among the bank notes '. . . we don't want your money – okay?'

'Well – what *do* you want?' It ought to have been an angry question, but the way it came out there was a pleading note in it.

Paul Mitchell's encouragement slowly changed to doubt. Then he swivelled towards Audley. 'What the hell *do* we want, David? That's a good question!'

Audley was watching her over his spectacles. 'Tell me about the safe deposits, Miss Loftus.'

'There isn't much to tell.' All the stuffing had gone out of her. 'Father gave me a parcel one day, and told me how to open a deposit – what to do . . .'

'In your own name?'

'That's the only way you can do it. And then he gave me other parcels . . . and there were other accounts . . . And I gave him the keys each time, of course.'

'Of course!' He thought for a second. 'And you always do what you're told – you didn't ask what was in them?'

Put like that it hurt, and she couldn't bring herself to answer it directly. But somehow it had to be answered.

'David – ' began Paul Mitchell.

'No. Let her answer.' Audley waved him off. 'Weren't you at least curious?'

There was no way of answering that without humiliation. 'You never met my father, Mr Audley?'

'No. That pleasure was denied me, Miss Loftus.'

The funeral came back to her: the rain gusting across the churchyard in sheets and falling through the saturated summer leaves of the trees on to the mourners – the smell of the wet earth and damp uniforms.

'He should have commanded a battle-squadron, Mr Audley – that's what they said. But all he had was me.'

She managed to look him in the eye. 'After he died there was a letter in his deed-box at the solicitor's with the keys. It's still there, so you can see it for yourself. And the keys, too.'

Paul Mitchell stirred. 'But he didn't say where he'd got it?'

'He said he'd taken a gamble. And he said that it was now all rightly mine, and no one else's. That's all.'

Audley nodded slowly. 'How much?'

It was the inevitable question. 'I don't know – not exactly. There are gold coins as well as bank notes . . . sovereigns, and also those South African coins.'

'Krugerrand,' murmured Paul. 'Nice!'

'Roughly – how much?' Audley wasn't letting her go.

'In bank notes . . . about £100,000. I don't know what the coins are worth. But there are a lot of them.'

'And the tax-man doesn't know about any of it!' Paul grinned like a schoolboy. '*Very* nice!'

'I don't know whether I should have reported it . . .' When it came to the crunch, pretending to be an unworldly schoolmistress lacked credibility, decided Elizabeth. But if she was to salvage something from the wreck she had to do her best. 'But if you think I ought to, then I will, Mr Audley.'

'Good Lord – I wouldn't!' exclaimed Paul. 'She doesn't have to, does she, David? I mean . . . can't we declare her prize-money between ourselves, as it were?'

Elizabeth's heart warmed to him. But also, at the same time, she had the impression that Audley was reading her like an open book.

'What you do with it isn't our business, Miss Loftus – as Mitchell said, we don't want it.' Audley closed the open book. 'But where it came from *is* our business.'

They were back to the unanswerable question.

'The notes will have numbers,' said Mitchell. 'Are they new ones, Elizabeth?'

The look on her face answered him even before she shook her head.

'Pity.' Almost unwillingly, he turned to Audley. 'That amount of money in used notes . . . means it's been professionally laundered, David.'

'It's not the money that matters.' Audley studied her. 'Tell me, Miss Loftus . . . did the parcels come to you after the trips to France?'

'I don't know . . . no, I don't think so . . .' Her memory sharpened as she realized the point of the question. 'No . . . there were more of them – he didn't go nearly that often . . . and . . . and they started before he went the first time –' she stopped suddenly as the absurdity of the connection became apparent.

'Yes?'

'He went to France to research the book, Mr Audley.'

'So?'

'It's absurd – it makes no sense.'

'It makes sense to someone, Miss Loftus.' He echoed Mitchell's words from the previous evening. 'That's why we need your help, you see.'

'My help?' Elizabeth was so grateful he'd dropped the subject of the money that she didn't frown.

'You're the expert on his book – you did all his typing, Mitchell tells me.'

'Yes – no . . .' Caution reasserted itself. 'I only typed the chapters when they were complete, he never discussed them with me or told me what he was doing. And he kept most of his notes in his head, it seemed to me.'

Audley nodded. 'But he was re-writing one particular chapter, I gather?'

They were back to the absurdity. 'Yes, but that was to do with Number Seven – the old *Vengeful* – ' She didn't want to discourage him, but it was no good pretending to knowledge she didn't possess ' – and I really don't know why, or what.'

Another nod. 'Perhaps not. But if we do come up with

anything new, then you'll be able to advise Mitchell here. You can be his technical adviser, in effect.'

She looked at Paul Mitchell. She could hardly refuse to help *him* now, Audley himself had made sure of that. And even apart from that moral obligation there was her money to be considered – they had made that her *prize-money*, and prize-money had to be earned in battle.

And that left her no choice at all.

'Very well, Mr Audley.' As she came to her no-choice decision it occurred to her that she'd been manoeuvred into this surrender by Paul Mitchell and Mr Aske and Mr Bannen just as surely as *Endymion* and the *Pomone* and the *Tenedos* had brought Decatur's *President* within range of the *Majestic*'s seventy-four guns. But Decatur had struck his flag then without loss of honour, so she could do the same.

Paul Mitchell smiled at her. 'It'll take you out of circulation too, Elizabeth. And that's probably just as well at the moment.'

She didn't know quite what to make of that, because she knew she couldn't trust him. But it sounded well-meant, and she wanted to believe that it was.

'I don't see how I can help you, Mr Audley. But if it really is Number Seven . . .'

'Ah . . . now we've been lucky there.' Audley had brightened with her surrender. 'Owing to Mitchell's . . . exuberance . . . we cannot put any questions to your burglars. But before your arrival on the scene they had collected all they wanted to steal, it seems. So at least we know what they wanted.'

Paul Mitchell nodded at her. 'Number Seven, Elizabeth.'

'The old *Vengeful*, Miss Loftus,' said Audley.

5

'Put on your seat-belt,' said Paul. 'Aske keeps telling me that I must wear it at all times. It's getting to be a habit.'

The belt clicked, and she had better keep her wits about her, snapped the sound of it. 'And now?'

'And now . . .' his foot went down on the accelerator '. . . and now . . . tell me about Number Seven, Elizabeth.'

'Where are we going?'

'Ah . . . you must have made quite an impression on David, because he's doing you a great honour – you should be pleased . . . *and* reassured – you're going to Steeple Horley.'

'Steeple Horley?'

'The Old House – *his* house . . . You'll like his wife – Faith is a great lady in her way – ' he snorted as he changed gear '– to be married to David Audley she has to be a great lady.'

Great lady? '*His wife*?' Elizabeth looked down at her creased and shapeless dress. It wasn't even very clean, either: there was something suspiciously like a stain right in the middle of it – she had last worn this dress when she'd helped the Vicar's wife with her meals-on-wheels for the old people of the parish. It was certainly not what she would have chosen to wear for a great lady. 'Oh Lord!'

'Don't worry!' He observed her consternation. 'I don't mean "grande dame", I mean she's sympathetic. And she's not a lot older than me – than you too, Elizabeth. Like they say, he married a much younger woman . . . and they live in this marvellous rambling old house under the downs – we haven't got far to go.'

Elizabeth was still appalled. Apart from the dress there

90

was her face and hair, which were irreparable. There was probably a mirror on the other side of the car's sun-visor, but she couldn't bring herself to look in it. Everything was bad enough as it was, but to have to meet another woman was downright unfair. She hunched herself up at the thought of it.

'Don't worry, Elizabeth!' He exerted himself to reassure her. 'It's a good sign – his inviting you to his home . . . you'll meet his daughter too – a skinny little blonde creature, the image of her mother, and very sharp like both of them . . . it means he's not about to peach about those safe deposit boxes of yours to all and sundry, I'd guess – for a start.'

'I thought that remained to be seen,' said Elizabeth guardedly.

'So it does. But although David's a damned tricky bastard, he's not mean with it. Putting one over on other people is what he enjoys, too – putting one over on the Inland Revenue, or whoever deals with death duties . . . that'll appeal to him.' He gave her another quick glance, but this time a fellow-conspiratorial one, which told her that under the skin, and in spite of their publicly abrasive relationship Paul Mitchell returned the loyalty and regard which David Audley felt for his subordinate – the same thing which had made the survivors of Father's old crew stand in the rain for him in their best suits so recently, in that secret society to which she had never been admitted.

'What's the matter?' Her silence bothered him.

'I have the feeling that I'm being press-ganged, that's all.'

'Hardly that. It's your knowledge we want, you won't be expected to fire the cannon and shin up the mast. And there can't be anything dangerous involved, not this time.'

'"Can't"? How do you know that? After what's happened already?'

Paul shook his head. 'David wouldn't invite you to his home if he was worried about anything. He's pretty careful that way – that's why the invitation is reassuring.' He drove in silence for a second or two. 'Surprising maybe . . . I admit I find it a little surprising . . . but damn reassuring nevertheless, Elizabeth. So tell me about Number Seven.'

Press-ganged or not – and shanghai'd might be a more accurate description for all that had happened to her during the last 24 hours – but press-ganged or shanghai'd or whatever . . . and reassured or not about her own fate and the fate of her inheritance, she had to trust to Paul Mitchell's judgement and David Audley's good faith, even though they were both men outside her experience.

'Where do you want me to begin?'

'Twelve *Vengeful*s,' said Paul, nodding at the road ahead, on which the homeward-bound Sunday traffic was thickening to slow him up. 'The Armada *Vengeful*, hanging on to Medina-Sidonia's shirt-tail up the Channel – King Charles's *Vengeful*, betraying him at Bristol in 1642, and Cromwell's 50-gunner in the First Dutch War, wrecked on the Goodwins . . . – then Pepys' *Vengeful*, scuppered by the Dutch in the Medway in '67 – then Rooke's *Vengeful* fighting alongside the Dutch at Gibraltar in 1704 – '

Was that his own research, or had he read Father's earlier chapters?

'Then Number Six, protecting our loyal American colonists from the French in '59, but eventually getting wrecked off Cape Hatteras in '81 trying to stop the French helping those revolting Yankee rebels – historical irony, you could call that, I suppose.' He drove in silence for a time. 'Number Eight – muzzle-loaders versus breech-loaders – I enjoyed Number Eight . . . He had a nice line in scorn, did your father – "the mechanics of incorrect decision-making, brought to a fine art in the mid-Victorian navy" –' he gave her a quick half-look, half-nod ' – and so to Number Nine – '

But he had missed out Number Seven altogether, thought Elizabeth, staring at the handsome profile.

'The armoured cruiser – "the ugliest *Vengeful* of them all, and in her day arguably the worst sailer and gun platform in the whole Channel Fleet" . . . But she was also the one that obstinately refused to sink when they used her as a target ship in 1897, wasn't she – "to the surprise and embarrassment of all concerned" – right, Elizabeth?'

Not just a handsome face, though: somehow, between last evening and the moment he'd bounced back into her life, and apart from whatever else he'd done, he'd read those carefully-typed pages closely enough to memorize passages from them accurately.

'Plus *my* Number Ten, from Jutland, and *his* Number Eleven, full-fathom-five off Finisterre, or wherever . . . and we don't need to worry about that submarine we gave to the Greeks after the war – we know all about that apparently, and it doesn't signify. So that makes the full *Vengeful* tally – right?' Another look, and then the profile again. And with that face and the self-assurance which went with it there would be equally good-looking and assured girl-friends in tow, if not an elegant wife close-grappled, so it was no use making silly pictures just because he was being gentle with her. She was merely business, and his gentleness was common-sense.

'Not quite.' To stifle that foolish ache she tried to concentrate on that business. 'You left out Number Seven, of course.'

'But you are going to tell me about her, Elizabeth – don't you remember?'

Elizabeth stared at the road ahead, on which the home-going traffic from the coast was thickening. She wished she was going home with them, even to another lonely evening.

'I remember that we started this conversation yesterday.'

'So we did. But yesterday you weren't exactly brimming with ideas. Quite understandably, in the circumstances, of course.'

'Yes . . . quite understandably . . . since I was brimming with alcohol – administered to loosen my tongue, presumably, rather than my brains?'

That earned her a longer look, a little rueful, mostly apologetic, but with a suggestion of respect which she found gratifying.

'Yes . . . I'm sorry about that. But it seemed a good idea at the time.' He smiled disarmingly. 'Anyway, I'm hoping you can do better on reflection.'

Respect was better than nothing, thought Elizabeth as she hardened her heart against the smile: if she couldn't have anything else from him, at least she could win that.

'But now that you've read Father's chapter you really know as much as I do. And you are the trained historian, not me.'

'But you are the expert on this, Elizabeth – not me.'

'No. I was only the typist. I keep telling you.'

For a minute or two he drove in silence. Then he shook his head slowly at the two small children who were waving at him out of the rear window of the car in front. 'No . . . I don't think "only the typist" could ever be a description of you, Elizabeth. You're always going to be a lot more than "only the typist". And that's not just my opinion . . . although it *is* my opinion.'

Elizabeth was half surprised, half shocked. 'You've canvassed other . . . opinions?'

'Of course! We don't go entirely blind into something like this, we know a lot about you. But it's Number Seven we want to know about now.'

Elizabeth was still grappling with the news that she had been . . . 'investigated' was the only word for it . . . by – by whom? 'Who are you, Paul? *What* are you?'

'But you know who I am, Elizabeth. You checked on me – and quite efficiently, too – the moment you left the fête yesterday.'

She stared at him. 'You were in that car – in St Helen's Street – when I visited Margaret's bookshop?'

'No. I wasn't in that car.' Suddenly his expression was intent. 'You spotted *that* car?'

'I didn't exactly "spot" it – I mean, I just saw it . . . I didn't really take any notice of it until I saw it again behind me, when I reached home.' His interest made her uneasy.

'But it could have been any car. Why did you notice it?'

'Well . . .' she floundered under his intensity '. . . I thought it might be you, as a matter of fact.'

'Why should I follow you?'

This was becoming awkward. 'Well – I don't know – I didn't know . . . I suppose I was a bit suspicious of you, that's all.'

'Christ!' He drew a deep breath, and then relaxed slowly. 'Phew!'

'It wasn't you?' She shied away from the proper question.

'No. I was round the corner, in another car.' He shook his head, but more to himself than at her.

The proper question wouldn't go away, it had to be asked. 'Who was in the car I saw, Paul?'

For a moment she thought he hadn't heard, as he raised his hand to wave back at the children. Then she thought it was more likely that he simply wasn't going to answer the question.

'It was a man who goes by the name of Fergusson.' He waved again. 'A freelance journalist from Canada.'

'A journalist?' Elizabeth was deeply suspicious of all journalists, both on principle and for their obstinate refusal to spell her name correctly in hockey reports and prize-lists.

'Actually, he isn't a journalist, and he wasn't born in Canada in 1942 – it *was* 1942, but it was in a makeshift hospital alongside the Krasnyi Oktiabr tank factory in a place they called Stalingrad in those days. And he certainly wasn't christened Winston Fergusson. His real name is Novikov.'

95

Novikov! The name came back to her clearly once she heard it pronounced for the second time, even though it had first come to her only indistinctly through the babel of her own thoughts beside the sitting room door – *Novikov* –

If I hadn't spotted Novikov –

'Josef Ivanovitch Novikov.'

The Russians, remembered Elizabeth – and this seemed the moment for them at last. 'A Russian?'

'A Russian.' He nodded. 'You know what the KGB is, do you, Elizabeth?'

That made it all fit, thought Elizabeth numbly, not so much without surprise as with an absence of feelings which was beyond surprise: it didn't make sense – the people . . . not just the terrible snake-man, but Paul himself, and little Humphrey Aske, and David Audley, with his kind-brutal face . . . and the violence, which was beyond experience. It didn't make sense, but it didn't have to make sense, it merely had to fit into its own ugly pattern, like some do-it-yourself kit for a science-fiction monster.

'Novikov is a KGB professional.' He took it for granted that her silence was a complete answer. 'Like, you might say, PhD, Dzershinsky Street University, Moscow. First Class Honours in Intelligence, Counter-intelligence, Subversion, Manipulation, Disinformation, Corruption and Violence, *cum laude* and so on.'

That *PhD* identified him as a Cambridge man – the very irrelevance of the thought steadied her. 'Are you trying to frighten me?'

'No. But if I am succeeding, that's fine. Because the bastard certainly puts the fear of God up me, I tell you!'

He spoke lightly, but Elizabeth stole another look, and saw the fighter-pilot's grin – the sub-lieutenant's deliberate false confidence which Father had written of, when the German Z-class destroyers had heavier armament and their E-boats were faster.

Just as deliberately, she turned herself against her own feelings. 'And what's your . . . PhD in, *Dr* Mitchell?'

'Ah! Good question!' He snuffled at the thought, as though it amused him. 'History, for a start – *The Breaking of the Hindenburg Line* was a thesis before it was a book, to be exact . . . But after that, you could say that I'm a Secret Policeman – with the emphasis on *policeman* . . . Or, as David would say, I'm a *submarine*, and Josef Ivanovitch Novikov is a *U-boat* – would that be an acceptable distinction for Commander Loftus's daughter?'

'Father hated all submarines, indiscriminately.'

'Hmmm . . . destroyer captain's prejudice . . . Then you'd better think of me as an anti-submarine frigate.'

He was mocking her. And, at the same time, he was steering her back towards the seventh *Vengeful*. But that wouldn't do any more, not after *Josef Ivanovitch Novikov*.

'Those men, at the house . . . were they – ?'

'KGB? I wish to hell that I knew! They certainly didn't behave like KGB – they were too bloody careless by half, thank God! Ugh!' He shivered at the memory. 'But then Josef Ivanovitch was careless, too – he wasn't lucky like me!'

'What?' She almost bit her tongue on the question: if he was ready to be indiscreet then she mustn't interrupt him.

'Oh – he was careless! He let me get a sight of him, when he was just slipping into his car to follow you, round the back of the church at the fête . . . I was thinking of going for a quick drink, actually.'

'In preparation for a boring evening?'

Instead of replying he put his foot down on the accelerator and overtook the children's car, and the next one, and the next one too, into the flashing lights of an approaching lorry which couldn't quite work up enough speed for a head-on collision.

Then he cleared his throat. '*I* was going for a drink, but *he* was going after you. It was careless of him to let me spot him . . . But if he took the risk that meant he couldn't afford to lose you – and you weren't routine after that – d'you see, Elizabeth?'

She saw – half-saw, didn't see at all, but saw enough to imagine his moment of truth, when this terrible Russian had surfaced in the wake of the dull Miss Loftus at the parish church tower restoration fund sale and fête: it was one of those enlivening occurrences which might have been amusing if she hadn't been at the other end of it.

'And we still don't know *why* – I suppose your burglars may have been contract labour, and he was keeping his eye on his investment . . . but I don't go very much on that – it doesn't have the right feel about it . . . But we're checking them out, by God! In fact, Elizabeth, after our mutual acquaintance Josef Ivanovitch we're checking *everyone* out –'

'Including me?' She tried to match his tone, even though now she was out of her depth.

'Including you, naturally! And for the second time . . . In fact, I did you this morning, Elizabeth – you've been double-washed, and wrung-out and dried on the line . . . and you're what we call "clean" – '

'"Clean"?' It was a reflex, not a question: she knew it was true, but the thought of being "double-washed, and wrung-out and dried" stung her. 'Are you sure?'

'We're never sure.' The joke was lost on him – if it was a joke. 'But we have to draw the line somewhere. Your closest known security-risk is two removes away, and that passes for white in our book. Which . . . presumably . . . is why you are privileged to meet Mrs David Audley in the very near future, as I've already said.'

Meeting Mrs David Audley, clean or dirty, wasn't something she wished to think about. 'You make me sound very dull.'

'Dull . . .' He tripped the indicator, swinging the car out of the line on to a side-road. Just in time, as the road sign flashed by, Elizabeth caught the legend *Upper Horley – 5* and *Steeple Horley – 5½*. 'Dull . . .'

Horley? She screwed up her memory, from the *Book of Wessex Villages* and *The Parish Churches of Sussex and Hampshire* in the bookcase in her bedroom, on the shelf dating from her childhood voyages of exploration in Margaret's company during the holidays, by bus or bicycle.

'Yes, I guess you could say "dull",' reflected Paul.

The Horleys, Upper and Steeple, had been just outside their range, tucked away under the Downs away to the east, or east-nor'-east, unserved even then by any traceable public transport.

'Or maybe "wasted",' murmured Paul.

But they had been on the list; or Steeple Horley had, for its gem of a church, complete with recumbent stone crusader and the re-used Roman bricks it shared with the much-decayed manor house built on the site of a Saxon hall mentioned in the Domesday Book –

Paul's last murmur registered suddenly, breaking her concentration. ' "Wasted"? What d'you mean – "wasted"?'

'Ah . . . well, you haven't exactly spread your wings for long flights since you came down from Oxford, have you, Elizabeth?' He raised one hand off the wheel defensively before she could reply. 'Just an observation, that's all.'

'I don't see that it's any of your business.' She felt herself bristling, but then the bleak truth submerged her anger as another signpost pointed them to the Horleys, in preference for a *No Through Road* to some unnamed farm.

'Someone had to look after my father.'

'Sure. And a house-keeper did that perfectly well when you were at school and at Oxford . . . Mrs Carver, No. 3, Church Row. *And* she's still hale and hearty – don't tell me he couldn't afford her, because we both know bloody well that he could have done.'

'I didn't know that. I thought we were . . . not exactly poor, but not rich.'

'Doesn't matter – forget it – ' he shook his head ' – *he* wasn't an invalid, your esteemed father, that's what I mean. He may have had a heart condition, but he didn't need a First-Class honours graduate to . . . to – how did you put it so graphically? – to "type his bloody books, and cook his bloody meals, and wash his bloody laundry" – eh?'

He knew too much – too *bloody* much – about Father, and Mrs Carver, as well as about the foolish Miss Loftus, who had let slip far too much under the combined pressures of fear and self-pity and brandy.

'But I suppose you thought it was your duty – right?' He slashed the word at her, almost contemptuously. 'You had to do your duty by him?'

Another signpost: *Upper Horley* left, *Steeple Horley* right – and it would have to be left here, because there was only the church and the 'much-decayed' manor the other way, the book had said.

Pride came to her aid. 'So what if it was – my duty?'

'Then do your duty now!' He fed the wheel to the right, to Steeple Horley and another *No Through Road* which had to end in half-a-mile under the steeple and the shoulder of the high downs curving above them. 'Stretch yourself for us, Elizabeth.'

It wasn't the thought of duty which stretched her – she had never even thought of duty in relation to Father: he had been there, sitting at his chair in the study, when she had come down from Oxford for the last time, and Mrs Carver had already been given her notice, and everything had been taken for granted, herself included . . . but perhaps that was what *duty* was – the thing that happened, and the state of mind which made it happen, without any conscious thought on either side, the giving and the taking being equally automatic.

But it wasn't that which stretched her now, it was the certainty that Mrs Audley was waiting for her half-a-mile ahead, or less – and that she needed Paul to help her –

God! What a mess I am – hair, clothes, face – !

The *Vengeful* – Father had gone back to France, to re-write the chapter –

But not *back* to France . . . that first writing had been just routine – just as she had been *just routine* when she'd first glimpsed Paul in the mirror, and he had seen her –

The car was slowing down – it was turning past a little cottage, into a gravel drive – past the cottage garden, with its apple trees already heavy with fruit, and the runner-beans, bright with their harvest to come, festooned over their bean-poles – and banks of blackberry bushes now, on either side – *but Father had gone to France to re-write the chapter –*

'It has to do with the survivors. The *Fortuné* sank some-where off the Horse Sands, but that was at night, and no one knows where exactly, and there were only four survivors. But there were also survivors from the *Vengeful* – they came ashore on the Normandy coast – he had a footnote about them . . . But . . .'

'Good girl!' He braked, slowing from his snail's-pace to stop altogether between the blackberry bushes, with the curve of the drive still ahead. 'But what?'

'They all died. Or the French shot them when they were trying to escape – there was a scandal, anyway. . . . But – I don't know . . .'

'Don't know what?'

'Just . . . don't know. But that's the only reason he could have had for going to France – the survivors who died in France – or how they died.'

'That's my *good* girl!' The car began to crawl forward again. 'That's what I needed to put you finally in the clear.'

'What – what you needed?' She caught a glimpse of a house ahead. 'What?'

'Because they didn't all die. At least one of them lived to tell the tale – and a very curious tale too, so David says.' The car crunched and slithered on the thick gravel as he braked finally. 'And here's Faith waiting to welcome you.'

6

The sound at the bedroom door disconcerted Elizabeth twice over: first because she was hardly ten minutes out of her bath, and was wondering what to do with her hair, never mind her face and her clothes; and then because it didn't sound like the sort of business-like knock she would have expected from Faith Audley – it was more like the tentative tap of a scholarship pupil who hadn't finished her essay on the Eleven Years' Tyranny of Charles I and hoped against hope that Miss Loftus wasn't in, or wouldn't hear if she was.

Only this time it was Miss Loftus who wished she wasn't in, or hadn't heard. But she was, and she had, and once again there was no escape.

'Come in!' She saw the lips of her bedraggled reflection in the dressing-table mirror pronounce the invitation.

The door opened slowly . . . too slowly, and not far enough before it stopped opening.

Oh God! thought Elizabeth. *Not Paul Mitchell – ?*

But neither Paul's face nor Faith Audley's ash-blonde head came through the gap – though an ash-blonde head *was* coming through, but at a level she had not anticipated.

A child – a child's face, like and yet unlike – *like* for its thinness and pale colouring, but *unlike*, with the gold-framed spectacles magnifying the eyes and the metal brace disfiguring the mouth which opened to speak.

'Mummy says – I'm sorry to *disturb* you, she says – but I heard your bath go down the plug at the back – she says, would you like the hair-dryer? And . . . *and*, she says – we can do your things . . . Clarkie can wash them, and tumble dry them, and iron them, and all that . . . *Clarkie –*

103

that's *Mrs* Clarke – and . . . *and* . . . Mummy says there's this – '

This, and the hair-dryer, and more of the miniature Faith Audley – *like* and *unlike* – slid unwillingly into the bedroom.

'It's a caftan.' The child juggled with her burdens the better to display the garment, allowing its material to ooze silkily over the hair-dryer. 'Daddy brought it back from the East somewhere years ago, long before he even met Mummy, and she's never worn it . . . Only, she says it'll fit, and she hasn't got anything else that will . . . But she says it's *very* beautiful.'

Elizabeth guessed that Mummy hadn't quite said all of that, or at least not for passing on. But Mummy was certainly right about the caftan.

'Come in, dear.' She remembered belatedly that she ought to be smiling, not staring the poor little thing out of countenance. 'You must be Cathy, of course.'

The child hesitated. 'I'm supposed not to bother you, Miss – Miss – ' her composure began to desert her as she searched for the right name.

'Elizabeth,' said Elizabeth quickly, searching in her own experience for the right approach. She had never taught children of primary school age, and was doubly nervous of one whose IQ went off the scale, if Paul Mitchell's judgement was to be relied on. 'Elizabeth Loftus.'

Cathy stared at her for a moment, wide-eyed, as though the name itself was a revelation. Then she advanced into the bedroom, dumped her burdens on the nearest chair, and presented her hand to Elizabeth gravely.

'How do you do, Miss Loftus.'

Elizabeth recognized the hallmarks. 'How do you do, Miss Audley. But if you will call me "Elizabeth" then I can call you "Cathy" – all right?' She smiled again as she took the little hand, but a cold memory came back to her as she did so, of just such another offer which Paul

104

Mitchell had made to her – an exchange of names designed to lull her into indiscretion when she was most vulnerable.

But the way Cathy Audley was looking at her suggested that David Audley's daughter could not be so easily deceived.

She released the hand. 'Is that all right?'

Cathy frowned. 'Daddy says . . . the names we use to each other are important. They all mean something – like, when he wants to be nasty to someone, he always says "Mister" – or "Colonel". But I don't believe I understand the rules yet.'

Elizabeth thought hard. 'You mean, like Treebeard not wanting to give his full name in *The Lord of the Rings*?' That wasn't at all what Audley had meant, but it was a carefully-fired long shot nevertheless, because this was the sort of child who would have read Tolkien.

The frown cleared, and Elizabeth watched the bridge build itself between them, half ashamed, but also half pleased with herself.

'Well . . . no, I don't think Daddy did mean that, actually – and he doesn't like Tolkien – it's Mummy who likes Tolkien. Daddy's favourite is Kipling.'

'And which do you like?' The shame faded and the pleasure increased. If this was the sort of game Paul enjoyed, it was dangerously addictive.

'Oh . . . I like both of them,' said Cathy loyally. And then looked around quickly. 'But I ought to go now, Miss – Miss – Elizabeth. Mummy *said* – '

'Don't go! You can show me where to plug in the hair-dryer.' The game played itself, almost. 'And you can help me dry my hair – I'd like that, Cathy.'

'Oh – yes . . . The point's just down there – by the little table – ' Cathy scurried obediently to obey orders dressed up in the uniform of appeals for help.

'Is Dr Mitchell still here?' She applied the Audley-Treebeard rule hastily.

'Paul? Yes. He's phoning Daddy at the moment – with the scrambler on, so it must be jolly important,' said Cathy over her shoulder, from under the table. 'He's staying for dinner – and I don't know when Daddy will be back, but Mummy's laying for five – *there*, it's ready now – just in case, she says . . . and that doesn't include me, because she says dinner will be late – ready!'

Elizabeth smiled as she lifted the dryer. *Five* counting everyone she could think of meant one more from some-where – maybe Humphrey Aske, whom Paul clearly didn't like?

'You switch on *there* – the little button . . . I'll hold it – I do it for Mummy,' said Cathy helpfully.

'"Scrambler"?' Mercifully, it was a very expensive hair-dryer, which made shouting unnecessary. 'What's that?'

'Oh . . . it's a thing that scrambles up words in the telephone, so no one else can hear them, except at the other end. Daddy doesn't know how it works, because he's not scientific – Mummy will tell you, if you're interested.' Cathy held the hair-dryer away for a moment. 'But don't you work for Daddy? I thought you did – ?'

That had been a mistake. But then perhaps this was all a mistake – to assume that the child knew more than was good for her, like all her pupils.

'What made you think that?' The sharpness of the question belied the false smile that went with it, warning her that she was still a beginner at Paul's game. 'Of course . . . I'm helping your father – *naturally* . . . but . . .' She pretended to be more interested in her hair, which was frizzing out abominably, as it always did. 'What made you think that?'

'Mummy said you'd had a bad time – that's why I'm not supposed to bother you – but you don't need to worry – not with all those men of Daddy's, I mean – '

'What men?'

'At the back – on the hill . . . and there are another two

down the drive, by Clarkie's cottage – I saw them when I came back from Lucy's. And Uncle Jack phoned – my godfather, he is – I know, because I took the call – '

'Uncle Jack?'

'Colonel Butler – don't you know him? He's awfully nice, and frightfully important – and, d'you know, he's got *three* daughters – but they're all much older than me, of course – do you have any sisters . . . or brothers?'

The mixture of prosaic family detail with the casual revelation of the guards Audley had set around his home for its protection – *her* protection – was somehow all the more frightening. 'No, I'm an only daughter – no sisters, no brothers, Cathy.'

'Me too. Rotten luck!' Sisterly sympathy loosened the child's inhibitions further. 'And Mummy too – although she was meant to be one of three, all named after Gloster Gladiators, you know – '

'What?' Confusion enveloped Elizabeth.

'Gloster Gladiators. "Faith, Hope and Charity" – they were three aeroplanes at Malta during the war. But Mummy's father – my *grandfather* – was killed before Hope and Charity could be born – he was an RAF pilot, you see . . . And Daddy's father was killed too – that's why I've got no grandparents, like everyone else . . . And *that's* why Daddy does what he does – and Uncle Jack too – like the Rangers in *The Lord of the Rings* – you remember, Miss Loftus, Elizabeth, I mean – Aragorn's people, who fought "the dark things from the houseless hills" in secret.' Cathy plied the hair-dryer expertly. ' "The last remnant of a great people . . . the Men of the West" – I always think that's a sad bit of the story, about them.' So that was what they'd told the child, thought Elizabeth. And it was a clever way of handling an inquisitive child, too – not to cut her off from the secret, but instead to make her part of it so that she could take it for granted.

'*Cathy!*' Faith Audley's voice came from somewhere outside the room. '*Are you bothering Miss Loftus?*'

Cathy switched off the hair-dryer and went to the long, low window. 'No, Mummy – I'm drying her hair. She asked me to.'

'Hmmm! Very well . . . Would you tell her, when she's ready, that Dr Mitchell is on the terrace, and he'd like a word with her?'

Cathy turned back into the room. 'You mustn't mind Mummy – she used to be a school-teacher, you know. She says that Dr Mitchell – did you hear?'

'Yes.' Any chance of pumping the child was gone now, and it hadn't been such a good idea in the first place.

'I think it's almost dry now, anyway.' Cathy surveyed her handiwork critically. 'It's going to be like those paintings Daddy likes – sort of Lady of Shalott-ish.'

Frizzy was the word. Elizabeth scowled at her reflection, waiting for the mirror to crack from side to side. 'Yes . . . it looks fine, dear.'

'Then I'd better go.' Cathy turned at the door. 'Good luck with Paul – and Daddy, and all that, Elizabeth. And long live the Dúnedin!'

The Dúnedin? Elizabeth stared at the door. The Dúnedin were . . . they were Aragorn's people, of course – the Rangers who hunted those 'dark things' . . .

Her eyes came back to herself, to her own eyes watching her in the mirror, dark-shadowed. It was obvious, what the child meant – so obvious, and also oddly flattering, to be type-cast not as just another school-teacher, like Mummy, but as one of the select brand of the Dúnedin, the SAS of Middle Earth . . . obvious and flattering – and quite wrong.

And, anyway, she must not keep one of the genuine Dúnedin waiting on the terrace, thought Elizabeth as she reached for the caftan.

'Ah – Elizabeth!' The genuine Dúnadan rose at her approach, looking at her strangely, from out of a welter of scattered type-script.

Strangely, as well he might with the way she looked, she thought, grasping the voluminous silken folds in an effort not to trip as she negotiated the stone steps. And then the whole scene around him took her mind right off her own bizarre appearance.

The suitcase from her interrogation – the pink files were the completed chapters from Father's book, the green ones his vestigial notes and rough drafts – and other things she couldn't place . . . but they were of no consequence compared with Father's *Vengeful* box, also gaping open – but *empty*!

Her eyes met Paul's and her mouth opened stupidly, and worried avarice progressed instantly to shame as he grinned at her.

'Don't fret – we haven't made away with your prize-money. Faith just doesn't like piles of loose cash lying around her house, that's all, so she's locked it all up safely somewhere.' He reached towards the empty box. '"*William Willard Pike – Surgeon, HM Ship Vengefull*" – I hope Dr Pike's medical skill was more reliable than his spelling . . . But who are these others, inscribed on the inside of the lid? *Amos Ratsey, Jas. O'Byrne, Octavius Phelan* and the rest? Would they be the ship's officers?'

'No.' It was a relief to cover her embarrassment with even half-baked information. 'Father thought they might be his grateful patients – the ones who presented him with the box of instruments when he joined the ship. But that doesn't really fit.'

'Why not?' He flipped the lid closed. 'Wasn't he a good surgeon?'

'Nobody knows . . . Father couldn't trace him on shore. But ships' doctors certainly weren't the cream of the profession in those days – a lot of them were failures and drunkards who couldn't make a go of it ashore . . . In fact, they weren't even rated as officers until the 1840s – they were warrant officers – or, technically, they were just

109

civilians, on the same level as the purser and the chaplain, you see.'

'I don't really see. But it doesn't matter.' He picked up the pages he'd been holding when she'd hobbled out of the French windows. 'This is what's fascinating – what a rotten old tub the *Vengeful* was!'

'She wasn't old. She was launched in 1805.'

'The year of Trafalgar! Okay – not old, but just rotten. Did we always build so badly?' He gestured towards one of the chairs on the terrace. 'I'm sorry, Elizabeth – my manners are appalling . . . Do sit down – would you like a drink? Sherry or beer . . . or something stronger?'

'Nothing, thank you.' He seemed to have forgotten yesterday completely. 'Does it surprise you that we built inferior ships?'

He shook his head. 'No, not at all, actually . . . We built the first dreadnoughts in 1905–1906 . . . But we didn't build a good capital ship until the 1912 estimates – the *Queen Elizabeth* class – up to then everyone else seems to have made a better job of it . . . But your father says we actually copied the *Vengeful* design – from the French?'

'That's right. It was based on a French frigate that was captured in 1797, and measured at Chatham – the French and the Spaniards always built better ships than we did . . . better sailers, with more guns. But it was the Americans who built the best frigates – Father called them "pocket-battleships" – he thought the *President* was the finest frigate ever built, but we didn't capture her until 1814 . . . By then we were actually cutting down ships-of-the-line – battleships – to take on their frigates, after what had happened to the *Guerrière* and the *Java* and the *Macedonian*.'

'But HMS *Shannon* took USS *Chesapeake*, I seem to remember?'

'Yes – but the *Shannon* was our best frigate – Broke was gunnery-mad – and the *Chesapeake* was their worst one – '

110

Elizabeth halted her enthusiasm in mid-flow, aware that it was Father who was speaking out of her mouth, and that none of it had anything to do with the *Vengeful* anyway.

'I once wrote a very bad essay on the War of 1812, you know.' He seemed to catch her incomprehension. 'Or, it was about Anglo-American relations in the early nineteenth century actually, only it got bogged down with the war of 1812 . . . But, of course, the *Vengeful* was at the bottom of the sea a month before the Yankees stabbed us in the back, wasn't she?'

He was putting her at ease again, decided Elizabeth. And that was something she no longer needed. 'You wanted to have a word with me, Mrs Audley said – ?'

He focused on her. 'Yes – that's right, Elizabeth. Now . . . this was the chapter your father was re-writing – the one about the seventh *Vengeful* – you made a guess about it, but you don't actually know?' He held up the original chapter, all her beautiful typing, without a single erasure.

'No. But there ought to be something in his notes.' She looked quickly at the suitcase.

'Yes . . . maybe. But I'd like to get the original details clear first.' He smiled. 'So . . . Number Seven was coming back from Gibraltar, via Lisbon, for a major refit – or maybe to be condemned as unfit – when she met the *Fortuné* off Ushant . . . in the early summer of 1812?'

'May 5th.' Her eyes were drawn to the typed pages. 'It's all down there.'

'Uh-huh. That was the usual route home, was it?'

'What d'you mean – usual?'

'Well, if they were going to run into trouble, it would be most likely close to the French coast, wouldn't it?'

'Trouble?' Now she could smile back – at his innocence. 'I expect that's what Captain Williams was hoping for. Frigate captains were always on the look-out for trouble – and prize-money. One good capture could make him rich . . . like a French Indiaman. There were still one or two of them around, even as late as 1812.'

'Instead of which he met the *Fortuné*, though – '

'That would have done almost as well. Prize-money *and* glory!'

'But the *Fortuné* was much bigger – 44 guns and 1200 tons to his 36 guns and 975 tons . . . and the French crew was substantially bigger too, and the *Vengeful* was desperately under-strength –' he started to riffle through the pages ' – it's here somewhere, the figures – '

'It doesn't matter – he wouldn't have thought twice about any of that.'

He frowned. 'Why not?'

'It isn't in there, but Father had me draw up an appendix about frigate losses during the whole war, from 1793 to 1815 – he liked appendices.' Elizabeth switched on her memory, and the neat columns of figures came to her photographically. 'We lost eighty-two of them altogether, but only nine of those were by enemy action – and that includes wars against practically every country in Europe, plus the United States . . . the rest were wreck or accident, and mostly wreck, like the *Vengeful*. But in the same period we sank or captured . . . oh, I think it was nearly 250 enemy frigates – 238, it was.' The way he was looking at her, she had to shrug modestly. 'I remember the numbers because Father made me total them all for him.'

'I see . . .' He grinned lop-sidedly. 'Now I understand what *Rule Britannia* meant! So Captain Williams thought he was on a statistical winner, in fact?'

'He'd have expected to win.' Elizabeth shrugged. 'He'd have been court-martialled if he hadn't fought, anyway.'

'But the Frenchman fought better than he expected, apparently?'

She had to shrug again. 'They probably did more damage to the *Vengeful* than he expected. But that was because she was in such a rotten condition, Father thought – and that came from the testimony of the

112

survivors from the prize-crew on the *Fortuné*, after she sank . . . The French always fought bravely, though.' She looked at him curiously. 'What's the object of all this?'

'Nothing really . . . The *Fortuné* couldn't have been waiting for the *Vengeful*, could it – she, I mean?'

'No.' She shook her head decisively. 'That's quite out of the question. With sailing ships in those days . . . no way. It's quite out of the question.'

'I see . . . So they met by accident, and they beat each other to a pulp . . . And after the surviving officer in the *Vengeful* had sent across his prize-crew to take over the *Fortuné* – including the good Dr Pike – ' he pointed to the surgeon's box ' – the worst storm of the year started to blow up . . . Is that the size of it?' He bent over the type-script again. 'Where is it, now? Ah . . . *"leaving the victor in a more desperate case than the vanquished, partially dismasted, and her remaining sails, spars and rigging much cut about"* – that was because the French aimed for the masts, on the up-roll, and the British aimed for the hull, on the down-roll . . . I'm getting the picture, you see . . . and that also accounted for the disproportionate casualties the French usually suffered, I suppose. Although your father is a bit imprecise on them – in fact, he's a bit vague about Number Seven's last voyage in general, wouldn't you say? Compared with the other chapters?' He cocked a critical eyebrow at her.

'Oh, I wouldn't say that.' And yet there was a germ of truth in it, thought Elizabeth. 'It was maybe . . . more conjectural than the others – '

'Conjectural? All right, I'll settle for that: conjectural, then?'

'There was a reason for that.' He was smart, but not quite smart enough. 'Everything about that last voyage came from the Court of Inquiry, after the *Fortuné* was lost on the way home, on the Horse Sands off Portsmouth – in the same storm that drove the *Vengeful* ashore on the French coast . . . So it all comes from those four survivors' testimony, Paul.'

'Oh . . .' His face changed, almost comically. 'Yes, of course – I'm a bit slow, aren't I!' He hid his confusion in a further study of the type-script. 'Four survivors . . . one carpenter's mate . . . and three illiterate able seamen – yes . . . and it was the carpenter's mate who let slip about how rotten the *Vengeful*'s timbers were – how one of the French 24-lb cannon balls went right through her, from side to side, just about the water-line – '

'You don't need to look – I remember it all.' She fired on the down-roll.

'You do?' He looked up, making no pretence of hiding his defeat. 'Tell me then, Elizabeth dear – '

It was impossible to resist that look. 'I had to type that chapter out again because Father wasn't satisfied with the carbon copies, that's why I remember . . . When the French surrendered Captain Williams was dead, and his first and second lieutenants were both dying – the French captain was dead too . . . and they had to put the prize-crew on the *Fortuné* – and they didn't really have enough men left for that – '

'They should have abandoned the *Vengeful* – that would be the third lieutenant who was in command – ?'

'He couldn't do that. He'd never have got his wounded off, not in that weather and with darkness so close.' Elizabeth shook her head. She could recall even now, from the typing and re-typing of that passage, how she had felt for poor young Lieutenant Chipperfield in the nightmare of his first command as Father had imagined it: the two battered frigates, both holed below the water-line, the screaming wounded . . . nearly a third of his own crew and more than half the Frenchman's dead and injured . . . and the dismounted cannon rolling around the decks as the gale rose, and with night falling. 'All he had time to do was to get the prize-crew across, Paul. It was the only thing he could do.'

114

'It was still the wrong decision. He should have concentrated on saving one of them – instead of which he lost both.' He stared at her for a moment, and then through her as his own imagination began to work. 'But maybe you're right . . . It's all too bloody easy to sit here in quiet and comfort, sipping our sherry, and making all the right decisions – same with *my* war, the '14–'18 . . . all too bloody easy . . .'

It *was* very quiet on the terrace. Elizabeth felt the tranquillity of the evening all around her, not only in the silence itself but also in the peaceful protectiveness of the old stone house and the great comforting curve of the downland ridge above them, in which the house nestled; and she could smell the evening smells, of honeysuckle and thyme and lavender.

But it was a false tranquillity – false both because their thoughts were concentrated on battle and sudden death, and pain and fear long ago . . . and because there were men on that hill, the child had said, and they recalled her mind to sudden death and fear and pain in the present.

She shivered, and found he was looking at her again.

'Sorry – I was . . . thinking.' He straightened up. 'And for thoughts there is drink! I'll have another – and will you change your mind?'

'I'll have a small sherry, Paul.'

'Good! So . . . next morning the *Vengeful* had disappeared, and the prize-crew reckoned she'd gone down in the night, and it was all they could do to stay afloat anyway . . . there – one small sherry! So they beat it as best they could for Portsmouth, only to come to grief themselves on the Horse Sands, which would have been in sight of home if it hadn't been midnight in another howling gale, poor devils . . . poor brave devils! Hence . . . one carpenter's mate and three seamen left to tell the tale.' He raised his glass in a silent toast. 'But the *Vengeful* didn't go down that night, did she! She lasted three whole days, before she piled up on – where was it?'

115

'Somewhere among the rocks of Les Echoux, Father thought. From where the survivors finally came ashore on the coast near Coutances, he thought they might have been making for one of the Channel Islands.'

'They had the damnedest luck too. If it hadn't been for the weather they might have made it. Instead of which . . . just another couple of forgotten epics. And two more for your statistics, Elizabeth – one French battle casualty and one English shipwreck. But two epics, nevertheless.'

She was glad that he'd got the point, which Father himself had been at pains to make, that the saga of the *Vengeful* and the *Fortuné* deserved to be told for its own sake and not just as the sad history of Number Seven.

'So that leaves us with another thirteen survivors to account for – the very last of the Vengefuls – right?'

'Yes. The crew of the jolly-boat,' Elizabeth nodded.

'The jolly-boat – "a hack-boat for small work", the OED says . . . which was presumably the only undamaged boat to get away from the wreck . . . and *not* a very jolly voyage, because two of them died soon after they came ashore, from injuries or exposure, or both . . . and they were all in a bad way, more or less.' He nodded back, and then his eyes shifted to the *Vengeful* box. 'And *that* came ashore off the *Fortuné* – the ship's doctor's box of tricks . . . presumably?'

She noticed that he was watching her intently. 'Father thought so. It was rather surprising that Dr Pike left the *Vengeful*, but maybe the French ship didn't have a surgeon. But that's the only way it could have been washed up on the English coast. And the carpenter's mate remembers him being on board the *Fortuné*.'

'But he wasn't one of the survivors.'

'I'm sorry?' Elizabeth's attention had strayed back to the box, with its inscription plates which it had been her duty to keep brightly polished, but which were sadly tarnished now.

'I said, he wasn't one of the survivors from the *Fortuné* . . . And from the *Vengeful* there was the third lieutenant, Chipperfield, and the little midshipman, Paget . . . and the gunner's mate, Chard, and the quartermaster's Mate, Timms – '

'*What?*' exclaimed Elizabeth in astonishment.

'Timms. And the six seamen – eight originally – '

'*But* . . . but, Paul – ' She was forced to curb her astonishment by the appearance of her hostess on the terrace.

Paul stood up, clasping the chapter to his chest. 'Mrs Audley – are you going to join us?'

'Of course not – not when you're talking business – and do make it "Faith", Paul, please . . . *Elizabeth*, are you all right? Are you absolutely famished?'

Faith Audley at the best of times, on neutral ground, would have demoralized Elizabeth. Maybe she was all Paul Mitchell had said – and, to be hatefully fair, from the gentle and sympathetic putting-at-ease with which she'd greeted her dishevelled guest, she probably was a nice woman. But that slender, elegant blondeness, and the equally stylish cut of the working-clothes, jeans-and-shirt, not to mention the expert make-up and hint of very expensive scent, was positively debilitating.

'No, I'm fine, Faith.' She was, to be accurate, absolutely famished. But there was also another hunger inside her now, which required more urgent satisfaction. 'Really I am.'

'I'm sure you're not . . . I've had to feed Cathy to stop her falling apart . . . But it won't be long – ' she switched her attention back to Paul ' – the office phoned again, Paul, to say they're en route . . . But meanwhile you are instructed to spill the beans to Elizabeth, David says – whatever the beans are . . . But I'm sure that means more to you than me – *entendu?*'

'*Entendu*, madame – Faith,' Paul Mitchell bowed. '*Bien entendu.*'

'Ye-ess.' She gave him a slightly jaundiced look. 'You and my David are two of a kind, I've always suspected. Which means . . . for Miss Loftus – for *you*, Elizabeth, beanz meanz troublez.'

'Not at all!' Paul protested. 'It means that your David reposes confidence in Elizabeth's superlative loyalty and common sense – beanz meanz secretz.'

'Hmmm . . .' Faith had the height to look down her nose at the world, and the right shape of nose for looking down. 'It sounds very much like the same thing to me. As long as *you* don't repose the same confidence in *them*, Elizabeth, that's all.'

Paul watched her depart, frowning slightly at that final, left-handed, half-affectionate insult.

None of that mattered, though – it was those names which mattered.

'One of them lived to tell the tale, Paul – you said that just as we arrived.' And *a very curious tale, too*; and it was irritating also – it was more than that, it was infuriating – how the effect of arriving at the manor house, and being met by Faith Audley immediately, had abated her curiosity until now.

'The tale?' His mind seemed to be elsewhere.

She pointed at the type-script. 'In Father's chapter – except for Lieutenant Chipperfield he never had the names of any of the survivors. He only had what that one sailor who reached Verdun told the senior naval officer there – that Chipperfield's party had escaped from the fortress at Lautenbourg, in Alsace – and the conflicting stories the French put out . . . it's all in there, darn it, Paul – ' the abstracted expression on his face irritated her further ' – but he had nothing on the midshipman, and the gunner's mate or anyone else.'

'Oh yes.' He surfaced from his thoughts. 'But I've got a much more curious tale for you now. And one that'll interest you much more, too . . . Number Thirteen, you might say.'

118

'Number – Thirteen? But there wasn't a thirteenth *Vengeful* –'

'Not a British one. But there is a Russian one.' He studied her, no longer smiling, as though the thoughts from which he had surfaced had sobered him.

'A *Russian* ship, Paul?' For a moment the jolly-boat's crew became insignificant.

'No, not exactly. Not a ship, that is.' He stopped, and Elizabeth sensed an unwillingness in him which hadn't been there before.

'Not a ship? What's the matter, Paul?'

'Nothing.' He shook his head. 'If David wants you to know, then I must assume it's all right . . . But it's a big secret, Elizabeth. And big secrets are heavy burdens to carry – and dangerous too.'

'But not here, you said.' The change in him made her feel uneasy.

'No – not here – of course!' He smiled suddenly, shrugging off his own doubts. '*Not* a ship . . . more like an idea. The Russians have these ideas, you know – bright ideas or nasty ideas, according to taste, and it's our job to see them off . . . like in that verse of the National Anthem that we never sing: "Frustrate their knavish tricks – Confound their po-li-tics".'

'The Russians, you mean?'

'The Russians among others. But *them* at this moment, for you and me, trying to do *us* down.' The last of the momentary cloud had lifted from him. 'It's too easy, really – *we're* too easy – there are a million ways of taking us to the cleaners . . . even you can think of examples, Elizabeth – from Klaus Fuchs and the Burgess and Maclean lot – all the bad boys and poor fools from Cambridge . . . before *my* time, naturally . . . right down to the professionals of today, with all their gadgets – and the Judas goats leading what they call "the useful fools" up the garden path to the knackers' yard – the brave sons of Ireland in the IRA and the honest pacifists in CND . . . Christ! I

119

sometimes wish I was working for the KGB – we make it so easy for them . . . But no matter! The point is that their knavish tricks don't happen by accident and haphazardly – obviously. They're *planned,* you see. Obviously.'

'Paul – '

'But bear with me, Elizabeth, because there's a point behind that point . . . Which is *how* they're planned – and I don't mean the routine stuff, like updating the NATO order-of-battle and so on, which has to go on all the time, but the really clever stuff – I mean the one-off high-grade operations.' He paused. 'Because they have these experts – dozens of them – who make a special study of us, and receive all the intelligence digests appropriate to their specializations. And they're expected to come up with ideas for development, most of which get turned down, but some of which go on to the expert-experts – top brass with brains *and* field experience. And *they* pick and choose from the short list, and run feasibility studies on their preferences. And if an idea comes up alpha-plus in their book it gets what they call "Project Status", and then it goes on up to the real top brass – the KGB politicals, who reckon to know which way the wind is blowing in the Kremlin as well as in the West. And *they* put a tick or a cross beside each project . . . and the crosses are sent back down the line marked "Must do better", or something . . . but the ticked ones – they cease to be projects and become operations. And once a project is given "Operational Status" it gets a code-name and goes off to the operational planners – and finally to the poor bastards who have to do the work, like our friend Novikov. Are you still with me so far, Elizabeth?'

'Yes.'

'It isn't difficult, I agree. And I suppose we do much the same thing, only on a much smaller scale due to our poverty.'

She frowned at him. 'And this is what you do?'

'Lord, no! I'm in Crime Prevention, not Burglary – I'm

in the Knavish Tricks Frustration Department, Elizabeth. It's their projects which are *my* operations.'

Elizabeth realized that she had once more been slow on the uptake, like any tiro, and Paul Mitchell was treating her more gently than she deserved. 'Yes . . . I'm sorry, Paul . . . And now what you're going to tell me is that there's a Russian operation which is code-named "Vengeful" – is that it?'

His face was a picture. 'No . . . no, that's not quite it. Because if that was the case we wouldn't be interested in any *Vengeful*, from Number One to infinity – and you'd be sitting safe at home in front of the telly now, Elizabeth.'

She had been slow again somehow – slow to the point of stupidity, although she couldn't see where this time. And he was smiling at her again too; but not his insincere smile, which always revealed a hint of teeth between his lips, but a genuine closed-mouth smile which creased his cheeks.

'This one's the pay-off, Elizabeth – the difference between Project Status and Operational Status . . . All you have to do is imagine Winston Churchill writing to Franklin Roosevelt in 1942 or '43 . . . *Dear FDR – About the invasion of Europe, we think the Normandy Project is the one we should go for, and henceforth we'll call it Operation Overlord. Yours ever, Winston* . . . Don't look so sad just because you can't run before you can walk, dear Elizabeth – it's simply that operational code-names by definition don't mean a thing, it's only project names which spill the beans. Just think what Hitler would have done if he'd picked up "Normandy" rather than "Overlord" – okay?'

Elizabeth could only nod, still ashamed, because getting anywhere too late was still just as bad as not getting there at all, and not boring him with lack of intelligence was all she had to offer him.

'Getting a Project Name is a very rare occurrence, like winning the pools. What's much more usual – in fact, what I've been doing the last year or two in my own specialization – is trying to work out in advance what the most likely projects could be, so that we can set about frustrating them.'

'How do you do that?'

He shrugged. 'How indeed! It's a bit like forecasting the future from the entrails of a sheep . . . we try to identify their project planners first, and then what they specialize in. And then we postulate the information they're likely to get, and so on.'

'But this time . . . you got "Vengeful".' Elizabeth hadn't concentrated so hard since her *viva* at Oxford, when she knew she was on the borderline. 'But this time it hasn't helped you.'

'What makes you think that, now?' He put the question casually, but she could sense the change from boredom to curiosity.

'Practically everything that's happened to me. Coming to see me was supposed to be just routine, for a start.'

'Everything is routine to start with.' He parried the truth neatly. 'Ask any policeman.'

'Researching single-ship actions of the Napoleonic War is routine? That's what policemen usually do?'

'I've done more unlikely things.' This time the teeth showed in the smile.

'I've said something that amuses you?' She didn't like that smile.

'No. I was just remembering that I once said much the same thing to David Audley, years ago – that what I was doing was an unlikely thing to do.'

'And how did he reply?'

'Oh . . . he said that the past always lies in ambush for the present, waiting to get even.' The smile vanished. 'But you are right: I didn't think your *Vengeful* – or any of your *Vengeful*s – could possibly have anything to do with *their* "Project Vengeful".'

'But you do now?'

He looked at her, but not quite inscrutably. 'Now . . . I also think of everything that's happened – to both of us. And I think of Novikov . . . because Novikov is real – he's not a Napoleonic single-ship action, or a crew-member from a jolly-boat – Novikov is KGB, and the KGB isn't a registered charity, or a funny set of initials to frighten the children with when they won't settle down, or any other sort of imaginary bugbear that doesn't really matter – ' he caught himself as though he could hear the change in his own voice. 'You have to understand what the KGB is, Elizabeth: it's the militant arm of the Soviet State outside Soviet territory – and inside it as well, but inside doesn't concern us – *here* concerns us . . . and I've seen it kill *here* – plan to kill, and then kill someone who got in the way of the killing, without a second thought – and that was a bloody "project" too, which became an operation . . .' Again he caught himself, this time scrubbing his face clean before he continued. 'So you've got to watch out for yourself now. Don't depend on Audley – don't even trust *me* . . . Faith is quite right, we're not really trustworthy, and we're not safe to know.'

Something had changed about him. The garden, and the quiet of evening, with the smells of honeysuckle and lavender, were the same. But he was different.

'Why are you telling me this, Paul?'

'Orders, Elizabeth. "Spill the beans", David said.'

She shook her head. 'No – why are you warning me?'

He looked at her curiously for a second, and then grimaced. 'You know too much now, Elizabeth.'

'But you said . . . David Audley trusts me now – ?'

He nodded. 'That's right. And in my experience that's a damn good reason for not trusting *him*, I'm sorry to say.'

123

7

'"He shot an arrow in the air" – or, to be exact, in the correspondence of *The Times*, which for his purposes was very much better – and it came to earth in the remarkable memory of Miss Irene Cookridge. Which was not at all what he expected, but much more rewarding,' said Audley. 'So you just read her reply for yourself, Elizabeth.'

He reached down the table towards Elizabeth, and she took the letter from him. But although she also caught Paul's eye between the silver candlesticks, with the flames sparkling on the glitter of the cutlery and glass between them – and Del Andrew's eyes too (less cautioning, more frankly curious) in passing – she still felt like the little girl who had found the answers in the back of her book, but still couldn't make her sums add up right –

'Elizabeth – Detective Chief Inspector Andrew, Special Branch – "Del" to us, apparently, according to my husband . . . Chief Inspector – Miss Elizabeth Loftus – Elizabeth to us.'

First, he was too young – or not first, since she had never met a Chief Inspector of any sort, let alone of the Special Branch . . . So first, was this the type – more like the young gipsy who'd come up the drive last month, trying to sell a load of asphalt 'left over from a job'?

'Hullo, Miss Loftus.' The sharp gipsy look was there too, sizing her up unashamedly.

'Chief Inspector.' She couldn't quite expel the surprise from her acknowledgement, and was embarrassed to observe the flicker of amusement in his dark eyes.

'And I'm Mitchell.' Paul drew the eyes away from her.

'I don't believe we've met before, Chief Inspector. But I've heard about you from Colonel Butler.'

'No.' There was the merest suggestion of an East London *naow* there, just as there had been the slightest hesitation in the aspirate of *hullo,* and the eyes were frankly appraising now, with a hint of wariness. 'And I've heard about you too, Dr Mitchell.'

'Nothing derogatory, I hope?' Under the light tone Paul also sounded just a touch wary.

The Chief Inspector smiled. 'You've just given two of my sergeants a lot of paper-work.'

'I think I'd better see to the ruins of dinner,' murmured Faith. 'Are you staying the night, Del?'

'I don't know, madam.' The Chief Inspector glanced towards Audley, while Elizabeth envied Faith's ability to handle eccentric situations gracefully.

'I think he is, love.' Audley waited until his wife had departed before continuing. 'To be exact, Paul . . . they've been tidying up your depredations of yesterday to make them fit for any god-fearing coroner.'

'I wouldn't call them "depredations".' The Chief Inspector cocked his head at Paul. 'In fact, I got some mates down my old nick who'd buy the first round for you, Dr Mitchell – and all the other rounds, and see you safe home when you couldn't stand up straight. They'd reckon you done them a favour.'

'Which reminds me – ' Audley moved towards an array of bottles in the corner of the room ' – it's Irish whiskey, isn't it, Del?'

'Thank you.' The Chief Inspector wasn't overawed by Audley. 'All the same, you chanced your arm with Steve Donaghue, Dr Mitchell. Very quick on his feet was old Steve – for a man his size.'

'Steve Donaghue – ' Paul swallowed. '*Was?*'

'Patrick Lawrence Donaghue – "Steve" to his friends, of whom there can't have been very many, because he had a nasty temper . . . yes, we've lost him, Dr Mitchell – to

125

your second bullet though, so we'll count that as self-defence, because he'd 'ave broken your back if he'd reached you. But he doesn't matter – he was just a thick heavy, and somebody would have done 'im sooner or later . . . And much the same goes for little Willie Fullick – someone would have done *him* sooner, rather than later, because he wasn't nearly as good as he thought he was – lots of talk, but no bottle . . . He reckoned he was Steve's brains – and God knows, Steve needed some brains . . . but he wasn't.'

'Willie . . . Fullick?' Paul repeated the name softly.

'Thank you – ' the Chief Inspector took his glass from Audley, and sipped, and nodded ' – very nice . . . yes . . . of course, there was no time for introductions – William Harold Fullick was the look-out man you put down yesterday in the garden . . . But at least he gave you the shooter, and that makes things easier for *us* to prove self-defence, like it made it easier for *you* with Steve.' Another sip, and a cold smile to go with it. 'Funny really – Willie was warned not to carry firearms, that it'd be the death of 'im . . . and it *was* . . . but it'd 'ave been the death of you, Dr Mitchell, if he hadn't – if old Steve 'ad got 'is hands on you.' He shook his head at Paul. 'Very careless, you were.'

Paul said nothing.

'But they don't matter – no one'll cry over those two . . . though no one'll buy you a drink for them, either.' The Chief Inspector stared at Paul for a moment, and then turned towards Elizabeth. 'But Julian Oakenshaw – Julian Alexander Carrell Oakenshaw – Bachelor of Arts . . . You are a very lucky lady, Miss Loftus, if I may say so – a *very* lucky lady.'

For the first time ever, Elizabeth wished she had a strong drink in her hand, like yesterday.

'But I think you probably know that – I shouldn't be at all surprised – '

'She knows it,' snapped Paul. 'So what?'

126

'So I shouldn't explain to her how lucky she is?'

'If she knows it – no.'

'Ah! You're worried because he didn't have a shooter – '

'I don't give a damn what he had – '

'He didn't *need* a shooter.' Suddenly Chief Inspector Andrew was all chief inspector, and a thousand years older than Paul Mitchell. 'Steve Donaghue maybe killed a couple of men in his time – he certainly crippled a few . . . and Willie Fullick never killed anyone most likely, because he couldn't break the skin on a rice pudding – though it wasn't for lack of trying, and 'e'd 'ave managed it sooner or later . . . with some poor old nightwatchman, or a sub-postmistress maybe . . . But Julian Oakenshaw killed seven people – six men and one woman – and he killed them slowly, and he enjoyed every minute of it . . . And each time we couldn't even prove he was in the same county when he did it, because he was a Bachelor of Arts and he was smart – and that's why my two sergeants are going to fix that report so you'll come up smelling sweeter than the biggest bank of roses you ever saw at Kew Gardens, Dr Mitchell – okay?'

The fact that it was all delivered unemotionally, like a traffic report on a Bank Holiday, served to silence Paul.

'I'm sorry, Miss Loftus – ' Del Andrew's dark eyes clouded sympathetically as he saw that, where Paul was merely silenced, Elizabeth was actively terrified ' – but Dr Audley here wants me to make this plain, so you don't misunderstand anything: this . . . this man Oakenshaw was a real bad bastard – a psychopath of the most dangerous kind – not just hard, but *bad*, and crafty with it . . . Not just your ordinary villain, like I was brought up with, but one of your maximum security throw-away-the-key swine, if we could ever have got our hands on him. So you were lucky, Miss Loftus.'

She nodded. 'Yes . . . I think I do understand that, Chief Inspector.'

The eyes – the darkest brown eyes she had ever seen – almost black-brown – darted towards Audley, and then back to her. 'Ye-ess . . . he said you would . . . So what you want to know now is that for his daily bread Julian Oakenshaw specialized in getting information – like, sometimes, where the really tricky burglar alarms were, an' the electronic gear . . . and industrial espionage, that was up his street too – he had a good analytical brain, and when he was briefed right he always knew what to look for . . . The only thing wrong with 'im was that, when the moon was full like last night, he preferred people to be difficult, so he could burn a pretty pattern on them first, before they told him what he wanted to know, before he cut their throats –' Del tensed suddenly ' – sorry, dear – but that's what he would have done, when you'd sung for him. And you would have sung, believe me – that was his stock-in-trade, gettin' results for carriage clients who weren't fussy about how he got them, just so they weren't involved: information was his business, an' that always came first. But inflicting pain was his pleasure, an' he liked to mix pleasure with business when the opportunity presented itself and the moon was full, an' he had a clear run.'

'And was that well known?' asked Paul.

'In the trade it was – we knew about it. But he was too fly to let anyone pin so much as a charity flag on him . . . like he never used the same talent twice to watch his back, and do his heavy work for him. That pair he had yesterday, that you sorted out . . . that was their first time as well as their last – an' the first time he picked two dud 'uns too, thank God!'

Mitchell looked at Audley. 'Then that doesn't fit, David.'

'You don't think so?' Audley seemed to know what didn't fit, but it evidently didn't worry him.

'I know so.' Paul caught Elizabeth's eye, but almost without seeming to see her. 'The KGB would never sub-contract an important job to a psycho – not in a thousand years.' He focused on her suddenly. 'It's just not their style, damn it!' He swung back to Audley. 'And with Novikov sitting in his car, trailing Elizabeth? It never *did* fit, David – Novikov careless is bad enough, but Novikov there at all cancels his connection with Oakenshaw.'

Audley shrugged. 'Maybe he was watching over his investment to check on the dividend. Who knows?'

Mitchell frowned at him, then at Chief Inspector Andrew. 'Is that what *you* think?'

'What do I think?' Del Andrew finished his drink. 'About this Novikov I don't think, because I don't know 'im well enough . . . an' the same goes for "style", 'cause I haven't been playin' this game long enough to suss it out. But Oakenshaw would have put his grannie through it if the money was right – that was *his* style . . . Only, having said all that, it wasn't Comrade Novikov who put the money up for this – you're spot on there, Dr Mitchell.'

'Then who was it?' Mitchell brightened.

'It was a right little villain named Danny Kahn – '

'Dinner's on the table,' said Faith Audley through the doorway. 'And you still haven't opened the wine, David – '

Danny Kahn?

The meal, whatever it was like – over-cooked or not – was purgatory for Elizabeth.

Danny Kahn?

HM Frigate *Vengeful,* 36 guns, 975 tons –

A right little villain, Danny Kahn?

Lieutenant Chipperfield, Mr Midshipman Paget, Gunner's Mate Chard . . . *Danny Kahn – ?*

It was purgatory because, by apparent convention, they didn't talk shop in front of Faith Audley during the meal

129

– that was plain from the start, from the way Faith controlled the conversations at both ends of the table –

Why should a man she had never met hire another man she had also never met to ransack her home and threaten to do such unthinkable things to her – ?

'Peckham, Mrs Audley – ' Del Andrew obstinately refused to call Faith anything but 'Mrs Audley'; Elizabeth had become Elizabeth, and although Drs Audley and Mitchell remained Drs Audley and Mitchell Chief Inspector Andrew plainly wasn't overawed by either of them; but Faith he kept at arm's-length ' – Peckham's the real world, all the rest is just a figment of my imagination – "pound note" country – '

Purgatory.

But in the end it came to an end, although not at all the way she expected.

'Very well.' Faith gathered them all. 'Now I'm going to stack the things, and then I'm going to bed. And Elizabeth ought to go to bed too.'

'I'll help you,' said Elizabeth dutifully, not wanting to help her, but only wanting to hear about Danny Kahn.

'I'm only going to fill the dish-washer, Elizabeth dear. Mrs Clarke will sort things out in the morning – '

'We need Elizabeth,' said Audley. 'And in the morning you're both going to be busy – you too, love.'

'Oh yes?' Faith looked at her husband suspiciously. 'How busy, exactly?'

'You're going to Guildford – or wherever you go to waste my substance – and kit her out for travelling from top to . . . ah . . . bottom – clothes, shoes, baggage to put 'em in, what she's not wearing – hair – everything, love.' Audley peered at his wife over his spectacles and the candles. 'Start at dawn, and Paul will meet you at twelve.'

'He will?' Paul sounded mutinous. 'Will he?'

'I can't possibly do that, David.'

'Cancel your engagements.'

'It's the time, not the engagements, David. And I go to London for my clothes, anyway.'

'There's a smart place in Guildford. I've seen the bills, by God!' Audley gave a snort. 'But don't worry about the money – Her Majesty will pay – '

'*I* can pay,' snapped Elizabeth.

'Hold on, Elizabeth!' exclaimed Paul Mitchell. 'With Novikov on the loose – never mind . . . never mind anyone else . . . you'd better think twice about going *anywhere*, damn it!' He swung towards Audley. 'And where *is* she going? And come to that – where am *I* going?'

Elizabeth looked at Audley. 'Where *am* I going?'

'You're not going anywhere,' said Paul. 'Because nowhere outside this house is safe.'

Audley looked at Elizabeth. 'She'll go where she wants to go – right, Elizabeth?'

'Now you're being devious, darling,' said his wife disparagingly.

'I hope so, love – that's what I'm paid to be . . . But I know if I say there isn't the slightest danger that will only offend you, even though it's true . . . so Aske and Bannen will accompany you tomorrow for the sake of reassurance, if for no other useful purpose, while you make your purchases, until Mitchell arrives to take her from you.'

'And then?' Paul sounded unreassured.

'Then, all being well, you shall both go *Vengeful*-researching somewhere even safer, in so far as that is possible. And you can still keep Aske, if not for protection then as a chaperone.' Audley came back to Elizabeth. 'Well, Elizabeth – are you game?'

'Don't agree,' advised Paul. 'He put the same question to me once – '

'And look at you now!' murmured Audley. 'But I'm not

going to argue with you, Elizabeth. You have a mind of your own, and can make it up for yourself.'

And that was true, thought Elizabeth – true now as it had never been before, even though she was still her father's daughter . . . And, in any case, the incentives hadn't changed.

But *that*, of course, was what David Audley was relying on: he knew his mark better than Faith or Paul did.

She looked from one to the other of them apologetically. 'I can't stay here for ever, can I?' she said. 'And I do need some new clothes.'

'No, it doesn't start with Danny Kahn,' said Del. 'It only finishes with him. It starts with our doing-over your place, Elizabeth – what we sniffed out as maybe of interest, after Dr Mitchell had finished with it . . . which was mostly a lot of junk and dead ends that wasted our time . . . But there was this quarterly account from this taxi firm in London for journeys right across town – Victoria all the way to Whitechapel, north of the river – regular journeys, costing a small fortune . . . an' that was when I first thought "aye-aye – something not quite right here" . . . so I got on to the firm, an' they remembered your dad – good customer an' all that – an' routed out his regular driver. And after I'd talked to him I dropped everything else, because I'd got this lucky feeling then.' He sipped his port and almost winked at her, she thought. 'Whitechapel tube station, that's where he was let off, an' picked up an hour later each time. And there's only three directions you can go from there – like, back where you came from, or on into deepest Essex . . . Barking, Upminster, Ongar . . . or you take the line through to New Cross Gate, under the river – which is the oldest tunnel under the Thames, built by Isambard Kingdom Brunel – Rother'ithe, Surrey Docks . . . all my old stamping grounds when I was a kid, but not the sort of place your dad'd go to, except maybe further on to

132

Greenwich and the Royal Naval College . . . But he wouldn't go that way, see?'

'But that's where he went?' said Paul.

'Sssh!' said Audley.

'An' that's where I really started to get lucky – lucky it was me, an' not someone who didn't know the area – but lucky first because his driver used to worry about him . . . nice old gentleman limping along alone, with his stick, down into that tube station, with his little brief-case – '

'Heavy little brief-case,' murmured Paul, looking at Elizabeth.

'So one evening he was late back, an' the driver went and inquired in the station . . . and he was told that there'd been a breakdown at Shadwell, which is the back-end of the East End, just before Wapping, where the tube dives under the river, an' comes up in South London at Rother'ithe. Which meant, of course, that he was doubling back across the river, just as a routine precaution, because he didn't want anyone to know where he was going – clever, but amateur, like you'd expect. But I *knew* I was on to him then, an' not wasting my time . . . Apart from being lucky, that is.'

Elizabeth observed the rapt expression on David Audley's face, half admiring, half smug, and knew that Chief Inspector Andrew hadn't been lucky at all; or, if he had been lucky, it had been the deserved luck of the clever man who takes the right path at each intersection out of that rare blend of intelligence and experience and instinct which passed for luck among lesser mortals.

'So . . . to cut a long story short . . . I ended up at the Jolly Caulkers pub right opposite Surrey Docks station, on the edge of all that rundown docks area, where there's a bloke behind the bar I used to be at school with. An' they know I'm a dick, of course, though I've been mostly up Bermondsey, Peckham way, out of Catford divisional nick . . . but I'm still nearly one of them, all the same. An' because this is a rush job, I flashed your father's picture around. An' someone says for old times' sake "Yeah – I saw 'im with Lippy once", an' I said "Lippy who?", and he says "Harry Lippman, what used to fence gear out of Redriff Road – but 'e's dead now" . . . Which was the only reason why he'd even said that much, of course – Redriff Road's just nearby, little 1920s council flats, just square boxes with iron railings in front – because Lippy was where I couldn't touch him.'

Sip. 'So because it's still a rush job I went straight to Deptford nick, where I'm known, an' up to my old mates on the first floor. An' they knew Lippy all right – "Harry Lippman, fence" – but they say the guys who really knew him are at Tower Bridge nick . . . So I went all the way back to Tower Bridge nick, on the edge of the bridge. And there's a guy there . . . he says Harry Lippman was the kind of fence they never really wanted to catch. They knew what he was doing – jewellery was his speciality, an' the more antique the better, but he'd handle any gear that wasn't too hot . . . only he wasn't tough or rough, he didn't upset people or hurt people – he was of the old school . . . If he'd have been an obvious nick, they'd have nicked him, but as he was careful an' they had a lot of worse villains, they didn't bother with him.' Del smiled suddenly and looked round the table. 'Besides which there was his war service, anyway, in his favour.'

'His war service?' Mitchell leaned sideways towards Del.

'That's right. Leading Radar Mechanic Lippman, RNVR, with a Mention in Despatches too.' Del turned to Elizabeth. 'And that was the same despatch your father figured in for his medal – Leading Radar Mechanic Lippman of HMS *Vengeful*, that's who Lippy was . . . before he went back into the family business and became *Harry Lippman – disposer of stolen property.*' Or "Retired general dealer", as his death certificate puts it.'

'What did he die of?' said Paul quickly.

'Arterio-sclerosis. In hospital – as natural as you like.'

134

Del shook his head. 'It was the next thing I checked – got half the staff out of bed . . . Nothing for us there. And it was about five, six months gone by.' Back to Elizabeth. 'Lippy handled your father's business right enough – would have been honoured to, by all accounts . . . very proud of his war service he was – British Legion treasurer, Old Comrades' Association – picture of his ship and his captain in the sitting room, above his medals in their case . . . Doing your dad a favour or two would have been right up his street – he had all the contacts, for money or gear, and he was recognized as an honest crook, so no one double-crossed him. In fact, right to the end, if anyone got done down or hurt in Rother'ithe, Lippy had a way of dealing with it . . . 'Fact, I reckon they *miss* him in Tower Bridge nick, the way things are down there now.'

Paul turned to Audley. 'Not the man to give Novikov the time of day, David.'

'Too right!' Del gave a snort. 'Maybe now they've got some weirdos on that patch today – young Trotskyites and Revolutionary Workers from outside, where it always used to be dockers who were rock-solid Labour – Ernie-Bevin-Labour . . . But Novikov would have stood about as much chance as a snowball in hell in the Jolly Caulkers in Lippy's heyday – he'd have ended up under a barge in the river, most likely. Lippy was on the Murmansk run in '44, and he didn't take a shine to what he saw at the other end, from all accounts.'

'So where does Danny Kahn come in?' said Elizabeth.

'Ah . . . now Danny Kahn doesn't come in with Lippy,' Del shook his head. 'Lippy wouldn't have given Danny the time of day on a wet Sunday afternoon, not if he'd have come to him on bended knees . . . Danny wasn't *family*, either in the general sense or the specific one, an' Lippy was a great family man – you can still see that in the street markets, and on a Saturday night, they say, when his daughters go out.'

'His daughters?'

'Yeah – three of 'em . . . They like to see their kids looked after, Lippy's sort . . . and some of the things he fenced, if they weren't hot – like if someone from pound-note country wanted to get rid of the family heirlooms on the quiet – he couldn't bear to get rid of some things so they ended up on his daughters . . . You go into any South London market, an' look at the women, an' you'll see they've got rings on all five fingers of both hands. They don't really trust banks, those people – they prefer to have their riches about them, on their wives and daughters . . . It's one way of looking good, and it's another way of investing your money away from the bleeding tax-man – mother to daughter, an' no questions asked . . . But Danny doesn't come into any of that . . . Although, funnily enough, it's through the family that Danny has got his dirty little hoof into the door – '

'Through the daughters?'

'Naow . . . Lippy's daughters wouldn't look twice at Danny's sort – they're married to accountants and solicitors and school-teachers, all strictly legitimate an' respectable, even if they are still South London – but he had these two brothers, see . . . an' one of them's okay, in Hatton Gardens, in precious metals – '

'Gold?' inquired Mitchell, almost innocently. 'Coins?'

'Yeah. He could handle gold coins easy enough . . . But the other married a gentile, that's got this no-account step-son, Ray Tuck – Raymond Darren Tuck, who's been sucking up to Lippy ever since he found he couldn't do nothing else, because it was too much like hard work . . . An' Ray Tuck's been running Lippy's errands – or was, until Lippy snuffed it – an' now he's tried to take over Lippy's operation.'

'Tried?' echoed Paul.

'Yes . . . well, of course, all he's got is the bad end, because the good ends don't want to know. Because Lippy's nearest and dearest criminal colleagues and clients have quickly sussed Ray Tuck out as a johnnie-cum-lately, an' they don't trust 'im. So they've decided to go elsewhere, an' all Ray Tuck's ended up with is the rough end of the business, that Lippy himself didn't want, but had to be polite to so as to afford the little niceties of life – I don't mean the really rough end, like Oakenshaw wanting to dispose of something – Lippy wouldn't have touched *that* . . . but . . . the dodgy end, where the risks are. So . . . the word is . . . sure as eggs is eggs, Ray Tuck is going to get himself nicked – or worse – '

'Worse?'

'Right. Because what Tower Bridge nick thinks, it's only a question whether *we* get him – or Danny Kahn does.' Del smiled at Elizabeth. 'And, finally to answer your reiterated question, *Miss* Loftus . . . Danny Kahn's a bright kid who could have gone far, but he decided to make his pile the easy way . . . 'Fact, I knew his dad, who was a runner before the Betting and Gaming Act came in . . . and as a result of his running he got this betting shop . . . an' Danny, who's got a few brains – which Ray Tuck hasn't – has managed to increase the empire, with a few snooker halls an' a bit of the other on the side, that can't be mentioned in polite company, an' even a bit of protection with his present West Indian partner, who is apparently just about due for a nasty accident owing to a sudden rush of ambition to the head . . . because Danny's real hard, and got a certain amount of bottle – again, which Ray Tuck hasn't got . . . So all Ray Tuck's got now is debts and an expensive girl-friend, both of which also belong to Danny, who doesn't care much about the girl, but does care about his money.'

'So Danny *could* take out a contract with Novikov?' said Audley.

'Danny *could* . . . and Danny *would*, if the price was right, and if Novikov undertook to get any stray reforming middle class Trots off his back, sure – Danny wasn't on the Murmansk run – '

'But Novikov *wouldn't*,' said Paul. 'Not if there was a

137

sub-contract involved – that would be . . . too dodgy?' He looked at Del.

'It's a mistake to think in certainties,' said Audley mildly. 'Novikov would do whatever he thought would work.'

'But it didn't work,' said Paul. 'The infallible David Audley messed it up.'

Audley's spectacles glinted in the candlelight. 'Now you're being what my dear wife would call "devious", Paul. And in the sense that she undoubtedly means, I would advise against that. Just keep an open mind, that's all.' He turned to Del Andrew. 'And what is your interpretation of all this?'

Del stared at Audley thoughtfully for a moment. 'Well, as long as you allow that it *is* only an interpretation . . . bcause this is as far as I've got, even under starter's orders – '

'An interpretation only, Chief Inspector.'

'Okay.' Del switched to Elizabeth first. 'Your dad shifted gear, not cash – '

'Gear?'

'Valuables. *Objets d'art* – anything from the Crown Jewels to a pretty picture of a Stubbs gee-gee, or the family silver. Because Lippy could handle that, and divvy up untraceable money for it, over a reasonable period. And he wouldn't have gypped your dad, his old captain. Point One.'

Audley pushed the port decanter towards him.

'Thank you . . . Point Two: Ray Tuck would gyp anyone. But he doesn't have the resources to do it, or the bottle to do it if it was tough, or the time – and most of all the time, because time is what he hasn't got . . . Even though I reckon he'd like fine to take over the late Commander Hugh Loftus's custom . . . And Lippy would have advised your dad against that, in any case. *But* . . . Ray Tuck has got big ears – '

'You haven't talked to Ray Tuck?' cut in Mitchell.

'If I had, then I wouldn't be guessing, I can tell you,' said Del grimly. 'But no . . . Ray Tuck is "unavailable" at the moment. And we've got a three-line whip out on him . . . so my only fear is that he's drifting on the tide somewhere around Wapping Stairs, after what you did yesterday, Dr Mitchell. Because I'm pretty sure it was Danny Kahn who contracted Oakenshaw to do this job – no proof, just m.o. and past history . . . Because I think that just recently Ray Tuck sold everything he knew about Commander Loftus, lock, stock and barrel, to Danny Kahn on a payment-by-results basis.'

'Why just recently?' said Mitchell.

'Because I don't think Ray Tuck knew who his Uncle's valued old friend was until just very recently,' said Del. 'To be exact – until his old friend died.'

'You're not telling us that he read *The Times* obituary, man – ' Mitchell began incredulously.

Del grinned at him. 'Your trouble, Dr Mitchell, is that you read the wrong newspaper. Because, while *The Times* had a boring obituary, the *Sun* had a luscious nude on page three – and a bloody marvellous picture of young naval officers and old ex-*Vengeful* heroes on page five, with a sorrowing veiled daughter, and her address, near enough . . . and a nice picture of Loftus of the *Vengeful* himself for good measure – a very neat piece of nostalgia on a day when there wasn't much hard news . . . Apart from which, the same touching scene was picked up on both BBC and ITN local news, partly because it was photogenic, and partly because of the row he made about the *Vengeful*'s renaming a year or two back – '

'So what do you deduce from all that?' said Mitchell sharply.

'I deduce, Dr Mitchell, that Ray Tuck saw it – or read it . . . doesn't matter which . . . and then he knew at last who the golden goose was – that's what I deduce. And because he hadn't time to suck the eggs, because of the way Danny's leaning on him for his money, he sold the whole goose – beak, feathers, gizzard, *daughter* and all. An' Danny reacted predictably, by not wanting to go on from wherever Lippy left off, just taking his cut like any honest villain, but going for the whole goose too. Because he's a greedy sod, an' because he's got his own troubles, with the recession, like any other businessman, and he's in need of capital just now.'

'Why did he call in Oakenshaw, though?' asked Paul. 'Why didn't he do the job himself?'

'Ah . . . now that's where the real guesswork comes in – though to my mind it also strengthens the rest of it.' Del paused for a moment, first considering Mitchell, then Elizabeth. 'Now, I don't know what your dad was up to, dear – it was dodgy, but I don't know what it was anywhere near, or how it fits in with what Dr Audley there wants . . . except that the name *Vengeful* comes into it somewhere . . . But I suspect it's not going to be easy to suss out, either way, an' I reckon Danny came to the same conclusion. Because, as I say, Danny's not stupid . . . an' after he'd thought about what Ray Tuck gave him I think he decided that he needed *real* brains – trained, analytical brains . . . a scholar, if you like. An' that . . . apart from being a nasty little murdering, torturing swine . . . was what Master Julian Oakenshaw was. An' Danny knew it, because he'd used Oakenshaw before, according to the skipper at Tower Bridge nick.'

'So where's Danny Kahn now?'

'That's the next piece that fits in,' Del nodded. 'Because Danny's gone to ground too, like Ray Tuck. "Off on holiday in foreign parts", his Number Two says. An' no forwarding address because he doesn't want to be disturbed, 'cause he's been working so hard, an' needs a complete rest.' Del's lip curled. 'But he was still around yesterday, and he hasn't taken his latest girl-friend with him. So my next guess is that, with Julian Oakenshaw not surfacing – and Steve Donaghue and Willie Fullick also absent without leave . . . and me going through the Jolly

Caulkers like the fear of God . . . Danny's running scared too. Because he'll not only know the Old Bill is asking about Lippy and Ray Tuck, but with his contacts he may even know that I'm no longer the same Old Bill he knows and loves, but one of the funnies from the Special Branch who can be a whole lot meaner.'

'And what are the chances of finding him?'

'Of finding Danny, Dr Mitchell? Slim . . . Danny's the sort that's smart enough to plan for a rainy day, is the Tower Bridge opinion. But with Ray Tuck, we've got a better chance – assuming that he hasn't already gone to the great dole queue in the sky – because no one's scared of him, like of Danny . . . and there's still one or two of Lippy's old mates that'd like to see 'im cut down to size for takin' Lippy's name in vain – Ray Tuck don't count as family any more, that's going to be his epitaph if Danny Kahn hasn't carved it on 'im already.'

Paul Mitchell drew a deep breath, almost a sigh. 'I don't see how we're going to get anywhere without one of them.' He looked towards Audley. 'And if Danny Kahn is in with Novikov by any remote chance . . . which I still frankly doubt . . . then they both know more than we do, David. So whatever you're planning for Elizabeth – I don't like it. Our best best is to keep her under wraps, and let Del here have his head, and give him all the manpower he needs.'

That was one score to Paul's credit, thought Elizabeth, observing both men through the candlelight across the table. Because Del Andrew and Paul Mitchell were chalk and cheese, and sculptured by their backgrounds to be competitors even though they were on the same side; and also, doing nothing would be as much against Paul's nature as against Del's – in that they were brothers, because doing nothing was boring, and because no one could shine while doing nothing. But here was Paul, nevertheless, conceding the short corner to Del.

141

'Wrong,' said David Audley, almost insultingly, pouring more port into his glass, and then offering the decanter to Elizabeth.

'No thank you, David. But why is Paul wrong?' She felt an absurd loyalty for Paul Mitchell now, in spite of his arrogance.

'Not wholly wrong, Elizabeth.' Audley pushed the decanter towards Mitchell. 'Del must have his head – a free hand to scour everything south of the river – I agree . . . But we still have the edge on Kahn and Novikov, my dear.'

'How?' said Elizabeth quickly, before Paul could ask the same question. Because it was her turn to fight now, even if she didn't know why.

'Because we have what Oakenshaw was going to take from you – ' Audley's hand had already been reaching inside his coat pocket ' – and most particularly we have *this* – ' he slid a piece of folded paper across the table to her.

It was a letter. Pale blue paper, shakily hand-written –

Dear Commander Loftus –

Elizabeth looked at the address – it was nowhere she had ever heard of: somewhere in Kent, near Tenterden . . . and, on the other side, was a name she had never heard of – *Irene Cookridge (Miss) –*

Dear Commander Loftus,

I saw your letter in 'The Times' today, regarding your wish to make contact with surviving members of the crews of the warship which bore the name 'Vengeful' during the first world war, or with any of their next-of-kin having material relating to their service, in connection with a book which you are writing.

While I do not have any connection with such persons, or any such material, I have in my –

Possession? The writing was small and spiky – elderly, guessed Elizabeth – and the pen had spluttered over the second double-*s* successively; but extensive experience with juvenile hands, and bitter experience with Father's own scrawl, made that *possession* beyond reasonable doubt –

– in my possession a slender volume relating in part to another vessel of that name, dating from a much earlier period in history; and while this does not answer your appeal it may provide you with a curious footnote to your researches.

Elderly, also beyond reasonable doubt. No modern education could have produced that semi-colon, never mind the particular words and the style itself: *Miss Irene Cookridge* was someone's great-aunt, or great-great-aunt, since she could not be anyone's grandmother.

This volume, which is hand-written, records conversations between my maternal ancestor, the Revd Arthur Cecil Ward, and the squire of his parish, Sir Alexander Gower, and it was among my mother's possessions which came to me on her death in 1952.

She couldn't help looking up as she turned the page, and catching Audley's eye twinkling at her.

'Gold, genuine gold,' said Audley. 'The stuff that dreams are made of – and the best is yet to come, Elizabeth.'

These conversations relate chiefly to the memories of my ancestor, who in his younger days had been a Chaplain to the House of Commons, and Sir Alexander who was an ensign with the Foot Guards at Waterloo. But there are also some twenty pages of the recollections of one Thomas (Tom) Chard, head gamekeeper on Sir Alexander's estate,

143

formerly a gunner's mate on a ship named 'Vengeful' during the Napoleonic War. This relates briefly to a desperate battle with a French warship, a subsequent shipwreck off the French coast, Tom Chard's experiences in captivity, his escape therefrom, and his adventures on the long journey home in company with other members of the crew.

All this, I appreciate, does not fall within the terms of reference, as laid down in your letter. Yet I venture to think that, since it has never to my knowledge been revealed before, it may be of historical interest in such a book as yours. And, needless to say, I would be only too pleased to make it available to you –

Elizabeth stared at Paul. 'You've read this?'

'Not read it. David told me about it . . . and he's talked to her – Miss – ?'

'Miss Irene Cookridge.' Audley nodded between them. 'And I have seen her book – half-leather, with a brass lock – but pure gold, both of them . . . Miss Cookridge and her book!'

'Pure gold, I'm sure – if I was finishing off the *Vengeful* book for Elizabeth.' Paul's face creased with irritation. 'But where does Danny Kahn come in? And where does Josef Ivanovitch Novikov figure? *Come on, David –* whatever pure gold Danny Kahn and Loftus may have found there, it's fool's gold when you mix Novikov into it – it's a con – it's a bloody classic con, in fact – '

'A con?' Del studied Mitchell sideways. 'Why a con, Dr Mitchell?'

'Because it's exactly the sort of thing that David would fall for – it's just sufficiently too bloody outlandish for anyone else . . . but it isn't too outlandish for *him* . . . And, David, we know that's the next likely ploy – to shoot us off at a tangent . . . I'm not saying we're not close, with Loftus . . . But frigate actions off Ushant in 1812 – and PoW escapes after that – it's simply not *on*. It's just too predictable, if they suspect you're on the job.'

144

'You're giving them too much credit, my dear fellow.' Audley waved a hand dismissively. 'They couldn't possibly have set up Miss Cookridge months ago, and written out her ancestor's memoirs in longhand, and aged the ink, and all that . . . just in case we came up with *Vengeful* out of Washington – it's quite beyond their capabilities, apart from the timing, even if they do have my number.'

Elizabeth could almost feel Paul struggle against this negative argument, and find nowhere to go.

'But, right or wrong, you're under orders now.' Audley came down to earth abruptly. 'So you'll do what you're told tomorrow, like everyone else.'

8

There were bells ringing somewhere out in the warm darkness of Laon.

'In the Champagne district of northern France, between Craonne in the east and Soissons in the west, lies the Chemin des Dames – "the Ladies' Highway". This name originally applied to a road built along the crest of a ridge by Louis XV for the diversion of his sisters, but has since come to refer to the ridge itself, some 15 miles long and for the most part nearly 450 feet high, and with numerous hog's-back spurs and deep ravines running south to the valley of the Aisne . . .'

Elizabeth's eyelids fluttered, but her brain again refused to stop working, feverishly and confusedly trying to assimilate her experiences, and to codify and file them for future recollection.

'No, madame – Madame has quite a high colour, so she thinks a blusher will add to her difficulty . . . But no! It is only that the flushed cheeks are always in the wrong place . . . so we need to relocate the colour – so!'

'It was here, on this fatal ridge, and by a matter of no more than a couple of hours only, that the German retreat from the Marne ended on September 14th, 1914: although neither side knew it, in the thick weather and bitter close-quarter fighting between isolated units of the British 1st Corps and the German 7th Reserve Corps on those formidable muddy slopes, the trench warfare of the next four years was born –'

It was no good – it was just too much . . . Louis XV and his sisters and their maids-in-waiting . . . and Paul Mitchell's Northamptons and Coldstreamers, and their comrades of the King's Royal Rifle Corps and the Royal Sussex . . . they all mingled together with Lieutenant Chipperfield's exhausted escape party in the mist and the rain on the Chemin des Dames under a hail of machine-gun fire and a deluge of 8-inch howitzer shells from von Bülow's Germans –

And . . .

'The eyes are not difficult – Madame has good eyes – the important area is not *over*, but *under* . . . and there one does not cover the whole area – that is vital – but simply touches out the dark bits, which make the *baggy* look . . . like *so* – I will do this eye, and then Madame will do the other, eh?'

'A private aeroplane?'
  'Not a private one, Elizabeth. Private planes are for millionaires and oil sheikhs. Just a business plane for a business trip – saves hassle, saves time . . .'

There were bells ringing somewhere, out in the warm darkness –

'Where's Humphrey Aske, Paul? Didn't David say he was coming with us?'
  'That little bastard? That's one of David's bad ideas – a chaperone! Do you want a chaperone, Elizabeth?'
  Wishful thinking! But hers, not his, obviously – sadly!
  'But he'll meet us over there, anyway – more's the pity!'

Over there had been the first clue –

'*All the British could do was to dig, as they had never dug*

147

before. Fortunately, the soil was good – at least before the rain began to drain off the crests – and the sides of trenches and "funk-holes" held up without revetment – '

'Madame's hair *must* be cut, and it must not be put *up* – no . . . *up* may seem sensible, but it is a great consumer of time, and Madame's hair is naturally fuller, and hair is getting fuller now . . . So Monsieur Pierre will shorten perhaps a trifle, and will add the highlights – the colour is *good*, but the highlights will accentuate – yes?'

' – which was just as well, since the enemy's artillery observers dominated the valley, while the British guns were still south of the river, firing blind. Here too, was the shape of things to come: this was to be an artillery war, and the man who could see could kill – '

'Christ! Elizabeth . . . what have they done to you?'

Dust and ashes: she had thought they'd made her presentable, and the cost of this summer suit would have started turning Father in his grave if she'd paid for it with his money.

'Don't you like it? Faith chose it, Paul – '

'Oh – the clothes are okay – trust Faith to go for the county look . . . But you've turned into your younger sister, and I've become a baby-snatcher – '

The man who could see, could kill –

'Isn't that the Channel, Paul – ?'

'On Madame's account?' This was to *Madame* Faith Audley, not to the nameless *madame* who had arrived with her, pressed neatly, but obviously not credit-worthy.

'I must settle up with you, Faith – '

'Settle up? Not *bloody* likely! David will pay – or Jack Butler will pay, don't you worry! You can't know what

148

pleasure this gives me, Elizabeth – soaking them, for what they've done to you . . . Take the money and run, Elizabeth –'

Expensive luggage, already packed with her new clothes, from the skin upwards –

Polite cough. 'Madame's cosmetics are all in the vanity case. And I have included both the Rimmel and the Clinique – the Clinique is not cheap, for the eye make-up, but it lasts very well – '

'All that?' Paul goggled at the cases, having already goggled at Elizabeth. 'It looks like, we're not going away – we're running away! Is that what you've got in mind, Elizabeth?'

'I don't even know where we're going, Paul.'

'Isn't that the Channel, Paul – ?'

He craned his neck round her. 'Looks very much like that, yes.'

'But I haven't got my passport.' Panic. 'I haven't even *got* a passport, Paul!'

He felt inside his breast-pocket. 'One passport. Though whether they'll recognize you from the picture we rustled up is another matter – '

The Frenchman in the funny little office on the even funnier little airfield regarded Madame – *Miss Elizabeth Jane Loftus – Occupation – Secretary – Place of birth – Portsmouth – Residence – England* – with the honest doubt any functionary should have had when faced with an enlarged press photograph of E. Loftus, as she had appeared in the Amazons 'A' Hockey Team (captain), and E. Loftus's younger sister, as processed by Madame Hortense and Monsieur Pierre, of Guildford, and dressed

149

by *Style*, also of Guildford, and Madame Audley, of The Old House, Steeple Horley.

'Miss Loftus is my secretary,' said Paul, deadpan and confident, observing the Frenchman's incredulity and offering his own passport in explanation, alongside hers.

The Frenchman looked at Paul, and then at his passport, and then at Paul again.

'Dr – Mitch-ell – '

Paul Lefevre Mitchell, Elizabeth read upside down – before the Frenchman turned the page. But then she decided that, however much she wanted to know the official description of Paul's occupation, it might seem inappropriate for his secretary to be interested in such detail.

'A business trip, Dr Mitchell?'

The false insouciance of the question first surprised Elizabeth, since she didn't think they bothered with such formalities any more. Then she felt insulted by it, in the guise of Dr Mitchell's secretary, and started to bristle.

'Yes,' said Paul. 'That is to say . . .'

The Frenchman caught Elizabeth's frown and quailed slightly.

'Historical research,' said Paul.

'Ah – yes!' The Frenchman studied Paul's passport again, almost gratefully, as though to confirm something he had known all along but had now skilfully established by interrogation. 'But of course!'

It occurred to Elizabeth that she might also feel flattered – or that Madame Hortense and Faith Audley between them deserved the credit for whatever insulting thoughts had passed through the man's mind – and then she felt a wave of contempt for herself at such silly imaginings.

'Un moment!' The man looked around for something, and didn't find it, and vanished quickly through a door behind him with both passports still in his hand.

'Either they've had some trouble here – ' murmured

150

Paul out of the corner of his mouth ' – or we're the first English to land on this field since 1940, and they've forgotten what to do.'

The sound of scurrying came through the open door.

'And either they're going to arrest us on suspicion of being escaping criminals, or they've lost their bloody stamp.' There was a hint of savagery in the murmur. 'But either way they'll remember us now, blast it!'

'Does that matter?'

'I had a bit of trouble in France . . . once upon a time.' Paul drew a deep reminiscent breath. 'So they'll have my name and number written up somewhere for sure . . . Not here, but somewhere . . .'

'What sort of trouble?' She knew he wasn't going to tell her, but having some first-hand experience of the sort of troubles he had she didn't really want to know anyway. And that unfledged thought itself was enough to make her feel what she realized she ought to have felt all along: not surprised, and neither angry with the Frenchman nor herself, but just plain scared.

Two thumps sounded from the inner office, saving Paul the trouble of not replying, and to her intense relief the Frenchman reappeared with a smile on his face and the passports in his hand –

'What kept you?' Aske smiled at her in his usual half-shy, half-friendly way, but eyed her appraisingly at the same time as he held open the door of a big blue Renault. 'Mmm! I like your new scent, Miss Loftus – very *chic* and expensive!'

'That's probably what kept us,' said Paul irritably. 'Let's get out of here. We should have come by the hovercraft, like I wanted to do.'

'Another three hours on the journey – if you're in such a hurry,' said Aske mildly. 'Where to now?'

'But no awkward questions.' Paul sat back. 'To the hotel.'

'They were inquisitive? Well . . . I suppose you're a bit out of the ordinary. This isn't exactly a tourist spot – it's just a stop-over to and from the coast, though the old city's very fine . . .' Aske looked over his shoulder at Elizabeth '. . . I got us into a place in the old city, I thought you'd like that . . . medieval walls more or less intact, and a nice little 17th–18th century citadel – not a Napoleonic PoW depot, of course – too small for that . . . the nearest one of *them* is Sedan, then maybe Longwy. Then Givet to the north, on the frontier, and the three to the north-west – Arras, Valenciennes and Cambrai. And the big one to the east, naturally – Verdun. I wonder you didn't prefer Verdun for your base, Mitchell, even if the escape party didn't break out of there. It was the main British prisoners' depot, after all.'

Paul merely grunted, but Elizabeth sat up.

'Oh yes – I'm an expert too, now – an instant expert!' Aske appeared to have eyes in the back of his head. 'I'm your man on British PoWs in France, and French PoWs in England, *circa* 1812 – and on the year 1812 too . . . a very interesting year seemingly, as years go. "The 1941 of the Napoleonic War", no less.'

'I didn't know you were a historian, Mr Aske,' said Elizabeth.

'I'm not. Politics and Economics were my student theatres of activity – and cookery at night school . . . I must not deceive you, Miss Loftus – I did say "instant" expert.' Aske snuffled to himself. 'In the division of labour yesterday, after you were removed from my charge I drew one of Dr Audley's old dons, Professor – now Emeritus Professor – Basil Wilson Wilder . . . once the terror of generations of idle Cambridge undergraduates, but now retired from the fray on Portsdown Hill, above Portsmouth.'

'Professor Wilder!'

'You've heard of him? You know him?'

'Yes – I mean . . . that is, Father had a frightful row with him a year or two ago.'

'Did he, now? I find that a little surprising. He seemed to me to be a really *darling* old gentleman, and he's certainly a positive goldmine of information on the period . . . What did they row about?'

'Oh . . . it was about a letter he wrote.' The memory of Father's explosive rages during the *Vengeful* renaming correspondence still made her wince. 'What did he tell you about the prisoners? Did he know about the *Vengeful* survivors?'

'Not specifically. But he did agree with your father's conclusion about them – that they weren't included in the Decrés propaganda letter to Napoleon in the *Moniteur Universel* with the allegedly full list of successful British escapers down to September, but they *were* in the Lautenbourg fortress in early August – and they *didn't* turn up anywhere else thereafter, and weren't listed anywhere else as having been recaptured or died of natural causes . . . He reckoned the French killed them right enough – he said that, apart from the conflicting stories the French told, sending them to Lautenbourg was suspicious in itself. Because no one had ever been sent there before, and no one ever was again. "Something fishy, but I don't know what" was his conclusion – and here's our hotel – ' he swung the car under a narrow archway, through a passage, and into a tiny courtyard ' – then we can have a *proper* session, once we've installed you – it's all *quite* fascinating, Miss Loftus – I haven't been involved in anything so absolutely *fascinating* in ages!' He turned to Elizabeth with an expression of disarmingly innocent enthusiasm. 'There's a sweet little café in the square – '

'We're not going to sit in any café.' There was anything but an expression of innocent enthusiasm on Paul Mitchell's face. 'For any "proper session".'

'No?' Aske took his disappointment philosophically. 'Then what are we going to do?'

153

'I've got phone calls to make. You deal with the bags. And I want to be on the road in twenty minutes.' Paul sounded a bit like Father on one of his off days.

'And then where?' Aske's obedience didn't include total abasement.

'Wait and see,' said Paul rudely.

Twenty minutes later he seemed happier; or maybe he was beginning to regret being such a bear, decided Elizabeth.

'I'm sorry to push you like this, Elizabeth.' He tried to smile, and then looked past her and gave up the attempt. 'Where's that obnoxious fellow, for God's sake?'

'Mr Aske is trying to get me a better room. He thinks the one I've got will be too noisy.' Enough was enough. 'Why must you be so beastly to him? Has he ever done you any harm?'

'Not so far as I know – and he's not going to get the chance, either.' He shrugged. 'I hardly know him, actually.'

'You just dislike him on principle?'

'On several principles. I don't fancy queers, for a start.'

'Queers?'

'God, Elizabeth! You're not that innocent, surely?'

She flushed – she could feel the blood in her cheeks, pumping at treble pressure because she *was* that innocent, but also because that explained her own unformulated doubts, and finally because such naked prejudice embarrassed her.

'It isn't a crime any more,' she said stiffly.

'No.' *More's the pity* was implicit there. 'I can see you've never been propositioned! But then you wouldn't be, would you . . .' He sniffed derisively. 'You're safe.'

That was more hurtful than he intended. 'No. I have never been propositioned.'

'I didn't mean that, and you know it.' The hardness in his face broke up. 'Damn it – if you want to be propositioned, just keep your door on the latch tonight – '

154

'No, *thank you!*' snapped Elizabeth.

He ran his hand through his hair, suddenly not at all the Paul Mitchell she knew and didn't understand. 'Shit! I always get this wrong, don't I! Frances, you *are* avenged!'

'Frances?'

'Doesn't matter.' His face came together again. 'I also dislike him *because* I don't know him . . . and in this game, if you have someone there to cover your back, that's not a comforting feeling. And I *also* dislike him because I associate him with someone I don't trust – someone I *do* know. And birds of a feather – ' He stopped abruptly.

'Hullo there – sorry I'm late,' said Humphrey Aske. 'I've got you an absolutely super room, Miss Loftus – quiet and comfortable – and a wonderful view across the old city.'

'Thank you, Mr Aske,' said Elizabeth, split disconcertingly down the middle between them. 'I hope it wasn't too difficult?'

He smiled at her. 'Not at all, actually. I just got them to swop Dr Mitchell's bags for yours. Nothing could be easier!' He turned to Paul. 'Now, Dr Mitchell – which way?'

'South, across the N2 as best you can, on to the D967, Aske.' Paul embraced Aske's enmity like a lover.

'You've been there before, then?'

Paul looked through him. 'To the Chemin des Dames? Yes, I've been there before, Aske.'

Getting out and down from the old city of Laon, through the narrow streets, and down the winding hairpin road to the plain beneath, wasn't so easy in the rush-hour; and crossing the N2 ring road was hair-raising, even though Humphrey Aske drove with relaxed excellence and courtesy; so the question on the tip of her tongue delayed itself until Aske repeated the first name on the road signs.

'Bruyères-et-Montberault?'

155

'About twelve miles, straight on,' said Paul. 'Then we cross the Chemin des Dames, and go down half a mile, to the British War Cemetery at Vendresse.'

'Why, Paul?' asked Elizabeth.

'Why what?' He was staring straight ahead. 'Why the Chemin? Or why Vendresse?'

'Why . . . all of this?'

He stared ahead for a moment, without replying. 'I like the cemetery at Vendresse. It's only a little one, but it's one of my favourites.'

'What a perfectly *macabre* thought – to have a favourite cemetery!' exclaimed Humphrey Aske. 'You normally prefer the bigger ones?'

'And an interesting one, too.' Paul seemed not to have heard him. 'Late summer 1914 – and then late summer 1918 – the two turning points. I'll show you, Elizabeth.'

'But that simply can't be the reason, Mitchell – just to show us something . . . of interest?' said Aske.

Elizabeth found herself wishing that he wouldn't ask the questions which were uppermost in her own mind, instead of leaving the answers to the due process of Paul's own reasoning.

'You ought to know the reason, damn it!' snapped Paul. 'The only good cover is what's true. I don't usually fly to France – that was a mistake. We should have taken the hovercraft and the autoroute. But when I do come to the Aisne, this is what I do – and this is what I'm doing.'

'And what makes you think we need a cover?'

'That's right, Paul,' Elizabeth agreed with Aske uneasily. 'David Audley said we'd be safe over here.'

'And we *are* safe, Miss Loftus,' Aske reassured her. 'Nobody can possibly know where we are, except those who need to know. So unless Dr Mitchell left your flight plan lying around – '

'The flight plan was doctored,' said Mitchell testily.

'Then no one knows. Because no one followed *me*, I assure you.' Aske giggled. 'No one follows me when I don't want to be followed, I promise you – not without my knowing, anyway . . . And, for the record, no one's following me now.'

'The French know,' said Paul.

'Two or three dim *fonctionnaires* on a tin-pot air-strip half the size of my pocket-handkerchief? Oh, come on!'

'Don't underestimate the French.'

'I don't. I know they've got a smart computerized system for checking up on *mauvais sujets* who intrude into their privacy. But the great and good Dr Mitchell surely isn't lumped in with visiting Libyan assassins, is he?' Aske paused. 'Or is he?'

Paul said nothing

'You don't mean to say you've got a record here?' Aske appeared more amused than frightened. 'In the line of duty, naturally – ?'

'I am known here,' Paul came dangerously close to pomposity. 'Both in the line of duty, as you put it, and in the line of military history. And that's why we're going to Vendresse – because if they do by any chance pick me up on their radar I want to be well dug-into that second line.'

'Ah . . . well *now* I'm with you!' Aske nodded. 'So what are you doing in Champagne? I rather thought Picardy was your stamping ground – the Somme and the Hindenburg Line, and all those *awful* places?'

'This is where trench warfare started for the British – in September 1914, at the end of the battle of the Marne.'

'Indeed? And so what are *we* doing, then? We're strictly 1812 experts . . . we don't know anything that happened after the battle of Waterloo.'

'In my case I've got a type-script of unpublished material on the origins of trench warfare – it was the basis of the opening chapters in the Hindenburg Line book. If you both read that you'll know enough.'

'How very jolly! All about lice and phosgene?' murmured Aske. 'Well, that's awfully clever of you – and we

157

shall become experts on lice and phosgene, and gas gangrene and mud, Miss Loftus . . . did you hear that?'

It was six of one and half-a-dozen of the other, thought Elizabeth. The truth was that when men weren't comrades they were children – and not-very-nice, potentially savage children too.

'Very clever . . . that ridge ahead must be your "Ladies' highway", Mitchell,' continued Aske, still mock-admiringly. 'Except that we're not actually here to study all those charming 1914 facts, we're here to sort out something which occurred in 1812, or thereabouts. So . . . even allowing that you're scared of the French . . . on account of heaven only knows what past misdeeds . . . we are rather going out of our way now, aren't we? Or are we?'

'Just drive, Aske,' said Paul.

'"Just drive"?' This time the mildness in Aske's voice was paper-thin. 'No . . . I know I said 1812 was fascinating . . . but don't you think it's about time you explained to me why it's so important?'

At the best of times that would have been a bad question to put to Paul Mitchell, reflected Elizabeth. But just now, and coming from Aske, it was like a spark in the powder-magazine.

'Paul – '

'I know I'm only one of the *lesser* breeds, Mitchell – *I* know that *I* don't have the confidence of the legendary Dr Audley . . . I'm only here to *do* for you . . . or die for you, as required, like a one-man Light Brigade, and you just point me towards the Russian guns.' Aske peered ahead. 'And if this is your famous Chemin des Dames I must say that it's rather a non-event . . . *But* I would prefer to be pointed at the right guns in the right century – even if it is the nineteenth century – '

'For Christ's sake – shut up and drive!' spat Paul.

'There's no call to be offensive – '

'Oh yes there is.' Cold rage almost choked Paul. 'You are now driving, Aske – ' he spoke slowly and clearly ' –

158

across ground over which real men charged real guns . . . Germans and Frenchmen and British . . . and . . . if you make one more silly crack then that will be the end of this fascinating trip for you. Understood?'

This time Humphrey Aske said nothing, and Elizabeth cringed in her seat, all her own questions equally stifled not only by the order and the threat, but also by the suppressed passion with which both had been delivered, for all that they were camouflaged under clarity.

'Straight over the cross-roads,' said Paul tightly.

The road continued for a little way, then dropped and twisted down the southern slope of the ridge, affording her glimpses of a river valley, of fields and trees and distant roofs below.

'On the right there – you can pull in under the bank.' His voice was conversational again. 'You come with me, Elizabeth – you stay with the car, Aske.'

It was, as he had said, quite a small cemetery, cut into the hillside out of the sloping fields: in size it was more like the little village churchyard in which Father lay, than the hecatombs of the war dead which she had seen in photographs; but there was no church, and the lines of identical tombstones were ordered with military precision, rank on rank up the slope, as in a well-kept garden.

Elizabeth followed Paul up the centre aisle, towards a small kiosk-like building which was open on the side facing them, having to trot to keep at his heels. When they reached it Paul opened a tiny metal door and drew out a book wrapped in a plastic envelope from the niche behind it. She watched him in silence as he pulled a biro from his inside pocket and signed the book, then offered both to her. 'Name and date please, Elizabeth.'

Elizabeth studied the list, and was surprised to see how many names from this summer there were on the open pages – even from this same month, and several from this very day – who had found this place in the middle of nowhere, and this book.

159

And there was space for comment, too –

'My grandpa brought me here, and told me about it' –

'I was here in 1918, and I remember' –

But Paul had written nothing except the date and his name – plain *Paul Mitchell* – so Elizabeth had no stomach to do more than the same – plain *Elizabeth Loftus*.

'What about me, then?' said Humphrey Aske, from behind her.

Elizabeth looked towards Paul, quickly and fearfully. 'Paul – '

'Yes, of course – ' he blinked just once, as though the late afternoon light was too strong for his eyes ' – you *are* here, I suppose, so you must sign. You're right.'

Humphrey Aske signed the book – just name and date – and meekly gave it back to Paul, who wrapped it up carefully and replaced it in its niche.

'Sometimes I get to be rather a pain,' said Aske simply.

'Yes.' Paul addressed the ranks below them. 'And sometimes I fly off the handle, and particularly in places like this . . . Because everyone's obsessive about something – ' he caught Elizabeth's eye ' – with your father it was the *Vengeful* . . . but with me . . . someone once said to me, she said . . . "one minute it's a field of cabbages, but with a machine-gun you can turn it into a field of honour with a single burst".'

They walked down the aisle together, and it was only at the end of it that Paul spoke again.

'The stories are all here, but we haven't time for them – the regiments and the names . . . they were older in 1914 than 1918 – there's even a general here, from 1918, who was younger then than I am now . . . two great British armies, so alike and yet so different – one so small, and the other huge – separated by four years of war, that's all.' He shook his head. 'But we've got to get on – '

He led them back to the car in silence, and she couldn't take her eyes off him.

'Turn round and get back to the cross-roads, and then

turn left, along the crest.' It was hardly an order, more an instruction, and almost a courteous one.

'And then where to?' Vendresse had also taken the sting out of Humphrey Aske.

'To a place called Coucy-le-Château. About twenty miles, mostly on side-roads. I'll direct you.'

'What is there to see at Coucy-le-Château?' asked Elizabeth.

'There's a village . . . and a ruined castle.'

'A medieval castle, you mean?'

'Yes. But the ruins are more modern – ancient and modern, like the hymns in the hymn-book.'

'What d'you mean, Paul?'

'I mean, there was once the greatest medieval tower in Europe there – there still was in 1812, anyway . . . the great tower of Enguerrand III of Coucy, who was a contemporary of our King John – he was also excommunicated by the Pope, like King John, I believe . . . But General Ludendorff blew up Enguerrand's tower in 1918, before he retreated, to remind the French he'd been there.'

They had turned on to the crest road, the fabled Chemin des Dames itself. Elizabeth's eye was drawn to a huge French war cemetery, with a sign to a German one nearby.

'Not that he hadn't been reminding them already,' continued Paul. 'He'd had the Paris Gun – the one that's always wrongly called "Big Bertha" – stashed in a wood just below the castle. Paris is only about seventy miles down the road, as the shell flies . . . I could take you to see the gun position in the wood, it's still there. But it's rather overgrown and depressing, so I won't.'

'So it's another of your 1914–18 places, where they've got to remember us – just in case?' If it hadn't been for Vendresse she would have spoken more sharply.

'It can be.' He nodded thoughtfully, then stopped nodding. 'But as a matter of fact it isn't.'

Elizabeth couldn't add up this reply to make a sensible answer of it, and Paul appeared to be in no mood to elaborate on it, but withdrew into himself. It was as though their passage across one of his old battlefields, on which every fold and feature had its significance for him, was inhibiting him.

Finally Humphrey Aske roused himself behind the wheel. 'You said . . . the tower – the Frenchman's tower – was still there in 1812. Was that meant to mean something, or could it have been 1912, or 1712?'

'No.' Paul shook his head. 'No.'

'No . . . what?'

'You'll be coming to the Laon Soissons road in a moment. You turn left, towards Soissons, and then almost immediately right, down a side-road.' Paul stirred. 'I meant 1812.'

Aske peered ahead. 'What have medieval towers got to do with 1812?'

Mitchell twisted in his seat, pulling his safety-belt away from his shoulder, and stared past Elizabeth out of the rear window, as though to get a last look at his old battlefield on the ridge.

Then he caught Elizabeth's eye. 'Your father came this way, our people think, from his rough notes.'

'My father?' She frowned at him.

'Or, if he didn't, Tom Chard certainly did – "along the high road above the river to the greatest tower I ever saw" – he must have seen a few great towers along the road from Lautenbourg, but this was the greatest . . . size and time and distance, that's how they worked it out . . . with a few other clues beside, from Miss Irene Cookridge's book, Elizabeth.'

'To – ?' But she had forgotten the name of the place.

'Coucy-le-Château.' He nodded. 'Because Coucy-le-Château is where Lieutenant Chipperfield died, they reckon.'

9

'You see, Elizabeth, this is a research project with a difference – or a whole lot of differences . . . like *time*, for a start, obviously.'

'You mean, we don't have much of it?'

'Maybe we don't have any of it. I don't know. I only know that I've taken years to reconstruct days . . . and your father, Elizabeth – he bumbled along after the *Vengeful* escapers for months and months, enjoying himself in the best hotels and the Michelin restaurants, picking up the odd fact here and there, but mostly useless information. But he wasn't worried about time, anyway.'

That was Father to the life in his later days, thought Elizabeth: in spite of the doctor's advice he had been convinced that the whisper of his heart in his ear was only a false rumour.

'But we have other things that he didn't have.' Paul half-smiled at her. 'Because, when you think about it, an intelligence department is well-equipped for this sort of enterprise: we have the manpower – trained researchers, who know how to ask questions, and how to interpret the answers – and we have the resources – '

'Huh!' Aske snuffled to himself. 'If the tax-payers could see us now! Or are we going to publish this time? A *Festschrift* for Dr David Audley – *1812: Defeat into Victory*? Will that balance the books?'

'And the contacts – manpower, and resources, *and* contacts – '

'Professor *Emeritus* Basil Wilson Wilder, no less!'

'Aske – '

'Sorry, old boy! A moment's weakness . . . But Wilder

is a contact – at least, if this is what your Dr Audley wants to know, he is . . . And that's still *ultra*-secret, is it?'

Looking from one to the other, Elizabeth almost smiled; because they were Lucan and Cardigan at Bala-clava, re-enacting history, with the one hating the other so much that he'd never let himself be stung into admitting that he didn't know why he was doing what he was doing. But since she was in this particular Light Brigade charge it was no real smiling matter.

'So you're not interested in the *Vengeful* any more, Paul? It's only the escapers now?'

He nodded. 'That's what your father was concerned with, Elizabeth. You were right.'

'After Miss . . . Miss Cookridge's letter?' Here, coming down off the Chemin des Dames ridge, *Miss Irene Cook-ridge* was no more incongruous than *Julian Oakenshaw* and *Danny Kahn* in the roll-call of names.

'Not just her letter, but the *Conversations* book as well. David had people working on it half the night, and me working on what they came up with this morning.'

'Doing what, Paul?'

'Plotting the route they took after they broke out of the Lautenbourg Fortress.'

Aske half-turned, then his mouth closed on his unasked question and his eyes returned to the road. But Elizabeth knew what was still plaguing him, because it plagued her equally; the only difference being that she knew that Paul himself didn't know the answer to it, and Aske thought he was being frozen out from the truth.

Why?

'And that was a minor epic in itself – a classic Colditz-style job,' continued Paul. 'Because they were shut up tight in an old barracks between the town and the citadel, and there was no way they could get through the barracks' perimeter into the town.'

Why? 'So what did they do?'

He smiled. 'They climbed up *into* the citadel. They

made ropes out of their bedding, and grapnels somehow – they were sailors, of course, and sailors are ingenious . . . And then they climbed down the other side, where the sentries weren't expecting anything. But it still must have been pretty hairy, because their ropes weren't long enough, and they had to make the descent in stages – that's the steep side of the Lautenbourg, which is alleged to be unclimbable. But they had these two ropes, which were just strong enough to bear one man's weight, and a thin one to pull the ropes back up for the next man. And the last man down fixed the knot so it would bear his weight, but then two of them could pull it free – risky, but ingenious, as I said.' He shook his head admiringly. 'Tom Chard – he made it sound easy. But that's one hell of a cliff, with the wall on top of it.'

'You know the Lautenbourg Fortress, Paul?'

'Uh-huh. I was down that way a few years back, when the French started restoring the battlefield of Le Linge, above Colmar.' He smiled at her again. 'It's a 1915 battlefield, you see, Elizabeth, Le Linge is . . . I just visited the Lautenbourg in passing, as it were. But then, oddly enough, I've visited most of the Napoleonic prison fortresses they used for our chaps in 1812 – a happy coincidence, you may think.'

'No coincidence,' said Aske. 'Just an historical progression, really.'

'Historical, Mr Aske?'

'Or Napoleonic, Miss Loftus. Napoleon was luckier than the British: he had all his PoW camps ready-built for him – all the old frontier fortresses that he didn't need any more, having advanced the frontier far beyond them, and beaten everyone in sight. But, of course, when *he* was beaten in his turn, the frontier went back to where it had started – and all the PoW camps became fortresses again . . . Arras, Cambrai, Verdun . . . Do you recognize the names, Miss Loftus?'

To a historian those were names to conjure with from

165

older wars, but Elizabeth knew what he meant: they were the great names of Paul's war, the sepulchres of three great European armies. And because Lautenbourg itself had been just such another fortress along that long-disputed frontier, it too had its 1914–18 battlefield.

And yet Lautenbourg didn't fit, nevertheless: of all Napoleon's British captives, only the handful of Vengefuls had been sent there, she remembered.

'Why were they sent to Lautenbourg, Paul? Did Tom Chard know that?'

Paul shook his head. 'He never even asked himself the question – and why should he? But what he does say is that they were marched towards Verdun at first, by easy stages. And then one morning a new escort took over, under a full colonel of the Gendarmerie – a hard man by the name of "Soo-shay" – and they went off in a different direction, and under close arrest, as though they were criminals.'

'To Lautenbourg?'

'Yes. And Lieutenant Chipperfield protested about it, because he'd given his parole in the usual way, and he expected to be treated according to the rules of war – like a gentleman.'

Aske gave a snort. 'Nothing unusual about that. Napoleon Bonaparte was a great man, but he *wasn't* a gentleman – he was always breaking the old gentlemanly rules, Professor Wilder says. Like encouraging his officers to break their comfortable paroles, and then complaining if a British officer he'd locked up broke out of prison . . . where they shouldn't have been put in the first place, once they'd given their word-of-honour . . . Because, the way the British worked it out, an officer could only escape after they'd shut him up in jail. If they didn't then he couldn't escape. It's funny really: if Napoleon had played the game there wouldn't have been any escapes at all, not of officers and gentlemen. But he did – so there were lots of them.'

Elizabeth frowned, trying to remember Father's original brief paragraph on the fate of the prisoners. 'But it was unusual – the way they were treated – surely?'

'It was, yes,' Paul agreed. 'What Tom Chard says is that they asked him a lot of silly questions . . . What it amounts to is that "Colonel Soo-shay" interrogated them, and didn't get the right answers. And then Chipperfield decided that, since they weren't being treated properly, and sent to the main depot at Verdun, they had a legal right to escape.'

'So they did!' said Aske triumphantly. 'It's exactly as I said. Or what Wilder said . . . *he* said . . . there's this famous quote, by some officer-PoW, about his word-of-honour being stronger than any French locks-and-bolts. Meaning, that if they broke the rules he was honour-bound to teach them a lesson. But you're right about Lautenbourg, all the same – "fishy", was how Wilder described that. But. . . . so shouldn't we be digging there first – at Lautenbourg, where they started – rather than here?'

Aske's voice was gentle now, and his question was innocently put, to conceal the suggestion in it that he still doubted the sense of Paul's actions. Yet there was also more to it than that, thought Elizabeth: having been repulsed once in his attempt to obtain a straight answer to the central question, he was manoeuvring to repeat it indirectly and obliquely.

'Here will do well enough.' Paul found it harder to maintain his politeness, but he managed it.

Was it simply because Aske was homosexual, and a stranger associated with someone Paul distrusted? Perhaps all that was good enough for him, the irrational confirming the rational, and yet there was surely an edge of something else which she couldn't place . . . If she'd been beautiful and desirable, and Aske had been heterosexual . . . *then* it might have been sheer masculine irritation – three was a crowd, and she hadn't concealed

her sympathy for Humphrey Aske, in spite of everything
. . . But she wasn't, and he wasn't, so it couldn't be that,
whatever it was.

'There – up ahead,' said Paul. 'I've brought you this way
so you can get a proper view of it. The first time I came here
I could hardly see my hand in front of my face. This is a
great country for mist and fog, summer and winter. Both
sides found that out in 1918.'

Elizabeth craned her neck to see.

'Coucy,' said Paul. 'Once upon a time it was better to be
the Lord of Coucy than a Prince of the Blood, they used to
say.'

A great castle . . . walls, with their massive interval
towers, stretching for half a mile – or more, disappearing
into the trees – crowning a high ridge above the plain.

'I'd much rather take you on to see the Paris Gun site, of
course – that's why I came here first, back in '73 . . . castles
don't mean a bloody thing to me. Battlefields are the places
to see, they're where it's all at.'

'Battlefields – ' Aske caught his tongue again, before it
could betray him ' – it's an impressive ruin, I must say . . .
Where do we go?'

'Follow the road up, through the gateway. Then I'll
direct you,' said Paul, in his Aske-clipped voice.

The road meandered up the ridge, twisting with its own
logic until it turned finally under the walls and towers to
skirt their circuit. Elizabeth felt herself pressed into silence
by the very weight of history, with Lieutenant Chipperfield
of the *Vengeful* sandwiched between medieval Enguerrand
III and twentieth-century General Ludendorff.

'Park here,' commanded Paul. 'From here we walk.'

Elizabeth looked round, to get her bearings. They had
passed through Paul's great gateway, but into a little town,
not a castle – a walled town, which must be what she had
glimpsed from below. And now they were in one corner of
the town, approaching another gateway, which must
belong to the castle itself.

No . . . the whole thing was on a bigger scale than that: this second entrance was only an outer gate, opening on to an immense grassy space dotted with trees – an outer ward much bigger than at her own Portchester, near home.

But Paul seemed to know what he was doing, turning away into the custodian's office with a curt 'Stay here', leaving them to kick their heels on an empty square of gravel.

'I've never heard of this place.' Aske blinked, and stared around as Elizabeth had done. 'But then, judging by the lack of enthusiastic sightseers, I'm not alone in that . . . or maybe this is *apéritif* time . . .' He kicked his way across the gravel like a bored schoolboy, to a curious collection of rusty iron. 'This is never medieval – more like industrial revolution . . . that iron trolley . . . and those look like I don't know what – railway lines? Except they're curved – ?'

The gravel crunched behind them. 'Slightly curved, for a circle with a ninety-foot diameter. But your dating is about right, Aske. Say, mid-1860s. Vintage Napoleon III.'

Another period, and from the wrong Napoleon. They both looked questioningly at Paul Mitchell.

'And also significant. Cardinal Mazarin tried to blow up the great tower in the seventeenth century, only he hadn't got anything powerful enough to do the job. But there was an earthquake in these parts in 1692 that cracked it from top to bottom . . . didn't bring it down, but cracked it – which is one of our main clues, as it happens . . . so when Viollet-le-Duc came to do his rescue job on the cheap for Napoleon III he fixed a couple of iron hoops round it, to hold it together. And these are bits of hoop – you can see more of them among the wreckage inside ´ . . . Ludendorff's explosive *was* powerful enough . . . Although it took twenty-eight tons of even what he'd got. Something like ammonal, I suppose.'

'What d'you mean "one of our clues", Paul?' She stared at the bits of old railway line.

169

'Not the hoops. The great crack – that's what fixed our chaps on Coucy here: '*A wondrous great tower, the like of which I never saw for its breadth and height, but very ancient; which yet stood, though split sadly by a fierce tremor of the earth in the days of the Great King, so it is said.*' Tom Chard wasn't a great one for French names, but he was interested in everything he saw on his travels, and he had a good memory, thank God! So he left us enough clues – an earthquake in the reign of Louis XIV, because no one ever called Louis XV or Louis XVI "great" . . . and a "wondrous" tower split by an earthquake can only be Enguerrand's – *wondrous* is exactly what it was, which was why Ludendorff blew it up, the bastard.'

Aske caught Elizabeth's eye a little despairingly, as if to share his conviction that they were even further from any sort of useful answer.

'And . . . that's why we're here?' he prodded Paul cautiously.

'Partly, yes . . .' Paul scanned the landscape ahead, as though he was looking for something in it. 'We're here to re-write a chapter in Elizabeth's father's book, as a result of Miss Irene Cookridge's recent revelations, actually . . . *Ah!* There he is!' He pointed up the pathway.

Elizabeth frowned along the line of his finger. 'Who? Where?'

Why?

'On the seat there. My old friend Bernard Bourienne. He made it!' Paul sounded childishly delighted. 'Come on – '

'Who's . . . Bernard Bourienne?' panted Elizabeth.

'He's a veterinary surgeon from Château-Thierry – '

'A *what*?' exclaimed Aske.

'He's also an enthusiastic amateur historian. In fact, there aren't many professionals who know more than he does about American operations in France in 1918 – all the best American bits in my Hindenburg Line book are thanks to him . . . and he's pretty good on the Chemin des Dames too.'

'Dear God!' whispered Aske. 'Into the trenches again – with a vet!'

Mercifully, Paul didn't hear him, he was already striding towards the man on the seat. 'I didn't think he'd make it – Bernard! Well met, mon vieux!'

'Paul!' Bernard Bourienne unwound himself – all six-foot . . . six-foot-two – six-foot-four – and, with the shock of dark hair on the top of it, matching the bushy eyebrows, finally more like six-foot-six. 'Well met, also, old friend!'

They embraced, in the continental manner which left Elizabeth slightly embarrassed. And then the Frenchman's dark eyes zeroed in on her, stripping her down and reassembling her in a fraction of a second, and yet somehow achieving this without the offence she would have felt in England.

'Bertrand – *M'sieur* Bourienne – allow me to introduce *Mamselle* Elizabeth Loftus, daughter of the late Commander Hugh Loftus, VC – '

The shock of hair came down to Elizabeth's level.

' – and my . . . my colleague and fellow historian, Humphrey Aske, of London University.'

'M'sieur.' Bertrand Bourienne gave Humphrey Aske a very brief glance and then a second and more searching one, as though the first had quivered some sensitive antenna hidden in the tangle of hair.

'Now, Bertrand – ' Paul pre-empted any return civilities '– I hope you've got something good for me, because we're pushed for time, as I told you on the phone last night.' He looked around. 'In fact, it must be almost closing time here, to start with . . . and I'd like my friends to see what's left of Enguerrand's tower before we get chivvied out.'

'Chivvied out?' Bourienne waved the threat away. 'My dear Paul, they do not *chivvy* me.' He drew himself up to his full height, adding the elongated length of one arm to it in a signal directed towards the gate-house. '*So!*'

Elizabeth followed the signal, but could see no sign of movement. Then she looked at the Frenchman and he smiled at her, lifting a finger to silence her as he did so. 'Listen, Miss Loftus.'

For a moment there was total silence, no voices, no sounds, not even any bird-song, which she might have expected in England. Then, out of nowhere – out of the air around her – there was music . . . not music she could place in any origin of time instantly – not the *Musak* of the twentieth century . . . but the sweeter sounds of a distant past, made by unfamiliar instruments and clear in the stillness of the evening.

'Oh – clever stuff, Bertrand,' murmured Paul irreverently. 'One day you'll have to do a *Son et Lumière* here – ending with a bloody great 28-ton *bang*, maybe?'

'Fourteenth century,' said Aske. 'Lute and hautboy – Enguerrand's background music, perhaps?'

Influence, thought Elizabeth, putting it all together just as suddenly as the haunting music had filled the open space between the trees and the towers all around her. Paul had said *contacts,* but that had been what he meant – and that had been Father's complaint in the latter days: *I haven't any influence any more – I can't make people do things for me – I don't know the right people . . .* This was what Paul had, which he had boasted of –

'Enguerrand's music, c'est vrai,' Bourienne acknowledged Aske's guess. 'Although I should have had them play *La Marseillaise* for you this time, Paul . . . if not the rataplan of the drummers of the Guard.'

They were moving now, as though by consensus, still lapped by Enguerrand's music, towards an inner gateway, much more ruined and overgrown, but also greater.

Paul turned towards his friend. 'So you *have* got something?'

'That . . . I don't know . . .' Bertrand Bourienne mused

on the question. 'I know that I have worked very hard for you, these last hours . . . and in a period unfamiliar to me – and also with material and people unfamiliar to me – yes!'

'Ha . . . hmmm!' Paul grunted unintelligibly, and Elizabeth sensed that he was trying to control his impatience.

'We're very grateful to you for taking such trouble to help us, M'sieur Bourienne,' she said carefully. 'And at such short notice.'

'No trouble, Miss Loftus. Assisting fellow-labourers in the vineyard is always a pleasure. And I understand the importance of checking new material when it arrives so inconveniently, with a book almost finished . . .' Bourienne nodded sympathetically '. . . though that is the mark of a true scholar, but naturally – and nothing less than what I would expect of my friend, Dr Mitchell . . . No, my only reservation – my only regret, even – is that this concerns an era of history with which I am not conversant in sufficient depth to be of real help, so that . . . with so little time at my disposal . . . I have been dependent on the charity of others. And to no great effect, I fear.'

'You mean that Dr Mitchell has sent you on a wild goose chase?' said Aske.

'No . . . *that* I do not mean.' Bourienne pursed his lips, and looked sidelong at Paul. 'I know him of old, and he has the historian's gift – the instinct for the one fact out of many . . . the one fact which cannot safely be left behind – the nose for the deep dug-out in the captured trench which is not empty, but full of Germans waiting to issue forth to take you in the rear as you move on.'

They were passing through the gateway now, with a labyrinth of ruined guardhouses, and steps descending into darkness, on one side, and a jumble of stones on a hillside on the other.

'And this is one of those dug-outs – those facts, I think,' said Bourienne. 'Even though I do not know this period, my nose tells me so.' He looked at Elizabeth suddenly,

173

nodding again, but this time thoughtfully. 'I think . . . you are wise not to leave this chapter behind you, Miss Loftus.'

'Why, M'sieur Bourienne?' She had come to the question at last.

He pointed to the stone-covered hillside. 'Do you not wish to see Enguerrand's tower?'

'I want to know why, first, if you please.' Once out, the *why* took precedence over everything else.

'Very well. If I have understood Paul correctly, you are concerned with the fate of a party of escaped British sailors who concealed themselves here, in one of the towers of this castle? Deserters – yes?'

'Yes.' If that was what Paul had said, then *yes*. 'Prisoners-of-war, though, not deserters.'

'No.' It was Aske who spoke. '"Deserter" was the official name for all escaped PoWs, on both sides of the Channel. Once they broke out they were regarded in law as criminals, the officers as well as the men. And over here, if they were recaptured they went straight to the dungeons in the punishment fortresses.'

'And in England they went to the hulks – the old wooden battleships rotting on the mud-flats, m'sieur. Which was worse, I have been told – is that not so?'

Aske shook his head slowly. 'Not worse than the hell-hole at Bitche – "the house of tears". And they reckoned Sarrelibre was worse than Bitche. Or so *I* have been told, m'sieur.'

The tall Frenchman looked down at the little Englishman for a moment, then turned back to Elizabeth. 'Let us say . . . it was a cruel age, Miss Loftus. Any man who escaped in those days risked more than mere recapture. But then any man who wore his country's uniform . . . that was also a cruel fate. And especially here in France, after twenty years of war, and the Law of Conscription, which was hated so much.'

'Like the Press Gang?'

'That I cannot say. But here . . . by 1812 the country-side was full of *réfractaires* – the evaders of conscription who were on the run . . . as well as deserters from the army. And, for the most part, the peasants and the poor people pitied them, and helped them. Or at least did not inform on them – ' he swung towards Paul ' – and *that*, Paul, is how these men of yours survived here for so long without discovery: they passed themselves off as conscripts – as fishermen from the west coast trying to return to their homes . . . Would that be right?'

'Exactly right, Bertrand, by God!' Paul nodded first to the Frenchman, then to Elizabeth. 'Tom Chard said that Chipperfield and the midshipman both spoke enough French to get by, but they passed off their accents as Breton – like pretending to be Scotsmen in Kent. By God! Bertrand – you've found them! That's brilliant of you!'

'*Moment*, Paul.' Bourienne cautioned Paul with a hand. 'It may be that I have *not* got them. None of the peasants who were interrogated admitted that these were Englishmen – '

'But the place and the time is right, Bertrand – '

'But not the numbers, my friend. You said four men, and these were not four men – they were three men and a girl.'

'And a girl?' Elizabeth's heart sank.

'A young girl. The sister of one of them, who was travelling with her brother, Miss Loftus.'

Elizabeth turned to Paul. 'Paul – '

'Bloody *marvellous*!' Paul beamed at her, and then at Bourienne. 'You're a magician, Bertrand. I never thought you'd find them, not in the time. But you have!'

'But . . . the girl, Paul?'

'Tom Chard mentioned a girl – obviously,' said Aske. 'Everything comes back to Tom Chard.'

'Not quite everything.' Paul cut back to the Frenchman, dismissing Aske. 'What happened, Bertrand?'

'Ah . . . now I am going to disappoint you! What

happened is not at all clear . . . I have this friend in our society – a local history society, you understand, Miss Loftus – and he has a colleague who is an authority on the times hereabouts of the First Empire . . . on the local administration under the Emperor Napoleon, and so on . . . a man who knows his way round the records and documents of the period – '

'Bertrand – '

'All right. You are in a hurry, I know . . . The fact is, for security purposes the country was divided into small districts, each with a police commandant, and the presence of this party was eventually reported to the officer at Chauny – I say "eventually", for it seems that they had lodged in one of the smaller towers here for ten days or more . . . the château as a whole had been derelict since the revolution, you understand . . . Yes, well . . . it was assumed that they were *réfractaires*, and a party of police was sent to arrest them. But when they searched the château they found that the birds had flown. Possibly they had been warned by the peasants . . . or perhaps they had a look-out. All that the gendarmes found was – a grave. A fresh grave.'

Elizabeth looked to Paul. 'Lieutenant Chipperfield, Paul?'

'Shh! Go on, Bertrand.'

Bourienne frowned at Paul. 'This was all routine so far, you must understand. Hunting deserters was one of their main tasks – *French* deserters . . . All through that previous winter, and into the spring, there had been a special drive to bring the conscripts to the colours as never before – every man or boy they could lay their hands on, the class of 1813 even. The whole of France was on the move, they said – the whole of Western Europe even. This was 1812, remember – '

'Russia,' said Aske. 'The great invasion! The dress rehearsal for 1941.' He nodded to Elizabeth. 'You remember what I said? This was the big year – 1812!'

'The year of Salamanca,' said Paul. 'One of David Audley's maternal ancestors was killed at Salamanca, charging with Le Marchant's cavalry in Wellington's greatest victory, as he never tires of telling us.'

'Greatest victory – phooey!' Aske sniffed derisively. 'Napoleon withdrew forty of his best battalions from Spain for Russia. Spain was a side-show, compared with Russia – like Greece and North Africa were side-shows in 1941 compared with Russia. Once they'd dealt with Russia – Napoleon and Hitler both – the rest was chicken-feed . . . they'd have taken England next after that. In fact . . . *in fact*, the only difference between the year 1812 and the year 1941 is that at the very end of 1941 the Americans came in on our side . . . Whereas, in 1812 the Americans declared war on *us*, old boy!'

'This is Professor Wilder talking, presumably?' Outside his 1914-18 War Paul wasn't so sure of himself.

'Professor Wilder and the facts.' Aske picked up Paul's uncertainty like a £5 note in the gutter. 'Wilder says the trouble with us is that we've been brought up on Arthur Bryant and Nelson – we reckon we're winning the war from Trafalgar in 1805 onwards. But the fact is that by the summer of 1812 we were *losing* it. Bad harvests . . . riots in the cities – the Luddites breaking up the factories and burning the corn-ricks . . . the pound falling against the franc . . . and war with the United States . . . *and* then Napoleon leading the greatest army of the age against the Russians.' He shook his head. 'In 1812, when poor old Chipperfield was being planted here, we were *losing*, believe me, Mitchell.'

'Hmmm . . .' Paul cut his losses at a stroke. 'So they found a grave, Bertrand. And did they dig it up?'

'They dug it up, yes.' Bourienne didn't quite know what to make of the Mitchell-Aske byplay. 'And that is when it started to cease to become routine, my friend.'

'How so? He died of natural causes, surely? Blood-poisoning or gangrene, or whatever?'

Bourienne waved a hand. 'What he died of, I do not know. But there was a British naval officer's uniform coat buried with him – that is when the trouble started . . . *en effet,* that is when the records start. Because until then it was no more than a police matter.'

'So what happened then?'

'Oh . . . it did not happen immediately. I do not know all the dates, but it was late summer, early autumn, when the coat is . . . is . . . disinterred. And then the commandant's report goes through the official channels, and eventually to Paris. And then – and then . . .'

'The shit is in the fan?' Paul grimaced at Elizabeth. 'Sorry, Elizabeth – and then, Bertrand?'

'And then . . . Colonel Jean-Baptiste Suchet, bringing the fear of God and the Emperor with him, and two squadrons of *gendarmes d'élite* from the Young Guard battalions in Paris – '

'Suchet!' exclaimed Aske. 'Meaning "Soo-shay", Colonel of the Gendarmerie?'

'Not the Gendarmerie, m'sieur – ' Bourienne shook his head ' – this Suchet was a colonel of the Marines of the Guard, and also a special *aide* of the Emperor himself . . . What you would call "top brass" – and not so much a policeman, I think, as – as – as, maybe a colonel of the general staff – or of intelligence, perhaps?'

Now they were really in deep, thought Elizabeth, looking quickly from Paul to Humphrey Aske. Because, with that one flight of comparative fancy, Bertrand Bourienne had lifted up Lieutenant Chipperfield of the *Vengeful* out of the category of escaped PoW into the realm of cloak-and-dagger.

'Indeed?' Paul seemed disappointingly unmoved. 'So just what did this fellow . . . Suchet do, to put the fear of God up everyone?'

'Ah . . . well, he dismissed the commandant at Chauny – for incompetence, one supposes . . . And he summoned the *adjoints* from Compiègne and Soissons and Laon, and

178

drafted both the local police and the soldiers from the garrisons to conduct house-to-house searches . . . Also, it would seem that he despatched messengers to St Quentin and Arras and Amiens, and even as far as Rouen – '

'What messages?'

Bourienne shook his head. 'Messengers . . . what messages, I do not know . . . And he interrogated many local people – peasants and farmers from Coucy here, and also from Folembray and Guny and Pont-St Mard – after he left there were complaints from several mayors to the Prefect, both about his behaviour, and the behaviour of his men . . . chiefly his men, for damage to property . . . and there were two assaults, and the rape of a respectable woman. After the troubles of the winter and the spring, when the conscripts had been combed out, there was much disaffection – even after he left – even with the news of great victories in Russia – false news, as it turned out.'

Bourienne shrugged. 'But after that there is little more to tell – little more than the records here contain, at least. This is the worm's-eye view of what you seek. If you wish for the eagle's-eye view, you must go to Paris, that is what my friend's colleague advises. There are many other records there, and it was from Paris that Colonel Suchet came.'

'Suchet does sound like our best bet,' agreed Aske. 'If he was top brass, someone must know about him. And now that we know he turned up here as well as at Lautenbourg –'

'Lautenbourg?' Bourienne frowned. 'In the Vosges?'

'That's where they escaped from,' said Aske.

'And Colonel Suchet pursued them all the way here?' The Frenchman's bushy eyebrows rose. 'But then that fits well enough – well enough . . .'

'Well enough how, m'sieur?' asked Elizabeth.

Bourienne considered her for a moment. 'I said . . . a worm's-eye view, mam'selle . . . and that is the truth . . . And there is little enough that I have been able to give

179

you, beyond what you already appear to know . . . the more so, as I myself know so little of this period. But there is one thing I do know, which every worm knows . . . and every student of history must learn to identify from the worms' memories – ' he paused for dramatic effect ' – and that is the heavy tread of authority . . . the tread of history itself crushing down on the worms.'

Elizabeth looked at him blankly.

'I do not know what messages Colonel Suchet sent – I do not even know why he pursued these prisoners. But it is clear that he wanted them very badly . . . enough to turn this whole region upside down . . . and it was not merely because they were escapers – of *that* I am sure.' He shook his head. 'They were not ordinary escapers.'

'What makes you think that?' asked Aske quickly.

'Partly because *he* was no ordinary policeman – and an imperial *aide* does not chase ordinary escapers.' Bourienne looked at Paul, and smiled. 'And partly because *he* has a nose for the dug-out full of Boches.' He came back to Aske and Elizabeth. 'And partly because I also feel the heavy tread above me – perhaps that most of all.'

'Hmm . . .' Aske wrinkled his nose doubtfully. 'A bit of circumstantial evidence, in fact. Plus a lot of mere instinct.'

Bourienne gestured towards the hill of rubble. 'This is Enguerrand's tower, Miss Loftus.'

Elizabeth blinked in surprise. 'Oh . . . yes . . . It was built on a hill, was it?'

'On a hill? But no! Here – where we stand – was the edge of a great ditch. The ruin of the tower fills the ditch and also makes your hill, mam'selle. And what we see is but the edge of a huge crater where the tower stood. The greatest single ruin in France is what you see here – am I right, Paul?'

'What?' Paul frowned abstractedly.

The Frenchman nodded. 'They were not ordinary prisoners? Am I right?'

'No, they weren't. I suppose I owe you that, Bertrand.' Paul grinned. 'But I don't yet know why.'

'But you knew before, nevertheless?' Bourienne nodded.

Elizabeth stared at Paul. 'How did you know, Paul?'

'I don't *know* – I'm guessing, like Bertrand.'

'They were sent to Lautenbourg, that's why,' said Aske. 'Sent there – and then interrogated about something. And then, when they escaped, the French pretended to the British that they didn't exist. And if they'd been caught I'll bet that would have been the truth. "Shot while escaping" is the standard formula.'

'Timing is the giveaway, Elizabeth,' said Paul, ignoring Aske. 'They met the *Fortuné* by accident – the *Vengeful* was wrecked – they came ashore . . . By the ordinary rules they would have been marched to somewhere like Verdun, and Lieutenant Chipperfield and the midshipman would have been semi-paroled there, and perhaps the warrant officers with them. That must be what Chipperfield reckoned on.'

'So what?' said Aske.

'So he didn't need to escape. Once he reached Verdun he'd be among friends, with a Senior British Officer to advise him what to do next . . . Or at least he'd be safe, anyway.'

'Where does *timing* come into this?' persisted Aske.

'At first they did march towards Verdun – they nearly got there, in fact. But then they were diverted to the Lautenbourg, and Colonel Suchet turned up. And then they were in trouble.' Paul looked at Elizabeth. '*Timing*, Elizabeth.'

He expected something of her – and since he could hardly expect her to be brighter than Aske it must relate to something he expected her to know, and to be able to put together as he had done.

'Timing . . .' Her mind stretched into Father's *Vengeful* Number Seven chapter, but to no avail. And Bertrand Bourienne, who knew nothing about the *Vengeful*'s last voyage, was looking frankly bemused. And Humphrey Aske –

The *Vengeful*'s last voyage?

'The French couldn't possibly have known that she'd be off Ushant – ' But now she was echoing her own answer to the question he'd put to her in the garden at the Old House ' – but she was at Gibraltar for re-fitting and stores before that . . . and then she called at Lisbon on the way home . . . ?'

'Come on, Elizabeth!' Paul encouraged her.

'Well . . . I suppose the French could have received news of her sailing from Lisbon, if they had spies there . . . if she didn't sail immediately – but meeting the *Fortuné* . . . that was still accidental, Paul.'

'You're just guessing – clutching at straws,' murmured Aske.

'Of course I'm bloody guessing!' snapped Paul. 'But our people say the time factor just about fits – allowing for the length of time it took to transfer information to Paris from Spain.'

'But that would take weeks – ' Aske stopped suddenly, and his expression changed. 'Ah!'

Elizabeth stared at Aske.

'That's what he means, Miss Loftus,' Aske nodded. 'The *Fortuné* doesn't come into the reckoning at all. But once the *Vengeful* survivors came ashore the news would have gone to Paris in a matter of hours, by semaphore. They always celebrated whenever one of our ships came to grief – the *Moniteur* would publish it, we can check that even . . . But . . . they didn't do anything about it. They just started the prisoners off towards Verdun, like always . . . and *that* also took weeks – don't you see?'

Belatedly, Elizabeth saw – saw the two additions of time, and what they might mean: on the one hand the days the *Vengeful* had been in Gibraltar, or Lisbon, and at sea, plus the time from the sea-fight with the *Fortuné*, through the shipwreck and the survivors' landfall, and the long trek thereafter across France towards the prison depot . . . and on the other, the odyssey of the information about the *Vengeful* from Lisbon to Paris, first from behind the British lines, from some French spy, and even through French-occupied Spain . . . which, with guerrilla bands watching every road, would have been hardly less slow and dangerous. And together those two additions of time and distance turned into snails creeping across the map, but converging on each other just short of Verdun and safety, when Colonel Suchet finally caught up with Lieutenant Chipperfield.

'So Suchet's our man now – "Colonel Soo-shay" who asked the silly questions – *goodbye* Tom Chard, *hullo* Mon Colonel,' said Aske to Paul. 'Because whatever it was the old *Vengeful* had on board, Mon Colonel wanted it, that's for certain – '

Colonel Jean-Baptiste Suchet –

The night-bells of Laon had stopped long since, but sleep still eluded Elizabeth as the roll-call of the living and the dead – the newly dead and the long dead – continued to echo inside her brain –

Colonel Jean-Baptiste Suchet and Lieutenant Horace Chipperfield . . . and Danny Kahn and Julian Oakenshaw – and Harry Lippman and Ray Tuck . . . and Harry Lippman and *Father* . . . and *Father* and Lieutenant Chipperfield – and Tom Chard and Abraham Timms and the little midshipman . . . and Colonel Suchet and Bertrand Bourienne . . . and Paul – and Paul . . .

And Humphrey Aske, and Chief Inspector Del Andrew – and Danny Kahn . . . and David Audley, and Faith Audley, and Cathy Audley – and David Audley and Josef Ivanovitch Novikov, and Paul – Dr Paul Mitchell of the King's College, Oxford – *Paul* . . .

And all the dead Tommies, lying so neatly, row on row, on their hillside in Champagne, below the road on which the king's sisters had chattered their way so long ago . . . and yet not so long ago as Enguerrand had built his tower . . .

Friends and enemies, heroes and villains . . . heroes and villains at the same time, according to whose side they were on – Suchet and Novikov and Audley and Paul . . . and whose side had Tom Chard been on, who had somehow beaten all the impossible odds to break free, and to live to tell the tale?

Whose side? And why?

The questions crowded behind the ghosts closing round her bed in the silence – whatever it was the old *Vengeful* had on board – what had Father been doing – what had he *done* –

Then, dissolving the ghosts and the questions both, and startling Elizabeth out of her mind as they vanished, there wasn't quite silence any more: there was the sound of a discreet *tap-tap* on her door – discreet, but insistent.

10

'Elizabeth – '

But whatever Dr Paul Mitchell, of the King's College, Oxford, whispered after that was lost to her as she scuttled back into bed, conscious more of Madame Hortense's taste in night-attire than of Dr Mitchell's post-midnight opening gambit.

The door closed out the light from the passage, and darkness sprang back into the bedroom.

'Christ, Elizabeth – I can't see a bloody thing!' Dr Mitchell blundered unromantically against the table by the door. 'Put the light on, for heaven's sake!'

Elizabeth drew the sheet up to her neck. 'What d'you want, Paul?' The silly question asked itself before she could stifle it.

'For God's sake – I want to talk to you!' hissed Paul. 'What did you think I wanted?'

Dust and ashes filled Elizabeth, turning to shame and then anger in quick succession. She let go the sheet – what did it matter what he saw or didn't see? – and leaned across to switch on the bedside lamp.

'What d'you want?' She glared at him in the knowledge that it hadn't been a silly question after all. 'I was trying to get some sleep.'

'I'm sorry.' He blinked at her in the light.

'So am I.' Disgust with herself hardened her voice. 'Well, what is it?'

His face set to match her tone. 'First . . . as of now, when someone knocks on your door in the night, you don't just open up, like Juliet for Romeo. You ask who the hell it is – okay?'

'Juliet for Romeo' was too close for comfort – too

humiliatingly and pathetically close, thought Elizabeth miserably.

'Second . . . I *am* sorry to disturb you, Elizabeth. But I have some news for you.'

'News?' It was on the tip of her tongue to reject the offer until morning, but that would be merely petty, and she was awake now anyway. And there was also something in that voice which didn't match the set expression. 'What news?'

'I've been on the phone to England. I've spoken to David Audley . . . and to Del Andrew, Elizabeth.'

It was sympathy – the news must be *bad* news. But what bad news could either Dr Audley or Chief Inspector Andrew have for her, who had no next-of-kin, no hostages to fortune?

'Yes?' She couldn't help him, he had to bite on his own bullet.

He stared at her. 'They think they know where – how – how your father got all that money.'

She had been wrong about not having hostages to fortune: she had a hundred thousand of them, and they were going to take them all away from her. She had been briefly rich, but now she was poor again.

'In fact, they're pretty damn certain. That Del Andrew – he's a fast worker . . .' He continued to stare at her, rolling the bullet around, unwilling to clench his teeth on it.

So it was worse than that: they were going to send her to prison . . . or was it Father, who was beyond their reach, who had committed some disgraceful act – even some treasonable act – ?

No – not some treasonable act . . . not Father – *never* Father! But . . . disgraceful? Dishonest?

'It wasn't his money?' Was that what the *Vengeful* had been carrying? The thought of some great treasure had been in the back of her mind all along, even though she had scorned the possibility of it – even though she knew

186

that the *Vengeful* was a long-lost wreck, and that the survivors could hardly have got away with anything of value –

Or could they?

'It wasn't his, no.'

Or could they? But if they had . . . of what possible importance could it have been to the French, who had plundered most of Europe, from the horses of St Mark's to the hard cash in the treasuries of whole kingdoms? And . . . and even more – even if Colonel Suchet had coveted it . . . there was no conceivable way that it could interest Josef Ivanovitch Novikov of the KGB –

'It was yours, Elizabeth,' said Paul.

She hadn't heard him properly. 'What?'

'It was yours.' Paul sat down on the edge of the bed, and started to reach for her hand, but then thought better of it. 'He stole it from you.'

She had heard him properly, she just didn't understand what he was saying. 'From . . . *me*?'

'Del Andrew took Ray Tuck – lifted him out of somewhere in the Essex marshes this morning, bright and early. And then made him sing by the simple expedient of letting him choose between singing and being turned loose on the street for Danny Kahn's boys to pick up . . . So Ray Tuck sang like a canary.'

That was the authentic voice of Del Andrew, thought Elizabeth irrelevantly, while thinking at the same time *From me?*

'The funny thing is . . . Ray Tuck sang true, and yet it was all a pack of lies, the song he sang, Del Andrew thinks – Harry Lippman's lies. Or maybe your father's lies, but we can't check on that now.'

'What lies, Paul?' All Elizabeth could think was *From me?* How could Father have stolen from her, who had nothing to steal?

'Oh . . . a cock-and-bull story about hidden treasure from the old *Vengeful* – how your father was picking it up

187

bit by bit from somewhere in France, and Lippy was fencing it for him. Which was a whole pack of lies, because there's no *Vengeful* treasure – or not this treasure, Elizabeth.'

She had to listen to what he was saying. 'How do you – how does . . . Del . . . know that?'

'At first he didn't. But Ray Tuck gave him the name of one of the buyers – a dead-respectable jeweller who'd never handle "dodgy" goods . . . apart from the fact that Lippy wouldn't have sold any to one of his "straight" clients, Del says, and the jeweller himself wouldn't have bought this jewellery anyway, without proper provenance for the record.'

'Jewellery? What jewellery? What . . .'

'Provenance? "Commander Hugh Loftus, VC – family heirlooms – *item*, one emerald-and-diamond necklace, with matching earrings, very fine – £12,000 . . . *item*, one diamond tiara set in gold, central stone umpteen carats, very fine – £15,000 . . . those are two we've been able to check. And also some small trinkets Lippy couldn't bear to part with, because he loved good antique jewellery, which he passed on to his daughter to wear on Saturday, down the market . . . having paid the full market price himself, of course.'

Listening was one thing, but grasping the sense of it was still another. 'Why couldn't it have come from the *Vengeful*, Paul? How can you be so sure?' She grasped at the word 'antique'. 'If it was old – '

'It was old, but not old enough.' He gazed at her sadly. 'About 150 years old to be exact – between 150 and 130, that is.'

Elizabeth made the subtraction dumbly, hopelessly.

'Early Victorian. Made by a jeweller named Savage who opened up shop in Bond Street in 1832, which his son sold in 1883 – they made the necklace and the tiara, anyway: their work is apparently quite distinctive . . . Lippy's buyer recognized it straight off, because Savage pieces are highly regarded in the trade – real craftsman's work . . . So naturally Lippy would have recognized it too, it was right up his street. Some of the rings and brooches he gave his daughter aren't Savage work – they're late Victorian and Edwardian, which is equally distinctive. So there's no possible doubt about it, Elizabeth.' He paused. 'And no doubt that it's yours, either.'

Elizabeth waited, oddly aware that her feet, which had been warm, were cold now.

'You see, Elizabeth, our Chief Inspector Andrew is an observant fellow, and he's done his time on the robbery squad, or whatever they call it. So when a certain Lebanese tycoon showed him a certain emerald-and-diamond necklace, with matching earrings, late yesterday afternoon . . . he remembered that he'd seen it all before, in a picture on the wall of a house in Hampshire he'd searched two days earlier . . . as worn by Mary, Lady Varney, wife of Admiral Sir Alfred Collingwood Varney – necklace and earrings, and a lot of other jewellery, tiara and rings and suchlike. "Got up like a Christmas tree", is how he remembered her . . . your great-great-grand-mother, Elizabeth – or would she be great-great-great?'

Great-great-grandmother, dripping with jewels, thought Elizabeth, the cold at her back now.

'The way Del sees it, the jewels very often pass straight down the female line, mother to daughter, grandmother to granddaughter, great-aunt to great-niece, with no publicity. Even before death duties came into the picture they were passed as gifts on the quiet, with no fuss and bother. Which is how they must have come to your mother, Del thinks. But she died when you were a baby, so . . .' he trailed off diplomatically ' . . . so that's how we think it was, Elizabeth.'

That was how they thought it had been. And that was how she thought it had been, too.

Paul shrugged. 'Del thinks . . . maybe Lippy tried to make it all sound difficult – or at least too difficult for a little wanker like Ray Tuck to try and get his hands on, anyway – '

'"Wanker"?' For a moment Del's vernacular flummoxed her.

Paul waved one hand vaguely. 'Small-timer . . . The idea of hiding it in France, and historical research, and all that . . . It never occurred to him that Ray would sell the whole idea to Danny Kahn – '

'Who's got a lot of bottle?' She tried to hold on to the absurdity of the dialogue because she didn't want to think of Father quibbling about the house-keeping bills.

'"Bottle"? Oh . . . yes . . . Danny Kahn's a whole lot smarter, yes – ' Paul rallied ' – smarter and even greedier, unfortunately. Not that he matters now . . .'

Not that anything mattered much – now, thought Elizabeth. It was an odd feeling, to be a rich woman again, so quickly, with Madame Hortense and M'sieur Pierre at her elbow to advise her, and yet to be so poor and lonely at the same time, in the traditional way in which unloved and unbeautiful rich women were supposed to be poor and lonely.

'We'll never know which of them made up the story for Ray Tuck.' Paul drew a deep breath. 'But anyway . . . that's the size of it, Elizabeth. And I'm sorry for disturbing your rest, but I wasn't going to tell you all this in front of that – that fellow Aske – '

'That "wanker" Aske?' It was better to smile than to cry: that was the lesson she must learn from his charade, for the future. 'He can't help being what he is, Paul.'

He stood up, carefully adjusting his dressing-gown. 'Just leave me my irrational prejudices intact, Miss Loftus dear. I have problems enough without that.'

'What are you going to do about it?' The cold was in her voice – she could hear it.

'Why – nothing, of course.' He stared at her. 'I mean, Del Andrew will put in his report to Jack Butler. But it isn't any of our business . . . and Jack Butler's not that sort of chap, I mean . . . And we had a deal, I seem to recall, eh?'

Prize-money, remembered Elizabeth. Father had lived in the wrong century for that, just as he had missed out on the battle-squadrons of dreadnoughts. But he had managed the next best thing with the Varney jewellery which should have been hers.

'You shouldn't think too badly of him, Elizabeth,' said Paul. 'He may have spent a fair bit of it, but he also put plenty away for you – tax-free, remember.'

But Elizabeth was remembering other things – the penny-pinching on the laundry, and the unpaid secretarial work. And what had nearly happened to her –

She sat up straighter in bed. 'Why did he tell that story about the *Vengeful*?'

'Maybe he didn't.' Paul shook his head. 'Maybe he just talked about the *Vengeful* research to Lippy, and Lippy spun the yarn on his own initiative.'

'Why should he do that?'

'Well . . . Del Andrew thinks Ray Tuck's eyes – and ears – were bigger than his stomach. He could have heard something or seen something – Lippy was getting sicker, so Ray Tuck was doing more of the leg-work around his place, and he could have heard something one day . . . And as Lippy didn't trust him he wouldn't have wanted him to believe that the Captain was sitting right on top of a lot of loot here in England – *there* in England – he made up this yarn about treasure to put him off the scent.'

Elizabeth almost smiled through her heart-ache: it was strange to hear Del Andrew speaking out of Paul's mouth, word for word.

'Don't go, Paul!' She had tried to throw her bonnet over the windmill, only to have it blown back into her face. But now she was desperately awake – and even more desperately lonely. 'Sit down, please – *please!*'

He sat down unwillingly. 'What can I do for you?'

What indeed! The rich woman had to think – and that was another lesson, to be learnt as she went along.

'You said . . . Danny Kahn doesn't matter – ?'

'Oh . . . Del Andrew will get Danny Kahn – don't you worry about him!'

'So what does matter?' Desperation honed up her wits to a razor edge. 'What – what on earth was there on board the *Vengeful*, that Colonel Suchet wanted so badly?'

For a moment he didn't reply – he was staring fixedly at the low frills on Madame Hortense's nightie. Then he shook his head and concentrated on her.

'Ah . . . well, that may not prove such an overwhelming mystery, Bertrand thinks – he was the first one I phoned after dinner.' He smiled at her a little ruefully. 'Contacts again, Elizabeth: it seems that Bertrand put his friend's colleague on his mettle – the one who knows all about Napoleon's times. Experts like demonstrating their expertise, I know the feeling all too well, it's quite irresistible . . . Apart from which, Bertrand shrewdly suspects, the mysterious Colonel Suchet sounds interesting in his own right – and I know *that* feeling, too.'

But if he knew it he wasn't demonstrating it now, as he had done at Coucy-le-Château, Elizabeth observed: if anything, he looked tired and rather worried, and somehow younger because of that, not older.

'The long and short of which is that we have a name and an address in Paris – and an appointment for 11 o'clock: Professor Louis Belperron, of the Sorbonne, editor of the *Annales historiques de l'Empire*, and author of books too numerous to mention – not to add innumerable contributions to the *Revue des études napoléoniennes*, and so on and so forth.'

'Paul, that's wonderful – ' Only his lugubrious expression cautioned her. ' – isn't it?'

'Yes. It's wonderful.' Whatever it was, said his face, it wasn't wonderful.

'Then . . . what's the matter?'

'The matter, Elizabeth . . . is that I spoke to David Audley last of all, after Bertrand and Del Andrew . . . that's the matter.'

Elizabeth frowned. 'But why . . . ? Doesn't he want us to see . . . Professor Belperron?' A spark of anger kindled suddenly on Paul's behalf. 'Isn't he pleased with you – with us?'

'Pleased? No, he's not pleased – he's bloody *delighted*! He's so damn pleased he's busy galvanizing his Professor Wilder on the *Vengeful* back in England . . . and probably half the research section as well, for all I know.' He drew a deep breath. 'He's so pleased that I've got to send Aske to Charles de Gaulle Airport tomorrow afternoon to collect him, so he can tell us in person how pleased he is . . . among other things.'

'He's coming to France?'

'And then we're all going on a jaunt to Lautenbourg – "Tell Aske to book rooms in a Michelin-recommended hotel – somewhere where the food's good" . . . sweet Jesus Christ! Where the food's good!'

In any other circumstances the prospect of actually visiting the scene of the great escape would have over-joyed her, but Paul's misery was infectious. 'That's bad, is it?'

'Yes, it's bad.' He fell silent for a moment. 'You don't know David Audley as I do.'

He made the prospect of Audley daunting. And yet at the same time the memory of the big man, with his strange handsome-ugly face and rough-gentle manner, excited her intensely: wherever Audley was, that would be the centre of things and the answers would be there.

'I know he likes you, Paul.' She tried to reassure him and to make amends for her treachery. 'In fact, I think he's fond of you, even.'

For an instant he stared at her incredulously, and then his expression blanked out; and she knew, but too late, that she'd said exactly the wrong thing.

193

'If I may say so, Elizabeth . . . that's a damn silly remark – '

'I mean – I meant, he *respects* you – '

'I don't care if he worships the ground I tread on.' He bulldozed over her. 'What *I* mean is what I said last night, only more so: I think the Russians are making a fool of him. The difference is that *now* I'm not just guessing. Because now the evidence points that way.'

'What evidence?'

'What evidence . . .' He got up, and walked round the end of the bed towards the open window. And then stopped suddenly. 'Put the light out, Elizabeth.'

She fumbled for the switch. 'What is it, Paul?'

'Nothing. Just a precaution.' He waited, and she guessed that he was accustoming his eyes to the darkness. 'In the field you take precautions, that's all. And this is the field, Elizabeth – "some foreign field" . . . but that's not what I intend it to be, for either of us . . . so, as of now, we take the proper precautions – okay? I should have done it before . . . I'm getting careless, like Novikov . . . or maybe not like Novikov . . .'

'Yes, Paul.' Excitement was only a thin skin on top of fear, she realized: 'the field' was no more than an abbreviation of 'the battlefield', where men died.

'What evidence.' He was a silhouette against a skyline faintly lightened by the illumination of the old city. 'It was always on the cards that they'd stage a diversion of some kind. What I don't know is whether you were planned to be that diversion, or whether they're bright enough – and quick enough – to take advantage of you when you turned up out of the blue . . . I just don't know . . .'

He was speaking as much to himself as to her, and she didn't dare disturb his line of thought. Because this was something she'd never seen before – never heard, never even remotely imagined: this was a man struggling with a problem which involved not only his comfort, or his business – his job, his livelihood, his income . . . even the security of his country, which he was paid to safeguard – but *his life* –

And her life too?

'If there was a Russian Audley running the operation I'd guess this is pure opportunism – that they didn't know about you, but you fitted the bill so perfectly that they dropped everything else in preference for you – in preference for the old *Vengeful*.'

It was strange, but she wasn't cold any more. The thought of Father, and what he had done, had chilled her; but now she was aware of the warm darkness all around her, and of the slightest prickle of sweat at her throat.

The silhouette changed, and she was aware that he had turned back inwards to face her. 'Guessing isn't evidence – if that's what you are about to say – I'm aware of that. But I'm not guessing when I say they have Audley-*watchers* over there, on the other side. I could even give you a name – the name of one of them whom we know about, if it would mean anything to you. And he's a scholar, like Audley . . . an archaeologist, not an historian, but a Russian Audley, all the same.' He nodded at her. 'He'd know very well how obsessed David is with the past. And if he knows Audley's in charge on this side . . . and that's a reasonable assumption by now . . . then the evidence starts to pile up.'

She wanted to say *What evidence?* again, but instinct ruled against it.

'Contemporaneity, Elizabeth – that's the first piece: unconnected things which happen at the same time, and then influence each other. Your father died . . . and Lippy died – and they were both old men, so that wasn't out of the ordinary . . . And Ray Tuck was in trouble, and Danny Kahn was greedy – that's nothing special, either. But all those were *your* contemporaneous events, not ours, do you see?'

Instinct still silenced her.

'Your *Vengeful*, let's say . . . But there was also *our*

195

Vengeful – or what David Audley made of our "Vengeful" – really *their* "Project Vengeful", which I'm inclined to think now has nothing to do with yours, Elizabeth. Nothing whatsoever.'

Instinct snapped. 'But, Paul, if – '

'He made a mistake – ' he overrode her ' – or, not quite a mistake . . . He wanted this job for himself so badly . . . or he didn't want someone else to get it . . . that he used your *Vengeful* to get it.' The silhouette nodded at her again. 'And maybe it was that someone else who put out the word that the great David Audley was at work – ' shrug ' – or maybe I'm doing *him* an injustice . . . maybe the Russians spotted me sniffing about – that's probably more like it. Because if I've added up two and two correctly I'm the one who hasn't been so clever. And that's what worries me, Elizabeth dear – if this is going wrong, then I'm to blame too. And I've got enough on my conscience already . . . like, sometimes I feel too much like the Angel of Death flying over the battlefield – '

'*Paul!*' His voice had become too elaborately casual for conviction when she could sense the mixture of fear and guilt emanating from him. 'If what you say is true – what about that Russian who was watching me?'

'Novikov?' The voice cracked. 'Elizabeth – Novikov is the best bit of evidence of all! Novikov is a pro – a top-flight pro!'

'Yes? So what, Paul? You spotted him – '

'I spotted him? Damn it, Elizabeth – even *you* spotted him! Doesn't that tell you anything? Christ! Do you remember when that little bugger Aske said "No one follows me when I don't want him to", or something like? Do you think anyone spots Aske on his tail when he doesn't want him to?' Paul momentarily lost his cool. 'Christ, Elizabeth! Novikov's ten times the man Aske will ever be – if he didn't want to be seen, neither of us would have seen him, don't you understand?'

This time it was the mixture of his anger and his self-contempt which silenced her.

'He followed *me*, Elizabeth – and I didn't see him, because he's better than me. But then he let me see him – and from that moment the old *Vengeful* was afloat again, with a vengeance – can you at least understand *that*? David Audley may have baited the hook himself, but it was Novikov who made the sinker bob up and down – and we all swallowed it, hook, line and sinker. And now it's stuck in my throat, and I can't bloody well dislodge it – that's what I'm saying!'

She could see most of it at last; part of it darkly, or indistinctly, because it was out of her experience; she could see the loom of it through the half-light and the mist, like some great three-decker bearing down on her with its gun-ports open and its guns run out and double-shotted, ready to blow her out of the water with one broadside.

'But . . . But haven't you told David Audley all this, Paul?'

'Oh . . . I've told him, Elizabeth – I've told him!' He paused. 'I told him last night, when I was guessing – remember? – and he told me to obey orders – remember?' Another pause. 'And I told him tonight, too . . . And he pulled rank on me – he told me to do my *effing* duty – and David only swears like that when he intends to, when he doesn't want any argument, and there isn't going to be any argument . . . But what I ought to be doing is pulling you out of here tonight, and running like hell for safety – that's what I ought to be doing! Because there's been something wrong with this operation from the start. And I don't like it.'

His vehemence frightened her into silence.

'Because if I'm right the Russians will be doing something pretty soon – something to make us believe we're on the right track, to confirm what Novikov did – anything to keep us from looking in the right direction . . . That's

197

why you must keep your door locked, Elizabeth – do you see?'

Now she wasn't merely warm, with that delicate trickle at her throat: she was clammy with his fear, which was more infectious than his unhappiness.

'Have you told this to Humphrey Aske, Paul?'

He drew in a breath. 'I haven't told him that I think David Audley's making a fool of himself – and us . . . if that's what you mean. But I've put him on second watch, keeping an eye on your door and mine from three-thirty onwards. And it's "Stand-to" for both of us at seven – ' his voice rearranged itself as he spoke, as though he had belatedly realized the effect he was having on her ' – don't worry, dear – we'll watch over you between us. You can sleep soundly tonight.'

That was one thing she wouldn't be doing. But now everything was unreal, and the prospect of what sleep might bring was as scary as not-sleeping.

'I'll go, then.' The silhouette moved from the frame of the window into darkness.

'No!' The thought of being alone panicked her.

'You'll be quite safe. We'll be watching – I told you.'

'No.' She could see the outline of him clearly, dark against almost-dark, at the end of the bed. 'Don't go.'

Silence.

'Very well. I'll stay here . . . there's a chair here somewhere – ' the darker outline moved as he felt around blindly ' – you go to sleep, Elizabeth.'

'No – I didn't mean that – ' But what did she mean? And if he did stay she would snore, and he would hear her snore ' – I mean . . . couldn't you be wrong, Paul?' But that wasn't what she meant, either: the truth was that she didn't know what she meant. 'I mean . . . David Audley said there wouldn't be any danger – that we would be safe over here, in France – ?'

'Yes.' He bumped the end of the bed, and the tremor ran through her. 'Yes, he said that, Elizabeth.'

198

She simply didn't want him to go, that was it: she was lonely, more than afraid, and she didn't want to be alone, as she had always been. That was it.

'So you could be wrong.' She didn't want him to go, and she didn't want him to sit down in the darkness in the corner of the room, and she didn't want him to stand up like Death at the end of her bed.

'Yes, I could be wrong.' He sounded far away. 'I've been wrong before – yes . . .'

He had been wrong before – but that wasn't what he meant now, his voice said.

'I was wrong once before, Elizabeth.' Just in time he saved her from saying something pointless. 'There was this girl I knew – woman, rather . . . *colleague*, rather – Frances was her name, and she was damn good . . . in fact, she was better than Novikov and Aske and me rolled into one – she was *good* . . . and pretty as a picture with it, and I adored her, Elizabeth.'

The darkness shivered between them.

'Which is dead against the rules – and against all common sense as well, which is what rules are all about: "gladiator, make no friends of gladiators" is the rule – and it's a good rule.'

She saw now why he had reacted against what she had said about David Audley's feeling for him.

'She didn't know, of course. Nobody knew . . . *She* didn't know, and *they* didn't know . . . because everything I ever said to her was the wrong thing to say – and it was . . . like, I was always trying to jump into bed with her . . . and I *was*, too – I couldn't think of anything cleverer to do, I suppose – and she couldn't stand the sight of me.'

Silence.

'But I could stand the sight of her – any time.'

Silence.

'So one day I looked at her. It was raining – and I was glad to see her . . . So I looked at her, Elizabeth, when I should have been looking somewhere else.'

199

Silence.

'And that was a mistake, Elizabeth. And she died of my mistake . . . in the rain, in my arms, Elizabeth.'

It was very strange, but only for one fraction of a second was she sorry for poor dead Frances. Because poor dead *pretty* Frances was still her enemy, and if ever there was a moment for defeating her enemy *it was now* – when the dark was her ally.

'Paul – please come in with me,' she whispered. 'I'm so frightened.'

11

Everything was just fine until Humphrey Aske turned on the car radio for no apparent reason, and then refused to turn it off, and finally started to talk nonsense. And –

'Yes,' he said finally. 'I think the great Dr Audley may have been careless somewhere along the line.'

'What do you mean, Mr Aske?' asked Elizabeth.

'I mean, Miss Loftus, that we're being followed,' said Humphrey Aske.

Actually everything hadn't been altogether fine even before, not really. But everything had been different; or, if not exactly recognizably different, at least not quite the same because she felt it had no right to be as it had been before.

Although *actually* . . . but then it might just have been the presence of Humphrey Aske at the breakfast table with them which had spoilt everything – and an unbearably bright and talkative Humphrey Aske, not in the least blear-eyed from night-watch – even, it was Aske who behaved as she so desperately wanted Paul to behave, noticing and complimenting her on the second of her elegant summer travelling suits, which Paul had studiously ignored in preference for one quick glance, which had almost been a stranger's frown, at her face.

And there, she had to admit to the mirror already, the wear and tear of the last almost-24-hours had done Monsieur Pierre's original work of art no good at all, which she had lacked the expertise to restore as it had been: what she had seen in the mirror was the truth of the fairy story, she had realized now – that Prince Charming simply hadn't recognized Cinderella the morning after, it had only been the size of her foot for the glass slipper which had identified that happy ending.

'Paris – no problem,' said Aske to Mitchell. 'There's hardly any mist this morning. I filled the car up last night, before I went to bed. Straight down the N2, through Soissons – the last bit's motorway, and we can whip round the *périphérique* and come off at the Pointe d'Asnières for the Avenue de Wagram – no trouble at all.' He smiled at Elizabeth. 'Be there in time for coffee, then M'sieur Bourienne's professor . . . then a nice elongated lunch at a little place I wot of . . . then the airport and the great Dr Audley himself . . . Then another motorway, with the foot down on the pedal, and supper in Alsace, Miss Loftus. *No problem!*'

On Paul Mitchell's face, Elizabeth observed out of the most oblique corner of her eye, there was a look of the purest hatred.

'What one *would* like to know – ' either Aske couldn't or wouldn't observe the same storm warning ' – *is* . . . if the great Dr Audley is coming to take the reins from your capable hands, Mitchell . . . which means that we are on to something highly promising . . . is – what is it? Isn't it time now that one was told why one may be required to do and die?'

It occurred to Elizabeth that, after the events of the last three days since the church fête, and more particularly after the events of last night which were already beginning to become unreal, she had some rights. So, just as Paul's mouth opened in a snarl, she kicked him hard on the ankle.

'Fff-aargh!' exclaimed Paul.

Aske looked at him curiously. 'I beg your pardon?'

'I'm not sure that Dr Mitchell knows any more than we do, Mr Aske,' said Elizabeth.

Humphrey Aske transferred his curiosity to her. 'Ah . . . now *that* hadn't occurred to me, you know – '

Paul grunted explosively. 'The fact is, Aske . . . I'm

202

not permitted to tell either you or Miss Loftus everything that's going on – for obvious reasons, which you should understand better than she does.'

What Miss Loftus understood, thought Elizabeth, was that Paul Mitchell was never going to admit to Humphrey Aske that he didn't know what he was really doing, and didn't like it either.

'But if David Audley wants you to do and die . . .' Paul reached down to rub his ankle '. . . I'm sure he'll tell you.' He straightened up. 'If it suits him.'

'Which it probably won't – I know!' Aske shook his head ruefully at Elizabeth. 'The occupational temptation of our profession, Miss Loftus, is to confuse essential secrecy with inessential secretiveness . . . with the predictable result that the left hand rarely knows what the right hand is doing. But a trip to Paris is better than nothing, I suppose.' He smiled suddenly and disarmingly at her again. 'We must just hope that the great Dr Audley is right, and we aren't simply wasting our time, however agreeably!'

She couldn't kick Paul again – she kicked him a bit too hard the first time. All she could do was smile and nod, and hope for the best.

And the best was that Paul drank his coffee, and pushed back from the table. 'If you're packed up, Elizabeth, then let's go,' he said. 'Get the car, Aske.'

But Aske, once he had manoeuvred them through the narrow streets of the old city, and round its descending hairpin bends, was still hell-bent on needling Paul into talking, even if his undeterred approach to the problem was as tortuous as their departure from Laon –

'I'll book the hotel when we get to Paris,' he began innocently.

Paul grunted.

'In Lautenbourg? Or will nearby do?'

'Suit yourself.'

'There's a place about ten kilometres away that does *glâce au miel de sapin*, according to the Michelin.'

No reply.

'How many rooms shall I reserve?'

'What?' the question caught Paul unguarded. 'What the hell d'you mean – how many rooms?'

'Don't take on so! Is Audley coming alone?'

Paul subsided. 'Yes . . . alone.'

'Four rooms then. And for how long?' Aske probed gently. 'And where after that?'

Again Paul didn't reply, and Elizabeth knew that this approach wasn't going to work either. All it would produce was another explosion.

'We are retracing the escape route between Lautenbourg and Coucy-le-Château, I take it?' persisted Aske.

There was only one way to defuse Paul, and she had to risk it. 'We do actually know the route then, Paul? Would that be from Father's notes or from Tom Chard's story?'

He drew a breath. 'A bit of both, actually. We've traced three places where he stayed, and they fit in well enough with Chard's account.'

'Yes, but – ' began Aske.

'Father got it right, did he?' Elizabeth blotted out Aske deliberately.

'Oh yes . . .' Paul gave her an uncharacteristically shy look '. . . he got it right. He was slow . . . and he let himself be side-tracked into investigating Abraham Timms, the quartermaster's mate, when he should have been concentrating on Colonel Suchet. But he was right.' He paused. 'And, to be fair, Abraham Timms sounds an interesting character.'

'Yes?' She didn't want Aske to break in.

'But then they were all interesting characters – '

'Hold on a moment,' said Aske. 'I want to pull in here.'

The signs of a garage came into view suddenly.

'You said you'd filled up last night,' accused Paul.

'Yes.' Aske unstrapped himself. 'Won't be a moment.'

The bonnet went up, and Paul fumed silently until Aske came back.

'All interesting characters, you were saying?' Elizabeth stepped between them again as the car pulled on to the road.

'Chipperfield was a natural born escaper – he thought one jump ahead all the time, it looks like, reading between the lines.'

'How – one jump ahead?'

'Well . . . first, he reckoned there'd be a big search, with all the stops pulled out – this is drawing conclusions from what Tom Chard remembered. And he did exactly the right thing, so our experts say.'

'What was that?'

'He had four or five hours' start, until daylight. They could have made five or ten miles before they had to go to ground. So if Suchet knew his business, he'd draw a ring round the fortress, maybe ten to fifteen miles out, and move in from there. Can't you go faster than this, Aske?'

'This is fast enough. So what did Chipperfield do?'

Paul sniffed. 'He went to ground in a vineyard half a mile from the fortress. They had scraps of food they'd hoarded, and four bottles of water, and they stayed put there for three days and two nights, not moving.'

'Ah! I like that,' murmured Aske.' So the ring moved in for the first day – but after that it would move out, on the assumption they'd broken through? Is that it? And then, of course, he'd keep inside the ring, never trying to break through it as it expanded? That's good thinking.' He half-turned towards Paul. 'And then what?'

'He moved in the least expected direction – southwards.'

'And why was that unexpected?'

'The obvious direction was east – across the Rhine into Germany. That was the way many of the escapers went from the other fortresses, because they reckoned the Germans wouldn't give them up so easily. And the most direct route to England was north-west – or they could have headed due north, and then turned west when they reached the Low Countries.'

'So they went southwards. And you think that was deliberate?' Aske sounded unconvinced.

'They were sailors, Mr Aske.' Elizabeth could see that Paul chafed under Aske's interruptions. 'They would always have known the points of the compass, with the sun or the stars overhead.'

Paul nodded. 'That's exactly right, Elizabeth. Chipperfield and Timms were both professional navigators. And all Tom Chard's recollections of their route are full of bearings and distances, as well as descriptions . . . like "we bore southward that day five leagues, which, for nature of that country, was very wearisome by reason of the steepness of its many hills and valleys".'

Aske considered the evidence briefly. 'So that would mean they were in the Vosges, would it?'

'The Upper Vosges. "Great trees, tall and straight, enough to spar mighty navies" is how Tom Chard remembered it – and the humming of the insects up above in the tree-tops, and the crickets in the high pastures . . . and the goats with bells round their necks – Chard was country-bred, and he noticed all the differences between Sussex and Alsace. Although in fact he was much more surprised by the presence of familiar things from home – the jays and the magpies and the robins, and the cranesbill and harebells and foxgloves . . . *and* the rose-bay willow herb, which tipped off your father about Abraham Timms, Elizabeth.'

'Tipped him off . . . to what?'

'That Abraham Timms was country-bred like Tom Chard, only much better educated – Chard said he knew the name of everything that lived, and what was edible and what wasn't . . . It's even possible that Chipperfield took Timms along because he knew how to live off the country. But most of all that he was an American.'

'An American?' Aske pursed his lips, and then nodded. 'Yes . . . well, there were a lot of Americans pressed into the Royal Navy – that was why they went to war with us. But where does the willow herb come in?'

'Which in his country was called by the savages "Fire-weed", according to Chard. "His country" and "savages" and "fire-weed" was what tipped Loftus off – not only that Timms was country-bred, but it was a *different* country. And the clincher that he was an American was when the waggon wheel broke, and Timms had to find wood to repair it – '

'What waggon wheel?' Elizabeth frowned.

'What waggon?' echoed Aske.

'The waggon in which they crossed half of France,' said Paul. 'They came down out of the Vosges somewhere near Gérardmer, so far as we can estimate. And first they bought a horse – Chipperfield had money. Tom Chard doesn't say how, but he had it – '

'PoWs always have money,' murmured Aske. 'And they often let the officers keep their personal possessions. Go on.'

'Then, a bit further on, they bought a farm cart. And a day later they filled the cart with hay, and Chard and Timms hid under the hay whenever they came near a village, because they couldn't speak a word of French.'

'Nice – very nice!' said Aske admiringly. 'Nothing stolen – so no hue and cry . . . and nobody suspects a couple of farm labourers with a hay cart when the word's out for four desperate characters! I like it.'

'Not even a couple of farm labourers,' said Paul. 'Chipperfield was smarter than that, Aske.'

'Yes? I'm going to stop again soon – at that garage in the distance. So just sit tight.' Aske slowed the car. 'A man and a boy, of course, I'd forgotten the little mid-ship-mite – '

'What?' Paul sat up irritably. 'For Christ's sake, Aske – what are you playing at?'

'It's like yesterday, old boy. You are doing the talking and I'm doing the driving – okay?'

The previous halt was repeated, with the additional detail of a few litres of petrol to top up the tank.

'Off we go again – just let me do up my seat-belt,' said Aske. 'So . . . the little mid-ship-mite, and the waggon, and the mysterious Timms . . . who was an American cousin far from home, eh?'

'What the hell's wrong with the car?'

'Nothing that need worry you, Dr Mitchell . . . A man and a boy, you were saying?'

The air, which had warmed up during their five-minute delay, crackled between them in the ensuing silence, and Elizabeth looked at Paul unhappily. 'A man and a boy, Paul?'

With an effort Paul tore himself away from Aske. 'Not a man and a boy, Elizabeth,' he addressed her deliberately. 'Don't you remember?'

It came to her then, suddenly but quite easily, out of nowhere . . . no, not out of nowhere – out of the far distant memory of an owl flapping noiselessly across a college garden unreasonably disturbed by strange lights and stranger noises, disappearing into the darkness.

It had been a weird open-air production, by some smart undergraduate who had gone on from Oxford to great things in television – *A Midsummer Night's Dream,* with Titania and Hippolyta and Hermia and Helena all cast from the sixth form of a local prep school –

'The girl, of course.' It was simple when you knew the answer. 'They dressed the midshipman as a girl.'

'Of course!' Humphrey Aske chided himself. 'Thirteen years of age, so the childish treble . . . or that delicious half-broken husky alto – no wonder no one spotted them! *Clever* Miss Loftus!'

'Clever Lieutenant Chipperfield, rather.' She could see that Paul was pleased with her, so this was the moment for becoming modesty. 'But he died at Coucy, Paul – how?'

'Just damned bad luck, that's how, Elizabeth.' His pleasure turned instantly to Chipperfield – identifying regret. 'The cart broke down at Coucy, and they tried to repair it with what they could scrounge. But while they were working on it there was an accident of some kind . . . Tom Chard's a bit vague about what actually happened, but it looks as though something gave way, and Chipperfield was crushed underneath . . .' he trailed off for a moment '. . . not killed, but very badly injured. Fatally injured, as it turned out . . . which is . . . rather sad, when you think about it.'

He was no longer looking at her, but just staring into space as though he could see pictures inside his head.

And that, thought Elizabeth, was what he *was* seeing: *rather sad* concealed the same insight which had informed his account of the last efforts of the British and German soldiers locked in mud and exhaustion on the muddy slopes above the Aisne – he had been there with them in their embryonic trenches, just as he was there now, dying by inches under the cart at Coucy-le-Château.

All those years ago, and long forgotten, it had been first relegated to one old man's memories, and to a few pages in a commonplace book which had become an old lady's family heirloom until Father's letter in *The Times* had re-animated it. But once it had been a Great Adventure until *rather sad* – she could almost love Paul for that under-statement of the unendurable truth it concealed: that this almost anonymous third lieutenant of the *Vengeful* had brought his comrades so far, in safety against all the odds, with pursuit long out-distanced, only to die slowly and painfully by cruel accident almost within sight of home.

'So what did Chard actually say, then?' Aske was quite oblivious to *rather sad*.

'Oh . . . he was still angry after all those years about the cart breaking down that second time.' Paul snapped himself back to reality. 'He said, if they'd used seasoned ash instead of green elm it would have been okay, and

209

Abraham Timms said that in his country there'd have been plenty of hickory-wood for the taking, which would have been even better – that was what Chard thought was interesting, because that was what he remembered all those years after.' He lòoked at Elizabeth, seeing her again. 'Which was all quite meaningless until your father saw it, and after "fire-weed" *hickory* was the clincher – and our experts zeroed in on it too . . . because hickory is the American equivalent for ash – "*Carya ovata,* or *Carya cordiformis*, which is frequently confused with walnut, was rare in Europe in the early nineteenth century, but common in North America, from New York State to Florida".' He smiled lop-sidedly at her. 'When you spend most of your time interpreting security tip-offs and Russian tit-bits a query about the origin of hickory-wood is like a breath of fresh air . . . But that's where your father picked up his final American clue – and why he went off at half-cock, following Abraham Timms for so long, instead of Colonel Suchet . . . not that Timms isn't a fascinating character, as I said.'

'What's so fascinating about him?' inquired Aske.

Paul shook his head. 'He doesn't really matter. It's Suchet who matters . . . all that matters about Timms – and Tom Chard – is that they had to bodge up the cart with inferior material, and it broke again while Chipperfield was underneath. And that was still bugging Tom Chard twenty-five years after – I think he felt that somehow he'd been responsible for his officer's death. He was a good man, was Tom Chard.'

'But not quite good enough,' murmured Aske, reaching down towards the dashboard. 'Let's have some music.'

Elizabeth had just started to think *but what happened next? Because if Tom Chard came safe home, what happened to* – and then a sudden burst of pop music drowned her thoughts.

'For God's sake, man – ' Mitchell leaned forward towards the radio.

'No!' Aske restrained him. 'Leave it on, Mitchell – not quite good enough – and we're not quite good enough either, it seems, old boy. Because we've got a tail.'

'What – '

'Don't turn round! Yes . . . I think the great Dr Audley may have been careless somewhere along the line.'

'What do you mean, Mr Aske?' asked Elizabeth.

'I mean, Miss Loftus, that we're being followed,' said Aske calmly. 'And don't you look round, either – and don't shout – I can see behind us perfectly well, and I can hear you well enough . . . The music's just in case they've got us bugged as well as bracketed . . . and there is still just a chance, with that and all the rigmarole I've been through, that they may not be quite sure I'm on to them – just a chance.' He looked at Paul. 'Well, Mitchell? What is your pleasure, then?'

Paul thought for a moment. 'What sort of a tail?'

'Ah . . . now as to origin, I cannot tell you, except that it is undoubtedly professional, as one would expect – never right behind us, in clear view . . . But as to content, that's easier, because they had to turn off after passing us when I stopped, and pick us up again when we continued . . . and then one had to overtake us – he's in front now – just to make sure we hadn't switched cars, or anything tricky like that.' He paused, and then half-turned towards Elizabeth. 'I had this feeling, you see, Miss Loftus, not long after we left Laon . . . this pricking in the back of the neck . . . that we were not *altogether* alone. But I couldn't be sure, not until now.'

'What sort of tail?' repeated Paul. 'What vehicles?'

'One Renault 20 saloon, blue, with driver and passenger. And one unmarked Citroen van, grey, with driver only. Though what's behind the driver – what wealth of ingenious gadgetry – I also cannot tell, of course . . . Hence the disgusting French equivalent of the Top of the Pops, Miss Loftus – just in case.'

Paul leaned closer to Elizabeth. 'He means we could be

bugged – with a voice pick-up as well as a directional indicator . . . *Damn!*' He turned back to Aske. 'Didn't you check out the bloody car?'

Aske sighed. 'Don't be silly, old boy. If these are pros I could strip it down, and still not find anything – you know that.'

'Damn!' murmured Paul. 'Damn, damn, damn!'

'I admit I maybe didn't take things quite seriously enough,' conceded Aske. 'But then we haven't been doing anything terribly serious, have we?'

'Damn!' said Paul again.

'Don't fret, old boy. This is what I'm here for – to keep you safe and sound. So long as they don't try anything crude we're in no danger . . . and with all this traffic around us I can't think that they have that in mind. And I'm sure I'm a *much* better driver than either of them . . . There's a passenger seat-belt in the back, Miss Loftus – put it on, please . . . Just in case . . . though one should always wear one's belt, in *any* case, of course.'

'Can you lose them?' asked Paul.

'Yes.' Aske leaned forward again. 'I think we'll have a *leetle* more background noise . . . Yes . . . But not here.'

'Where then?'

'Oh, Paris is the place. Lots of nice fast traffic, lots of different lanes . . . They have us boxed in, so I shall lose them on the *périphérique* – the one in front at the Saint Ouen intersection, or at Clignancourt . . . and then I'll get the one behind into the wrong lane just before Clichy, and I'll slip out there. We'll need a little luck, but not a lot.'

Elizabeth began to feel almost reassured.

'I can only give you a few minutes, though,' went on Aske smoothly. 'Because if they know their business – if there's a directional bug in this car, which I assume there is – they'll be on to us again quick enough . . . and if

212

they've got more back-up waiting for us, that could be awkward . . . You can never be absolutely sure of losing a well-organized tail – I know, because I've outsmarted my Bulgarian friends more than once . . . But I can put you down round a corner near the Avenue de Wagram, and then I can ditch the car further on . . . So not to worry, eh?' Aske checked his mirror. 'Here he comes now, tucking himself nicely behind that Saab . . .'

Elizabeth fought the desire to look over her shoulder. 'Who are they, Paul?'

. 'Ah . . . now that's the interesting question, Miss Loftus,' said Aske. 'But it can hardly be the French just watching over us, I'm afraid.'

'Why not?'

'What have we done to annoy them?' Aske's shoulders lifted. 'Nothing, so far as I am aware – certainly nothing to justify this VIP treatment . . . even if our Dr Mitchell has something of a record . . . No – if they didn't like us they'd simply pick us up and boot us out, without much ceremony. That's more their style, you see.'

'It could be the French, Elizabeth,' said Paul.

Aske snuffled. 'You're making pretty pictures, Mitchell. Pretty pictures to suit yourself – what they tell us never to do!'

'Pretty pictures, Mr Aske?'

'That's right.' Aske nodded at the road. 'To be spotted by the French – that's just bad luck . . . But to be picked up by the KGB . . .' He shook his head sadly '. . . that's both good and bad, I suppose.'

Elizabeth couldn't for the life of her see how being pursued by the KGB could be good.

'Shut up, Aske!' snapped Paul.

· 'She has a right to know, old boy. It's *bad*, Miss Loftus, because it means our security is bad – or because theirs is too damn good, alternatively . . . But it's also good, because it means that we've got the swine worried enough to take all this trouble – which means that Audley knows

213

what he's doing, however odd it may seem to us.' He turned to Paul. 'So do tell us what happened next in 1812, Dr Mitchell – do tell us more about the old *Vengeful* and All That – '

12

The weight of scholarship surrounding them in the ante-room to Professor Louis Belperron's study was at once reassuring and oppressive: the room was high-ceilinged, almost a square box, and every inch of it not taken by its two doors and single window consisted of shelving cram-med with old books. And from these, in the absence of the slightest breath of fresh air, there emanated a dry smell of old paper, ancient leather and glue, and of the dust of ages which had gathered on that combination.

'Well, if Professor Belperron doesn't know about Col-onel Suchet, then no one does,' concluded Paul from his reconnaissance of the shelves.

Elizabeth stared out of the window, down into the bustling avenue below. The contrast of that bustle, after their dodge'em car drive through the maelstrom of the peripheral motorway, and their final rush from the car into this old apartment building, with this sudden peace and quiet . . . that contrast ought, she felt, to be calming, but somehow it wasn't – it was more like the uncalm stillness of an examination room before the exam.

'Can you see Aske?' asked Paul.

'No.' It didn't seem likely to her that she would be able to spot Humphrey Aske in that throng, but the unlikely gave her the lie even as she spoke. 'Yes.'

'Where?' He craned his neck over her shoulder.

'Down by the corner of that side-street.' Perhaps it was because, in all that movement, that one slender figure was unmoving at the apex of a corner-shop window – unmov-ing except for his head, as he switched his attention through the points of the compass.

'Well, at least he's keeping his wits about him,' said Paul ungraciously, turning away again.

Aske completed his survey, but instead of crossing towards the entrance into the building he then walked quickly a few yards up the street, to disappear under the awning of a café.

'He seems to do his job rather well,' said Elizabeth.

'Adequately, yes.' Paul was studying the shelves again.

'Even though you're horrible to him.'

'Hmmm . . .' He seemed more interested in the books. 'I cannot bring myself to love Mr Aske, certainly . . . or trust him either, come to that.' He lifted a volume out carefully, and blew the dust from it. 'And the prospect of travelling with him to Alsace, which could have been a pleasure . . . that frankly appals me, Elizabeth. And not least because he brings out the worst in me . . .' He opened the book. 'Which I would prefer you not to see.'

This, Elizabeth realized suddenly, was the first time they had been completely alone since last night – since last night a thousand years ago. And Aske hadn't reappeared yet.

'You mean . . . going to Alsace with me . . . you wouldn't have minded that?'

'Yes.' He closed the book, put it back, and selected another, not looking at her. 'I'd enjoy showing you the Lautenbourg. And I'd show you the battlefield at Le Linge, that's fascinating . . . And we could come back *via* Verdun, and the ossuary at Douaumont, and the woods at Mort Homme . . . and then I'd show you the Somme, and the canal at Bellenglise, where my grandfather was killed in 1918, with the glorious 46th Division – he commanded his battalion that day, September 29th . . . and Vimy Ridge, and Loos . . . you'd enjoy all of that, Elizabeth.'

Elizabeth looked at him in a state of emotion beyond surprise, almost into shock, at the prospect of being dragged from one hideous battlefield to the next – 'ossuary', if she had it right, was only one degree short of

216

'charnel house', or 'bone-yard' even . . . But he was quite oblivious of that; rather, he was probably doing her the greatest compliment he could think of in offering to share his obsession with her – *where my grandfather was killed in 1918* even . . . and Loos, so far as she could recall, was a miserable flat landscape of ugly mining villages pock-marked with old overgrown coal-tips, which he was offering to her like some fabulous beauty spot, the Lake District combined with Salzburg.

'I'd like that very much, Paul.' As she pronounced the lie, another shock hit her, crumbling her preconceptions into rubble: *that it wasn't a lie* – that she would willingly and happily tag along in his wake, learning why the 46th Division was so glorious, and admiring the dreariness of Loos – that if that was what turned him on, then it would damn well turn her on too. 'I'd like that.'

'Yes . . . well – ' He pushed the second book back in its slot ' – another time, maybe . . .' He selected another book.

'Yes – ' She mustn't sound too eager – not even when her instinct was to grasp that offer before it could blow away. 'Another time, of course.' But her desperation increased as she felt *another time, maybe* already receding into forgettable platitude.

He looked up from his book. 'But when David arrives maybe we can pack Aske back home . . . David is a different kettle of fish – he's even trickier, but he's family, in a way.' He grinned at her, half shyly. 'And . . . with David we wouldn't have to – ' he caught the next word before it could escape as one of the doors rattled and opened.

Aske's head came through the opening, followed by Aske himself. 'Pooh!' He sniffed the air critically.

Now she'd never know what *we wouldn't have to* . . . what? thought Elizabeth, swearing silent words she'd never spoken aloud. Explain? Worry about? Pretend? Sleep in separate rooms? It wasn't fair to blame Aske, but the not-knowing was painful.

'Where the hell have you been?' snapped Paul, as though he too had left out some unspoken oaths.

'I'm not late – it isn't eleven yet,' protested Aske, looking from one to the other of them. 'And, anyway . . . apart from tucking the car out of sight . . . I've been looking around, just in case. Watching your back, in fact.'

'Hmmm . . .' Paul controlled the worst in himself. 'Well?'

'We seem to have slipped our followers, at least for the time being. And no one's going to steal our baggage, that's for sure.' Aske smiled at Elizabeth.

'Why not?' asked Paul.

'Because it's parked behind a police car. Of which there are three in this vicinity. Perhaps they're expecting a smash-and-grab . . . Plain clothes, of course. But I can always smell a copper, they have an air of bored possession all of their own . . . But they'll serve to inhibit the opposition, if they do find the car.'

Paul regarded him with distaste. 'You still don't believe it could have been the French behind us?'

'More than ever, old boy.' Aske cocked an ear at faint sounds coming from behind the other door. 'If this stakeout is for us, then they already knew we were coming here, so there'd be no point in following us. Whereas those fellows who followed us so enthusiastically didn't know where – ' this time it was the click of the door handle which cut him off finally.

The gaunt woman who had shown them into the anteroom reappeared, opened her mouth to address Paul, but then saw Aske.

'M'sieur – ?' She looked from Aske to Paul.

'M'sieur is my . . .' Paul strangled on the admission '. . . my colleague.'

From the frigidity of their own welcome Elizabeth had already decided that the gaunt woman was the sort of secretary who regarded all strangers as intruders on her employer's privacy, and Humphrey Aske's standard nervous smile had no melting effect on her suspicious expression. But she held the door open for them nevertheless.

Elizabeth led the way, only to find herself in another ante-room, identically book-lined, but with a table and chairs. On the far side of the table, framed in another doorway, stood a small plump man, almost a miniature man, whose high bald head rose out of puffs of white hair above his ears.

'Professor Belperron – it's very good of you to give us your time,' said Paul deferentially.

'Dr Mitchell?' The Professor glanced down at the card Paul had given to the secretary.

'Yes. And this is Miss Elizabeth Loftus, daughter of the late Commander Loftus VC . . . and . . . Mr Humphrey Aske, of London University.'

The little man acknowledged them one by one. 'Come this way, please.'

The study was twice the size of the ante-rooms, and had twice as many books, together with all the paraphernalia of learning overflowing an immense desk on to the floor: papers and periodicals and books full of marking slips and box-files – Father's desk, in the high days of his writing, had been not unlike this, though on a much smaller scale. Behind the desk there was a high-backed chair, and in front of it were three ordinary chairs like those in the second ante-room, set precisely in a semi-circle as though waiting for them.

The little man walked round the desk, stepped on something which increased his height by several inches, and climbed into his chair. Although she couldn't see them, Elizabeth imagined his little legs swinging in mid-air.

He indicated the three chairs. 'Please . . .'

They sat down.

'The King's College, Oxford.' He put Paul's card on his blotter. 'I knew the late Master.'

219

'Sir Geoffrey Hobson?'

'It was during the war, in Normandy in 1944.' The little man picked out one of several pairs of spectacles from a small tray on his desk. 'He was in command of an armoured regiment.' He peered at Elizabeth through the spectacles, then selected another pair. 'Tilly-le-Bocage was the place, and he was *Colonel* Hobson then.' The second pair seemed to suit him better. 'But it is Colonel Suchet in whom we are interested now.'

'Yes.' Paul leaned forward. 'Perhaps I should explain – '

'Please! The circumstances have been explained to me: there is a book almost completed, but now there is fresh material – yes? And it is this material which has led you to Jean-Baptiste Suchet?'

'Yes.' Paul sat back. 'Or, to be more exact, our material concerns a party of British PoW escapers. Suchet interrogated them before they escaped, and he was still chasing them two months later, so it seems.'

Aske stirred. 'Which would make him either a superior variety of policeman or an intelligence officer of some sort, we think.'

'No.' The Professor shook his head. 'At least, not in the Abwehr or Gestapo sense . . . He was a gallant soldier – indeed, he was an escaped prisoner himself, and a most daring one. Twice he escaped, once from Chel-ten-ham, but unsuccessfully – '

'Cheltenham?' Paul looked at Aske.

'He broke his parole, that means,' murmured Aske. 'French officer prisoners were always paroled.' He gazed intently at the Professor. 'And the second time?'

'From Portsmouth – '

'The hulks!' Aske nodded. 'That's where they sent the bad boys . . . and the hulks were no joke. I'll bet he didn't love the British after that.'

'That is true.' The Professor returned this intelligence with interest. 'It was a terrible punishment – some might say inhumane.'

'No worse than the *souterrains* in the French fortresses. In fact, better a ship on the Portsmouth mudflats than below ground at Bitche or Sarrelibre,' said Aske coolly. 'Some might say that, Professor.'

Men! thought Elizabeth critically, as she felt the temperature drop: unless she came between these unlikely adversaries they would be into the ancient Anglo-French argument next, as to which nation was the more wicked.

'If Colonel Suchet had a score to settle – ' she tried to include both of them, and Paul too, in her silly question ' – could that be why he wanted so badly to recapture them, Professor?'

'Ah . . .' The Professor turned politely towards her '. . . no, Mademoiselle . . . That is to say, whatever Colonel Suchet may have felt personally, he was far too busy to pursue them for personal reasons. He had other duties, you see.'

'What other duties?' asked Aske.

'You are a student of this period? An expert?' The little man studied Aske intently.

'A student,' admitted Aske cautiously.

'Of naval history.' For once Paul came to Aske's rescue. 'British naval history.'

Professor Belperron almost smiled. 'Then you will perhaps be acquainted with the name *de la Rousselière*?'

'No.' Aske had guessed he was about to be put in his place, but had evidently decided to cut his losses quickly. 'I've never heard of him.'

'I'm surprised.' Surprised and gratified. '*Berthois de la Rousselière, chef de bataillon du corps de Génie* – major, Royal Engineers, as Colonel Hobson would have translated it.' The Professor cocked his head at Aske inquiringly, with false innocence. 'Or perhaps Lieutenant Robert Hamilton?' He smiled. 'Captain Hamilton, as he became?'

'Naval history is Mr Aske's field, Professor,' said Paul.

'Oh, but Robert Hamilton was a naval officer, Dr

221

Mitchell,' said the Professor, his good humour thoroughly restored. 'He was a lieutenant in the Royal Navy of His Britannic Majesty King George III . . . and then a captain in the Royal Navy of His Most Christian Majesty King Louis XVI – he was doubly a naval officer . . . But, to be fair, perhaps a little before . . . before your period, Mr Aske? And yours, Dr Mitchell?'

But neither of them was falling for anything this time, observed Elizabeth: each face bore the same expression of obsequious interest of students at the feet of the master, even if those little feet might be swinging in mid-air.

But that was not necessarily appropriate to the daughter of Commander Loftus VC, she decided: heroes' daughters could take narrower attitudes.

'He was a traitor, you mean?'

'A traitor? Ah . . .' He gazed at her, then raised his favourite hand expressively, to indicate a finer balance. 'In those days loyalties were not so simply defined. He was a Scotsman, and the English – the *English* – they did not appreciate his excellence as a navigator and a map-maker – they did not promote him . . . So he promoted himself into another king's more grateful service, to make maps, not of Cherbourg and Brest, but of the Medway and Portsmouth.'

'That still sounds like treason,' said Elizabeth.

'Perhaps. But the frontiers of treason are rarely so clearly defined.' He smiled at her. 'I remember Portsmouth in 1944, Mademoiselle. I was in a tank landing-craft of His Britannic Majesty King George VI, waiting to invade France, and not far from the mud-bank on which Jean-Baptiste Suchet was held captive in one of Mr Aske's hulks . . . And I remember thinking, as I looked up towards the forts on the hills above – the forts which the Lord Palmerston built to protect the naval base from his French enemies in the reign of Queen Victoria . . . I remember thinking that if I fell into the hands of my own countrymen in France . . . that I had already been sen-

222

tenced to death *in absentia* by the Vichy Government.' He spread both hands. 'Traitor – renegade – patriot . . . we take the side that we must take, and do what we must do, which seems best to us. And it is the winning and the losing which decides what we were.'

'Yes – very true. And most interesting,' said Aske. 'But if Hamilton served King Louis XVI, what has he got to do with Major de la Rousselière and Colonel Suchet, who served Napoleon Bonaparte?'

'Major de la Rousselière served the King, Mr Aske, not the Emperor. And the King invested him with the Cross of St Louis for his distinguished and daring services – in 1779.' The Professor sat back and regarded them benignly.

'What services?'

'He was a spy, Mr Aske, who specialized in British naval bases. And in 1779, having closely examined all the dispositions of your defences in and around Portsmouth, and working also with the detailed maps supplied by Captain Hamilton, he drew up a blue-print for the seizure of the Isle of Wight, Gosport and Portsmouth in that order. All of which were then to be turned into a "French Gibraltar" thereafter.'

'Huh!' snorted Aske.

'Oh . . . do not be too contemptuous of the might-have-been, Mr Aske.' The Professor shook his head, still good-humoured. 'The planning was sound – the troops were available . . . General de Vaux and the Marquis de Rochambeau were to command them . . . and you must remember that your army was then busily engaged in losing the war in America, against General Washington, at the time . . . It is true that circumstances changed, to render the Franco-Spanish naval squadrons helpless at the crucial time . . . But the plan was sound – the same strategic concept as that the French and the British applied seventy years later, when they set out to take the Crimea and Sebastopol from the Russians, in fact.' He smiled. 'And all this is a matter of record, in the archives of the English section in the Ministries of Marine and War here in Paris. It is well-known, even.'

One of the great *might-have-beens,* thought Elizabeth. History was about what happened, and its whole weight endowed the facts after the event with inevitability. But, against all that, there had been so many close-run things – all the useless but tantalizing historical cul-de-sacs down which her pupils too often strayed when they were dissatisfied with the facts – *'But if Henry of Navarre had not been assassinated, Miss Loftus . . .'* or *'If Mary Tudor had executed Elizabeth – '*

Professor Belperron leaned forward suddenly, elbows on his blotter, hands clasped. 'What is *not* well-known – what has never been remarked on until now, except in mere footnotes, because it was overtaken by greater events, and bore no fruit . . . is what Colonel Suchet was doing in 1812, my friends.'

Now he was not addressing them, but the students of some future class in the ante-room with the table and the chairs: this, translated through what Bertrand Bourienne had said to Paul on the phone, was what must be 'interesting' about Colonel Jean-Baptiste Suchet.

'It comes down, Mr Aske – ' the Professor focused on Humphrey Aske as his main target ' – to a question I had never thought to ask myself before, of 1812 . . . Which is: *after Russia, what next?'*

'The same question Hitler must have asked himself in 1941,' said Aske, nodding to Elizabeth and Paul in turn.

'Good. Exactly that – *good!'* From *main target* Aske was transformed into *most promising student.* 'As with Hitler, so with the Emperor: after the defeat of Russia – the reckoning with England, Mr Aske.'

Elizabeth shivered. Suddenly the Professor wasn't a little mannikin swinging his legs under his desk, or even a brave Resistance fighter swinging the same little legs on a landing-craft in Portsmouth Harbour in 1944, before D-

Day. He was the old hereditary enemy of all those battles, from Hastings in 1066 through Tinchebrai and Bouvines and Agincourt, and Fontenay and Blenheim and Saratoga, and Trafalgar and Salamanca and Waterloo – of all those trumpet-calls and drum-beats which had summoned the two neighbours to waste their genius killing each other in fools' quarrels over the centuries.

'But then it would have been the whole world against England, Mr Aske – the infant United States as well as the whole of Europe – '

'Britain, Professor Belperron,' said Paul. 'Britain and the Royal Navy, actually.'

Belperron nodded. 'I give you the Royal Navy, Dr Mitchell – incomparable, always magnificent . . . but over-stretched by 1812, with the Americans at sea, and a hundred French ships-of-the-line in a dozen European ports, and another hundred on the stocks . . . and the capacity to out-build you from Norfolk in Virginia to Brest and Copenhagen and St Petersburg and Venice . . . the whole world, Mr Aske – not in 1940, or 1914 – or 1588 or 1779 . . . but the whole world in 1812 – '

'If the Tsar Alexander had given in, Professor,' said Aske. 'But he didn't, did he?'

'But he *should* have done, Mr Aske. After the Emperor reached Moscow – which Hitler never reached . . . And if the Tsar had made terms then . . . what next, Mr Aske?' The Professor shook his head. 'There was no Churchill in 1812 – there were only nonentities – Mr Spencer Percival had been assassinated by a madman, but he was nobody in any case . . . and Lord Liverpool, his successor – he was nobody also . . . and the Duke of Wellington in Spain, with his little army – after Russia, Mr Aske, the Emperor could have ordered half-a-million soldiers to Spain. And where would Wellington have been then?' The *if* of 1812 was beginning to assume terrifying proportions in Professor Belperron's imagination, and he spread his hands as though to embrace it. '*Make peace*, Wellington would have said – because he was a realist. But that might not have been good enough for the Emperor, because he was a realist too, and he knew how England was not to be trusted – England and Europe – England and Austria, and Prussia, and Austria, none of them were to be trusted . . . But England most of all – so England must be dealt with finally, as the trouble-maker and the paymaster among all the others.' The Professor nodded first at Aske, and then at Mitchell, and even at Elizabeth. 'She must be taught a lesson – that is what I now think he decided. A – the word escapes me – but a lesson she would not forget, anyway.'

'A salutary lesson – "salutory"?' Aske smiled. 'So he dusted off de la Rousselière's 1779 Plan for Portsmouth – was that the salutary lesson?' He glanced sidelong at Paul. 'And, of course, our dear Colonel Suchet himself had a nodding acquaintance with Portsmouth, didn't he! Mud-banks and hulks, and all that . . . plus a well-founded dislike for the English, as a result – he'd be the ideal man to put his heart and soul into the project, obviously – ' he came back to the Professor ' – obviously?'

Paul frowned. 'What evidence have you for this?' He ignored Aske. 'Apart from circumstantial evidence?'

Belperron nodded. 'He withdrew all the Hamilton maps and the Rousselière plans from the archives of the Ministry of Marine in the autumn of 1811, to the Ministry of War, where he had a small staff of officers working under him. It is my belief that these officers – and there were engineers and naval experts among them – that they were bringing the Portsmouth Plan up to date on the basis of fresh intelligence from England.' He nodded again. 'Also . . . he solicited reports from Admiral Missiessy on the condition of the squadrons in the Channel and Atlantic ports, and on the construction programme – and from Count Emeriau and Admiral Cosmao on the numbers of trained seamen in Toulon and Genoa, who could be transferred north, to bring the crews of those ships up to strength.'

'But . . . except perhaps for those maps . . . all this is still circumstantial,' said Paul. 'Is there any real proof that there was a new Portsmouth Plan, Professor?'

'Circumstantial . . . up to a point, Dr Mitchell. It is even true that the plans prepared by Hamilton and de la Rousselière were not the only ones Colonel Suchet called for – indeed, all this I already knew, from other researches, though I must confess that I never assembled it in this fashion until now . . . for none of it came to fruition. Because in December – December 1812 – all the maps and plans and charts were returned to the Ministry of Marine, inevitably.'

'Why inevitably?' asked Elizabeth.

'The Russian disaster, Mademoiselle. For after that Colonel Suchet was no longer working to strengthen the fleet – he was stripping it of men for the army, in preparation for the European campaigns of 1813. The Portsmouth Plan perished in the snows of Moscow.'

'If there ever was a new Portsmouth Plan, Professor.' The retreat of the *Grande Armée* encouraged Aske to advance again.

But Professor Belperron smiled. 'Oh, there was a new Portsmouth Plan, I believe that now, even though I have not had time to prove it yet. Not conclusively . . .'

He had something else, thought Elizabeth. He had had it all along, and he had just been waiting for the right moment to let it out of the bag, to impress them.

Paul caught her eye, and grinned – Paul had come to the same conclusion, and that grin told her that he was quite prepared to be impressed if that gave him what he wanted.

He even kept the grin in place for the Professor. 'You know . . . I don't think you've been quite straight with us, Professor,' he said.

The little man, who had been concentrating on Aske, now frowned slightly at Paul. 'Pardon, Dr Mitchell?'

'What we want to know is why Colonel Suchet was so keen to get our fellows from the *Vengeful* back into the cooler – which should also give us the answer why they were treated the way they were, and shunted off to the Lautenbourg, instead of to Verdun, or somewhere like that, where there were other prisoners.' Paul leaned forward again. 'Well, my old friend Bertrand Bourienne told me that you know more than any man alive about what was happening in France in Napoleon's time, and particularly the last five years of the First Empire – he said, if you didn't know, then no one knew, by God!'

For a moment Elizabeth was afraid that he was laying it on a bit too thick, but then she saw that the Professor was visibly disarmed by such confidence.

'Dr Mitchell . . . I fear your friend overrates me – '

'I don't think so. I think you know *exactly* what Suchet was after . . . Or, you've got a pretty damn good idea of it.'

Aske sniffed. 'Well, it's pretty damn obvious, I should have thought: somehow the poor devils had tumbled to this new Portsmouth Plan of his – it can hardly be anything else, can it?'

Belperron's eyes glinted behind his spectacles. 'Can't it, Mr Aske? Can't it?'

Aske opened his mouth, and then thought better of what he had been about to say, and said nothing at all.

Belperron shook his head. 'To tell the truth, my friends, I do *not* know exactly what Suchet wished to suppress – I have had far too little time . . . only a matter of hours . . . to look for the necessary confirmation of what I *believe* . . . All I have at this moment is another name – and another name connected with Colonel Suchet – and the known facts about *him* . . . a most interesting man . . .'

'What man – what name, Professor?' asked Paul, dutifully on cue.

'James Burns – no, I am sure you will never have heard of him, Mr Aske. James Burns, merchant – import-export, as we would say now . . . James Burns, of London, New York . . . and Portsmouth, Mr Aske.'

'Another traitor?' Aske's mouth twisted. 'Or another renegade patriot?'

'No, none of those.' The little man shook his head. 'This time – another spy, Mr Aske. Even perhaps a super-spy, since you British never caught him – never even suspected him, so far as I am aware . . . though I know nothing of his subsequent history as yet.'

Whatever happened to Father's book on the twelve *Vengeful*s, there was a book here – or at least a learned article in the *Annales historiques de l'Empire* in the making, thought Elizabeth. It was surprising that Belperron was prepared to let so much slip.

'How was he not a traitor – or a renegade, Professor?' she asked.

'Because he was not an Englishman at all, Mademoiselle,' said Belperron simply. 'He was an American – an Irish American.'

'But also a *French* spy – a spy for France?'

'Ah . . . now there again we are on those debatable frontiers! Where should a good American – and an Irishman . . . an Irishman in any age . . . where should such a man be when England is at war? And in those days, after the Irish Rebellion of 1798, in which my country assisted so inadequately and disastrously?'

'In Portsmouth, apparently,' said Paul dryly. 'And we let him import-export from there, did we?'

Belperron shook his head. 'In England I am not sure that he was *James Burns – American* . . . not from the way he continued to move at will between the two countries after the Americans had declared war on you. What he did in England, except that he traded in naval stores . . . American timber and cordage, and the like . . . that I do not know. But here in France it was in military equipment – in British greatcoats and boots for the French Army –'

'In *what*?' Paul's voice cracked.

'British greatcoats and boots – the *Grande Armée* wore them both into Russia . . . imported through Hamburg, of course.' The Professor smiled his little coldly-amused smile again. 'You must understand how the Industrial Revolution and the French Revolution came to terms with each other, Dr Mitchell, and how honest neutrals were caught between them – it was not a business as conducted in later war. Because in those pragmatic days an honest trader could also obtain licences to break the rules, to the advantage of all parties.'

'And James Burns was good at getting licences?'

'That is what I think, Dr Mitchell. As yet I am not sure.'

'But you're sure he was a spy?'

'James Burns was a client of Joseph Fouché's Ministry in 1805, and again in 1808 – and a close colleague of Colonel Suchet in 1812 – that I *know*, Mr Aske.' Professor Belperron brought his hands together. 'James Burns had a dream . . . of confusion to Albion . . . *that* is what I believe.'

'With the Portsmouth Plan?'

'With *his* Portsmouth Plan. Which was very different from those of de la Rousselière and Hamilton – very different, and much more outrageous . . . but perhaps also much more dangerous to England.' The little man switched from Aske to Paul. 'And which Suchet, of all men, would have recognized, where Fouché would have discounted it.' He shrugged. 'Though, to be fair, the time was not ripe in Fouché's day, as it was in Suchet's.'

This time they both waited, now that he was altogether wrapped in his own cleverness.

'Some of this I know . . . and some of it I am guessing, on the basis of what I was told last night, which has made me put facts together with guesses . . . to make an instant theory, you understand? No more than that.'

They nodded, and Elizabeth nodded too, to encourage him.

'Good . . . Now it may be that your escaped prisoners somehow knew of de la Rousselière's plans, Mr Aske – Dr Mitchell. I do not know how . . . but it does not matter.

Because, if his plans were good in 1779, they were bad in 1812 – they were plans which would not have attracted Colonel Suchet, I suspect. And also because he would have had in mind the invasion plans of 1804–5 – the massing of a great army on the Channel coast to conquer England, not merely to raid it, or capture a foothold.'

Aske snuffled. 'He would probably have had the Royal Navy in mind also, Professor. And the battle of Trafalgar.'

'Very correct, Mr Aske. *Always* the Royal Navy . . . But by then the Royal Navy without Nelson. And the Royal Navy was stretched all the way to the war with America, with the best part of the British Army fighting in Spain, and the rest of it in Canada fighting the Americans . . . And 1813 would not have been 1805 in Europe either, Mr Aske: Suchet was planning for an invasion in which the Emperor no longer had to worry about the armies of Austria and Prussia and Russia, as he had had to do in 1805. This would have been his last battle, you must remember, Mr Aske – his very last battle!'

That silenced Aske, as Elizabeth herself could hear the echo of his own words from yesterday: *In 1812 we were losing the war* . . . And that had been before this image of a defeated Russia, with no catastrophic retreat from Moscow.

'But you are right to remind us of your navy, Mr Aske – it was your navy which frightened the German generals in 1940, before the Battle of Britain, not the RAF . . . And the very idea of seizing a defended port, like Portsmouth, in a *coup de main,* with its warships there at anchor – *ridiculous!*' Belperron waved a hand dismissively. '*I* remember the Canadians coming back from Dieppe in 1942, what there was left of them . . . That made it certain we would not try to seize a port in 1944, but would invade across the open beaches – as the Emperor planned to do in 1805, up the coast from Portsmouth, where you built your equally ridiculous Martello Towers in those days – along the same beaches where William the Norman landed in 1066 . . . No, Mr Aske, the pattern of prudent invaders down the centuries has always been the same: get as much of your army ashore first on some likely beach – then seek battle with your enemy's army and invest his strong places. But do not make your assault on those strong places from the sea in the first place – *that* is the lesson of history.' He sat back confidently.

'So what was James Burns's "Portsmouth Plan", then?' asked Paul. 'Because Portsmouth would have been a strong enough place. Apart from whatever garrison there would have been, there'd be the navy itself – the ships at anchor. You'd never have got a ship into Portsmouth harbour, Professor, let alone a man ashore.'

'You are right,' agreed the Professor. 'But, you see, there was no need to get a ship into the harbour, Dr Mitchell, and no need to put a man ashore. *Not when they were already there.*' He paused momentarily. 'The hulks, Mr Aske – have you forgotten the hulks?'

'Christ!' exclaimed Aske. '*The hulks!*'

'The hulks?' Paul turned to him.

'The prison ships. There was a whole line of them right there in the harbour – jammed with French prisoners!'

'Fourteen ships, to be exact, Mr Aske,' said the Professor pedantically. 'Your old prizes of war from France, like the *Prothée*, from which Colonel Suchet escaped, and from the Spanish and Danish fleets . . . and your own old worn-out battleships – fourteen ships containing over nine thousand men . . . Wretched prisoners – embittered prisoners – all the men who had escaped and been recaptured, officers among them . . . desperate men, Mr Aske – Dr Mitchell . . . and also trained soldiers and sailors, with trained leaders among them.'

'And right there in the harbour,' Aske repeated. 'Christ!'

'And on shore too – right there in the harbour,' said the Professor softly. 'Behind the old Roman walls of Portchester Castle . . . another seven thousand men. And just across the water, in the prison at Gosport . . . thousands more. Over twenty thousand men in all.'

For a moment neither Paul nor Aske spoke, then Paul drew a deep breath. 'Evidence, Professor?'

'For 1812 – little as yet, Dr Mitchell.' The Professor shook his head. 'As yet I have not had time, and I am guessing . . . But for James Burns' earlier plans there *is* evidence – plans which were discounted at the time, in spite of all his powers of persuasion.' He paused. 'He argued that the troops guarding the prisoners were of the poorest quality – the sweepings of the British army and navy, officered by pensioners and rejects . . . He argued that both the hulks and the land prisons were organized to keep unarmed men from breaking *out* – not to prevent a handful of armed and determined men breaking *in* . . . To be precise, he asked for two hundred men, two hundred British uniforms, and a thousand muskets. After that he said he would capture what he needed, and burn what he did not want. And with that he could take Portsea Island, occupying the fortified lines across the isthmus, and would hold it until relieved by the invading armies.'

Aske looked at Paul. 'It would have been a bloody massacre – either way.'

The Professor shrugged. 'It would have been chaos and confusion, and death and destruction, of that there can be no doubt.' He wagged a finger at them both. 'But it would have appealed to Colonel Suchet, of all men – that is important. Because he knew the hulks, and he knew Portsmouth. And even if he did not plan to land the invasion army at Portsmouth, he would appreciate the value of such a terrifying diversion – I am sure of that.'

Paul rubbed his chin, looking first at Elizabeth, then at Aske. 'I think we have to go away and think about this one.'

Aske frowned. 'What d'you mean, think about it?'

'Well, for a start . . . going to Alsace can serve no

233

useful purpose, not now.' Paul thought for a moment. 'We have to begin again with the *Vengeful* – how the devil can Chipperfield have got wind of any of this?'

'Perhaps he didn't,' said Elizabeth. 'Perhaps Colonel Suchet was just trying to make sure . . . ?'

'Perhaps we ought to have another look at the *Fortuné*?' said Aske tentatively. 'We could do that over here, with Professor Belperron's help, maybe?'

'Professor Wilder could tell us about Portsmouth,' said Elizabeth. 'He's a tremendous expert on everything to do with its history – even Father admitted that.'

Paul nodded. 'Wilder's a good bet, Elizabeth.' He looked towards the little Frenchman. 'If you could keep digging at this end, sir . . . if you could spare the time, that is?'

Belperron had been watching them curiously, his eyes darting from one to the other. 'Well . . . if that is all that you want . . . there will surely be other documents, it is only a matter of knowing where to look, and what to look for, and how to look at it – ' He stopped abruptly as Paul stood up.

'Of course. Isn't it always?' Paul started to shrug, then turned the shrug into a little bow. 'And you have pointed us in a promising direction, Professor. We are indebted to you . . . But we mustn't take any more of your time.'

'Yes.' Aske stood up in turn, taking his cue from Paul.

'Elizabeth,' commanded Paul.

'Yes.' She stood up obediently, but she was conscious that something had happened which she had missed, only she had no idea what it was.

Belperron stood up behind his desk, unnaturally tall. For a moment he seemed undecided as to what to say. Then he returned the bow. 'I will be interested to hear from you, Dr Mitchell. We must keep in touch,' he said stiffly.

'Absolutely right – we must keep in touch!' Paul's enthusiasm was as false as the Professor's height. 'Please don't bother – we'll see our way out – '

Aske was already opening the door. Elizabeth found herself sidling through it almost crab-wise.

'Most grateful, Professor – ' she heard Paul say as she collided with one of the chairs in the second ante-room.

Paul closed the door behind him. 'Is there a back-entrance, Aske?'

'Christ! I don't know!' said Aske.

'What's happening?' said Elizabeth.

Paul went to the window. 'There's something not right about this.'

Aske nodded. 'I agree. *Definitely* not right.'

'I don't understand – ' Elizabeth heard her own voice crack. 'What – ?'

'Can you see anything?' said Aske. And then, when Paul merely shook his head, he turned to Elizabeth. 'He didn't ask enough questions – he gave us too much, much too easily – he was scared, if you ask me – ' he switched to Paul ' – right?'

'And he's not the only one, by God!' murmured Paul, still craning his neck at the window.

'Scared?' Whatever they'd seen, she hadn't caught the slightest glimpse of it. But now she was joining the club to which they both belonged.

'There has to be a back-entrance,' said Aske decisively. 'Let's get out while we can, Mitchell . . . I'll go first – that's what I'm bloody-well paid for – '

He took two steps towards the door, but it opened before he could grasp the handle, and he skipped back as though it had tried to sting him.

Elizabeth was simultaneously aware of Aske jumping back, and Paul turning from the window towards the open door, and of her own frozen immobility.

And of what was in the doorway.

'Nikki!' exclaimed Paul. 'What a delightful surprise!'

13

Emerald green – emerald green was by any reckoning a
dangerous colour for a woman to attempt.

But this woman could get away with it, with her pale
complexion and the flaming red hair – except that it wasn't
red, thought Elizabeth enviously, but that painter's colour
which stopped the man who'd been talking to you in mid-
sentence and made him lose the thread of what he was
saying.

'*Nikki!*' The second time Paul managed to substitute
pleasure for surprise. 'How delightful!'

The woman in the doorway gave him a cold smile.
'Captain . . . Mitchell, is it?' The eyes took in Aske, and
dismissed him; and then took in Elizabeth, and lingered
on her for just half a second longer – the eyes were green
too, damn it! – and then dropped her, coming back to
Paul. 'It's been a long time, Captain – six years?'

'Seven, more like – since Hameau Ridge, Nikki – far
too long!' He wasn't pretending his regret: even the best
liar couldn't electrify his lie so well. 'We should have
contrived a Hameau Ridge Old Comrades' Reunion ages
ago.'

Mid-thirties, decided Elizabeth critically. But still
almost flawless, and seven years ago didn't bear thinking
about.

'But what brings you here?' This time there was a slight
loss of conviction in Paul's voice.

'You do – as you well know.'

'*I* do?' He frowned. 'But why? What am I supposed to
have done now?' The frown deepened. 'You're not going
to tell me that this is . . . *official*?'

'Official – what?' said Aske. 'What's going on?'

'What indeed!' Paul gestured helplessly. 'I'm sorry, Humphrey – and Elizabeth . . . but this, apparently, is Mademoiselle Nicole MacMahon, of the French security service – which bit of it I'm not quite sure.' His voice tightened as he spoke. 'But if this is official business then I don't need to introduce my friends to you, Nikki, because you'll already know who they are . . . Only, as for what's going on – I'd like to know that, too.'

Mademoiselle MacMahon looked at each of them in turn again. 'Captain Mitchell – '

'No. Not "captain". That was strictly acting and temporary – and unpaid, as it happens. If you want to be formal, Nikki, it's "Doctor Mitchell" now – PhD, Cantab.' He shook his head suddenly, as though to dispel unreality. 'Only I just don't see why it has to be formal.'

She looked at him, almost sadly so it seemed to Elizabeth. 'Very well – Paul.'

'That's better!'

'It isn't better. I had hoped you would not be tiresome, Paul. That is why they sent me – because we know each other, and you wouldn't try to play the innocent.'

'I'm not going to be tiresome, Nikki. But this is one time when I can't avoid being innocent. Because that's what I am – what we *all* are.'

Nikki MacMahon sighed, and then indicated the table. 'Sit down, please.'

They sat down facing her, examinees again.

'So you are innocent, Paul. Which means that you are not in France in a professional capacity, concerned with any matter of security?'

'No, I didn't say that.' Paul's face was expressionless. 'I am in France professionally. And I *am* concerned with a security matter.'

'What?' The delicately-pencilled eyebrows rose.

'A matter of the greatest importance to my country, in fact . . . in 1812, that is.'

Nikki MacMahon's lips compressed into a tight line.

'In 1812, Nikki . . . if what Professor Belperron back there says is even half right – ' Paul jerked his thumb over his shoulder ' – your little Corsican Tyrant was planning to do our dear old Farmer George a terrible mischief. That's the security matter we're interested in – and I'm interested in it as a professional historian. And that's the beginning and the end of it – ask anybody – ask Miss Loftus here . . . It's her father's book I'm commissioned to finish, you see.'

'I know about the book, Paul.' Nikki MacMahon had recovered from that brief moment of irritation when she'd been out-manoeuvred. 'I know about your escaped sailors at Coucy – I know about Colonel Suchet – I know about all that.'

'Well, then – ' Paul spread his hands ' – if you know about all that, then what the hell are you doing here?' Then he frowned again. 'You must have talked to my friend Bertrand Bourienne? Yes . . . well, I hope you didn't frighten the life out of him, that's all! But if you talked to him . . . and I suppose you were listening in back there to what was said in Professor Belperron's study – of course you were!' He shook his head at her. 'I *thought* there was something funny about that – it just never occurred to me what it was . . . But – *okay* – I hope you enjoyed what you heard! So ask poor old Bertrand, and ask Professor Belperron anything you like too. But I'm afraid they'll only be able to tell you the truth, plain and simple, Nikki.'

Whatever the truth was, it wasn't plain and simple, thought Elizabeth. And yet it *was* also the truth, that was the twisted strand of irony in Paul's display of injured innocence – the truth which he himself could make no sense of.

'I see.' Nikki MacMahon's smile was halfway into a sneer. 'So it is merely the year 1812 in which you are interested?'

'1812, yes. And maybe 1813 and 1811. And I could throw in 1805 and 1779 now, I suppose.' Paul shrugged, then turned to Elizabeth. 'We shall have to replace that whole chapter, of course. But we've got something much better already. And if I can argue Nikki here into clapping us in jail for a few days I shouldn't wonder but that we might have a best-seller, Elizabeth.' He came back to the Frenchwoman almost lazily. 'The Press would like that – on both sides of the Channel, Nikki . . . how you caught your wicked English spies 170 years too late – they'd really enjoy that.' Then he shrugged again. 'Of course, it won't exactly polish up the image of the *Direction de la Sécurité du Territoire* . . . But you can't win 'em all.' He looked at his watch ostentatiously. 'So shall we just be on our way, then? It's lunch-time, and I'm more than ready for Humphrey's favourite restaurant.'

The green eyes blazed for a fraction of a second, then became ice-cold again, and Elizabeth warmed herself in the chill of their coldness. Whatever had happened those seven years ago, there was more rivalry between them than affection, and no rivalry for her to fight.

'No,' said Nikki MacMahon.

No, thought Elizabeth: this formidable woman would never let any mere man walk away from her unbruised, not if she could help it, and least of all an English man.

The woman turned suddenly to Aske.

'Mr Aske – if Dr Mitchell is a professional historian . . . tell me what you do for a living?'

Paul stiffened. 'Oh – come on, Nikki! You know who we both work for, one way or another – you said that's why they gave you this job . . . So Humphrey works with me, you know *that*. But what you probably don't know is that he's an authority on early nineteenth-century naval history – is that the answer you want?'

'I want Mr Aske's answer, Paul. Mr Aske – ?'

Aske sat back. 'I wouldn't dream of being uncivil, Miss MacMahon . . . but if you were a man I'd say it really wasn't any of your damn business – beyond what's on my

239

passport, anyway.' He smiled at her. 'Which says "Civil Servant", as it happens.'

Nikki MacMahon switched abruptly back to Paul. 'Where did you go yesterday afternoon?'

'After we landed?' Paul packed insolence into his pause for innocent reflection. '*Ah* . . . did you lose us for an hour or two? Well . . . let's see . . . we signed in at our hotel in Laon, and dropped off our bags . . . Then we went for a spin in the country before meeting Bertrand . . . Then we went back to Laon, and had a drink, and had our dinner – the *profiteroles* were delicious – and had another drink . . . and then we went to bed. Do you want more detail than that? Did you dream of anything subversive to the Republic, Humphrey?'

Another flash of green fire. 'Where did you go before you met M'sieur Bourienne?'

'We took Elizabeth to see the Chemin des Dames, where the French Army mutinied in 1917. I wanted to show her the British War Cemetery at Vendresse, Nikki – you know my weakness for visiting British war cemeteries in France. I remember taking you to the Prussian Redoubt Cemetery on the edge of Hameau Ridge, back in '74 – you remarked on the way the poppies grew there, as I recall . . . They don't grow nearly so well in Champagne as on the Somme – do they, Elizabeth?'

He was cruel, thought Elizabeth. But then, he was fighting on another disadvantageous slope, against heavy odds, so there was no room for weakness in his tactics.

'Yes – that's what we did.' She nodded at Nikki. 'I signed the book there, Mam'selle – ' she wanted to add *It's a lovely sad place,* but that would have been an insult to those poor dead Tommies, to add the truth of what she had felt.

The green eyes pinned her momentarily. 'Yes, I'm sure you did, Miss Loftus.'

Hating herself, Elizabeth frowned. 'I beg your pardon?'

Nikki turned from her. 'Your cover was always good, Paul. You haven't changed.'

'Cover?' Something stopped him from denying the charge. 'I seem to remember your cover back in '74 was pretty damn good, if you want to talk about covers, Nikki.'

Nobody was deceiving anybody, thought Elizabeth. Yet they were both bound by the rules of a game which she didn't really understand, even though she was now one of the players.

'Mr Aske – ' Nikki came round to Humphrey Aske again, as though still searching for a weakness in their defences, but now with a hint of weariness in her voice ' – why were you nosing around so long outside, after you'd parked your car? Why didn't you come straight here?'

Aske shrugged unrepentantly. 'Just habit, I suppose. I always take a professional interest in stake-outs, even when they're as amateurish as yours, Miss MacMahon . . . I thought the local police must be up to something – I never imagined your people could be so *gauche* – we'd never set up anything so crude in London . . . I was looking to see who it was for – it never occurred to me that it was for *us,* Miss MacMahon!'

When it came to insults, Aske had nothing to learn from Paul, Elizabeth was reminded. They were both professionals.

'No?' The Frenchwoman countered him with bored disbelief. 'Just habit . . . and you are such a good driver, aren't you?'

'A good driver?' Aske feigned bewilderment. 'Yes. I've done a bit of rallying in my time, and I've been round the circuit at Brand's Hatch . . . Let's say I'm a good driver – possibly a very good one, if it's of the slightest interest to you.'

'Not a great deal. But losing those cars which were following you – that was just habit too, Mr Aske?'

'Good Lord! You even had a tail on us?' Aske's tone was mocking. 'That was a bit antediluvian, surely? I mean . . . doesn't your budget run to directional devices?' He

241

thought for a moment, and then shook his head as though mildly surprised. 'It wasn't even awfully bright, either . . . if you already knew where we were going . . . ?'

'You didn't lose them, then? On the *périphérique*?'

'Was that where I lost them?' He indicated mild interest, edged with amusement. 'I'm sorry to disappoint you, but in Paris I do like to drive like a Frenchman – it's a little conceit of mine . . . I'd say it looks rather as though your drivers are like your stake-out: just not up to the job.'

'Not *my* drivers, Mr Aske.' The perfectly painted lips again compressed momentarily – lips already a tiny bit too thin for perfection, Elizabeth noted: add a few years, and that would be an unforgiving mouth.

But then the face round the mouth turned towards her, and it was her turn for the next broadside.

For what we are about to receive – that was the way they waited for it in the old navy –

'*Nikki* . . .' Paul cut into the instant of silence before the crash of the *coup de grâce* '. . . I've taken about as much of this nonsense as old acquaintance allows, for Hameau Ridge's sake. But now I'm getting close to pulling rank on you.'

'Rank?' The challenge turned her back to him. 'What rank, Paul?'

'Try me and find out.' Paul regarded her obstinately. 'If you're not going to tell us what's happening then arrest us or let us go. But no more questions.'

But this wouldn't do, decided Elizabeth: he had picked up her silent distress signal, but was hazarding his own safety in order to save her. And she wasn't going to be humiliated like that by either of them.

'It's all right, Paul.' Her confidence flooded back with the sound of her own voice: if Elizabeth Loftus could *viva voce* First Class Honours from the borderline against two hostile examiners, what could this French bitch do that could frighten her? 'If Mademoiselle MacMahon

242

wants to ask me anything, she's welcome. I don't have anything to hide.'

The green eyes came back to her, uncompromising but also at least no longer so dismissive. And that in itself pumped more adrenalin: it was better to be scared than to be nothing, she discovered to her surprise.

And *get in first* signalled the adrenalin –

'After all, it's my fault that Dr Mitchell and Mr Aske are here, Mademoiselle.' It was no different from sighting the enemy's quarter-deck in the v-notch of the carronade, and then pulling the lanyard. 'My father commanded *Vengeful*, and I asked Dr Mitchell to finish his book.'

It pleased her to drop the *the* from *Vengeful*, as Father always insisted, and she was the more rewarded by the very slightest suggestion of doubt in those green eyes.

'I wasn't going to ask you any questions, Miss Loftus, as a matter of fact . . . I thought it just possible that you might not know what was happening to you.' The doubt faded. 'But now I think I may have been wrong.'

Bluff. Or, if not bluff, what could they do to her?'

'Wrong about what, Mademoiselle?'

Aske sat up suddenly, as though stung. '*Not* your drivers, Miss MacMahon? *Not* your drivers?' He looked quickly at Paul, then back at the Frenchwoman. 'Whose drivers, then?'

'Good question, Humphrey!' said Paul. 'Whose drivers, if not theirs? And the right question too, because it gives us our answer in one.'

'Answer to what?'

'All this. The VIP treatment!' Paul nodded. 'Mademoiselle MacMahon's newest masters don't give a stuff for the British, but they don't want any unscheduled trouble with their Russian friends at the moment, not with all the deals they've got going.'

'With the Russians?' Aske repeated the words incredulously. 'What the devil have the Russians got to do with what we've been doing?'

'I can't imagine. But if I had to *guess* . . . I'd say that we're all the victims of . . . a misunderstanding, shall we say?' Paul looked at Nikki MacMahon hopefully. 'How about that?'

'A misunderstanding?' She received his olive branch as though it had nettles entwined in it.

'That's right. Because . . . contrary to what you have assumed . . . Humphrey and I are on leave, and we're strictly devoted to 1812. And if you can prove anything else, you can lock us both up and throw away the key – and we'll come quietly, too.'

'But I don't have to prove anything – '

Paul lifted his hand. 'I haven't finished. You have a nasty suspicious mind, Nikki – or your bosses have . . . But if the roads behind us are crawling with KGB heavies I can't honestly blame you altogether.'

'That's very generous of you, Paul.' She seemed to relent slightly. 'You're about to blame them, are you – for also having nastier and more suspicious minds?'

'Ah . . . now you're beginning to get my drift.' He smiled. 'But I don't altogether blame either of you, actually . . . Because, you see, Nikki, before I started my leave I *was* engaged in an activity which surely interested them . . . Nothing that had anything whatsoever to do with France, I assure you . . . but something they certainly could take exception to. Only, you appreciate that I can't tell you what.' He shrugged disarmingly. 'But I suppose it is just possible they thought I was still hard at work – quite incorrectly, as it happens.'

Elizabeth became aware that her mouth had dropped open, and closed it quickly. It wasn't so much that he was craftily offering the French security service Peace With Honour, as that he had so quickly and ingeniously interwoven truth with lies, and fact with fiction.

The emerald-green shoulders drooped. 'Paul . . . do you know how many cars they sent to Laon?'

It was in the balance now, as he shook his head.

244

'Five, Paul. And ten men. *Ten men, Paul!*'

It was still in the balance.

'We were afraid there was going to be a bloodbath.' Nikki stared at him. 'And you're lying – of course.'

It was going the wrong way.

Paul gave a tiny shrug. 'Well, if I told you the truth you'd never believe it. Just let Elizabeth go, that's all – she was led astray by bad company, you can say.'

'No.' Nikki shook her head again. 'It's all or none.'

'Better make it *all* then, because I promise we'll go quietly. But if we have to stay we'll make trouble, I promise you *that,* too.' He nodded. 'Starting with a phone call to the British Embassy.'

'You can have one call, Paul.' This time Nikki nodded. 'From the departure lounge. Your plane leaves in two hours. The seats are already booked.'

14

As Elizabeth reached for the bell-chain which hung beside the big iron-bound door a narrow window under the eaves above swung open.

'Oh – hullo there! I thought I heard a car.' Cathy Audley's little bespectacled face peered out of the window. 'You're early . . . but come on in – it isn't locked.'

Elizabeth set her hand on the latch, and then remembered Humphrey Aske and turned back towards the car.

'The daughter, is that?' He made a face. 'You go on, Miss Loftus, and I'll bring in your luggage . . . And then you'll have to protect me. I'm not at my best with little girls.'

He wouldn't be, thought Elizabeth waspishly, and then despised herself for becoming infected with Paul's prejudices.

The trouble was, it was not an infection which could be shrugged off easily once it was in the blood, even though Aske of all men had treated her with his own brand of courtesy, diffident but unfailing; it wasn't anything he said, or anything he did – it was what he *was* which made her irrationally uneasy, and there was nothing to be done about it.

She forced her mind away from him, and stepped into the house – and was uneasy there, too: it was like coming home, yet not coming home – home, because here, still guarded, she could feel safe, and *she who outlives this day and comes safe home* . . . and because the home from which she had been plucked on Saturday could never be home again for her after what had happened in it.

'Elizabeth!' Cathy pattered down the great polished

staircase and skidded breathlessly to a halt in front of her. 'You're early – sorry, but Mummy's gone to Guildford with Daddy – but the old gentleman's here, and I've put him in the library with Mummy's *Guardian* and a glass of sherry.'

What old gentleman? There was simultaneously too much and too little to grasp there at one go: they were expected, which was fair enough from Paul's phone call, which had brought two cars to Gatwick . . . and Humphrey Aske had driven one of those with all his Brand's Hatch skill . . .

But what old gentleman?

'That's fine, dear – ' Gently now, gently: to be taken for granted by a child as an equal was a high compliment, not to be trifled with ' – how long has he been here?'

'Oh not long. Do you know, Elizabeth – he has hair coming out of his ears?' Cathy nodded. 'But he's terrifically polite – he calls me "Miss Audley" and stands up when I come into the library, would you believe it?'

Elizabeth had hoped for better than that, but while she was searching for another approach the door clicked behind her and Cathy's magnified eyes looked past her.

'Hullo. Who are you?' The child frowned.

'I . . . am Eeyore's brother,' said Humphrey Aske. 'Do you know who Eeyore was?'

'Yes.' The eyes filled with suspicion. 'He was a donkey.'

'Correct. So people put burdens on me. And they beat me at regular intervals. And that makes me a donkey.'

And that did indeed make him a donkey, thought Elizabeth, even though he was doing his best with *Winnie-the-Pooh*. Because he had chosen the wrong child to patronize.

'Cathy – this is Humphrey Aske, a friend of your father's,' she said hurriedly. 'Mr Aske – Miss Audley.' She grinned at Cathy conspiratorially.

'*Ee-ore*,' said Aske self-consciously.

'How do you do, Mr Aske,' said Cathy.

'I'm bad-tempered, actually,' said Aske. 'Nobody's offered me a thistle for ages.'

'A – *what?*' Cathy regarded him incredulously.

'I haven't had my lunch, little girl,' Aske sighed. 'And I haven't had my tea, either.'

Cathy wilted slightly at *little girl*.

'You don't happen to have a thistle, by any chance?' inquired Aske, before Elizabeth could intervene.

'Cathy – '

'Would you like a glass of sherry, Mr Aske?' said Cathy icily.

This time it was Aske who wilted.

'It's all right, Cathy,' said Elizabeth. 'We've just come back from France, you see.'

'Or, to be exact, we've been thrown out – on our ears . . . or maybe on some other part of our anatomy, eh?' Aske gave Elizabeth a rueful half-grin, ignoring Cathy Audley.

'Oh!' Cathy's ears pricked, and she turned to Elizabeth. 'Is that *persona non grata*? Daddy explained that to me just recently – "grata" agreeing with "persona", he said.' She came back to Aske. 'Which means you've been caught red-handed, he said.'

Aske's mouth opened wordlessly.

'What did they catch you doing? Or shouldn't I ask?' Cathy over-fed his confusion before turning again to Elizabeth. 'Of course – Daddy was going to France, wasn't he! I even gave him some money to buy that smelly after-shave for Uncle Jack, for Christmas – Paco – Paco – Paco . . . *Paco* – did they catch you doing something too, Elizabeth?'

'They didn't catch us doing anything, really,' said Elizabeth.

'Ah – now that is strictly true.' Aske had recovered his cool. 'But they did catch us doing *nothing*, and sometimes that's just as bad as being caught doing something.'

Cathy nodded seriously. 'That's like at school: if they

ask you what you're doing, and you say "nothing" they never believe you, they think you're doing something bad. Poor you!' She nodded again, sympathetically this time, then frowned suddenly. 'But where's Paul? I bet they didn't catch *him*!'

So Paul had made another conquest. But instinctively Elizabeth decided to leave his reputation intact.

'No, they didn't catch him, Cathy.' Anyway, there was an element of truth in that: Paul had always been way ahead of them in expecting the worst. 'He's gone to London.' Besides, there was another and more pressing matter. 'Hadn't we better go and meet the old gentleman?'

'Yes – ' Cathy's answer was cut off by a sudden bleeping, muted but insistent, which seemed to come from inside her ' – *oops!* That means Mummy's puddings have to come out of the Aga!' She produced a slim pocket calculator from her smock. 'I got this for my birthday – it's jolly useful, because it reminds me of things . . . He's in the library, Elizabeth – just down the end of the passage there. Can you find your way while I take the puddings out of the oven?' She started to turn away.

'What old gentleman?' Aske called after her.

'The one that knows all about Elizabeth's ship, Daddy says – Daddy asked him to come, he says – ' Cathy disappeared through a door in what was presumably the puddings' direction.

Aske looked at Elizabeth. 'A disconcertingly precocious child, as well as a typical only child – *persona non grata* indeed!'

'She's probably learning Latin, that's all,' said Elizabeth defensively.

'A typical Audley child, more like. "Grata" may agree with "persona", but she doesn't agree with me, Miss Loftus. And who is this old gentleman who knows all about your ship?'

'I don't know – except he has hair coming out of his ears and is apparently very polite.'

'Ah! Now that is a positive identification on both counts, if ever I heard one!' Aske perked up. 'Let us go and meet the great Professor Basil Wilson Wilder, Miss Loftus – down the passage, was it?'

Elizabeth followed him into the green-shaded gloom of the passage, the windows of which were half-obscured by the wistaria on the front of the house. There was no help for it, but she felt daunted by the prospect ahead, not so much because two elderly professors in one day were too many, as by the memory of Father's enraged correspondence with this same Professor Wilder, both in public and in private, over the *Vengeful* renaming. The two men had never been friends after an earlier Wilder review of *From Trafalgar to Navarino*, which had mildly disagreed with Father's assessment of Collingwood. But after the *Vengeful* letters even the mention of the Professor's name had been taboo.

Aske held the door open for her, courteous as ever.

It really was a library, not merely a room with books in it: it was as totally book-lined as the ante-rooms in Professor Belperron's apartment, except that the book-spines were much more colourful, and the room itself was beautiful, with its oak-beamed ceiling and intricately geometric Persian carpet on an unpolished stone-flagged floor, and a great blaze of flowers in the open fireplace, and –

And there, on a low table in front of the fireplace, was Father's *Vengeful* box – her *Vengeful* box –

The old gentleman rose slowly from an immense leather chair, his back to her, refolded his *Guardian* unhurriedly and placed it on the box, and turned towards her.

'Miss Loftus, I presume?'

Age . . . yet with that indefinable twinkle, not of second childhood, but of victorious longevity, a quality Elizabeth had only observed once before, in a very old lady – a great lady, who had somehow combined age with inextinguishable youth, and had made it beautiful.

'Professor Wilder?' It had never occurred to her that a man could achieve that same beauty; but of course it had nothing to do with being a man, any more than it had to do with age – it was the triumph of mind over both those conditions.

'Mr Aske – we meet again!' The tiniest nuance of . . . it was not distaste, for this man was long past any desire to wound any other creature, whatever his second sight saw hidden in it . . . it was more like sympathy neutralizing the instinctive but unfair emotions which Paul had for Aske, with which he had infected her. 'What a pleasure!'

'For me too, Professor.' Aske's voice thickened, as though he was unwilling to admit his own feelings sincerely. 'But what brings you here – to us – hot-foot?'

'Hot-foot?' Wilder tested the image. 'In this age of the motor-car that is almost a contradiction – *my* feet become cold with inactivity when I am carried urgently from one place to another . . . not like Roger Bannister, with his four-minute mile at Iffley – or Pheidippides carrying the news of Marathon to Athens, eh?' He smiled. 'But *hot-foot* nevertheless – yes!' He transferred the smile to Elizabeth, and then re-edited it to seriousness. 'Miss Loftus . . . we have never met until now, but as one of your school governors I have heard of your prowess with our history scholarship girls, and I have admired your results from afar. You have a rare gift, I think – rare, because those who have it tend to gravitate to university teaching . . . But you have not, and I am glad of it.'

In that instant all Elizabeth's plans for enjoying her ill-gotten gains as a rich woman went out of the window: if this old gentleman thought she must teach, then she must teach.

'I very much regret that circumstances have militated against our meeting until now. But that is in the past – ' he twinkled at her ' – and now we meet at last!' He became suddenly serious. 'I was sorry to hear about your father's death, my dear. Because . . . in our time we had our differences, for which I must take my share of the blame, I fear . . . but he was a considerable scholar in his own field.'

'Differences' was an understatement, and the lion's share of the blame for them had been Father's, but he was burying the past gently and generously for her benefit.

'In the circumstances, it would not have been appropriate for me to write to you – I do not think you would have wished that. Yet . . . in these new circumstances, I am glad of the opportunity to be of service to you.' He frowned slightly, and cocked his head, and looked into space just above her shoulder. 'You know, I have been practising that little speech in preparation for you, and it sounded perfectly admirable inside my head. But now that I've heard it . . . it does sound not only pompous, but thoroughly insincere.' His eyes came back to her. 'Perhaps I had better not ask you to give me the benefit of your doubt. So shall I say rather that I find your quest vastly interesting? Will that do?'

Aske advanced from behind her into the corner of her vision. 'But I didn't tell you what the quest was, Professor.'

'No . . . *you* didn't, Mr Aske.' Wilder bent down and lifted the *Guardian* off the *Vengeful* box for a moment. 'But your . . . friend, Dr Audley, has rectified that omission.' He looked at Elizabeth. 'All the relevant papers your father collected are in there, Miss Loftus . . . together with photo-copies of the Irene Cookridge material.'

'And what did Audley ask you to do with it?' inquired Aske.

'To study it, Mr Aske, to study it . . . To let my imagination range freely over it. What else?' Professor Wilder answered inquiry with inquiry. 'When you came to ask me about the prisoner-of-war usages of the time, you indicated a certain urgency. David – Dr Audley – re-iterated that urgency. And he gave me a secretary and a

252

young man to do my leg-work, which served to emphasize the urgency. But urgency is no friend to the historian – urgency is for the journalist, it is the necessary spur to his skill, his art . . . For the historian what is required is time and tranquillity, for the slow sifting of the facts, and for the gradual and hesitant advance towards glimpses of truth – that is the historian's art.' He smiled at Elizabeth. 'There! I'm doing it again! And all you want to know is what I can imagine for you!'

Elizabeth smiled back. 'And what can you imagine, Professor?'

He stared at her, and suddenly he was no longer smiling.

'A tragedy, I think, my dear. Or perhaps not altogether a tragedy, because if two men died for this box of your father's two men were also saved in some sense by it.'

'For the box?' Aske frowned at the *Vengeful* box.

'Two men died?' said Elizabeth.

'Lieutenant Chipperfield and Midshipman Paget.' Wilder nodded. 'Two good and brave young men. But didn't you know that?'

'I didn't know about the midshipman, Professor. We've only traced them as far as Coucy-le-Château.'

'Where?'

'Coucy – ' But of course he couldn't know – or Audley hadn't told him about that. 'Where Lieutenant Chipperfield died in France, Professor.'

'Ah! The great tower? You've been following them in France, I was forgetting! I have been tracking them in England – Tom Chard and the American, Timms.'

'That leaves a gap in the middle, between Coucy and here,' said Aske. 'But obviously they crossed it somehow.'

'You haven't read Miss Cookridge's papers?' Wilder seemed surprised. Then he gestured towards the box. 'But that can be easily rectified.'

'Don't bother, Professor – just tell us.' Aske looked at Elizabeth. 'We're used to having the facts doled out to us one by one. I think they wanted to see how much we could make of them as we went along.'

Wilder studied them both for a moment, as though he didn't know quite what to make of that flash of bitterness. 'There isn't much to tell, Mr Aske. After Chipperfield died they went on towards the Pas de Calais.'

'With Paget dressed as a girl?'

'At first. But not for long.'

'He didn't like being a girl, I'll bet.' Aske nodded.

'He took command, Mr Aske, nevertheless.'

'At the age of thirteen?'

'He was a warrant officer and Chipperfield naturally passed on the command to him. "*Mr Chipperfield instructed Mr Paget as to his wishes, and these we did then execute to the best of our power*", that is what Tom Chard said. It was the old navy, Mr Aske: the Lieutenant gave them their orders, and the orders lived on after he was dead.'

'So they headed for the Pas de Calais . . .'

'For Dunkirk. That was almost certainly the plan from the start – to steal a boat at Dunkirk.'

'Why Dunkirk?'

'Because the Dunkirkers were celebrated for their pro-British sympathies. Only the year before we'd released a couple of dozen of their people – men they particularly wanted – in gratitude for the way they'd treated the survivors from a wrecked Indiaman. And there'd long been an unofficial live-and-let-live understanding between the navy and the local fishermen. Also Napoleon himself notoriously disliked Dunkirkers – and they reckoned he was more their enemy than King George, who at least didn't conscript their sons and get them killed . . . If Chipperfield had ever served in the Channel Fleet he'd have known that. And I think he did know it.'

'And they did steal a boat,' said Elizabeth.

'Not without difficulty – with tragedy, in fact.' He sighed.

'That was where the midshipman got it?' said Aske.

The Professor gazed at him for a moment, then nodded.

'The boats were guarded, inevitably. And the beaches themselves were patrolled – indeed, while they were lying up in the dunes the patrols were increased, with the addition of soldiers as well as mounted gendarmes.'

Aske caught Elizabeth's eye, but didn't interrupt.

'After four days their water ran out, and they were of a mind to give up the attempt, and try again later. But then there came a thick sea-mist, and they chanced it.' Wilder paused, and then lifted a hand in a sad little gesture. 'Paget was killed as they were manhandling the boat into the sea – a mounted gendarme came out of the mist behind them, and took one shot at them – "*but one ball was discharged, yet that a fatal one*" . . . I suspect those are Parson Ward's words, rather than what Tom Chard said. But that's probably true of much of the Chard narrative, it's a sight too pedantic in places for an unlettered man, though the sense is right . . . No, what I think Chard meant was that the odds against a French policeman hitting what he was aiming at with a cavalry carbine were about one in a million. But this was that one-in-a-million that had the boy's name on it.'

After all they'd been through, thought Elizabeth, after all they'd achieved against impossible odds, it had been a too-cruel end for Chipperfield and Paget both, who might otherwise have lived to be admirals. But then how many other admirals and generals – and prime ministers and surgeons and scientists . . . and good husbands and loving sons – had been cut off by chance bullets ahead of their time? Even Father's shell, which had only maimed him, had changed history to bring her here. But there was no point in mourning any of these mischances; one could only trust that the cause had been just, the quarrel honourable, as King Harry's soldiers had hoped before Agincourt.

'So he handed them that box,' Wilder pointed at the *Vengeful* box on the table, 'and he died.'

'*That box?*' repeated Aske incredulously. 'Are you

telling us that they carried *that box* all the way from . . . from Lautenbourg – no, all the way from the *Vengeful* – ?'

'That's what it looks like. "The surgeon's case", Tom Chard calls it.' Wilder nodded. 'That box, I think – yes.'

Aske stared at the box. 'But – for God's sake – what was in it?'

Then he looked at Elizabeth. 'Did you know this – about the box?'

Elizabeth shook her head. 'What was in the box, Professor?'

'That bastard Mitchell played his cards close to his chest!' murmured Aske savagely to himself.

'Mitchell?' inquired Wilder.

'Never mind him, sir.' Aske blinked. 'What was in the box?'

'Nothing, Mr Aske. It was empty.'

'You mean . . . they lost what was in it?'

'I mean just what I said: it was empty when they opened it. If Tom Chard is to be believed . . . and I see no reason why he shouldn't be . . . neither he nor Timms had ever seen the inside of it until they opened it for themselves. Lieutenant Chipperfield brought it with him from the *Vengeful*, and he took it with him when he escaped from the fortress. And he gave it to Midshipman Paget, and Paget gave it to them. And they opened it – and it was empty.'

Elizabeth and Aske stared at each other, and it was a toss-up which of them was more at sea now, thought Elizabeth – at sea in an open boat, shrouded in mist, with an empty box for company.

'So what did they do?' Elizabeth broke the silence.

'They rowed all that day, and most of the night.'

'In the fog?' said Aske, suddenly irritable.

'They were picked up by a fishing boat, off Ramsgate. They were lucky, Mr Aske.'

'Lucky?'

'They could have been rescued by the navy – by one of the blockade ships.'

256

Aske nodded. 'Then it would have been back to duty? But the fishermen didn't turn them in, you mean?'

'That is correct.'

'So they deserted – "R" for "Run" – I remember, Professor. They'd had enough of the Royal Navy!'

Wilder nodded. 'Also correct. And it would have been worse for Timms – if he'd chosen to be an American, anyway.'

'Of course! Because the Yankees were at war with us by then!' Aske whistled through his teeth. 'It would have been Dartmoor Prison for him – would it?'

Wilder inclined his head doubtfully. 'They might have taken a more lenient view. They weren't always uncivilized. But there was that risk, certainly.'

It was no wonder they'd *run*, decided Elizabeth. Life ashore if you were poor could have been no picnic anywhere in those days. But life afloat in the twentieth year of the war with France would have been a worse bargain. And if any men had done their bit, Tom Chard and Abraham Timms had done theirs.

'And yet that isn't the whole truth, I suspect,' said Wilder gently. 'I think . . . from what Tom Chard said between Parson Ward's lines . . . I think they still reckoned they were under their officer's orders.' He paused. 'I think that they were simple men – Timms less simple than Chard, but both essentially simple men.' His eyes fell to the *Vengeful* box. 'It is possible that I am imagining too far now . . . but they had their orders . . . and they had *that* . . . and simple men tend to approach life's problems literally.'

'And what was their problem?' Aske sniffed. 'Other than keeping out of the press-gang's clutches?'

'It was very simple – and very complicated. They had the surgeon's case, by which the Lieutenant had set such store . . . *but they didn't know what to do with it, Mr Aske.*'

The box was beginning to hypnotize Elizabeth: it had

come ashore from the *Vengeful*, against the odds of shipwreck; and it had travelled to Lautenbourg – and out of Lautenbourg, down an unclimbable cliff; and it had travelled across France in the midst of a twenty-year war, and had come through the waves from the dying midshipman into a stolen boat – and then into a Ramsgate boat, good luck cancelling bad – and finally ashore . . . the odds building up and multiplying all the way . . . and somehow, in the end, to Father, and to her . . . and now it was *here*, in a strange house, hypnotizing her.

'They'd have done best to chuck it overboard,' said Aske. 'If it was empty – '

'But they didn't.' Wilder sounded almost triumphant in his statement of the obvious. 'It is here. So that was what they didn't do – that, at least, is certain!'

'So what did they do with it?' Aske swivelled towards Elizabeth. 'How did your father get it, Miss Loftus?'

Elizabeth looked at Professor Wilder helplessly. 'His crew gave it to him – the survivors – ?'

'They bought it from White and Cooper, Antiques, of Southsea, Miss Loftus.' Wilder nodded. 'Binnacles and barnacles, and a wealth of maritime knick-knackery, much of it spurious and all of it over-priced, according to David Audley's young man. But old Mr Cooper – who was young Mr Cooper then – remembers buying it, and selling it . . . And he bought it from the intestate estate of Mrs Agnes Childe, of Cosham, with a job lot of junk, because he wanted some choice items which had been included in the lot, which he had spotted . . . And, fortunately for us, old Mr Cooper is old enough – and rich enough – not only to remember his sharp practice, but to exult in it . . . *And* to remember that Mrs Agnes Childe was *née* O'Byrne, of Ratsey and O'Byrne, ship's chandlers and merchants of Portsmouth – two very old-established families of Hampshire, in business and commerce . . . and in Parliament too, after the Reform Bill of 1832, in the Whig interest.' He was looking at Elizabeth now. 'Agnes married the Honourable Algernon Childe, who got himself killed in 1915, at Ypres, with the Grenadiers. Which left only the old lady, with all her family debris – the Honourable Algernon being a younger son, with nothing to his name except his name . . . But it's the other names that ring the bell – eh, Miss Loftus?'

She knew then. Even before he reached down and opened the box-lid, *she knew*, because she had polished those names dozens of times.

'*Amos Ratsey, Jas. O'Byrne, Octavius Phelan* . . .' he read from the plate inside the lid. 'All the names of Dr William Willard Pike's grateful patients – *"With the Respectful Compliments of Amos Ratsey, Jas. O'Byrne, Octavius Phelan, Edward MacBaren, Chas. Lepine, Michael Haggerty, Jas. Fitzgerald, Edmund Hoagland, Thomas Flower, Patrick Moonan of Portsmouth, Southsea and Cosham"* – grateful patients all . . . Or maybe not, perhaps?'

'Why not, Professor?' asked Aske.

'Who were they, Mr Aske? Men of some substance, undoubtedly – Ratsey and O'Byrne were, certainly!' He nodded. 'They did not combine their enterprises until 1815, but in 1812 they both held valuable contracts for supplying naval stores, and did business in the dockyards. And after the war they branched out into war surplus in the South American trade – guns and uniforms as well as stores and provisions . . . for the freedom fighters of those times – all quite respectable, as well as being profitable.' He smiled. 'Men of substance – such men as might well respectfully compliment their physician on his patriotism, and could afford to buy him a new set of the tools of his trade.'

'So what, then?'

'So who were the rest of them? Amongst my friends and contacts locally, and among the excellent employees of the Central Library and Museums staffs, not one of those names rings any bell as a local gentleman in the

Portsmouth district of that time.' Wilder shook his head. 'There was a Tom Flower who plied his trade ferrying officers to their ships – a one-eyed fellow with an exemption certificate in his pocket, to keep the press-gang off his back . . . And a "Jim Fitzgerald" jailed for sedition in 1814, for damning the King's eyes and wishing Parliament hanged, among other things . . . But neither of them sound like Dr Pike's grateful patients.'

'Well, you'd hardly expect to trace everyone from those days, surely?'

'You'd be surprised, dear boy. It was a much smaller world then. I would have expected more than two at the first trawl.' He looked at Aske shrewdly. 'And I would certainly have expected Dr Pike himself.'

'Dr Pike . . . himself?'

'There was no physician of that name practising in the Portsmouth region in the first twenty years of the nineteenth century. And neither is there a Pike in any naval list my friends in Greenwich can turn up.' The shrewd look came to Elizabeth. 'Pandora's box, you have here, my dear: we open it, and whatever there may once have been in it, only mysteries pop out of it now.'

Aske shook his head. 'He needn't have been a Portsmouth man – but that won't do, will it! Not if Ratsey and O'Byrne were local . . .'

'No. But he could have been signed on by the captain of the *Vengeful* in a foreign port on a temporary basis – ship's surgeons came in all shapes and sizes in those days. Only the same objection still holds good – the inconvenient Messrs Ratsey and O'Byrne – how did he know them, then?' Wilder shook his head back at Aske.

Aske made a face. 'But even if we can trace them all somehow, in the end . . . that still won't tell us what was in the box.' He looked sidelong at Elizabeth. 'Even if we were in a position to guess, we can never know, not now.'

'No, Mr Aske,' said Wilder. 'But we could try another

guess . . . which would make the contents of the box, if any, altogether unimportant.'

'What?' Momentarily Aske had been wrapped up in his own imaginings; which, Elizabeth supposed, were of Colonel Suchet's ultimate Portsmouth Plan. 'If any?'

Wilder spread his hands. 'We are assuming, quite reasonably, that the box contained something of value. But suppose, Mr Aske, that it was *the box itself* which was the thing of value? What do we have then?'

Elizabeth stared at the box. 'A list of names – '

'A list of names! Precisely, Miss Loftus. Amos Ratsey, Jas. O'Byrne, Octavius Phelan – a list of names where no one would look twice at them, even if that was what he was looking for.'

'Good God!' exclaimed Aske. 'Not "Jas." for "Jasper" – "Jas." stands for *James* – James O'Byrne – *James Burns!*'

'Ah . . .' Wilder picked up Aske's excitement. 'That small adjustment means something to you, does it?'

'James Burns does, by God!' Aske stepped round to get a better view of the inside of the lid. 'And half those other names are Irish – that fits too.'

'More than half, dear boy,' amended Wilder mildly. 'Am I to assume from this that James O'Byrne, *alias* Burns, was a French agent? And the others were his friends? His spy-ring, or whatever the term they favoured then? A Franco-Hibernian group, anyway – wild geese come home to roost, eh?'

Had that been his guess all along, wondered Elizabeth; but because he hadn't lost his good teacher's preference for drawing out his pupils he'd let them come to it in their own way?

'Franco-Irish-American, perhaps.' Aske's second thoughts were more cautious. 'We've still got a lot of checking ahead of us . . . but it does fit some of *our* facts quite well – don't you agree, Miss Loftus?'

Elizabeth nodded, yet found herself drawn to the

expression on the old man's face: it was as though he was willing her to go on, to build more elaborately on their card-house of guesses.

A tragedy, he had said. And there was a hint of sadness in that look of his, which reminded her of that.

'Amos Ratsey and James . . . Burns,' she began tentatively. 'If they were spies, they were never caught, were they?'

Wilder shook his head. 'No. They both flourished like the proverbial green bay-tree after the war. That is a fact – a historical fact.'

'Huh! They cut their losses, and joined the winning side,' said Aske. 'But after the retreat from Moscow they didn't have much choice – Moscow, and then the failure of the American invasion of Canada . . . and then Napoleon was beaten at Leipzig, and Wellington crossed the Pyrenees from Spain – what else could they do but keep their heads down and hope no one rumbled them?'

Amos Ratsey and James Burns had lived to keep their secret – a secret which Tom Chard hadn't known when he told his part of the tale, years afterwards, to Parson Ward. But that wasn't the tragedy – it was more like the luck of the Irish. So what –

'What I'd like to know is how the devil Agnes – what was her name? Agnes *née* O'Byrne, anyway – how she got hold of *that*?' Aske pointed at the *Vengeful* box. 'Chard and Timms must have brought it ashore. But what did they do with it then, I wonder?'

That was it: Humphrey Aske had been tracking her own thoughts, but somehow he'd overtaken her on the home straight.

She stared at Wilder. 'They gave it to James Burns, of course. Is that what they did, Professor?'

'I don't know, Miss Loftus.' He stared back at her. 'Yet that would seem like another very fair guess . . . Or, let's say, I can think of no other way it could have become an O'Byrne family heirloom.'

Aske frowned. 'Why on earth did they give it to him?' He shook his head. 'Timms and Chard weren't spies, for God's sake, were they?'

'That they were not, Mr Aske. I think they were good men and true – true to their salt, even the American. I believe that they must have come ashore with it, but they didn't know what to do with it. So they read the names on the lid – or Abraham Timms did – the names and the places . . . and they decided to deliver the box to one of those names. They may have looked for Ratsey first – or maybe O'Byrne was the first name they traced.' He shrugged. 'It's even possible they were aware they ought to give it to someone in authority, but they couldn't do that, could they?'

'You're darn right! Not if they were also busy deserting! Even going back to Portsmouth would have been like putting their heads in the lion's mouth – that would be one hell of a risk for them. But why should they want to do that?'

'Why indeed?' Wilder's voice was gentle. 'Why do men do brave deeds – if I knew that I would be wiser than I am! How did the O'Byrne family get the box? We don't know – but they *did* get it . . . And why did O'Byrne keep the box?' He smiled. 'But he *did* keep it, for here it is – and that was an irrational act. And that is what men do, Mr Aske: they act irrationally, as their instincts prompt them to do.' He stopped smiling. 'Or it could be that Chard and Timms were simply keeping faith with men they admired – "*a noble-hearted and humane officer*" was how Tom Chard described his lieutenant – and little Paget was a "*high-spirited young gentleman*" . . . Keeping faith is another irrational act, more often than not. But men will persist in doing it.'

Elizabeth shivered. 'How awful!'

'Awful?' Aske snuffled as though amused. 'If it's true, I'd like to have seen Burns's face when they turned up with it – it must have put the fear of God up him!' He

263

chuckled. 'And then the relief when he twigged they were deserters! I'll bet he filled their pockets with guineas to enable them to make themselves scarce, too . . . If it's true it's a damn good story, I'll say that for it!'

Elizabeth was scandalized. 'But it's an awful story, Mr Aske! The lieutenant and the midshipman – they went through all that, and then they died for nothing – *absolutely nothing!*' The enormity of the *Vengeful* tragedy suddenly enveloped her. 'They all died for nothing, really –'

'Chard and Timms got away, remember!' Aske moved to make amends.

'But they gave the box to Burns – of all men – '

Aske seemed to be trying not to smile. 'But it didn't matter either way by then, Miss Loftus. There wasn't going to be an invasion by then, anyway. It was all for nothing from the start – that's what I mean. Don't you see the irony of it?'

Irony? thought Elizabeth. It was the uselessness of all that courage and endurance and ingenuity which cut so deep. The irony was merely an insult added to that injury.

'But cheer up, Miss Loftus.' Aske managed to make the smile almost kindly. 'Professor Wilder may still be quite wrong, you know. There could be other explanations – dozens of them . . . We don't know who Dr Pike was yet, for a start – or how he and his amazing box got aboard the *Vengeful* . . . And Timms could have been an American agent – a sort of prototype CIA man – and we don't know how he joined the *Vengeful* either . . . All we know is that we've a lot more work to do. But now at least we know where to start looking.'

Professor Wilder reached down to close the lid of the box, replacing the *Guardian* on it as though to cover up the dark tale he had conjured from it. 'And I can probably help you there. I have contacts on both sides of the Atlantic.'

They were both trying to jolly her out of her depression,

but she couldn't be lifted so easily. There was something malevolent about that box – and about the long-lost *Vengeful* herself, too. The *Vengeful* was to blame for everything, it seemed to her suddenly.

'She was an unlucky ship.' The words discharged her feelings. 'She killed them all – all but two.'

'My dear . . . they were all unlucky ships, the *Vengeful*s,' said Wilder softly.

'What?' She looked at him in surprise.

'Didn't your father ever tell you? They had the reputation for being killers. Great fighters too, to be fair – *"Storm and tempest/fear and foes/They'll be with her where/the Vengeful goes"* – that's what they used to say about her. Didn't he tell you?'

She shook her head.

'That was one reason why they re-named the thirteenth *Vengeful*, my dear. Add unlucky thirteen to a bad-luck name, and that's a sure recipe for disaster.' He pointed to the box. 'And the navy's got too much riding on *her* for anything to be allowed to go wrong this time.'

'What d'you mean – this time?' She didn't understand.

'It's in the paper today.' He stooped and picked up the *Guardian* – it had been the newspaper, not the box, at which he had pointed. '*"Wonder ship on missile tests"* – ' he passed the paper to her ' – you can read it for youself.'

Elizabeth took the paper automatically. There was a large, slightly blurred picture of one of those ugly modern warships, all top-heavy with modern gadgetry, which were so different from the greyhounds of Father's time.

She read the caption: *"HMS Shannon, the Navy's new anti-submarine command vessel, leaving the pier at the Kyle of Lochalsh base for trials with the air-dropped Stingray anti-submarine missile and the new generation heavyweight torpedo'.*

And the story was in bold type below the *Wonder ship* heading: '*High ranking American and NATO naval officers shipped aboard the latest addition to the Royal*

Navy's anti-submarine capability, the command vessel HMS Shannon, yesterday.

'They left the new pier at the Kyle of Lochalsh for a demonstration of anti-submarine warfare in Europe's only offshore range, the British Underwater Test and Evaluation Centre, in 10 square miles of the inner Sound of Raasay, off the west Ross-shire coast of Scotland.

'The "Shannon" will show off weapons systems which the Government hopes to sell to NATO on the top-secret range, which boasts a multi-million pound installation of sea-bed hydrophones and cable links to a mainland computer . . .'

'What wonder ship?' asked Aske.

'The *Shannon*,' said Elizabeth.

'In attendance will be a small fleet of auxiliary ships and one of the Navy's nuclear-powered attack submarines, HMS "Swiftsure", which it is thought will be playing the part of a Soviet intruder . . .'

'What's that got to do with us, for heaven's sake?' said Aske a little tetchily.

'See for yourself.' Elizabeth handed him the *Guardian*.

'Wonder ship on missile tests?' Aske wrinkled his nose at the headline, and then studied the text briefly. 'Very interesting, I'm sure . . . But, more to the point, Professor – can you give us the names of those contacts of yours? I think we'll be needing them.'

Wilder inclined his head. 'In anticipation of just that request, Mr Aske, I have prepared a little list for you.' He produced a long white envelope from his breast pocket. 'For the Americans I have also written brief letters of introduction. For the English, it will be sufficient to mention my name . . . And now I must be away, regretfully.' He bowed to Elizabeth.

Aske looked at Elizabeth quickly. 'But won't you stay, Professor? I'm sure Mrs Audley will expect us to ask you to . . . and we do still need your brains, sir.'

'No. I think you'll do very well without me.' Wilder

spoke with the resolution of a grandee. 'Besides which, at my age one becomes a creature of habit, and my house-keeper has a steak-and-kidney pie and a bottle of Beaune waiting for me . . . And these August evenings are closing in, and it will be dark soon, and the forecast is for rain . . . and I have an hour's drive ahead of me. So thank you – but no.' He turned for a last time to Elizabeth. 'Miss Loftus . . . it has been a pleasure. And I hope you will regard me as a friend now, and will call on me. I see far too few young women these days.'

'Professor . . .' In any other circumstances she would have been flattered by that, and would have reacted to it somehow. But her mind was bobbing wildly in the *Shannon*'s wake, somewhere between Kyle of Lochalsh and the inner Sound of Raasay.

'I can see that your brain's full of new thoughts!' He smiled impishly. 'And that's what makes the historian, Miss Loftus – the sudden fertilization of knowledge by intelligence, to breed some tiny embryo of truth! Nurture it, Miss Loftus, nurture it and cherish it!' He swung back to Aske. 'Now, Mr Aske – ?'

Aske gave Elizabeth another of his quick looks. 'Yes, Professor . . . Allow me to see you out – '

They went, leaving Elizabeth to her own thoughts, which were carrying her on an irresistible tide past the old *Vengeful* on the rocks of Les Echoux and the *Fortuné* on the Horse Sands, towards the *Shannon* –

The door-latch clattered again eventually.

'That wasn't overwhelmingly civilized, Miss Loftus, if I may say so,' Aske chided her. 'The old boy expected a more graceful dismissal, after all his trouble, you know.'

She heard him, but the words hardly registered; she could think only . . . *if I can see it, why can't he see it?*

He shook his head. 'Maybe he wasn't quite expecting a peck on the cheek. But you could at least have shaken his hand.'

Her confidence ebbed. If it meant nothing to him when

267

it was so obvious, then perhaps it *was* nothing – a thing long since considered and discarded.

'Now the poor old boy believes you still haven't forgiven him for whatever it was he quarrelled over with your father – '

Whatever it was?

' – and we still may need his help, Miss Loftus.'

He didn't know! It seemed impossible to her. But then, when she remembered how contemptuous Paul had been of him, and how Paul had gone about everything, it suddenly didn't seem so unlikely – it almost became inevitable, rather –

'Miss Loftus?' He had realized at last that she was only half listening to him.

'Don't you know what they quarrelled about, Mr Aske?'

'Does it matter?'

Did it matter? Even if he didn't know, Paul did – and Dr Audley must know too . . . Was it possible that they hadn't seen the wood for the trees? Or was there simply no wood to see?

'It was over the *Shannon*, Mr Aske.'

'Oh?' His glance flicked to the *Guardian*. 'Well, I hardly think that matters.' He sounded as though he was finding politeness difficult. 'Does it?'

'She was originally named the *Vengeful* – until about eighteen months ago, when they were fitting her out. Father got very angry about the re-naming.'

'Did he, indeed?' He started to yawn, then quickly put his hand to his mouth. 'Mmm?'

'Doesn't that . . .' Diffidence almost froze her, but for a tiny red spark of anger which his boredom kindled '. . . doesn't that suggest anything to you?'

'Well . . . to be honest, Miss Loftus, the only thing I can think about at the moment is my dinner. That's what the Professor's steak-and-kidney pie did for me, I'm afraid.' He indicated the door. 'Shall we go and see what that precocious child is up to?' He smiled. 'Then – '

The spark blazed into fire. '*Mr Aske!*'

He raised his hands. 'All right, all right! The *Shannon* was once the *Vengeful*. Then so what?'

'Can't you see? Isn't it possible that we – that *you* – and Dr Mitchell and Dr Audley – that you've all been following the wrong *Vengeful*?'

He looked at her strangely, no longer bored, but with an expression in which so many emotions conflicted that there was no room for any one of them. 'What do you mean – the *wrong* – ?'

She had to get it right. 'This finding out what really happened in 1812, Mr Aske – you don't really care about that – you *can't* care about it . . . It's what's happening *now* that you care about – about . . .' she licked her lips '. . . about what the Russians are doing.' She forced the bogey-name out, even though it sounded unreal to her, on her own lips: she shouldn't be telling him this – it had nothing to do with her.

'The . . . *Russians,* Miss Loftus?' He seemed to sense her embarrassment, but was not disposed to help her. 'The *Russians*?'

Only her anger sustained her. 'Paul told me about this thing – this Project Vengeful – '

'He told you *that*?' Aske's own anger sparked suddenly. 'He had absolutely no right to do any such thing! That's quite appalling!'

'But he did, Mr Aske.' She hated Aske then, as irrationally as she loved Paul, so that both emotions were equally painful to her. 'He trusted me.'

'That's what's so appalling!' snarled Aske. 'My God! I'll see him hang for that!'

'You'll see him hang?' Elizabeth's loyalty fixed itself irrevocably on Paul. 'But you'll phone London first, Mr Aske.'

'I'll phone London?'

'That's right.'

'Why?'

Why? But she wasn't going to argue with him. 'Because I want you to do that – that's why.'

Not for Humphrey Aske was Paul's Theory of Contemporaneity – that would only make him laugh at her, and at Paul too!

'That's not a reason, Miss Loftus. I'm not about to make myself a fool for you.'

Then more fool he! But she wasn't, in her turn, about to explain why the timing of the Russians' *Vengeful* Project and the re-naming of the *Vengeful* made sense to her: if that was foolishness, it must be hers, not Paul's. That was the least she could do for him.

'Then I'll phone London, Mr Aske. Cathy will give me a number – she's precocious enough for that. Or there'll be a number somewhere – I'll go on phoning until I get it, starting from 999 and working upwards, even if I'm still trying to find it when Faith Audley gets back – and then she'll give it to me.' She looked down at him obstinately. 'And then we'll see who's the fool – you or me.'

'I already know who the fool is.' He tried to stare her down, and she felt his will harden against hers, as it had never hardened before. But that only made it a straight contest, and in a contest she outnumbered him – all the ghosts from the past crowded behind Commander Loftus's daughter: Lieutenant Chipperfield and Midshipman Paget, and Tom Chard and Abraham Timms, who had kept faith and had done their duty after their fashion, even though faith and duty had made fools of them.

His will crumbled against such odds. 'Very well. I give you best, Miss Loftus – I'll telephone for you, if that's what you want. But on your head be it. What do you want me to say?'

'Just remind them that the *Shannon* used to be the *Vengeful*.'

'Is that all?' He seemed on the point of refusing again, but then thought better of it. 'All right. But you stay here while I phone – if I have to make a fool of myself I'd prefer to do it by myself. I'll do it on those terms only.'

'Thank you, Mr Aske.'

He stared at her. 'I think I'd rather you didn't thank me, Miss Loftus.' Time stood still as she waited: the effort of imposing her will on him seemed to have drained her energy, and she found it impossible to concentrate on anything except the need to wait patiently. The house was very quiet, she thought.

Then the door opened, and Aske was staring at her again. 'I'm sorry, Miss Loftus,' he said.

'Sorry?'

'I owe you an apology.' His lips tightened. 'We have to go to London now – at once.' The skin had tightened on his face too, heightening the cheek-bones and jaw-line with stress; except that such a transformation must be in her own mind, imagined out of the change in his manner.

'We've got to go to London?' she echoed him stupidly.

'*You* have. I have to take you there.' The stretched skin shivered. 'I spoke to David Audley. I told him what you said about the *Shannon* – and the *Vengeful*. He was . . . he was rather upset by it, Miss Loftus.'

Her mouth opened. 'David Audley?'

He nodded. 'I spoke to him. He's getting a message to Kyle of Lochalsh, to our security people there. They're going to abort the trials, Miss Loftus.'

Her mouth closed, but her brain swirled. 'You spoke to . . . David Audley?'

'Yes.' He gestured urgently. 'Come on – *at once* means what it says in our business. It means *drop whatever you're doing and move* – ' he turned on his heel and opened the door for her.

She couldn't think straight. 'But, Mr Aske – '

'Come on, Miss Loftus – *now!*'

She went through the door. The passage was dark now, no longer green-shadowed, with the feeble light of the distant chandelier in the hall blackening the windows.

He overtook her at the entrance, reaching past her to lift the heavy iron latch on the outer door.

She didn't want to go outside, even though outside was only blue-grey, and much lighter than the yellow gloom around her.

'Quickly, Miss Loftus – ' He handed over her raincoat.

Cobwebs of rain drifted around her, and the wet smell of the countryside entered her lungs – the smell of growing things, sharpened by a distant hint of autumn to come.

Aske crunched past her on the gravel, reaching this time for the car door – swinging it open for her.

No!

He was already moving round the front of the car, as though he took for granted that the open door must suck her in, regardless of her own free will.

She straightened up. 'I can't go just like this, Mr Aske. I must say goodbye to Cathy.'

She didn't wait for his reaction, but turned on her heel back towards the house.

Through the door again – then to the doorway into which Cathy had disappeared – through that door –

A waft of warmer air and light engulfed her simultaneously: the kitchen was huge and bright with the innumerable reflections of electricity on copper pots hanging in descending size from a great beam, and Cathy herself was bending over the kitchen table – a great expanse of ancient working surface which looked as if it had been not so much scrubbed as holystoned colourless like the old *Vengeful*'s quarterdeck, only by generations of kitchen-maids under cook's eagle eye.

'Oh, Elizabeth!' Cathy half-straightened up over her own small area of chaos in the expanse. 'Something's gone wrong with Mummy's *crèmes brûlées* – they haven't brûléed properly, darn it!'

'Where's your father, Cathy?'

'He isn't back yet.' Cathy bent over the chaos.

'But you said he went somewhere with your mother?'

272

'Um – yes.' Cathy prodded one of the messes tentatively. 'They went to Guildford to look at curtain material.'

'Together?'

'Uh-huh. She's been on at him for ages – it's for his study, so she says he's got to like it. And when he couldn't go to France she said she'd got him at last.' The child looked up again. 'He was waiting for you, but he didn't expect you so early – he'll be back any moment, I should think.'

'He didn't go to London?'

'Why should he go to London?' Cathy looked puzzled. 'The curtain shop's in Guildford.'

'Could he have changed his mind?'

'Why should he do that? It's a super shop.' Cathy licked her finger. 'He didn't, anyway.'

'How do you know, dear?'

'Because he left the telephone number. He always leaves it, when he knows where he's going, in case an urgent message comes. So if he'd changed his mind he'd have phoned. That's the proper drill, you see, Elizabeth.' The child spoke with all the certainty of someone who knew her drill and was proud of being a Ranger's daughter. 'And he wouldn't leave Mummy in Guildford – there are no buses home . . . What's the matter, Elizabeth?'

The front door clattered.

'They'll be back soon,' Cathy reassured her. 'They must be caught in the traffic.'

Elizabeth walked quickly round the table and picked up one of the *brûlées*.

'Miss Loftus!' said Aske sharply from behind her.

'You're right, dear.' She scrutinized the *brûlée* closely. 'Could it be something to do with the sugar you used?'

'*Miss Loftus!*' He sounded close to brûléeing himself.

'I was just coming, Mr Aske.' She allowed herself a touch of irritability, but then smiled at the child. 'I would leave them, if I were you, Cathy dear – they'll be all right.'

She set the *brûlée* down among its fellows. 'But now we must go, dear – ' she started moving as she spoke.

'What?' squeaked Cathy. 'But, Elizabeth – '

'Must go!' She blotted out the child's voice with her own as she accelerated out of the kitchen. 'Give my love to your mother, and tell her I'll be back soon – ' Aske was standing aside for her, but was looking past her at the child, *and that wouldn't do* ' – come on, Mr Aske, then! Don't just stand there!' She checked her advance momentarily, long enough to shepherd him ahead of her before the child could betray them both, almost pushing him. Yet even as he moved, he did so crab-wise and doubtfully, still looking past her, as though spiked on a dilemma.

'Elizabeth!' she heard Cathy call behind her.

'That poor child!' snapped Elizabeth severely at Aske. 'You didn't give me a chance to explain – she won't know what to think . . . Do you want me to go back? Have we time for that? Surely we have?' She slowed down perceptibly.

'No.' Aske's doubts resolved themselves. 'We must go – you're right. I'll get David Audley to phone her.'

The delicate spatter of rain had increased to a drizzle slanting out of a uniformly grey-black sky pressing down on them, out of which the dark had come prematurely.

'A damned dirty night,' said Aske. 'And by the look of it there's most of it still to come. Fasten your seat-belt, Miss Loftus. The roads are going to be slippery.'

Elizabeth fastened her belt unwillingly: it was like snapping her freedom away.

Then the engine was alive; and in quick succession the headlights blazed ahead, darkening the half-light, and the windscreen wipers swept the rain away contemptuously.

'Where are we going?' She tried to push back the reality with a matter-of-fact question as the car moved forward.

Fact – matter-of-*fact*: they had turned themselves inside out with so many theories, these last twenty-four hours, that the fact of his deliberate lie filled her mind like a monstrous plant in a hot-house which had stifled all other growth.

'London,' he answered eventually. 'I told you.'

'But where exactly?'

'One of our places. You don't really need to know, and I'm not at liberty to say, anyway – sorry.' He shook his head apologetically.

She tried to think. 'Paul said we should stay inside the house, and not go anywhere.'

'Yes. But Dr Audley says otherwise, and he outranks Dr Mitchell. He's the boss.' He braked suddenly, and swung the wheel. In the half-gloom Elizabeth missed the signpost and could see only that they had taken a more minor road at a junction.

She tried to look over her shoulder. 'I think you've taken the wrong road – '

'This is a short-cut. Don't worry.'

They were never going to meet Audley and Faith coming back from Guildford on this road, thought Elizabeth.

'You must be tired,' said Aske solicitously. 'Why don't you lie back and close your eyes, and leave the navigation to me? I'll wake you up in good time.'

'Yes . . .' She was aware of the truth of what he had said: under her present mental confusion and disquiet she was bone-weary. So much had happened so quickly, and all of it so strange and so frightening, that it was no wonder she couldn't think straight – that she was starting to imagine things . . . and it was all beyond her understanding in any case. There was nothing she could do . . . there never had been anything she could do, from the start she had been helpless, pushed one way, then pulled another – it was her rôle in life, it seemed. 'Yes . . . perhaps I will.'

'That's right . . . You can let the seat back, if you like – there's a catch down by the side somewhere.'

'Yes.' She fumbled between the seats.

'Don't undo the safety-belts by mistake . . . When we've had our little talk with Dr Audley I'll put you into a nice hotel for the night,' he said soothingly.

A little talk with Dr Audley, she thought to herself almost lethargically – she could feel the seat-belt releases, but not the seat-reclining catch, darn it! – but that was one thing she wasn't going to have . . .

'Then you can dream about Lieutenant Chipperfield, and Mr Midshipman Paget, and Chard and Timms, and all the rest of them,' murmured Aske.

Elizabeth's hand found the catch, and closed on it.

Lieutenant Chipperfield, and Midshipman Paget, and Tom Chard, and Abraham Timms – they had all been trapped by misfortune, far from home and in a hostile land –

The car slowed.

'What is it?' asked Elizabeth.

'There's a phone-box just ahead.' Aske brought the car to a halt, and Elizabeth saw the dim-lighted box in the headlights. 'There's another routine call I've just remembered I ought to make, in case anyone phones the house. I won't be a moment, Miss Loftus.'

They seemed to be in the middle of nowhere, with no other light in sight through the rain-blurred windows of the car, and only a road sign warning 'Bend' picked out in the dipped beams as an evidence of civilization.

She stared at the shadowy figure in the phone-box, and a terrible certainty consumed her, driving out everything else – a certainty built out of innumerable small happenings cemented to that one great lie by an instinct which was suddenly so strong that she could feel her hand on the seat-catch shake –

Treachery!

Treachery? But if *not* treachery – if she was *wrong*?

No. *No, no, no, no, no – treachery!*

'Well, that's all right, then!' said Aske cheerfully, glancing at her quickly as he let out the clutch. 'But you haven't put the seat down yet – you'll doze much better with it down.'

The car was accelerating fast. Elizabeth could see the red reflectors of the bend in the distance.

'I can't find the catch,' said Elizabeth hoarsely.

'I'll find it for you – ' he took one hand off the wheel.

Faster – the rain slashed down on to the screen –

'No – I've got it now!' said Elizabeth.

'Fine. Sweet dreams, Miss Loftus, then.'

There were no sweet dreams, only nightmares in which the red reflectors burned like eyes, increasing in numbers as the car entered the bend.

Elizabeth released Aske's safety-belt and twisted the wheel into the red eyes.

EPILOGUE:
The fate of the hero's daughter

The car door slammed outside, but Mitchell discovered that he didn't want to get up now, after having listened so attentively for so long for any slightest distant noise which might herald Audley's return: somewhere along the line of time marked by the ticking of the grandfather clock in the corner he had ceased to expect good news and had started to fear the worst, his unwillingness told him.

And the fear only took hold of him more strongly as he glanced down at the papers on the desk in front of him: his own hand-written account of the untimely passing of Patrick Lawrence Donaghue, William Harold Fullick and Julian Alexander Carrell Oakenshaw, each of whom had died by the hand which had wielded the pen; and, beside it, impeccably-typed, Del Andrew's report on the three dead men – *Copies to the Prime Minister's Office (restricted); the Home Secretary (restricted); the Director of Public Prosecutions (restricted); The Acting-Director, DI/R & D (Col. J. Butler, CBE, MC).*

Everything was relative to the occasion, he thought. For the past three days he had been worried sick about all this, and it had been in the back of his mind, warping his judgement and disturbing his concentration the whole time except for that one hour with Elizabeth, when he had exchanged need for need.

But now the bill for that one hour had been delivered, and he couldn't pay it: he didn't give a damn any more for the three men he'd killed, yet the thought of Elizabeth, whom he had failed to preserve, was a cure for the original sickness more expensive and painful than he could endure.

It was no good: he had to make himself get up – he

couldn't put it off any longer. What was coming, was coming whether he wanted to hear it or not.

He got up, and walked to the door. He felt stiff with sitting, and very tired, and cold inside and out – the house itself was cold now, he could feel the chill of it on his cheeks and on the tip of his nose.

Not again, he prayed to himself, *not again.*

The sound of the door seemed unnaturally loud, as all sounds always did in the small hours. But it wasn't the only one loose in the Old House; there were other noises night-walking in it now.

Not Elizabeth – Frances he could accept, had learned to accept – but not Elizabeth too, for Christ's sake!

A board creaked loudly, and he saw Faith Audley halfway down the staircase, enveloped in a red velvet dressing-gown with a fur collar, her pale hair unbound, like a ghost out of the Old House's past. Then the kitchen door at the end of the passage ahead of him banged open, and Audley came through, and he was nothing like any sort of ghost: rain glistened on his face and plastered down his hair, and he carried a bulging brief-case under one arm and an untidily unfurled umbrella under the other.

'What the hell's going on, David?' said Mitchell.

Audley blinked vaguely at him. 'You may well ask! There's a gutter blocked above the kitchen door, and I got a face-full of water as I came in, and I can't see a thing!'

Faith Audley swept down the last of the stairs and relieved her husband of his burdens, setting them down at his feet.

'We've been very worried, David,' she said tightly.

'Oh?' Audley produced a huge silk handkerchief and began to dry off the lenses of his spectacles. 'I should have phoned, of course – yes.' He held up the spectacles to the light. 'But I'm here now.'

Faith caught Mitchell's eye. 'Not worried about you – about Elizabeth. And Mr Aske.'

'About Elizabeth?' Audley brought the spectacles down

slightly, so that for an instant he was observing Mitchell through them. 'What do you know about Elizabeth?'

'We don't know anything about her.' Mitchell heard the sound of desperation, rather than righteous anger, in his voice. 'Where is she, damn it?'

'But you're worried about her?' Audley hooked the spectacles over his ears with maddening clumsiness. 'Why?'

There was no point in letting anger take over from desperation. 'When I got back from London she'd gone – they'd both gone. And you'd gone too . . .' Steady. 'I told Aske quite specifically that he wasn't to let her out of the house.'

'And I told Paul that you were worried when you left,' said Faith.

Audley cast a reproachful look at his wife, then came back to Mitchell. 'So what did you do?'

'I phoned the Duty Officer, of course.' *Steady!*

'And what did *he* say?'

To hell with steadiness! 'Damn it, David – you know what he said! Where the hell is she? What's happened?'

Audley's face became obstinate. 'What did the Duty Officer say?'

This time Mitchell refused to catch Faith's eye. 'The first time he said there was an all-points alarm out on her, and I was told to sit tight. And the second time he referred me to you, fairly politely . . . And the third time he told me to get the hell off the line, he was busy – okay?'

'Okay. So he told you – to go to bed, and mind your own business!' Audley was adamantine. 'So why aren't you in bed minding it?'

'Ff – Elizabeth *is* my business!' *Is* or *was*? he heard himself cry out in pain 'Where is she?'

Faith Audley stirred, tossing back the pale mane of her hair. 'Where is she, David?'

Audley dropped Mitchell instantly, as though he didn't matter, frowning and pointing at his wife accusingly.

'Come on, love – we have a treaty on this – this is *business* –'

'But she was a guest in my house, David.' Obstinacy slammed head-on against obstinacy. 'And she wasn't – *isn't* – one of your people . . . So *I* have a right to know – I don't care what lies you tell Paul here – *I* want to know – *right?*'

There was some ancient quarrel here – something between them that Mitchell couldn't even guess at, but cared about less.

'David – '

'No, Paul!' Faith cut him off. 'Leave this to me . . . David – I *will* have an answer.'

'All right, love.' Audley caved in directly, and so quickly that he took Mitchell by surprise. 'She's alive. And she's safe. My word on it.'

'Thank you, David.' This time Faith Audley didn't catch Mitchell's eye, she stared directly at him as though to confirm the truth of her husband's given word. 'And now I'll go back to bed again.' She gave them both a sudden tired smile, not of understanding, but of relief. 'If you two have things to discuss, the study will be warmer than out here. But don't stay up too long – you both look exhausted.'

As Mitchell followed Audley the words began to sink in: *alive and safe – alive and safe – alive and safe*. He was aware that they were incomplete words, and that they might have other implications. But for that moment they were all he could handle – *alive and safe* was enough for this moment, that was all.

'What's all that on the desk?' said Audley. He took three steps and peered down at the papers. 'What on earth are you bothering with this for?' He frowned accusingly at Mitchell. 'You should have been watching over Elizabeth Loftus – not messing with this!'

Mitchell came back to reality. 'There was a message waiting for me at Heathrow when our plane landed.'

'About this? From whom?'

'From Del Andrew. Or . . . not exactly a message – he just tipped me off that CI 6 was sniffing around, and I'd better get my report into the pipeline before they made it official.'

'Damnation!' Audley smote his forehead. 'That makes two mistakes I've made – three, counting tonight – ' he glanced at the grandfather clock ' – or this morning . . . God, I'm slipping!'

'What mistakes?'

'Your Elizabeth Loftus, for one.' Audley looked at Mitchell keenly. 'You like her, do you? That's the reason for this inquisition, is it?'

Steady again. 'I think she's quite a woman – if you must know, David . . . Yes – I *like* her.'

'Yes.' The look became rueful. 'My dear wife told me as much a couple of nights back – she knew, and I couldn't see it! I said she wasn't your type, and she isn't . . . But *she* said I'd better watch out – that you'd get awkward if things started to go wrong.'

Curiosity. 'And that was your first mistake?'

'That was my *third* mistake. My first was not to realize quite how bright she really was – *is*, thank God!' He drew a deep breath. 'It never occurred to me that she'd put the whole thing together – or half the thing . . . and the most dangerous half, too! God Almighty!' He shook his head.

Humiliation. What had Elizabeth put together that Paul Mitchell had missed?

And double humiliation: unlike Elizabeth, who didn't know Audley as he did, he ought to have known that there was something to put together, because with Audley there always was. And what made it worse was that, in a sense, he *had* known all along –

'I really am rather an idiot,' said Audley. 'I thought I'd got it worked out so well, for once.'

'Oh, yes?' If that was the case, then there was no point

in exploding, Mitchell decided. 'But just tell me one thing, David – I am curious about one thing . . .'

Audley blinked at him. 'Yes?'

'Can you tell me what the hell I've been doing?'

'Ah . . .' Audley blinked again, and then looked round the room. 'Now . . . if we were in the library I could show you, from David Chandler's book on Marlborough. But then, as you're a military historian, you won't need to read about it – you'll know it already.'

'Know what?'

'The battle of Ramillies – 1706.'

'What about the battle of Ramillies?'

'He won it by a diversion: he lured all the French troops to his right flank by attacking there. Then he hit them in the centre.'

A nasty suspicion crystallized in Mitchell. 'Are you telling me that I've been on the right flank of your army?'

'No . . . that's not the point – ' Audley's face creased ' – the point is that Marlborough didn't actually *tell* the troops on the right that the real attack was in the centre, any more than Monty told us in Normandy that our job was to draw off all the German armour so that the Americans could break out elsewhere.' He gave Mitchell a twisted smile. 'We wouldn't actually have mutinied if we'd known . . . but he was right not to tell us. Because the Germans would never have believed that we were the main attack if we hadn't believed it first ourselves, you see. And, in a way, we were *right* to believe in it, Paul, because our diversionary bloodbath was essential to the breakout – it was all the same battle. And I like to think, when I remember absent friends, that we had the place of honour in it, if not the glory.'

Mitchell's eyes strayed to the reports on the table. 'The place of honour' was gift-wrapped bullshit for his benefit. But that 'diversionary bloodbath' was an accurate description for what had happened on Saturday evening.

Or worse than that, even. 'So those three – ' he pointed ' – I killed them . . . as a diversion?'

'Ah . . . no, you mustn't think of it like that. You saved a valuable life – perhaps a very valuable life. It was like saving a child from three mad dogs – you had no choice.'

'But it wasn't planned – it wasn't part of any plan?'

'It was better than we'd planned.' Audley paused. 'We had to convince Moscow that we were chasing the wrong *Vengeful* – just for a few days they had to believe we were off in the wrong direction, and we had to give them those days. And you yourself said that the old *Vengeful* was exactly the sort of hare I'd be tempted to chase – so they thought so too, which was why they let you spot Novikov so easily, of course.'

'But they didn't know about . . . those three . . . and Loftus's money?'

'Not a thing. But when they did, they must have been as pleased as I was – that was a pure bonus for both sides.'

'But how did they know?'

'Because we made damn sure they did – '

'Wait!' Mitchell felt the plot thickening around him too fast. 'You said "the *wrong Vengeful*". So which was the *right* one?'

Audley shook his head. 'Your old *Vengeful* was the right one for you, Paul – and it still is.' Then he grinned. 'But as your Elizabeth knows, I suppose it's unrealistic not to tell you too. And you'll be less trouble knowing than not knowing . . . The real *Vengeful* was the *Shannon*, of course.'

Of course. Stupid. Obvious. *Damn!* 'The *Shannon*?'

'We had our own word on that long ago – that the Russians were planning something . . . Not the actual project name, but just that they intended dealing with the next generation of our anti-submarine systems.' Audley looked at him. 'We don't have many secrets worth having, but if there's one area where we can still claim to be ahead, it's anti-submarine work.'

That was true, even if it was only the natural legacy of the past, in which Britain alone of all other countries had twice nearly been beaten by the submarine, thought Mitchell.

'And their plan was made before the *Vengeful* was renamed? Before she became the *Shannon*?'

Audley nodded. 'That's right. It was as simple as that.' He paused. 'So Oliver St John Latimer and James Cable set up a counter-plan. An in-depth anti-espionage system, you might say . . . And that Latimer's a fat slug, but he's a bloody good operator – better than everyone except me, in fact.' He gave the grandfather clock a calculating look. 'As of two hours from now we're set to take out the biggest Russian espionage operation of the decade, Paul. Not in the full glare of publicity, *alas* – which was what Jack Butler and I wanted . . . It seems that there are political considerations which rule that out – we're only allowed Philby and Maclean and Blunt in public . . . But for once we're about to impress NATO and our American cousins, and we're going to sell maybe a billion pounds' worth of anti-submarine systems over the next decade into the bargain, if we're lucky. And not even a Labour Government – or an SDP one – can quarrel with that.' He looked at Mitchell suddenly. 'Do you understand, Paul?'

Mitchell could only nod. The stakes had been raised far beyond his limit, but at least he could nod.

Audley gestured towards the papers on the desk. 'Which is why I don't think you've got anything to worry about there. We've got too much riding on this operation to let anyone make waves about those three . . . apart from the fact that you were only doing your duty as our diversion man, in any case. And we had to have that diversion.'

'So you knew about their *Vengeful* operation long before the Americans told us about it?'

'That's right. But when we learned that the Americans knew about it we were pretty sure the Russians would be close behind them, and we didn't want them to abort the *Vengeful* one – not after all the trouble we'd gone to. We had to reassure them somehow.' He half-smiled at Mitchell. 'So Jack Butler gave me the job of making a fool of myself . . . and I came up with the old *Vengeful* as an opening ploy – I was going to make a mystery of it somehow . . . Or, if it refused to stand up, we'd got a contingency plan to make something out of the other *Vengeful* – the submarine that was transferred to the Greek navy in '46.' He nodded at Mitchell, and then pointed to the papers again. 'But then those three turned up . . . and Novikov. So what we had was better than I'd hoped for – Commander Loftus's mysterious riches, and three dead gangsters . . . *and* the real mystery of the old *Vengeful* herself – that was a gift from the gods, because it was just the thing to help them believe that the so-clever Dr Audley was about to be too clever for his own good. With a little help from them, of course.'

Mitchell looked at him reproachfully. 'Why didn't you trust me? For God's sake!'

'I wanted to. But it wasn't my operation, and Latimer wanted you to be out of it.' Audley shook his head. 'The trouble was . . . I think the clever Dr Audley *was* a little too clever for his own good' – another shake ' – it never ceases to amaze me how what is basically *simple* becomes distorted and complicated by the human factor – I've *never* been able to make exactly the right allowance for that, you know . . .'

'Like what, for example?' Audley in this self-critical mood was too revealing not to encourage.

'Oh . . . I never expected that smart policeman of ours to crack the source of Commander Loftus's ill-gotten gains so quickly . . . Not that it mattered – but it might have mattered.' Another shake. Then he looked at Mitchell. 'And the French putting that red-headed beauty of yours on you – after they'd picked up the KGB so quickly: I didn't plan for you to be expelled from

France like that, or not until our *Shannon* Operation was complete.'

'No?' The memory of an icy Nikki MacMahon seeing him off from the departure lounge still rankled with Mitchell too.

'No. We were meant to be sleeping soundly in Alsace by now – you and I and your Elizabeth . . . with Comrade Aske watching over us. And after a good Alsatian dinner, too.' But Audley wasn't smiling. 'That's how the big things go wrong – from too many little miscalculations.'

'But . . . nothing big has gone wrong?' *Safe and alive* comforted Mitchell. He might never see Elizabeth again now; and even if he did he would never be able to convince her that he hadn't known about his true rôle – that they had both been ignorant foot-soldiers in the same battle. But *safe and alive* was better than nothing – with these stakes and these players it could pass for a happy ending, near enough.

'No. Nothing seems to have gone wrong . . . not so far, anyway.' Audley gave the grandfather clock another look. 'So long as they believe Aske and Elizabeth are both dead. And there's no reason why they shouldn't . . . and even if they are jumpy at this end, there's not much they can do to unscramble their set-up in Scotland now, with Latimer's chaps already closing in – '

'Dead?' Mitchell's jaw dropped. 'Aske . . . and Elizabeth?'

'Accidentally dead.' Audley adjusted his spectacles on his nose. 'They ran out of road about five miles from here this evening, on the Three Pigeons bend just outside Buckland. You may know the place – it's on the back road about a hundred yards before the Three Pigeons pub. It's a notoriously bad place – the bend's deceptive and the camber's wrong, which is why the highways people put up the posts with the warning reflectors there, on the edge of the concrete culvert – a bad place at the best of times.' He shook his head. 'It was pelting down with rain, and he was probably driving too fast. And he was tired . . . tired and scared, I'd guess . . .'

The moment was unreal because what Audley was telling him had all the hallmarks of a cover story being rehearsed – the circumstantial detail exact, the reasonable hypothesis for what had actually been an entirely different event, even the note of regret in the voice. Mitchell could remember staging similar lies himself in his time.

'There really has been an accident?'

Audley frowned. 'That's what I'm telling you. They skidded and went straight through the posts into the culvert, on the back road there – but she's all right, I tell you.'

'What the hell was Aske doing on the back road?' Mitchell couldn't place the bend, but he knew the Three Pigeons, he'd fortified himself there long ago, in Frances' time, before a sweaty session in this very room.

'He was making sure he didn't meet me, if you want an educated guess.' Audley pushed at the spectacles again.

'But what does he say?'

'He's not saying anything. He's dead.'

'*Dead?*'

'He went through the windscreen.' Audley's rugger-player's chin jutted out. 'But that didn't kill him, it only cut him up and knocked him out. Only then he rolled off the bonnet into the ditch head-first, and there's always eighteen inches of water in that ditch, even in summer. And *that* killed him.' The voice matched the chin. 'He drowned in eighteen inches of water, Mitchell. And six inches of mud.'

Mitchell's mouth dried up. 'And Elizabeth?'

'She's all right – I told you!' Audley's aggressive tone became defensive. 'Three cracked ribs, and a few bruises . . . and a bit of shock, naturally. But she's a tough girl, is your Elizabeth – women's hockey is a tough game, I'm told . . . And her seat-belt saved her, anyway.'

Seat-belt?

'We've got her down as DOA – "Dead on arrival" – like Aske.' Audley's voice became suddenly softer, almost apologetic. 'I was afraid you might have heard that on the grapevine somehow – it's the official version at the moment. But actually we've got her safe in Hadfield House, under wraps.'

Safe in the safe house again, thought Mitchell automatically.

'She's *okay.*' The big man looked at Mitchell helplessly for a moment. 'I don't lie to my wife. If I have to lie to her, I refuse to tell her anything – or is that too Irish for you to understand?'

Seat-belt, thought Mitchell. 'I don't believe you.'

Conflicting emotions of anger and honesty warred on Audley's face briefly. 'I've talked to her. You can talk to her tomorrow, Paul – in fact, I *want* you to talk to her tomorrow.' Something almost approaching sympathy came out of the conflict. 'That is the truth, Paul.'

Mitchell shook his head. 'I believe *that.*' He searched for the right words. 'But . . . I didn't like Aske, David – I hated his guts, I admit that . . . But if there was one thing he was good at, it was driving a car. He was a bloody good driver – and he was proud of it.' There were no right words: there were only the known and observed facts. 'And he was a careful driver too – he *always* wore his seat-belt, no matter what. He was meticulous about seat-belts – I know, because I travelled with him. So don't give me *accident.*'

'No . . . you're right, of course.' Audley paused. 'I was going to tell you, but I thought it could wait until we'd both had a few hours' sleep.' Another pause. 'We're both pretty tired.'

'Not too tired for the truth. Come on, David.'

'Very well.' Audley blinked. 'She killed him, Paul.'

'She . . . *what?*' The statement was too outrageous for belief. '*Elizabeth . . . ?*'

'Not deliberately.' Audley was committed now. 'She

didn't know the culvert was there – she didn't know he'd end up face-down in eighteen inches of water . . . But she did it – she admits it.'

'Did what?' Belief struggled with disbelief.

'She pressed the button on his safety-belt as she saw the red warning reflectors ahead. And then she twisted the steering wheel.'

Paul swallowed. 'For God's sake, David . . .'

'Why?' Audley gazed at him. 'Because she's a very clever young woman, Paul – and a tough-minded one, too. We both agreed on that, but we still underrated her criminally . . . At least, I did. And so did Humphrey Aske – in his case fatally.'

Unwillingly Mitchell began to accept what he was being told. He had never doubted the steel in Elizabeth's backbone, in spite of her long years of the servitude which she had accepted as duty. But now he had to add a quality of ruthlessness to it which he found hard to take, even if –

'*Aske* – are you telling me that *Aske* . . . ?'

'Was one of theirs?' Audley nodded slowly. 'The fact is, your Elizabeth Loftus did what I never imagined she could do: she guessed that the *Shannon* was the real *Vengeful* – quite extraordinary!'

'How the hell did she manage that?'

'It was something Professor Wilder said, apparently – she was a bit confused about it . . . But then she added up two and two. Only *then*, unfortunately, she told Aske about it after Wilder had gone, and insisted that he phoned London . . . Which he pretended to do, but didn't. Because that was the one connection Moscow couldn't allow, of course.'

They stared at one another.

'Yes . . . we've had Comrade Aske tabbed for about six months.' Audley sighed. 'Naturally, he was left in place, where he couldn't do any real harm – the usual procedure . . . I think the plan was eventually to try and turn him, but I don't think it would have worked, myself . . .

Because, gay or not, I have the feeling that Comrade Aske was a hard man under his camouflage . . . But we put him in the bank for a rainy day – and then this came up, when we needed someone of theirs to keep them well-informed on how far off-target we were. And he fitted because Latimer had been cultivating him, and Latimer also likes to keep a rival eye on me – everyone knows that, including Moscow, where they all spy on one another just the same way. So we arranged for Latimer to instruct Aske to do just that.'

Mitchell felt a surge of anger. 'You gave me your word that Elizabeth would be in no danger – and I gave her *my* word!'

'I didn't think there was any danger – '

'Not with Aske?'

'Aske was why there was no danger – that was the point, Paul. Aske was her protection, and yours: as long as he was there, helping you chase the wrong *Vengeful,* he'd make sure the KGB didn't do either of you any harm – your safety was vital to him.'

'He didn't keep the KGB off us in France, by God!'

'Nonsense! Now you're not thinking at all, man! Aske put them on to you, like Novikov, to reassure us that we were on to something good. They wouldn't have touched you – they were there to be seen.' Audley grimaced suddenly. 'The trouble was, the French saw them too. And *that* wasn't in the script – I wanted us all safe in France, enjoying ourselves, with Aske urging us on to greater and even more useless efforts . . . And that was my first mistake, if you like – underrating the French . . . But then, I still couldn't imagine how anything could go wrong. You were still hot on the *Vengeful* – the old *Vengeful* – or on those fellows who escaped from Bonaparte's clutches, anyway . . . And if you got a bit bolshie I could rely on Aske keeping you up to the mark.' He half shrugged. 'So I whistled up Professor Wilder – I'd had him working on 1812 angles, just in case you didn't come up with anything, ever since Aske first interviewed him, just as I had Del Andrew working on Loftus. But that turned out to be the worst possible thing I could have done, almost.'

Almost! Wilder plus Elizabeth had almost encompassed – what?

'What was Aske going to do . . . with Elizabeth?'

'That's another thing we're never going to know.' Audley gazed at him thoughtfully. 'She convinced herself he was going to kill her, and maybe that was what he was going to do . . . that, or have someone else do it – he made a phone call down the road somewhere – an ambush, with a flesh-wound for him, would have bought them time, and he might have thought he'd get away with that.' He paused. 'But it's irrelevant now, in any case. Because I've assured her she was right, and that's what we're sticking to. For her sake, Paul – okay?'

What Mitchell had tried not to think about was staring at him now, with cold eyes: Elizabeth had killed a man, deliberately or not. 'How is she taking it – what she's done?'

Audley reflected on the question for a moment before replying. 'Remarkably well. Anguished, rather than hysterical. She kept saying "What else could I do?", and she wept a bit. But all things considered she's pretty steady.' Audley watched Mitchell attentively. 'Does that surprise you?'

There was something not quite right, not quite healthy, about the big man's glance. 'I don't know. Should it?'

'You know her better than I do.' Audley was almost casual. 'Granted she knew he was lying to her – that he *couldn't* have talked to me . . . and there were a lot of other things she put together . . . it was still a pretty drastic thing she did – for a spinster schoolmistress, don't you think?'

Yes, it was! thought Mitchell. But because the treason of that thought hurt him he reacted against it instantly.

'She's been through some pretty drastic experiences – for a spinster schoolmistress.' He thought of himself. 'Maybe she was tired of being pushed around by everyone.'

'Yes . . .' Audley sounded disappointed. 'And then there's the bloodline, of course . . .'

'The bloodline?' Mitchell added Commander Hugh Loftus, VC to the list of pushers-around – perhaps him most of all!

Audley nodded. 'By Loftus, out of Varney: a captain's daughter and an admiral's grand-daughter . . . What *my* daughter would call "a shield-maiden". Or don't you go on that sort of thing much?'

Mitchell smiled. 'My father was a conscientious objector – remember?'

'That's right.' Audley was unabashed. 'And your grandfather a battalion commander at twenty-eight. So you come from a line of fighters one way or another, which illustrates my point.' He reached for his brief-case. 'I've got some interesting stuff for you here, telexed from Washington by our kindly CIA cousins.'

'What?' The sudden change of subject threw Mitchell for a second, then he recalled Audley's technique. 'Oh?'

'Yes. It's all rather comical, really . . .'

'Comical?' Mitchell watched him extract a folder from the case. 'Comical' wasn't a word he'd have chosen.

'Yes . . .' Audley flipped open the folder and peered at its contents. 'Our kindly cousins are to blame for our present predicament . . . If they hadn't got wind of Project *Vengeful*, neither Moscow nor London would have run scared – they would simply have converged on their collision course, and you and I . . . and Miss Loftus and Comrade Aske . . . would not have become involved.' He turned a page. 'But they did, and when the President gave Project *Vengeful* to the Prime Minister he also instructed our CIA cousins to give us every assistance, as befits their old wartime allies.'

'What's comical about that?'

Audley looked up. 'What's comical, my dear Paul, is that the first request we made was for them to disinter facts from the year 1812, when we were last at war with each other. And that tickled them no end – in fact, Howard Morris sent me a special SG: "Have given this Immediate Maximum Effort classification – like Amy Carter's homework".' He shook his head at Mitchell. 'What those poor innocent American academics made of Howard's IMAXEF teams arriving on their doorsteps I simply cannot imagine.'

Mitchell refused to be drawn further.

'Wilder gave us two lists of names.' Audley consulted the folder again. 'Living Americans who might be able to tell us about dead ones, as he put it.'

Mitchell weakened. 'Why Americans?'

'Ah . . . well, he knew you and Aske were in France, because I told him . . . And when he knew that he said I ought to check the American end, just to be on the safe side.' He scanned the page under his nose. 'I've never heard of any of his live Yankees here, but some of the other names . . . Abraham Timms at the top, naturally . . .'

'Tom Chard?'

'No – no Tom Chard here. But *Amos Ratsey, Jas. O'Byrne, Octavius Phelan* – aren't they the fellows from Miss Loftus's *Vengeful* box?'

'What about them?'

'Nothing about *them* – they did unearth a couple of references to a Michael Haggerty, who was an associate of an equivocal Irish American named Jim Burns . . . and there's a *Michael Haggerty* in the *Vengeful* list. But it's a common Irish name, and they've got nothing more at all on him than that. Whereas they've got a lot on Abraham Timms . . . It seems he became quite a distinguished man in the later post-war period – *"self-taught scholar and naturalist; corresponded with Sir Joseph Banks and John*

James Audubon; issue one son, Thomas Chipperfield Paget Timms, note names" – that's what it says: "*note names"* – ' he looked at Mitchell ' – the names are rather touching, don't you think? His fellow escapers?'

'Yes.' Mitchell frowned. 'What did the cousins find out about them?'

'Nothing, I'm afraid. There's only Timms, and Haggerty – two mentions, associate of the egregious Burns, who was a merchant of some sort, always lobbying Congress to make war with the filthy British – no – no, the really interesting one – and also the most surprising one – is the one you least expect, which shouldn't be there at all, Paul.' Audley looked at him slyly.

'Who?'

'The owner of the *Vengeful* box, Dr William Willard Pike, no less!' Audley bent over the page. 'The CIA liked the sound of him – or, if not the sound, then the smell . . . because it's a smell they know, I suspect – even at this length of time – the authentic whiff of the enemy within the gate!'

This time it wasn't a question of not being drawn: it was as though Audley was talking to himself.

'This is pure Howard – pure Howard!' Audley shook his head admiringly. ' "*There are two schools of thought about Dr Pike, another known associate of Jim Burns (who in our day would have undoubtedly have been wasting our time running hot Armalites across the Canadian border for the IRA to shoot Limeys in Crossmaglen). They both disappeared from the scene here in 1812, never to return, ostensibly to do George III a mischief. But for my money – and for that of Professor John Kasik, who is nobody's fool – Pike was a British double-agent, who lit out one jump ahead of Burns with whatever passed for microfilm in those days in his pocket, on the first boat (which was a Portuguese brig bound for Lisbon) with Burns in hot pursuit in a Yankee trader licensed for Plymouth and Antwerp. Kasik and I can't prove anything, but we've both got a 'pricking of thumbs', as you and William S. of Stratford-upon-Avon would say. So forget Timms and check out Burns and Pike. Ends message".'*

Mitchell had heard of Professor Kasik – had even corresponded with him on an American aspect of *Watch by the Liffey*, as the best-known living authority on Irish Americans. But that recollection was secondary to his growing sense of unreality over this turn in the conversation. Their interest in the true story of the old *Vengeful* ought to have ended, yet Audley seemed as enthusiastic about it as ever.

The big man was smiling at him. 'We're checking what we can of this in the Bodleian, in FitzGerald's monumental history of the Paddies in America, as well as Kasik's own book. But Howard's chaps probably gained access to a lot of unpublished material, so our new boy, Phillip Dale – the thin one – is burrowing into the old Foreign Office archives. If Pike was one of our agents he ought to turn up in association with some of Richard Wellesley's bright boys of the period there. Our very own ancestors, in fact!'

Was it mere academic interest? But it couldn't be that, surely – surely? Mitchell's brain ached with tiredness.

'If he is . . . the Portuguese brig accounts for him being in Lisbon, and he picked up the *Vengeful* there, while Burns was putting out a general alarm for him. Which, of course, could be why the French eventually became so interested in the *Vengeful*, eh?'

The Portsmouth Plot, thought Mitchell. If Pike had had information about that which couldn't wait, then that could be why he had trans-shipped to the less-damaged *Fortuné* after the battle.

It was all supposition – all pictures from a distant planet of a drama enacted long ago, in which the competing actors had been dust and forgotten for generations, mixed with the earth enriched by infinite millions of the long-dead heroes of lost causes. But if, when the Last Trump sounded, it was all of immense importance in some ledger of human courage and constancy in adversity, it added up to nothing in the cruel and selfish priorities of now.

'What's the point of all this, David – the object of it?' He hated the question even as he asked it, but it was the only honest question left to him in the extremity of his weariness.

'The point – the *object*, my dear Paul . . . is *your* Elizabeth – potentially *our* Miss Loftus.' Audley's voice was gentle, almost sad. 'The object and the point is to make your history repeat itself in her . . . through you . . . for us – do you see?'

'No. I don't see.' A huge disquiet enveloped Mitchell.

'No. Then perhaps this is not the time – '

'This is the bloody time!' Mitchell flogged himself awake. 'What are you up to, David?'

'My duty. Or . . . what I conceive to be my duty.' The fatigue showed in Audley too. 'They've pissed us around something shocking this time – you and me both, and your Elizabeth – Latimer has, anyway, to get him out of trouble! So now we must take our profit from it, if we can.'

'What profit?'

Audley considered the question. 'I want you to go to Hadfield tomorrow – or today, as it is now – to see Elizabeth Loftus. And I want you to chat her up – I want you to be very nice to her . . . I want you to offer to finish off her *Vengeful* book, as you promised you would do in the first place, Paul – ' A little twitch of pain there: Audley always knew when he was being devious ' – you can even take my name in vain, if you have to – but not too much, for safety's sake – '

'Why?'

'Why me? Because she mustn't hate me too much!' The pain became pure. 'Why you? Because you're the ideal man for the job – she knows you, and maybe she likes you . . . and I know *you* like her. And isn't it true that in Lieutenant Chipperfield's day the best press-gangs were always made up of men who'd been press-ganged them-selves?'

It was like being swallowed by a boa constrictor: you went in still alive, but in the end the crushing pressures and the stifling digestive juices made you an accepted part of what had swallowed you.

'She's *ideal*, Paul.' Audley willed him to accept the compact. 'It was in my mind that first time I met her, after what you said. What's happened since only confirms it – she's the finest natural recruit I've met since I set eyes on you back in '74 – ' the smile mixed pain with happy memory ' – in some ways she's maybe even better than you, actually.'

The shared memory tore Mitchell back to the British Commonwealth Institute for Military Studies – to the packed shelves of the Great War Documents Room in which he had been researching the West Hampshires' attack on Fontaine-de-Bois, when he had first locked horns with Audley.

But only for an instant, because he knew at last what they were both about – *dear God, he knew!*

'She's perfect,' said Audley, sharing the knowledge with his press-ganged press-gang commander. 'Independent means and no ties – unmarried, and not likely to be – no inconvenient boy-friends, no nosy relatives – '

Dear God! Audley must once have had a conversation like this with someone about *Paul Mitchell* – with Colonel Butler maybe, or old Brigadier Stocker or even Sir Frederick Clinton . . . but – *history was repeating itself now* with *Elizabeth Loftus* for *Paul Mitchell* –

No!

'You'll have to go carefully.' Audley took his silence for agreement, and stared into space. 'You'll need profes-sional advice before you pop the question – '

* * *

No! Never mind *Paul Mitchell* – they must have considered *Frances Fitzgibbon* like this, once upon a time, and he wasn't having *Elizabeth Loftus* go the same way – *no!*

'You look doubtful.' Audley had come down out of space a moment too quickly, to catch his expression.

'Yes – ' Mitchell choked on the admission.

'Yes. It *is* a responsibility.' Audley nodded understandingly. 'But, when you think about it, Paul, recruitment is one of the most important jobs we have – in peacetime.' He nodded again. 'In wartime, it's easy – we get the cream then. But in peacetime . . .' the nod became a shake of the head '. . . that's when we have to keep our eyes open for natural talent.'

A terrible heresy sapped Mitchell's faith: it could be that Audley was right – she was clever, and more than that – she was intuitively quick . . . and more than that – *more than that* – she was resolute – *she had killed a man!*

'But if you'd rather not do it I won't force you. It isn't a job to everyone's taste.' Audley looked at him, and then brightened. 'In fact . . . I could always ask James Cable as soon as he's free again – he's ex-RN, and the Cables are an old naval family. She's bound to like him.'

Elizabeth would like James Cable – everyone liked James Cable, thought Mitchell miserably. So it wouldn't make a damn of difference if he refused: Audley had it all worked out; and, what was worse, he probably had it worked out *right* this time, just as he had once done in the case of a certain Paul Mitchell.

Apart from all of which, it was up to Elizabeth to make up her own mind, for better or for worse – it was her *right*, just as it had once been his, and he had no right to influence her.

Then, suddenly, his own thought echoed in his head: *for better or for worse* –

'Well? Will you do it?'

Mitchell heard the rain beat against the windows. He could see his reflection mirrored in their blackness, distorted by the leading of the diamond panes. It reminded him of his first sight of her, in the mirror at the church fête. She had been scowling in his direction, and he had thought to himself that she was even plainer in the flesh than her picture in the file. But that first glimpse had been just as much a distortion of the true image as his own in the windows.

Audley stretched wearily. 'You can sleep on it if you like. She'll keep for a few more days.'

For better or for worse – the idea flowered in Mitchell's brain, opening like the speeded-up film of a natural growth which normally took far longer to mature. For a second it astonished him, it was so far from anything he had thought himself capable of imagining. But then it surprised him that he had not thought of it before, it was so beautifully simple.

'No – ' He tried not to smile foolishly 'no – '

Merely thinking of it gave him all the rights he needed; if he managed it she would be beyond Audley's reach – and it would serve Audley right for the use he'd made of them both.

'No, I'd like the job, David.'

Audley looked pleased. 'You think you can win her over, do you?'

That was the big question: she might turn his offer down in favour of Audley's. But then, he didn't need to tell her about Audley's offer at all: The beauty of the thing was that Audley was giving him the perfect opportunity to plead his own case, free of interruptions.

'I'll have a damn good try,' he said. 'You can depend on that, David.'

It was a double-cross. But, like they said, love and war were about winning, not fair play.